The Hand of Yemanjá

Claudio Tapia

Black Rose Writing

www.blackrosewriting.com

ISBN: 978-1-61296-170-5

PUBLISHED BY BLACK ROSE WRITING

www.blackrosewriting.com

Printed in the United States of America

Title is printed in Arabic Typesetting

For Mo & Camil

We all look for ways to shed our skins from time to time,
for a chance to look at the world through borrowed eyes.

For Nick -

The Hand of Yemanjá

Enjoy the READ An
-thanks for helping this
to the next plane.

Claudio

Lydia

It would still be hours before the mist completely lifted from the bay. The surface of the water was calm, tear-choked; glass colored black by the sky hovering right above it. Genoa was at half veil, a city poised in mourning.

The mayhem around her is complete, infectious; like the scene of a tragic accident and an endearing reminder every time of how Lydia's countrymen only seem more hysterical than is usually the case. Families, by far, are the rowdiest; especially the provincials in that perpetual state of panic about having to make sense of themselves in the face of changing times.

Lydia steps back to look at the string of trunks and crates queued like a trail of domino stones on the deck and hones in on the two valises halfway down the middle belonging to her. She tallies each piece, but not necessarily counting them. Rather, she seems taken in by the mathematics of it and the poetry that begs to cling to farewells in general.

She is then struck by the thought of how the next time each piece of luggage will touch solid ground again it will be on the western shores of the Atlantic Ocean somewhere. And for a moment her eyes light up as the coil of human circumstance reveals itself, the melodrama.

A young couple crosses her field of vision; entwined, looking vacantly eager and as unprepared as the rest of them. But it is mostly the children that distract her as they dart about, all cut and groomed to look like tidy monks and hoisted into the best rags economic hardship will allow. She asks herself whether she will actually miss any of this, but neither with the need to come up with something of an answer, nor in any way to underline the fact that she is probably quite incapable of such a thing anyway; too practical to have ever developed the kind of sentimental streak everyone else apparently has.

The passenger list counts five hundred and twenty-two souls in total. And the majority of them crowd the larboard side of the ship now for a last glimpse, a whiff, of things that will soon no longer be. Lydia and only a few others stand facing away from the dock and the city all together, scattered along the stern sharing nothing but the view. They look conspicuous; they always do, those few, if only for the fact no one has come to wave them off — outcasts either by law or intent in the process of shedding skin.

The movement of the ship as it jolts loose from the dock is faint and subtle at first. But it is unmistakable; she is physically disconnected now as well. With effort she manages to tear herself loose from the view and turn her attention to one of the ship's officers, who is calling out names for the luggage to be collected and for the quarters to be confirmed and assigned. And for the hundredth time that morning her eyes drop to the documents in her hand that sum up in pompous prose only the vague parameters of what is happening: that today is the 14th of November of the year 1902 and that a week earlier she paid for a second-class passage on the vessel she is now standing on; the Ostia Antica, the youngest of three ocean-faring sisters bound for Buenos Aires.

<><><><><><><><>

She excuses herself entering her cabin, cabin number ninety four, bumping both her suitcases on just about everything she could bump them on.

"Good morning" she says, feeling both sets of eyes belonging to the Scazzo sisters piercing through her.

"Could you tell me which one of the empty bunks I might be allowed to occupy?" she asks, her voice faint but not from exertion. Rather it is the wall of animosity she crashes up against that takes the vibrancy out of it somewhat.

"Top and bottom," answers the older of the two, pointing the half-empty glass in her hand through her bare feet dangling over the edge of the bunk.

Lydia lets her things fall on the bottom mattress, the horsehair inside it barely giving way under the thud it produces. She then straightens herself to face the two women and says, "My name is Lydia," simply and openly. "I am traveling to Buenos Aires."

"I am Benedetta and that there is my sister, Domenica" the older one says, half suppressing a giggle mixing with a yawn; her tone not sharp but nowhere near amicable either. "We are not going that far," she adds. "We'll be out of your hair as soon as we get to Madeira. Just a few days."

"It will not be a problem" Lydia replies, still testing the waters on whether the woman's brutish tone is intentional or that she is flat-footed in other ways as well.

But it is her sister, Domenica sitting on the opposite bunk who speaks: "We hope we will not inconvenience you, Miss" — the sarcasm there well exceeding sharp, landing somewhere near downright hostile and it leaves Lydia wondering if the stench of liquor in the cabin might have something to do with it.

Barely rousing the air around her Lydia turns to search the younger woman's face, all the while the wheat-in-June color of her eyes dancing with astonishment and contempt, and replies, "I am sure you will do fine, Domenica; just fine" - taking her time to let her words suck the air right out of the narrow enclosure that is to be her home for the next six weeks.

"What's in Buenos Aires?" Benedetta then asks, not so much out of curiosity as in an attempt to divert the bullets away from her sister.

But Lydia takes her time to disengage her eyes from Domenica before she turns, letting it be clear that even if it is to be for only three days that their lives will be entangled she still requires good manners, no matter who they are or how drunk.

"I am not sure yet," she turns to answer. "Work I hope. What's in Madeira?"

"Not very much really" Benedetta answers somewhat hesitantly and most probably wondering why, whenever she drinks too much the words that form so eloquently inside her head almost never come out of her mouth actually sounding that way. "We are going there to visit our brother," she says. "He owns an orchid farm outside of Funchal. We plan to stay six months, if he doesn't ship us off before then."

"Work?"

The question springs too naturally to Lydia's lips. So much so that it needs no verbs or much of a sentence around it for it to seem like the fairest assumption as to why two young women might want to travel to a place like Madeira in the first place.

But still, the sisters double up laughing, lifted both into the hilarity of it all before Lydia fully understands from the elegant tang of their perfume and the fine quality of their gowns that traveling second-class was probably not part of their initial plan. She turns away and pretends to fumble around with her luggage, embarrassed as she was raised to be, about her own small-town background. She catches herself wanting to be invisible again, as she tends to, whenever she is confronted by the frivolity of city people and their careless and unintended cruelties.

But it angers her foremost that embarrassing herself like that makes her think of her parents and how their unsophisticated ways have taught her through the whip of shame to begrudge those whose definition of earning a living does not necessarily involve breaking a sweat. But she quickly remembers that this is the very reason she boarded the Ostia Antica in the first place: to rid herself of precisely that; having to make excuses for who and what she is.

"That'll be one way to get us out of his hair," says Domenica, sniffling and still trying to catch her breath from her roar of laughter grinding down rather joylessly now.

All taunting seems absent from the younger woman's voice and manner. And this now gives Lydia the opportunity to examine her more closely – to store in her mind for future reference perhaps, how of the two Domenica is by far the prettier one and ironically the one that also seems the most bitter.

"Actually, it was our sister-in-law who invited us," says Benedetta, "to keep her company while our brother tends to his nursery, which is pretty much all he does nowadays, from what we hear. If you ask me," she hiccups, "our sister-in-law just wants to have us around as an excuse to paint the town red now and then," she adds leaning forward and bringing her tone down to a drawn out and ostentatious whisper.

Lydia takes the two-and-a-half steps required to cross the cabin to look for a place to hang the dress she bought for herself on the day she got her ship card, and which she intends to be wearing on the day she arrives in America, regardless whether or not she has the kind of shoes a work in black silk like that really demands.

"I don't think I have ever painted a town red," she then says. "Or any other color for that matter either."

Another salvo of laughs swells around her but dies out before it has even begun to really roll and makes way for an all-together different undertone, which she is unable to quite place. She pretends to study the microscopic detail on the surface of the wall when a light tap on her shoulder makes her turn. She encounters Benedetta Scazzo's extended hand dangling an empty glass in front of her.

"Maybe" Benedetta says, as she pours whatever is in the bottle in her other hand into the glass, "in the few days we have together we could teach you how a young lady gets to paint towns - or ships – red," she adds conspiringly again followed by a fast, twitchy wink. "Who knows, we may properly prepare you for when you arrive in Buenos Aires."

"You've been there?"

"Now that's a place that will paint you red, if you're not careful," Domenica says.

"No, I haven't but I know people who have," Benedetta answers, as she retouches her sister's glass and then her own, which she has stuck in between the mattress and the board around her bunk.

Lydia has yet to hear any real or even somewhat believable description of that place. Whenever people speak of Buenos Aires it is in the way one usually ventures to describe food or drink, or the basic parameters inside some emotional landscape few are ever able to really put into words and becomes all the more luring because of it. Fact is that there are few first-hand accounts to provide any certainty at all that such a place even exists and might thus ever be lifted past the abstracts of mere colors and shapes.

Lydia pushes down Bendetta's prune brandy and as she feels her muscles convulse in protest to the rasp of it she feels strangely hopeful too that perhaps, who knows, in raising a glass with the likes of these two, women whose floors she might have been mopping only yesterday, is proof that there is indeed more to what she can turn herself into, eventually, and that there is some grander reason for why people are boarding ships nowadays.

11

<><><><><><><><>

A cautious knock sounds on the door. In unison and with glasses still raised the women look up and watch it open with matching modesty.

The flustered, pinkish head of a man somewhere in his upper fifties precedes a perfectly rounded belly. His upper lip reaches no higher than the middle bunk and with his feet he pushes a large suitcase out in front of him.

"Yes?" Benedetta Scazzo asks; her voice spiked with horror.

"No, don't bother yourselves, please," says the man. "I will manage just fine. Thank you."

His thyroidal eyes appear to dance wildly behind the spectacles anchored midway down the bridge of his nose. But even as he looks up the rims still dig themselves into his eyebrows.

"My, it is all ladies!" the man says in a shrewdly reluctant pose, half to himself and half toward what has naturally become his audience. "I didn't know – didn't expect – is this right? Now, let me see if I read this correctly...."

He fumbles inside one of his coat pockets, and adds: "Well, it would seem I wasn't mistaken after all. Yes, that's correct. That is what my confirmation says: cabin number ninety four," he flounders on, unfolding a sheet of paper with the Doria Shipping Company emblem recognizable at the top and matches it with the numbers scratched in white chalk on the side of his suitcase. "I was assigned this cabin – ninety four, there it is. See?"

"Yes I see. But as you can see this is a women's cabin" says Benedetta Scazzo, her assertiveness matching her near-corpulence rather beautifully. "You surely don't expect to be occupying this cabin, do you?"

"Well, miss, if it makes you feel any better, I will not stop you from moving to other quarters. Until you do, however, would you be so kind as to point out which bunk is not yet occupied?"

"This is insane," now Domenica too takes up arms, pulling herself up from the side of her sister's dress to keep from toppling over. "You surely do not...."

"I am afraid, Miss, that this is the cabin I have been assigned. Would you like to have a look at my ship card?"

"No, not really, no. What I would like to do is have a word with the ship's captain instead."

"Don't let me stop you. But in the meantime would you be so kind?" the little man insists.

Domenica blinks her eyes not quite getting her focus right and while she steadies herself by hooking her elbow behind the board of her bunk, looks like she wants to offer her thoughts on the situation. No words slurred or otherwise, come out of her however.

So Lydia offered hers.

"I don't believe there is such a thing as a women's only cabin," she says. "At least, not in second class. Are you sure this is where you need to be?" she adds, turning to Benedetta who, for no other reason than the fact she has been standing the longest, seems like the most sober of the two just now.

"Yes, we're in second class all right. But they never said we would be sharing our sleeping quarters with men."

She sifts through her travel bag for her documents just to convince herself.

"I believe I can see how this may be upsetting for you," says the little man. "But let me prepare you, because by the looks of it we can still expect two more passengers to share this cabin with, if the ship is indeed filled to capacity as I understand it is."

"I believe the gentleman may be right," Lydia comes back. "I was told that it isn't at all uncommon for passengers traveling without family. Besides, considering I was sharing a dormitory with over sixty other people back in the city, spending the next six weeks with five doesn't really sound that terrible when you think about it."

In a flash Lydia realizes how evident her inexperience has just become, but foremost what her contribution to the conversation might ultimately have done to the fragile truce she seems to have established with the Scazzo sisters. But it is when she notices the little man straightening his back that she wishes she had kept her mouth shut good and proper.

13

From the doorway he seems to project himself like a seasoned actor and beams like a toy soldier with confidence and enough lung capacity to last him a Verdian belcanto or two, and orates:

"My name is Emilio Toffolo. I am an administrator for the region of Emilia-Romagna. I am traveling on official business to Brazil, if you must know. I am a gentleman of impeccable upbringing and take offense at the lady's insinuations that my intentions might be anything less than honorable."

He looks at each of the women with a disarming air about him that is probably the basis on which he has built far more than just a career as a government official. And which, as a result, if it doesn't necessarily make him more likable, it most certainly classifies him as perfectly harmless.

"I will do what I can to be a good travel companion to you all," he adds before he lets his chin drop on top of his buttoned up shirt by way of completing his theatrics.

<><><><><><><>

Lydia tries to open the window to add a breath of air to the scant few square meters she is standing on, but the rounded glass has been corked inseparably into the hull of the ship. She feels she might suffocate and decides to find the deck again after several pulls. Without a word to her cabin mates she takes her leave and sets off to wander the labyrinth of corridors in search for it.

Once outside it surprises her how large the deck seems and how far it appears to stretch before her, now that most of the passengers have moved below deck. All she can see are the scattered ones now, the outcasts, still moving about in a compulsive tread, airing private and sultry thoughts in the wind. A few of the younger couples she has seen earlier share coats and coarse blankets now to cover a knuckled embrace. They hardly look up as she passes them.

Every now and then she tosses a flighty glance in the direction of the red stripe of the Genovese flag, harpooned into the back of the ship like an insult to the thing the Ostia Antica really stands for. Or at least what it stands for to her. The city has faded by now and out to starboard the coast is indistinct, green and mountainous and hidden behind low-hanging clouds. On occasion, the ship will blow its horn in salute to the coastal towns some of the passengers on board have come from. And each time it does small groups will hurry outside for one last glimpse of a coastline that is in as many ways familiar as it is strange to them now.

Her hair has been pulled back, but she keeps wiping invisible strands away from her face as she takes in her surroundings. Her face is without expression and it reveals the same detachment that has clung to her for the past eight days, that two-dimensional mask that has always distinguished her so, in good ways and otherwise.

The question whether she will miss any of this, again, is like an echo that keeps bouncing through it all, yet comprising neither words nor any other kind of recognisable shape. And in the end it has left her unmoved besides. The water is choppy and still leaning toward a mournful, darkish grey. She wraps her hands around the railing and stares over it mind a blank and without realising it her lips shape words; unhinged and random but words nevertheless.

She reaches into her coat and with something that is halfway between annoyance and genuine curiosity, she re-reads the bureaucratic prose on her traveling papers to see if she can still recognise herself in any of the half-truths proclaimed in them. She runs her fingers over the emblem of the Doria Shipping Company and then skips to the bottom passing right over the segment that pronounces her free of tuberculosis and glaucoma, to the section which specifically declares her NOT-married — "the most accurate part of the entire document," she whispers to herself in a shaky, baptismal voice.

"Did you know that the Ostia Antica had its maiden voyage only two years ago?"

Startled she turns and finds Emilio Toffolo's magnified eyes are holding her in a soft but strangely devious little smirk behind his spectacles. In the light of day now she can sense a Hepatitic aura surrounding him, which she had not been aware of before.

"Did our cabin mates chase you off at last, Signore?"

"Hardly, Miss. I assigned them the care of a bottle of some outstanding anisette and left on my own accord."

She returns his smile and goes back to staring toward the water.

"How long have you been standing there?" she asks, the deliberateness in her words betraying how much she is plotting the conversation ahead.

"Long enough to hear you talk to yourself, dear," he replies carelessly, in a boyish tone.

"I believe I will forgive your impertinence, Signore, but only because you managed to dodge the wrath of our cabin mates so eloquently today."

"It wasn't my intention to eavesdrop, Miss, but you just happened to speak as I was approaching. And don't worry, I have heard people say prayers before."

"What makes you think I was praying?"

"Oh, it just sounded like you were having it out with someone."

He moves to her side and props his elbows on top of the railing, just short of having to tiptoe in order to reach.

"Susano'o is the god of the sea in the Shinto religion of Japan," he begins. "I am saying this only because it sounded as if you were praying, that's all. See, in Japan it isn't uncommon for sea travelers to spill a couple of words into the waves, much in the way you did yourself just now. That is if your words had been a prayer, of course; for protection perhaps, on the long journey ahead or for it to bring you luck in whatever is next after you get to where you are going."

"Well, it wasn't – a prayer I mean. And if there were such a thing as a god of the sea, what makes you so sure it would be a man anyway?"

"You would have to take it up with the people of Japan, I suppose," the functionary replies. "And besides, I don't think he would care in the least if you preferred to think of him as something other than a man."

"It sounds like you have been there."

She can hear the back of his palate tremble, as he releases an indistinct giggle – modest above all. And this is how she knows he will snore like a doubled up pig in his sleep. But before she is able to complete the image of Emilio Toffolo, the government functionary from Bologna sleeping, he is already talking again.

"No, Miss. I have never been to Japan. I just like to read. And I don't mind telling you that I am not much of a traveler either. The fact that you find me on board of a ship is quite exceptional."

For a moment she feels like telling him that she likes to read as well, but feels he probably wouldn't believe her if she did. He will only need one good look at her shoes to see that she might as well be illiterate. She decides to change the subject.

He stares at the coastline in the kind of silence that might as well be a scream that he already knows all about how things stand with provincial little girls like her.

After a while, he dry-smacks his lips a couple of times and adds:

"You never introduced yourself back in the cabin."

"I'm Lydia", she answers flat, but politely enough. "Just Lydia."

"Just Lydia... Should one call you Just or Miss Lydia then?"

"I like the sound of that. But Lydia will do," she says, not exactly hiding the fact she is more than a bit ruffled by his sense of humor.

"Very well, Lydia, just Lydia, did you know that this ship is considered to be just about the most technically advanced piece of machinery operating the trans-Atlantic routes out of Genoa and Naples?"

"No I did not, nor do I want to know how many tons of steel we are standing on. I don't care to know at how many knots we are currently navigating either, or over how many cubic kilometers of water, Signore. As a matter of fact, the levels of iodine in the Mediterranean, on average during the month of November, don't particularly interest me much either, you must know."

"No, I didn't think so," says Emilio Toffolo, his palate making that collapsing sound again; the short roll of a swine-like snore as the only indication that her harshness might have struck him in some way.

"You know, Signore, while I was standing here, before you spoke to me – when you thought I was saying a prayer to your Japanese God – I had just come to a most interesting conclusion."

"A conclusion?"

"I am starting to realise that there isn't a single soul on this ship who isn't in some way a big liar."

The functionary squints his eyes and observes her over the rims of his glasses for a better, less-filtered look.

"Please explain."

"See, does it matter anymore that I am anyone's daughter? I am clearly a lot of the things I wasn't only a year ago. And take the documents in my pocket. Those are now the only proof that says I am anything at all. Does it matter anymore that I lied about my age – and that I made myself out to be two years older? I feared they wouldn't let me travel otherwise. Who is going to split hairs on a thing like that?"

"No one I can think of," the functionary says.

"Consider the distance I will end up covering, Signore, before a thing like a birth certificate will mean anything again," she says, pushing her steady glare into him, but with her attention turned elsewhere completely. "Is it then still necessary for me to have been born right there in the interior, behind those mountains no one here can even see? I don't think there is a soul who would care – and I certainly don't. I could just as well have made myself out to be Greek, anything. I have come to the conclusion that this is the reason any one of us is on this ship in the first place."

"Because deep down we are all liars?"

"No, Signore, because imagination is now the only limit that binds us."

It surprises her she is being this forthcoming with what in essence is still a complete stranger and especially because only minutes earlier all she had wanted was to be by herself.

"May I ask where you are going?" the functionary says, quite ignoring her still rather insubstantial view of a world, which he figures until today had not extended much beyond the outskirts of her hometown.

"For now let me just stick to Buenos Aires," she replies.

She begins to move away from the railing toward the centre of the deck to escape the cold lashing of the wind and inquires with something in her voice resembling the steel they are standing on, "Brazil is it, for you?"

"Oh yes, Brazil. Yes," he answers, attempting to look and sound surprised.

"May I ask what's there?"

"Like I said before, official business. Well, somewhat official anyway.

There is also a small matter of the heart I mean to resolve while I am there."

"That really doesn't tell me much at all, Signore."

He straightens himself up and looks like a ten year-old boy again, who has just put on a soldier's hat in front of the mirror for the first time.

"Lydia, man has been crossing oceans for all the wrong reasons for centuries, is the way I see it. But not only wrong reasons, if you know what I mean."

With his miniature hands he grabs the lapels of his coat, as he orates again with the same theatrics she had witnessed of him earlier.

"And this time around," he adds, "I am crossing it for both; both right and wrong reasons. And that, Lydia, is the realisation I came to recently."

"I am still not sure I understand. But if you say so, then let that be it. And I wish you good luck."

She disperses her focus away from him, too stealthily for it to have been anything even remotely resembling movement. It is more like a shift in the light-fall on her face that tells him she is about to walk away. At once he reacts, engaging her again.

"Have you noticed, Lydia, how the ship is filled to absolute capacity with passengers?"

"I suppose," she answers him somewhat irritated, though at this point her annoyance is little more than a light surge of static across her skin.

"Well, given that we have now left the last Italian port, doesn't it strike you as odd that the only other persons you and I are sharing a cabin with are the two young ladies I left behind to finish off a bottle for me?"

"I don't see what it is you are driving at, Signore."

"Well, there are still two empty bunks in our cabin and considering the ship is probably filled to capacity, like I said, it makes sense that we would be sharing our cabin with at least two other passengers. Haven't you wondered how that could be?"

"Now that you mention it, I suppose it is odd. How do you know two more people have not joined our two drunken cabin mates since we've been out here?"

"Over the years, Lydia, I learned a thing or two about how to make

19

the whole travel experience less taxing for myself. And that the most important thing is to inspire officials at the shipping company to think of creative ways to accommodate me; that for the right amount of money just about anything can be arranged, in order to provide me with all the comforts I need. In the end it should only be a matter of, well, price, of course. The trading spirit of our countrymen has yet to fail me in this regard, I must say."

He shifts his weight from one foot to the other, as if he were looking for the right balance that will allow him to continue talking. But he times the interval of his words perfectly and beats her each time she thinks she might at last be able to get away.

"And this, my dear, is how I get to share a cabin, which should accommodate five other passengers, with only three other ladies. Two of whom, I might add, will be traveling only a small portion of the way."

"You are very crafty, Signore. So why suggest that more people might be joining us when we were in the cabin earlier?"

"Oh, I don't think it would have helped our cabin mates to warm up to me, had I admitted paying a small fortune to travel with only the three of you. And no, I am not crafty at all. I just happen to be very rich, that's all, which isn't really very fair to those who truly are crafty but still get to travel in the lowest pits of these ships."

"And what makes you think the Scazzo sisters will warm up to you now, after I tell them about all this?"

"My feeling is that the Scazzo sisters — even if they do find a way to crawl out of the bottle of anisette I brought for them, won't hear one word of this. Besides, why would they care? If anything they are benefiting from it."

"Is that how you figure the situation?"

He rubs his hands like a mouse that's found itself trapped inside a breadbasket.

"My guess is that you are a practical young woman and that you really ought to be thanking me for the opportunity to share your cabin with only me, after we set sail out of what, Madeira was it?"

She takes a small step toward him, much in the way a man might do only seconds before he lands his fist on the smaller man's teeth. But her eyes sparkle not only with scoff but also with a tinge of pity.

"I don't know what you take me for, Signore," she hisses in a dosed tone, "but you must know that traveling third or even fourth would not mean a thing to me. So," - limiting her words to him alone, even though there is no one else even remotely near - "please don't think for a minute that you have obliged me in any way."

He leans back but without actually taking a step away from her. "Sooner or later you would have noticed the conditions in which some of our fellow passengers are traveling," he says, "and you would surely have brought it up yourself I wager. I thought it was best if you knew right from the beginning, from me."

"If you're so rich, Signore, why even go through all the trouble?"

"Lydia, there are things not even money can buy. And something tells me that that is exactly why our cabin mates aren't traveling on first either — because there are things not even their money can buy either.

Would you like me to show you the lowest decks of the ship? Are you even aware of the fact that there actually is such a thing as third and even fourth class on this marvel of technical ingenuity?"

He extends his arm in the direction of the stairwell and adds, "Please join me in a walk. I think it will enlighten you as to what crossing the Atlantic can look like."

Her brow hardens, as she holds him in that granite glower that always makes her seem older than she really is. She looks to be deep in thought, moves her hand across her face taming real strands of hair this time and rests her gaze on the coastline crawling behind the fog. Lydia is an objective soul; at twenty-three she knows this much. And this is how she foresees that she will always be a foreigner no matter where she goes. She knows she will always embrace whatever crosses her path, as she will be able to discard all of it on a whim. But still, during those eight days she wandered through the city waiting to embark her grip had never loosened on the bundle in her hand — her documents, her identity, the last thing that connects her to the mountains fading in the distance.

She follows the functionary as he leads her through the maze of semi-darkened hallways and corridors, leading yet to more stairs and shapeless spaces. She senses her countrymen in the shadows around her but cannot see them. In the mash of dialects and accents she feels herself moving ever deeper into the uncouth, dust-ridden simplicity of the provinces.

After a long winding, she finds herself standing in the confined vastness of what looks to be the cargo hull. The paraffin fumes mixed with the stench of small-town cooking, settle on her skin immediately. She calculates how high the surface of the water stands on the other side of the steel around her and notices how the engines are many times more deafening here than on second class, the grinding of the steel set in tones much lower.

"Welcome to America," says Emilio Toffolo, his voice pulling her back to a place that has stunned her rather thoughtless and light. "If Italy were a soup, Lydia, this would be the grease that is skimmed off the top. This is what America is really about dear: discarded filth, in the hope it will one day bring forth civilization"

"I am part of this, you know. And in a way so are you," she replies, ignoring as best she can his likening her to filth, and that he used a metaphor for greasy soup to do so.

She pauses and bites her lip, as though pulling at something that is heavy and unwilling to give.

"All I know is that you are no better, Signore."

"But I never said I was, Lydia. Out at sea my money means nothing. I just commented on what I believe we are all part of, including myself by all means."

She looks around her. The Neapolitans seem to have populated one side of the hull, segregating themselves from the rest — the men standing and the women spread out on blankets in the sawdust strewn about to add something of an organic quality to the steel. Their conversations are more animated than those she had been used to hearing around her hometown. Yet, they seem to have put up something of a wall around themselves that not only feels exclusive but uninviting. Somehow there seems to be a difference between the two.

The children appear shunted, probably by the stagnant air and without realising it the question springs to her lips, "Why aren't they out on the deck?"

"That is exactly what I asked myself the first time I saw this," the functionary answers after a moment or two. "And I decided that it has probably something to do with the docility that comes from being faced with the unknown or something to that effect. It is only a theory but I'm afraid they remain here for the very simple reason that somebody in a starched uniform told them to.

But they will start to venture out, in a few days is my guess," he adds, "once we begin to navigate further into the tropics and the heat and the stench becomes harder to bear, even for them."

He pauses for a second and lifts the back of his tiny hand to wipe the tip of his rather flattened nose.

"It could be that it is also hard to look at the coast of a country they have rejected just today. Wouldn't you say?"

"Or a country that has rejected them?"

"If you wish."

"What did you mean when you said that not even your money could buy passage on first-class? I don't understand."

In the dim light she can see the functionary's face tightening.

"Do you want the short or the long answer to that question?" he says.

"It was just a question. I don't know."

"Well, without complicating my answer too much, I have powerful enemies who have seen to it that I will never travel the seas first class again."

"But that sounds ridiculous."

"Not if you consider that I have made great progress against people like that in the last few years, to where they would resort to such childish measures."

"Who are they?"

"Look around you, dear. There is one man who finances this journey for most of the people you see. He is the person who has single-handedly

23

depopulated entire towns all over Europe as well, to make the journey to America in search for whatever he's convinced them they are not finding here.

Like I said, Lydia, there are many reasons for crossing an ocean. And for this man it is to destroy Europe by depopulating it. He has said so himself, you know."

"You are not making much sense."

"So you want the long version after all."

"Well, it looks that for the next six weeks I will not be going anywhere, Signore, so, please."

Again he throws her a devious side-ward glance before he fills his nostrils with as much of the smell of boiled cabbage as he can and then turns to face her.

"Let me see, Lydia, my guess is that the reason you are here is probably to find work... in Buenos Aires, perhaps. But my guess is also that it isn't mere economics that has put you here. I can see a strong taste for adventure in you as well. Perhaps you feel there is something noble even, in exploring the unknown.

See, I believe there are three kinds of travelers There are economic travelers, the adventurers and those who see the expansion of our world as a convenient opportunity to disturb the order of things.

You, dear, are part of an exodus, one that will change the world for good. The man I am talking about, the one who wishes to disturb the order of things is also among those who say war might be coming, revolution and whatnot. What this man does is incite fear and in doing so, for years now, he has been chipping at the very basis of the world we know."

"Well, as long as it is for the better I suppose there is nothing wrong with wanting for things to be different."

"They're zealots, Lydia. Idealism is quite another thing!"

"Is this part of your official visit to Brazil?"

"Yes. I am going there to disprove some of the claims this man has made, the promises he has made to thousands of our countrymen and his lies about why they should head out that way. I am hoping that once I get to Brazil I will unmask him for the fraud I believe he is."

"And one man is able to prevent you from traveling first class?"

"He is the one that organizes almost every crossing to America. He is the one who is single-handedly responsible for the economic success of every shipping company in Italy and most of those around Europe too.

Sure, I can buy myself all kinds of extra amenities. But I will never actually travel first class. He has personally seen to that, in an attempt to demoralise me I suppose."

"That sounds very childish indeed. I assume it is quite a coincidence then that I have never heard of this man."

The functionary's face brightens. But a moment later it reveals he is in actual pain. It reminds her of a grindstone and the sharpening of knives the way his smile shrinks before her very eyes and his lips pull to the side as he tries to look away.

"Is everything alright, Signore?"

"Yes, dear. It's just some indigestion. That's all."

But he looks pale and tired— and saddened most of all; perhaps from the battles he tried to tell her about, the ones that in essence will always seem pointless to her — battles he has probably been losing all his life.

"The way I see it," he manages, barely, "this is the one man on this God's earth truly worth destroying."

"And I hope you do, Signore. I sincerely hope you do."

<><><><><><><>

The port cities of Genoa and Naples are virtually crawling with individuals and families waiting to board vessels west, leaving as frequently as three times a week these days. Lydia has made a point of staying clear of them as much as she can, however, figuring that as long as she remains in motion her chances of having to engage with any of them are probably the smallest. But at the Via Balbi it is almost impossible to not get drawn in with them in some way and be thus reminded of how her own appetite for travel and discovery isn't at all that unique.

In all there must be dozens of these transit houses, as they are called. Many of these have sprouted around the harbour over the years to accommodate the ever-growing stream of warm bodies entering the city from the countryside bound for the Atlantic. Every topic of conversation, from the docks to the train station along the Corso has in some way to do with that journey west, as well as the adventures one can expect whilst on it. Each story is more fantastic and hard to believe than the other, to a point where after a while it becomes difficult to distinguish fact from fiction, inflated to disproportion by the hysteria of some kind of common destiny.

No matter how hard Lydia tries there is just no escaping these soon-to-be citizens of a continent that in the end no one seemed to know very much about. No matter where she turns she finds her impulse to transport herself beyond every horizon just for the sake of changing who she can be, smeared by exaggeration and most often utter ignorance.

In between tales of the savages that come out of the Venezuelan jungles to kill the men and steal the women out of the newly founded towns, or the epic storms one is likely to experience out on the open ocean, Lydia is also able to pick up some useful information about the trip she is about to brave. And this is how she learns that her ship card will include two daily meals during her journey, that these are always served on the second deck and for instance that by the time they reach the coast of Brazil, there will be a shortage of fruit and vegetables and therefore, that it is advisable to feed on as many of those as one can before embarking.

As she twists her way through knots of history preserved in granite and marble along the streets of the port city; corridors radiating straight out of the bay and into the hills, a strange melancholy begins to settle over her, one that seems tied to her own need to be disconnected and detached somehow from the things she sees. More than ever before she hopes to get lost, to dissolve. And that perhaps, in a moment of illumination by some cathartic glance at some insignificant object, she will at last discover something, anything, which will bring her a sense of belonging to the things she is about to part with forever.

On the fifth day before her departure, after crossing the piazza Dante with the steady tread of someone in the habit of having to kill time, her feet involuntarily slow down before a window displaying a particular kind of spectacle that captivates her at once.

In the window she can see men sitting around tables cluttered with glassware and ashtrays filled with debate and worldly conversation. Everywhere cigars are being pressed to lips behind long moustaches which, years later, she would have been reminded of when admiring the tusks on walruses basking in the sun, along the coast of southern Chile.

She isn't sure what actually makes her stop and is downright baffled when she opens the door to enter a place that is by no means in the habit of serving women and even less women as young as she.

The throaty sound of men conversing and laughing moves past her in a steady wave that is muffled by thick curtains against the walls and plush carpets that cover the marble floors in random patches. The smell of liquor mixing with the smoke and the essence of coffee gives the salon the strange lure of a syrupy boil; an odd kind of density, she finds.

She sits down at one of the few tables still free near the back. It feels good to let the weight off her feet for a while; to feel her hands glow and tingle from the wet November outside. She carefully observes her surroundings without actually gawking and immediately picks up the trail of a cigar that is considerably sweeter and more flowery than its Arabian counterparts around it. As inconspicuously as she can, she tries to locate its origin and soon discovers that it is coming from the table right next to her; from two men engaged in talk conducted in a rather focused and complex tone — the way conversations between men can sometimes sound casual and business-like at the same time.

But it is the scent of what she later will learn is Costa Rican tobacco that strengthens her resolve to push forward and let fate unveil a world that just has to be so much larger than anything she might have ever imagined.

◇◇◇◇◇◇◇◇

She remains on deck until deep into the night. The weather has cleared and from the sparkle of the stars hangs the harsh winter that falls over Europe that year. She is a shadow against the night sky now. She imagines the rock of Gibraltar still invisible in the distance like a jab in the horizon, like a crack in a window, which the eye accustomed to seeing it there no longer really registers. She wonders how she will ever know for certain if it had been there at all, now that she is about to pass it in total darkness.

That first night she tries to reflect on all the choices she still believes she herself is making, but there is still too much she feels she needs to see, out there. Later, as she listens to her cabin mates snoring their boozy tunes to their own imperfect dreams, she wonders if any of them will ever live up to the promises they made to her today. Is she really that naïve to think the Scazzo sisterss will ever look her up? It's quite unlikely they will even remember her after Funchal.

Emilio Toffolo had been right; there is definitely something adventurous to the idea that one can become anything one wishes. And that is exactly how she feels when she makes herself out to be an orphan whilst getting on the ship and also why her documents make no reference whatsoever to the fact she had been volunteering as an apprentice to the nuns at the midwifery back home.

She has been delivering babies since she was fourteen. She knows she is skilled. But like the aquarelle painting she passed in the city earlier that week, discarded by the side of the road and smeared out by the rain, she hopes her own history will too soon wash off, as though one could seduce the future by rejecting the past somehow.

She wants to test herself in every way possible, to embrace destiny without some kind of legacy that might predispose her. All she wants to take with her on this journey, in order to measure herself, is her name and a simplified version of it at that. She wants to feel the freshness of being nothing more and nothing less than just a young woman with her gaze fixed on the future. She wants to fit herself with a brand new coat, one that may or may not be right for her at first or match the amber-green of her eyes, but one which she will alter until she has achieved a perfect fit.

Gibraltar passes like a shadow, only the lighthouse in the distance is able to give it shape in the night. There is nothing she recognises beyond it, either the coast of Europe to her right or the African shore to her left. She is a needle tip in the space between two continents that never touch. Both are shrouded in blackness now, as today both have come to represent all the things that are still alien and undiscovered.

She grabs hold of the railing and looks into the water again, the Atlantic now, officially. But all she really notices is that it too is black and deep and that it smears past her today.

In the early morning of the third day they dock in the port of Funchal, on the island of Madeira. If Genoa had been a platter of sorts, of mountains draping into the sea, Funchal is most certainly similar only set much deeper and colored brighter when in comparison. When the Scazzo sisters had talked about orchids, there had been no visual reference or any way Lydia could have linked their careless and meager descriptions of this place to the sight now spread before her.

And speculation soon leads her to think that their brother, the orchid farmer, probably came out this way for reasons that are quite a bit more poetic than how her cabin mates had sounded when they talked about him. But now, with the color-splattered hills before her it is hard to imagine a place more perfect.

Next to Benedetta and Domenica Scazzo, only a handful of passengers disembark that morning. In the distance, set against the kaleidoscope of color that surrounds the town, Lydia sees a man she takes to be the orchid farmer greeting his two sisters. He looks older than she imagined him and quite a bit more handsome than the picture she had painted of him in her mind. She can see him cupping their faces and kissing each of the women twice on the cheek, and how first Domenica and then Benedetta in turn grabs a hold of him, in order to steady herself on the uneven stones of the road.

He is dressed in shirtsleeves and there is something unmistakably peasant-like about him, yet mixed in with the elegance of a man who clearly owns things and might at times stick his hands in the ground because he chooses to and by no means because he might otherwise go hungry. She watches as their luggage is loaded onto a horse-pulled cart and aborts her wave as soon as she realises that they will not wave back. She then returns her attention to the hills behind the town, taking in all she can before Madeira too becomes a memory.

She finds Emilio Toffolo hidden away in the cabin. His bunk is covered with sheets of paper, himself poled in the middle, either rising from it or sinking right into it. He clenches a pencil in between his teeth and looks up rather bewildered when she enters.

"Lydia, what do you make of this?" he asks her almost gasping for air, as he lifts his spectacles from his nose to his forehead and then back again.

"What I make of this, Signore Toffolo, is a man probably somewhere in his mid-fifties, who appears to have dug himself into a heap of paper."

"Hmmm, you are cruel."

"What should I make of this?"

"Listen: the Brazilian Homestead Secretary of the State of Porto Alegre, and the Mayor of the city of Santa Cruz do Sul," he begins, as he often starts his endless rosy monologues, whether or not anyone is listening. "...they have jointly extended the disposition, for agricultural purposes, of one hundred hectare of high-grade arable land for the symbolic amount of one Mark, to no less than four hundred citizens of the German city of Reutlingen. Do you believe this?" he adds, waiving a fistful of paper at her.

"Please, Signore Toffolo, I didn't understand a word you just said to me. How do you expect me..."

"How can I put it any plainer?" he sighs with exasperation, pressing his palms together, as if he were begging for compassion and endurance from no one other than the All Mighty himself whilst crumpling two or three sheets of paper in the process. "Why would the state authority and the city of" – he searches through the papers for the proper facts – "Santa Cruz do Sul, give away land? Why? See, this is what Ulisse Paxi is luring people to America with – with these kinds of fables."

He pulls his glasses from the top of his head and then puts them down beside him on the bunk.

"Our cabin mates have gone ashore," she says, though knowing that he will not react. She watches his spectacles drift away from him until they finally disappear under the paper. She makes sure to remember the exact spot where they have gone under, for when he finally realises they have gone missing and he looks to her to help him find them.

"I will go straight to Porto Alegre - and when I get there I will verify that this is a pure fabrication on the part of that bastard, Paxi — and expose him for once and for all as the cheating snake that he is."

She sits down on the bunk opposite him and leans forward with her elbows on her knees, studying him like some rarity from another world, one which she feels determined to comprehend, however.

"I think I saw the orchid farmer today," she then says. "He had come to meet his sisters."

"Do you want to know how many deeds were submitted for review to the joint regional counsel in Bologna last year alone? That is how many properties were offered for sale in the region of Emilia-Romagna — just last year? And this isn't something that has just started to happen either. It has been happening for years — all over the country!"

"Have you ever been on an orchid farm?" she asks, eyes turning in the direction of the window and the sky beyond it.

"And who do you think is going to stop Ulisse Paxi from depopulating our country?" says Emilio Toffolo. "I'll tell you: me. You can count on it, even if I have to follow that rat across the seven seas to unmask him for what he is."

"They tell me orchids do not grow in Italy. Stubborn as far as flowers go, fit to grow only under very unique conditions. Tropical flowers. Very stubborn...."

"What happens, Lydia, is that when the market gets flooded — when everyone decides to sell, property prices plummet. And when this happens everybody loses, the country loses...."

Now and then their eyes meet — rather, they briefly cross trajectories before focus returns to its respective universe, expanding but never actually touching.

As he continues to waive sheets of paper in the air in one of his many heated sweeps, Emilio Toffolo then stops in the middle of his sentence, as if he hit a brick wall and has to brace himself before he realises where he is. He takes a mouthful of air and then leans back against the board of his bunk, his correspondence, legal documents and notes going limp around him.

"What on earth are you talking about?"

"I am telling you what I learned about orchids these past few days and about how difficult it is to grow them – especially farm them in large numbers," she replies.

"Have you heard one word of what I have been telling you?"

"Not one word. But neither have you."

"How can you talk about – what, orchids for heaven's sake, at a time like this?"

"The same way you seem to ramble on about – what, property value, while docked at an island off the coast of Africa that happens to be covered with flowers."

"Madeira isn't covered with flowers, Lydia, any more than there are mountains of gold in America – well, at least not everywhere in America. The point is..." he stammers, but she interrupts him before he can finish his sentence.

"But it was covered with flowers when I looked at it, Signore. When I looked it was."

Her words sound final; her logic simple and so clear that he finds himself unable to answer. He laughs instead, in a way she has not heard him laugh before. It reveals something stale and stagnant inside of him as well, something that surfaces out of him almost like an apology. It seems to make his body shudder as his breath travels forcefully out through his nose and mouth.

"We have been on this tub for almost four days," he then says, "and we still have weeks to go to either reach the coast of America or the bottom of the ocean, and I still haven't seen you eat. Lydia, if I promise you I will not rant about matters that will bore you – and if you promise to never talk about tropical vegetation again, I will consider joining you for supper tonight."

"I would say that that's the smartest thing you've said all day."

It will still be more than an hour before the evening meal is served on the second deck. It is only now, seeing it empty for the first time that Lydia fully gets a sense of what a colossal space it is. Without the hordes of passengers cluttering it, details like the lacquered wood of the walls now become visible to her. It appears to have been treated to such extent that she cannot imagine it requiring more than a single wet rag to keep the whole deck close to spotlessly clean. And for reasons she isn't quite able to piece together, the sensation of stepping through the bowels of some stately dwelling descends upon her. She takes her time to admire the thick rafters arching across the ceiling and the polished Turin Marble beneath her covering certain parts of the floor – had she known by any stretch of her imagination, of course, what Turin Marble actually looked like.

Seemingly at random, Emilio Toffolo seats himself down at one of the tables, but she already understands enough about him to know that nothing he does is ever quite random; that he is too methodical and too much bound by form.

"It looks like we have the place all to ourselves," he says, as he positions a small valise on his lap, which he has brought along from the cabin.

"But not for long, is my guess," Lydia answers brightly, as she lowers herself across from him.

None to her surprise he produces a bottle of liquor from the valise – cider of some kind, the one he says he has been hiding from the Scazzo sisters; saving it for a special occasion - and that he considers her company special in some way Lydia now decides to reward appropriately by letting the red of her cheeks deepen some.

Their conversation commences naturally, as it often does. Though, as always, they talk about things that are revealing but do not reach deeper than what is appropriate at this stage of their friendship. Eventually, she does manage to poke her questions deep enough to where she slowly begins to learn more about who he is and how deeply, for instance, his hatred for this man named Ulisse Paxi actually goes - and how that hatred might compare with the love he has for Brazil and whatever is waiting for him there.

"I suppose everything I do, I hope to do with passion," is his answer at last, once she finds the right moment and the right words to ask him about it, but which tells her nothing at all.

Meanwhile, the dining hall begins to fill with passengers. And before long they find themselves surrounded by strangers again; being drawn into conversations ranging from politics to the weather and back again, to even some analysis of the current political and economic situation back in a country that could interest her as much and as little as any other.

At some point they are drawn into an exchange with a middle-aged woman who, so they soon learn, is also traveling to Buenos Aires. She is accompanied by her thirty-year old son, a rather sullen number, Lydia finds, from what is visible behind a blank, dull-greyish mask. Their conversation is lively with trivial quack about everything and nothing at all. As it turns out the woman has recently been widowed and in the way she interrupts herself on occasion to make sure her son combines his vegetables, potatoes and stew in just the right proportions on his fork and points to the napkin laying in his lap before he drinks from his glass of water, it is evident that now with her husband gone, she has turned her smothering affections toward her son. It is impossible to gauge whether or not the rather lifeless young man, with his dormant eyes and pale skin is himself even aware that the cause of his father's demise will soon mean the end of him as well, at the hands of his own mother.

It does not surprise Lydia much how readily outsiders are willing to assume that she and Emilio Toffolo are father and daughter traveling together, for this will most likely be the case with anything else they might wish themselves to be seen as. They seem to understand very well how unnecessary it is to actually explain things and that the more they interact with others the thicker becomes the smoke screen they are able to raise around themselves at any time. It isn't that they set out to be deceitful; it is just that out at sea their true identities aren't really relevant.

They are in tune, she and the functionary; even the most skittish bit of eye contact is enough to hoist them both into any kind of role they choose. It becomes Lydia's first taste of the kind of freedom she always imagined her crossing west would eventually bring her: to be able to become whatever the moment demands, to renew herself at will.

Especially the loners, the conspicuous ones, she finds, bask in precisely that kind of freedom now, growing and becoming more visible the more ocean they put behind them.

A man unexpectedly appears at their table. He introduces himself as Tomasso, nothing more; only a first name, without decoration, a thing Lydia can certainly appreciate. Judging from the deliberateness of his gestures, to Lydia he seems like the kind of man who has never had to manifest himself by way of words much, the kind of man whose opinions are always either pointless or non-existent. Nevertheless, he speaks tellingly; of a wife and about children, whom he will send for as soon as he finds proper employment in Argentina. But it is the blade scar above his eye, his swollen knuckles and his remorseful glare that tell different stories altogether.

Pretenders, they are all around them now and all intriguingly ill-fitted to carry the histories they have brought with them. There are priests with moist, quivering lips, who dream of opening up orphanages in the jungles and hookers with theatre aspirations. There are industrialists and merchants with fingernails the color of soil; palms green with callous. There is talk about progress, the way children might talk about building tree huts, and talk about the dawning of a new age of artistic advancement and so on; about quick monetary gains sure to be found in places most of them have never heard of before, all eager to discover and all for the first time able to freely express personal fantasies.

It is liberating to be surrounded by masks and by farce. Lydia has never felt so deceived before; yet never this much in her element. She feels she can at last begin to grasp the concept of where she is going, the true essence of what she set out to do. Out of the corner of her eye a sudden change in Emilio Toffolo catches her attention. His otherwise rather attentive bearing and eager slouch have gone from lively to sullen and tense in just moments. It is as if the bridge they have pulled taught between them a second earlier has snapped. His eyes are no longer directed at her or even toward the circle they temporarily form with the others. From one moment to the next the functionary seems off in the distance, piercing his eyes through the bodies continuing to fill the hull. His gaze has become a glare, dark and felt, like heavy doors closing to his kind soul in a deep and resonant clunk.

She follows his eyes fixed like nails inside their sockets now and traces them all the way to a man sitting on the other side of the mess, engaged in conversation as they are, with four or five rows of tables separating them.

It is a man she has never seen before, because if she had she would surely have remembered. But she needs no explanation. From how the functionary had described him to her there is little doubt that the man he is glaring at can be no one other than the very beast that lurks inside his dreams at night: Paxi.

It frightens her to think of what this means and what the following weeks will in fact bring in light of this. And if indeed it is a coincidence at all that Emilio Toffolo's sworn enemy, whom he so religiously has vowed to destroy, is traveling with them on this hunk of steel that is now no more than a speck out in the middle of the Atlantic.

He sits facing them though at a distance large enough to where immediate eye contact will always seem accidental. She studies him, spies him and thinks how odd it is to look at a man she has already learned to dislike before she has ever even laid eyes on him. She can see his legs crossed out in front of him and how the wash-blue smoke from his cigar dances its way up over the black sleeve of his jacket and crawls over his shoulders before making for the ceiling. It makes him look like a volcanic bulge ready to burst and his mere presence seems to send tremors through the crowd in front of him. There is something treacherous about him no doubt. But most of all she understands now as well that he is the most beautiful man she has ever seen.

It is just impossible for her not to stare, for her eyes to not slither over every angle and line of his impeccable suit. He is arrogance become flesh; on occasion a played-down but deliberate bend of his wrist is enough to stiffen the crowd in his immediate vicinity and achieve close to absolute silence around him every time he releases a puff of smoke.

She can see the functionary struggling to pick up the thread of whatever he might have been talking about only a minute ago. But to no avail; everything seems lost on him now, his gaze continuously sliding off in the direction of the man against whom by the mere looks of it at least he will never stand a chance.

"Is everything well, Signore," she hears the widow ask.

"Oh yes, dear," the functionary answers. "It is just that I was reminded of a business matter waiting for me once I get to Brazil. Nothing for you to worry about," he adds with a smile that is complacent and removed.

"You didn't say that your business interest in Brazil was actually traveling with us," Lydia then says, unsuccessfully trying to mislead their table companions by striking a tone that is familiar, though nowhere near cryptic enough to go completely unnoticed.

The functionary turns slowly toward her, showing the kind of tension on his brow that suggests a fatigue of the spirit, of a man who has been reminded once too often of his own futility, and adds, "I am sorry I wasn't more clear about that, Lydia. But now that you have seen what my business interest looks like, wait until you actually make its acquaintance."

"I am not too sure that I really want to," she replies.

"My dear, the Ostia Antica isn't large enough for you not to; especially, if you are going to be on it for a month and a half."

"To tell you the truth, Signore, the prospect of coming face to face with your so-called business interest between now and the day I set foot on shore again, actually does thrill me, perhaps more than you might want to know."

"Oh, but I do know and that it would probably thrill you even more to take a closer look at it — as disturbing as the thought may be."

Their table companions slowly disengage and turn to each other for conversation that isn't entirely held in riddles.

"Were you going to tell me that your nemesis was not some person you simply enjoy hating from a distance, but someone who is actually traveling with us?" she asks, as soon as all ears have gone deaf around them.

"I'll give you one even better than that, dear" the functionary replies "I followed Ulisse Paxi on this trip."

Meanwhile, the smoke from Paxi's cigar has traveled through the hull. And once it reaches their table she wonders if she should ever tell Emilio Toffolo that she has smelled it before, and that sometimes it even comes back to her to evoke images in her own dreams. She only hopes it won't show that she herself is now somewhat at a loss for words, or why her own gaze has now grown distant.

After that evening, in cabin ninety-four, the name Lissy Paxi will not be mentioned again. But that doesn't mean, of course, that with every word Lydia and the functionary exchange from then on, they will in some way refer to him and perhaps the fact that destiny is now bound by design. Constantly, and in the most unexpected places, Lydia will catch the scent of Paxi's cigars now, or think she will recognise his voice in passing, even though she has never heard it before. Out on the deck, in the breeze sweeping past her, the scent of his tobacco will sometimes reach her or as she moves down the maze of corridors on the lower decks the sugary roast will stop her dead in her tracks, but never accompanied by the apparition of the man it ultimately belongs to.

"Odd thing: smell" she will say sometimes to the functionary, as he sits slumped over his papers on his bunk, or as they stroll together over the deck to watch the sun setting on the bow. But Emilio Toffolo rarely reacts to these little tests of hers. Whenever she tries to tempt him, her words are always a precipice that opens before him; one he always takes great care not to look into. Even so, she pushes, though always with measure.

And in this way, in the weeks that follow, riddles become the most common mode of communication between them, even if it has become quite clear by now that Emilio Toffolo is not going to budge. Their conversations always veer back to the more tangible realities around them — like the fact the tropics are upon them, heavy and thick.

She can feel the guttural breath of the equator in the sanding of the clothes on her back. And it makes her feel not only savagely unprepared but undeserving in some way, as well.

And in this particular discomfort she isn't alone. Everyone around her seems to progressively slip into a mangy kind of calm that makes even the occasional fistfight less frequent as the days wear on. And here too, a very specific set of smells Lydia will from now on come to associate with migrants and sea travel. It is like a foreboding of a heat none of them have ever felt before, the kind that makes bananas spontaneously sprout out of the leathery vegetation and spiders grow to the size of a man's hand, so she will later learn. As the tropics envelop them, she also discovers other characteristics that distinguish the equator from the temperate Mediterranean coasts, namely how the outbreaks of diarrhea on the lower decks have become more frequent, and that no one dares to speak out the word Cholera.

It isn't to say though, that the sanitary conditions on the Ostia Antica are any less than those at any one of the port cities back home; rather it is the heat of the tropics itself that causes them to deteriorate. She begins to notice how the stories she had overheard in the hotel at the Via Balbi about disease and lice during the trips west and about the quarantine periods of several weeks at some of the ports of destination seem less exaggerated now and more like some unavoidable part of it all. And in this way, days also become interchangeable, the one identical to the last and dreadfully similar to the one that will soon follow, all against the backdrop of sky, ocean and sun.

On the morning of the twenty-second day they dock at the port of Salvador. By now, one could have almost forgotten there had been a destination at all. The days have become so seamlessly woven into one another that it actually startles Lydia when she feels the engines begin to vibrate at a lower frequency inside the walls. It pulls her out of her sleep at once.

"Signore, are you awake?"

"I hardly ever sleep anymore. Of course I am awake," he replies.

"Is that what I think it is?"

"That, dear, is the sound of Salvador da Bahia; America," he says turning away in his bunk to face the wall, annoyed apparently by something she cannot quite put her finger on.

"At least I still have them; dreams that is," she replies, as she throws on her clothes and slams the door behind her.

She walks out onto the deck and toward the bow, eager to see the glow of the city. But that distinct face of civilization when looked upon from a distance: light, is missing. The sea is as black as it had been on all other moonless nights, except for some scattered specs now indeed, in the distance, but which could just as well have been from other ships lying still in the water.

Nevertheless, the excitement in the others on the deck around her, who have also come out to witness their long awaited arrival, is undeniable, even if this isn't yet a coast but little more than a break in the monotony of weeks at sea. And however feeble the lights, they are lights and this means the Atlantic has been crossed.

Hours go by before the specs multiply from half a dozen to a dozen and a half and on to a bundle that might represent something of a town at all. Three in the morning becomes four and then five, and when the sky behind her finally begins to pale, only then do the contours of the Brazilian coast and the town behind it begin to acquire shape.

It is nearing six when once around the bend, on the other side of the peninsula and facing the All Saints bay, the brightly painted stucco fronts and the towers of the São Francisco Church finally become visible. The city bears a resemblance to large, crooked teeth poised in a smile, like racks of windswept clamshells staked in the sand. There is a taunting optimism to the view; a gaiety to the whole arrangement and the deliberate absence of symmetry rouses her senses. It makes her want to reach, to touch in disbelieve like some curious child.

She spots several members of the crew nailing announcements on the walls along the deck, outlining the itinerary for the two days they will be docked here before continuing South to Rio de Janeiro. Disembarking is to begin at ten that morning and for which, so the announcements read, they will need their ship cards and all other documents for identification, including medical statements, etc, meant to satisfy the local port authorities – most ironically, she feels - as to one's true or rather assumed identity, good health and some measure of noble intentions.

It is well past ten o-clock when the gangway is finally extended and secured on one of the piers. The passengers whose voyage ends here, along with their luggage are queued in front of it to disembark first. But it strikes Lydia how reluctant they seem, as if only now have they been able to see the difference that exists between fancying a new beginning and actually having to start anew. She counts no more than about thirty individuals in total - sun-roasted rural types, primarily Calabrians, looking dazed and marked and not all too sure of the heroic thing that they all have come to represent.

In the crowd Lydia spots the widow she had been talking to on the day she saw Paxi for the first time. Slouching next to her she also spots her lurid son looking even more bludgeoned than he had looked that evening.

It has been twenty-two days exactly since any of them has last set foot on solid ground. But still it surprises quite a few of them how unsteady they feel once they step onto the pier.

For no other reason than the fact the widow and her son are two familiar faces single filing over the ramp ahead of her Lydia begins to follow them, as they move inside the herd toward the city. All Lydia wants is to move, to cover distance on her own volition for a change. She wants to see the town. But then again the thought she is about to do so compels her far less than the thought in itself that she has actually made it here. She wants neither company nor to be by herself; she wants to be invisible again, the way she best remembers herself: neither noteworthy nor bland and always likely to get lost in a crowd.

A cobblestone road runs along several workshops and a large market hall that lines the embankment. A natural fifty-meter fault in the rock divides the upper and lower towns, with a set of cable cars as the only visible means of transport between them. Lydia in turn observes the widow and her son watching the Elevador Lacerca, trying to see the scenery through their eyes. She wants her first impressions of America to be tinted somehow, for the whitewashed architecture and the thick, languid tongue that is spoken here to become palpable through an indirect and slightly alien experience. She feels this might protect her from disappointments.

The Africanness of this town runs through its streets like a caramel surge that is interrupted here and there by the infusion of blond hair into the local gene pool, a result of European shipping visiting this coast over the course of more than a century. Never before has the suggestion, which is entertained by some that Africa might somehow be visible in the dark complexions of some of her countrymen, seem more erroneous than on this day; because, if such a connection could at all be made amongst Italians, then the faces of Salvador clearly represent the very heart of it, a plunging right into the core of the African continent itself.

Lydia still follows the widow and her son and through their eyes, in safety, she sets out to further explore the town. In particular, she enjoys walking through the old centre, the Pillory, the whipping post, as it is still called - a tantalising irony, given that slavery has only been abolished in northern Brazil – at least by law – only less than thirty years prior. It is as if that specific chapter in this city's history is still being kept alive in the smiles on the faces around her now: blatant and in celebration of human endurance itself it seems. She thinks of the functionary and only now begins to see how defeat can also often be a choice.

She notices the widow suddenly halts and pulls at her son to do the same. She observes how they cross themselves and then hurry toward the doors of the Cathedral.

"Indeed" Lydia whispers to herself, "there is much to be thankful for." – as she too enters the cool shadows after them.

She waits for her eyes to get adjusted to the dark, as the details of the gold-plated baroque walls slowly become visible to her in timed succession. Almost immediately she catches sight of the widow again inside the crowd of believers, as the woman plunges forward with a candle in her hand, which she obviously means to light and sheath at the main chapel. Lydia takes a moment to observe further; again, to get some sense of where she is and notices that the son has temporarily managed to disjoint himself from her side. Lydia scans the crowd in search for him. But soon enough she feels the vacuum of his presence slightly to the side of her, trailing his eyes after the figure of his mother moving in the direction of the gilded Christ.

She is sure he has not seen or recognised her – but then again she also knows how invisible she can make herself be sometimes, when she really wants to. She does her best to measure the level of emptiness that shows in his eyes as he looks at his mother ritualise grief for them both – and quite possibly the fact that he himself has never been alive to begin with. She has never seen anyone this soulless, this empty of hope; has never stood witness either to a man so chained. And again, this too, reminds her of the functionary.

At that moment she feels something inside her break, not anything as cathartic as a snap really but it is like something unwinding, a collapse of sorts, like rotted fruit falling earthbound in the dead of night. Whatever it is, it confines the widow and her son in her mind to something like a page she is about to turn. And as far as turning pages, within that one instant she also understands how the functionary too will soon belong to the past.

She turns and walks back out into the light again, feeling nauseated by the smell of incense, which has begun to mix itself with the moisture on the skins of the faithful around her. It is as though the actual turning of that page has already begun and she now finds herself at a moment in time in which movement, action, are already beyond the grasps of will, where one is left with no other choice but to indeed push forward.

Lydia returns to the ship, but she decides to not head back to the cabin just yet. She is unsure of how she will react to Emilio Toffolo still ruffling paper there, his cynical and hopeless words and the inevitable stench of liquor growing on him for almost a week now.

Except for the boys who do most of the sweeping and the mopping around the ship, the Ostia Antica is completely deserted. There is a tense calm similar to the calm that generally descends right before a tropical downpour. She can feel that morning's early rise in the soreness of her feet and legs, but she is back on them the moment she attempts to sit on one of the benches; right back to pacing and to hankering like a caged beast after the moment they will break free from the dock again and she will at last continue her journey south.

But distraction isn't long in coming. In the thick stir of the breeze the unmistakable sweetness of Costa Rican tobacco moves past her. She steps toward the railing where thin strands of smoke waft from the lower deck and unlike on other occasions, this time she can actually hear a man's voice at the source. He is talking to a young girl down on the pier who stands looking up at him into the glare of the sun. He is not speaking Italian but what she now recognises as Portuguese, though in many ways different from the Portuguese she had heard from the dockworkers back in Funchal. Their conversation is harsh, taunting, yet playful; not unlike children throwing around a ball.

From this angle Paxi looks rather uncouth, with his cotton shirt open across the chest and the tan of his skin shimmering even in the shadows. She contemplates his every movement and in particular she feels drawn by his hands; how they come up to his lips for a puff of smoke and then rests on the lacquered wood of the railing.

The girl on the pier cannot be more than about twelve or thirteen years old. She is wearing a faded dress fit for little more than the mopping of a floor - a savage looking creature with a wayward smile on her tarred face. Lydia takes a step back so as not to block the sun shining into the girl's face and remain unseen and free to take in every bit of Paxi from this unlikely angle.

At some point Lydia senses a pause in their conversation. She sees him reaching into the pocket of his vest hanging loosely from his shoulders for a coin, which he then holds up triumphantly for the girl on the pier to see, clearly in a gesture meant to entice.

That he then tosses the coin does not really surprise Lydia, for everything in his pose suggested that he would – or, as a grimmer prospect perhaps that he indeed would not and that he only meant to be cruel. What he does do however, is so much beyond the boundaries of cruelty that it first freezes Lydia's feet to the boards of the deck before fury ignites her toward heights unknown to her.

Instead of throwing the coin in the direction of the young girl he aims it at the narrow patch of water between the side of the ship and the pier. And if this isn't enough to appall and invoke the kind of hatred Lydia isn't too sure she can ever either forget or forgive, the young girl then, without hesitating, dives into the water after it.

Lydia hears herself shriek and darts down the steps and over the ramp, her feet barely touching the ground as she moves. By the time she reaches the pier the girl already lay panting on top of the boards, blowing the salt and the oil out of her nostrils with Paxi's coin clenched tightly between her teeth.

It is like every time her hand lands on the girl's face Lydia temporarily descends back into her own body before she promptly rises out of it again in the kind of rage she never thought she was capable of feeling let alone express. She doesn't notice that Paxi has followed her off the ramp and is now standing behind her as she flogs the girl with everything she has. Yet, in no way is he attempting to stop the beating. Finally it is the trickle of blood mixed with the tears running down the young girl's face that makes Lydia remain inside herself long enough to will her hands to stop beating her. And once she has, her attention instinctively turns to him.

"If you ever do that again I will personally throw you down after it. Do you hear me?" she growls, hammering hot spikes into the devil himself in front of her. "And you..." she then adds, turning to the girl again still doubled up at her feet and covering her face with both hands, awaiting the next salvo of strikes to descend upon her.

"No, you tell her," Lydia reconsiders, directing herself toward Paxi after all. "You tell her, if she ever does anything like that again, I will personally see to it that she doesn't come up for air. Tell her!"

With her eyes piercing she follows him as he lowers himself to convey the message and as he does Lydia feels her hands glow again with the urge to strike the two of them now.

After he has whispered words into the girl's ear he straightens himself and stands facing her.

"I think she understands," he says with an amused glimmer in his eyes, yet with nothing of the arrogance Lydia had in fact expected. "She's promised she will never dive for coins again," he adds almost earnestly.

For a second he seems to study her more closely, treating himself openly to the details of her face.

"I'm quite impressed, Miss - but not so much by your passion as by your naivety. Did you stop to consider what else a young girl like this will

45

do for a coin?" he asks, extending his arms to cover the bay and the city around it.

"Don't you worry, Signore Paxi," Lydia answers, somewhat in control of herself again. "We will not get a chance to find out."

She pulls the girl to her feet and wipes the blood and the tears off the side of her face with the hem of her dress. She cups her hand under her chin for her to spit out the coin still in her mouth. But the girl looks up at her and it is clear that it will take a lot more than a beating for her to part with that. No matter what Lydia might still do to her, the coin in her mouth is hers; she has squarely earned it.

Lydia concedes with a hint of recognition and leads the girl toward the ship.

"What do you think you are doing?" Paxi calls after them.

"I am going to wash this girls face," Lydia replies without turning.

"But you can't do that."

"You could always try to stop me, Signore Paxi," she says, as he begins to move slowly after her in disbelief, as if only now were he actually witnessing something that is out of the ordinary somehow.

"You can't take this girl on board, Miss. The crew... "

"The crew isn't here. Besides, after what you did, the least we owe her is to clean her up."

"After what I did to her? If I recall correctly, it was you who stood beating her like a dog just now. So, what is it exactly you feel I owe her?"

"You are right, it should have been you who got a beating. And that is why I am going to tend to her."

"Wait," he pleads, as he picks up his step to catch up. "Have you thought how the other passengers are going to react to you bringing a Negro on board with you?"

"No, I have not. She is a young girl you knew would do anything for a lousy coin. And you put her in harm's way for your own amusement. It is you, Signore Paxi, who should be ashamed to show your face to the rest of the passengers."

"You obviously know my name."

"Doesn't everybody?"

"Perhaps, but you have no right to pass judgment"

"I only pass judgment based on what I witness with my own eyes, nothing more."

"Don't use the public lavatory. Someone might see you," he says.

"I don't care if someone sees me."

"Miss, as I mentioned before, there is a lot to be said for your passion but there is still a lot more that can be said about your lack of experience. You shouldn't overestimate our countrymen. You can use my quarters to do all the cleaning you need. Nobody will bother you there," adding, "it's this way."

He starts in the direction of the bridge, a part of the ship Lydia has not been to before. It is the area reserved exclusively for senior members of the crew and the first class passengers; a three-level, tower-like structure with the actual bridge at the very top, which is also, and quite logically, the highest point of the entire ship. Each of the two levels beneath it is made up of four luxury suites surrounded by windows and separated by corridors on the inside. Although the quarters aren't exactly spacious, it is the attention to detail and level of decoration that makes them lush.

He leads the way through the door. The musky scent of his tobacco permeates everything inside. Every object seems to come alive with it. His bed is made impeccably. Every crease has been smoothened to such an extent that the cotton of the sheets could as well have been silk. Lydia wonders to what extent this is a man for whom perfection has long since ceased to be some kind of an ideal but an everyday reality. And thus what it is he actually dreams about, at which level dreams even played inside of him.

He throws a couple of fresh towels on the edge of the sink with a bar of soap on top of them. He points to the faucet in a downplayed gesture and turns around to face her.

"Feel free to use anything you need," he says. "I believe I have everything here."

"Believe so too," Lydia replies in a voice that is much thinner and much more reluctant than she had wanted it to be.

He moves in the direction of the door and hesitates, turning one last time.

"I suppose a lot of people know who I am," he says, "Or think, at least, that they do. Usually it doesn't affect me either way. But for some reason it flatters me that you did."

He smiles at her only with his eyes, not wanting her attention to divert away when he says, "I wanted you to know that."

She doesn't quite smile back. But the hatred eases out of her face somewhat.

"The only problem, however, is that I still don't know who you are, Miss," he says.

"And I am flattered that you would see that as a problem, Signore Paxi. My name is Lydia," she replies, pushing her hair away from her face.

He stares into the empty space in front of him for a moment, as if to let her name resound inside his head before he speaks again. She might have expected a question to follow, that he might require more details about who she is, but it is the completeness with which she says her name that makes him reconsider asking her about it.

She watches the door close and stares at it for a moment. Then she turns her attention to the young girl still standing in the middle of the room, looking like a hatched chick rolled in mud. She motions for her to move closer and leads her toward the sink. She wets one of the towels and as she begins to wipe the dirt and dried blood from the girl's face she notices how as the filth disappears the girl's skin actually becomes darker instead of the other way around. The girl does little more than just stare into the mirror, blinking only as a reflex when the wet cloth rasps over her eyes. She seems without emotion and Lydia wonders what could possibly, amongst all of life's injustices, have hardened a child in this way and not quite sure if she wants to learn the full answer to that question.

"What you need is a proper bath, young lady," Lydia says as playfully as she can make herself sound and stops to look around the room. "Now that we are here we might as well take advantage of the situation. Wouldn't you agree? Who knows when we will get a chance again to indulge in the comforts of first class," she adds.

She throws a fresh towel on the bed and moves around the tub. It doesn't surprise her that the water that runs out of the faucet is actually warm, as the tub begins to fill. She starts removing the clothes off the girl's back and again she feels rather shaken by how passive and unmoved the girl seems. And again she prefers not to think of where and how a girl her age might have learned to disengage herself so completely.

"I am Lydia. And now that you know my name, I would like to hear yours," she says, using her hands and some different expressions on her face to make sure the girl understands; she is determined that she should at least achieve this much.

The girl appears to soften somewhat, either from the clean, septic smell of the soap in the water, or perhaps the sound of Lydia's voice after all. As the girl slowly sinks into the tub an unmistakable sign of pleasure is revealed when the lids of her eyes briefly close.

"What's your name?" Lydia finally whispers, thinking that there must be some universal sound to this question to which only one answer is possible, in any language.

But the girl just looks up at her, empty still, still quite unable to be reached.

"Where is your mother? Where do you live? Do you have any brothers and sisters? What were you doing on the pier?"

As Lydia's questions become more pressing and her tone more interrogating, the gaze in the girl's eyes just grows blanker, as she removes all light out of them again.

Lydia wraps the towel around the girl's body, which is still in the initial stages of morphing into young-womanhood. She plucks one of Paxi's shirts from the closet for her to wear and watches the girl look at herself in the mirror, as if at something she cannot entirely connect to. But then, right when Lydia has all but given up, the girl says effortlessly, in near flawless Italian:

"Edmilce. Mi chiamo Edmilce."

"See, I knew you could talk," Lydia whispers in a voice winded with amazement.

It is as if from one moment to the next a gag has been removed from the girl's mouth and at last she has been given a voice with which to speak, even though she still pantomimes and draws figures in the air between them to communicate the broad parameters of who she is. Yet, it is clear to Lydia that the thread that normally runs through childhood, or most certainly should, the skeletal structure that creates memories and a sense of origin linked to future, seems missing – as though the young girl's world were one that exists only in the now. Her stories are fragmented and sketchy, as she consistently refers to herself in the third person when she speaks.

"I want to get us some food," Lydia announces after a while, feeling strangely energised by what she has heard.

But it shames her, too how the efficiency with which a young girl can fill her large eyes with vigour one minute and then flick off her soul so completely the next, makes her even a bit jealous. In their erratic attempts to communicate, holding monologues in kin languages but which are also fundamentally different in their everyday use, Lydia does feel she has been given a glimpse of what America can also be: a place where poverty exists like any other and can thus be characterised as any other place on earth by the universal struggle to stay out of its clutches.

"Do not go anywhere," she says. "I won't be long. And if the gentleman comes back," she adds, "tell him that you are waiting for me. Under no circumstance are you to let him send you away. Understood?"

She can read from the girl's face that she does understand and also that food at this point is incentive enough for her to do exactly as she is told.

Lydia looks around the room at Paxi's personal belongings lying about and realises how valuable some of them must look to a child that sleeps on stone floors at night – but also how little those same objects probably mean to that same man.

Outside the cabin, an unruly festive mood has been brought on board by her fellow passengers returning from a day on the town. It annoys her to be standing in the middle of it. Especially in light of the thing she is considering and even if this thing is still just a fantasy from which she can be easily dissuaded.

She opens the door to her own cabin and as expected, she finds the functionary seated on the bottom bunk reading some of his famous manuscripts.

50

"Well, look who's come home. If it isn't my long lost cabin mate, the impeccable Lydia-just-Lydia."

"Signore Toffolo, I need your help."

"You know, dear, whenever people say that to me it usually is because they want money."

"That may be exactly what I will soon be asking of you."

"What's the matter? You look like you had a scare. Are you in some sort of trouble?" the functionary says, his face turning grave and motherly, the way it often does whenever he is distracted enough to feel any form of concern for things that are not necessarily contained within either his notebooks or documents.

"Not exactly, but I may run into it before long."

"Heavens, Lydia, what's on your mind?"

She sits down opposite him and digs her eyes into his, as if she were looking for an answer to a question she isn't sure she can dirty with words just yet. And in a similar way he searches hers.

"I met a young girl today. I can't tell you all the details, so you're just going to have to trust me."

"What girl?"

"A child really."

"A child? It amazes me sometimes, Lydia, how easily you forget you yourself are still one."

"To cut a long story short, Signore, I believe this child will be in serious danger if she remains here."

"In danger of what? What sort of trouble? Where?"

"Just trouble; here in Salvador. And you're welcome to fill in the blanks on that. She's a street child and I want to find a way to keep her on the ship."

"Where's she now?" he asks, a stony shadow falling over his face.

"I am hiding her. I left her so I could arrange for some food. I need to find a way for her to travel to Buenos Aires with me. I know I cannot keep her hidden for three whole weeks. And if it comes to that, I want to ask you to help me pay for her passage. We have four extra bunks right here and all I will eventually need is money to let her use one of them."

A cacophonous silence fills the cabin, as the functionary's eyes dart from one end of it to the other, digesting what he has just heard. Eventually, his gaze settles on hers again, holding her in a judicial glower that cannot fully veil how much it tickles him as well to be made accomplice to such a preposterous thing.

He finally says, "Does it concern a Negro?"

"Yes."

"And does this Negro have traveling papers, Lydia?"

"It would surprise me very much."

The hint of a devious chuckle passes over his lips.

"It'll please you to know, Signore Toffolo, that you're not the first person today that says how naïve I am. Just in case you are about to point that out to me now."

"Who else knows about this?"

"What, about the fact she is here or that she will be traveling with me to Buenos Aires?"

"I haven't agreed to partake in any of this — and it is already a fact she will be traveling with you to Buenos Aires?"

"Either way; with or without your help, yes, I believe the possibility is very real that she will."

"Who else knows about this?" he repeats.

"I told you I couldn't tell you everything; not now. You are going to have to trust me."

"If I am going to be asked to take part in anything like this, Lydia, the least I can ask for is to know all the details."

"I cannot give them to you."

"Do you really think they are going to let you do this? Do you think you can bring a Negro child on board of a barge full of Italians, who one by one are fiddling with nerves strung so tight about what's to become of them that they pass the time brawling amongst themselves? And you want to confront all five hundred of them with this insane project of yours?"

"I believe you understand my predicament, from front to back. Now, will you help me?"

"Of course I will help you. Bit of advice though: keep her hidden for as long as you can. I will be delighted to meet her."

Lydia holds the door slightly ajar and rests her head against the side of it, smiling back at him.

"Her name is Edmilce."

<><><><><><><><>

Coming around the bridge she notices the lights inside the cabin have been turned on, which means Paxi has probably returned. Under one arm, wrapped inside a cloth, she has a loaf of bread and a dried sausage, which she has charmed off one of the members of the kitchen staff, along with a jug of fresh milk, which she holds in her other hand. She knocks on the door and notices her breathing accelerating as soon as he appears before her. his sleeves rolled up past his elbows and smiling down at her.

"The girl told me you were on your way back," he says, searching her face like some simpleton demon.

But the way she looks back causes him to step aside before long.

She finds the girl seated on the bed. She is eating pumpkin seeds over an old newspaper and spitting the shells into the same pile she is picking them from.

"She says you went out to get some food," Paxi says, glancing at the mess of shells on the bed. "I hope you don't mind, but I got those around the docks this morning."

He comes around toward her.

"I figured she might enjoy having some while we waited for you."

"That was very kind of you," Lydia responds, scraping her throat. "But my guess is she could use something a bit more substantial."

She places her provisions on the table and begins to unwrap them.

"Now, there is an interesting definition of a substantial meal," Paxi comments in Portuguese, after releasing a thin little whistle, followed by a wink in the direction of the bed.

In response the girl lets a faint glimmer of a smile pass over her eyes and continues her chewing and spitting unhindered, as she watches them like a pair of exotic birds engaged in some weird prenuptial dance.

"Well, it was all I was able to get my hands on," Lydia protests, though also quite willing to laugh at herself a bit, even if outwardly she remains stern and focused on the grave business of cutting sausage and

53

pouring milk into finely polished crystal, which Paxis sets in front of her.

In silence they watch the girl eat — not ravaging the food like some beast but rather, and much to their surprise, well-mannered and quite in control of herself.

"A sign of upbringing after all," Paxi whispers.

But once the first gulps of fresh milk begin to disappear down her throat and her shoulders sink with pleasure, Lydia feels oddly relieved that the girl is indeed starved after all.

"I see you found some clothes for the child to wear," Paxi says, no longer bothering to mask the sound of his voice by whispering.

"I couldn't put the rags she was wearing this morning back on her. I hope you don't mind, Signore. And besides, you seemed to have plenty more, if you are referring to the shirt."

"I appreciate your reasoning. Though it might interest you to know that the shirt you picked for her is in fact half silk and half Egyptian cotton, made for me personally by my Milanese tailor."

"Ah, Milan," Lydia replies simulating tedium.

"Yes, a Milanese tailor — but living and working in Chicago going on ten years now," he adds. "As a matter of fact, the only wearable item I own that was actually made in Italy — or anywhere else in Europe for that matter are my boots. And those were indeed made in Milan, but out of washed bear skin from the Appalachian Mountains in Virginia."

He lifts his foot off the ground a bit to better demonstrate the workmanship he is talking about, seeming quite confident somehow that Lydia will be able to appreciate it — or understand it even.

"It seems like an awful long way to travel to get yourself some clothes, if you ask me," she says.

"Not if you consider that over the past twelve years I have spent no more than two months out of every year in Europe —or Italy- for that matter. You could say I prefer the style of the New-World."

"You always seem to be referring to yourself in some way or another. Why is that Signore Paxi?"

Their eyes only brush in passing.

"I befriended an Austrian doctor some years ago, who seems to be making quite a name for himself. He told me that I betray what he called a - narcissistic streak almost of pathological proportions - every time I open my mouth. This doctor — well, he says that this self-indulgent side to my character, even though quite a liability, is also part of my charm."

Paxi smiles but it is as if she were looking back at him from a great distance.

"He says he found my arrogance amusingly childlike, too" he adds.

Paxi leans forward, frowns and then says in a mock German accent, "Herr Paxi, I have concluded my analysis. If it weren't for your name and your wealth, you would be sadly ill equipped to survive in the world of grown-ups, you know.

I disagreed, of course," he says whilst turning to face himself in the mirror.

But Lydia's attention has long since gone back to the girl whose cheeks are puffy with bread and her eyes fixed and glistening from the sight of him talking like a madman. Lydia stands up unimpressed and moves to the window that overlooks the stern. It is nearing ten and most of the passengers outside have begun to retire to the levels below. She feels thankful for the night approaching, for the cover of dark that will soon allow her to carry out the plan that has been forming in her mind.

"I want to thank you, Signore Paxi, for your kindness," she says turning to face him. "After the business on the pier I feel you have proved you are the gentleman I sort of suspected you would be — even if you have the tendency to talk about yourself far more than I thought you would."

"If it means you won't unleash your wrath on me again, Lydia, rest assured, it has all been worth it."

"I am not as unforgiving as you might think," she says, sparing a laugh.

"Lydia, I don't believe you really know what it is I am thinking."

"We should be going," she announces and takes a step in the direction of the door.

He moves to block her path.

"I feel I do have the right to ask you what you are planning to do though," he says, all playfulness removed from his voice now.

"I don't know what you mean," she says, her lips tensing and colorless again.

"If you would like, Lydia, I can see to it the child makes it safely off the ship. As you know, the crew will not take lightly to finding out she was here. I will be able to explain if someone sees her. That is, of course, if that's what you were planning to do yourself — show her off the ship."

"To tell you the truth, Signore Paxi, I am not exactly sure what I am going to do."

He begins to pace around the room, as if he were searching for the right words that might lie hidden in the objects around him - in the leather-bound books stacked on the nightstand or the jingling of the metal, as he runs his fingers through a tray of silver and gold cuff links next to the sink. His movements give off the illusion that his feet might be lifted off the ground at any moment, the soles of his boots grinding that softly over the floorboards.

"Lydia, you know who I am. And surely you must also know at least something about what it is that I do."

"I have heard people talk about you. But not always in a bad way, if that's what you mean."

He laughs.

"I wonder who you have been talking to!"

"I am curious to hear what you have to tell me, Signore Paxi. Maybe you will explain to me what your Austrian doctor thinks is wrong with you; because I am afraid I didn't quite follow the first time."

He laughs again.

"Would you have a seat, Lydia?"

He slides out a chair from under the table for her facing the girl, who has pushed aside the bread and the sausage on the table and is now mechanically crushing shells with her teeth again, still without taking her eyes off the two of them.

Lydia hesitates but accepts, more out of curiosity than anything else.

"I am not going to give any speeches, Lydia. I give enough of those. But I do want to tell you, before you walk out of that door again, a little bit more about me."

He opens one of the drawers of the bureau near the end of the bed and flips open the top of a wooden box lined with cigars, the ones that have so tormented her these past weeks with a scent that has forced her to

56

think about herself in ways she never has before. She shifts in her chair, shocked by the thought that he is about to light one.

"Do you know what I think is the most valuable thing we own?"

She just blinks her eyes, ghost-like.

"It is choice. I believe the most important thing we own is choice; the freedom, the right, to be something different from what others would condemn us to be. It is actually quite simple."

She glances at the girl and then quickly lets her eyes drop.

"I don't think I could agree with you more," she replies thinly.

"Then, why don't you give her that right?" he says pointing his finger at the child. "Ask her what she wants, what it is she would like to be. Give her the right to choose."

"But she is a child, Signore."

"Yes and so are you. What do you really know about this child, Lydia? Did you even bother to learn anything about her?"

"As much as I could in the brief time we were here, most certainly!"

"In the time you were off to arrange this sumptuous meal you've brought for her," he says with benign sarcasm, "I was able to learn a thing or two myself. Did you know our young friend was orphaned at the age of about four? She isn't quite sure, see. From the little she does know about herself, she arrived in the city trailing by the hand of some older child she refers to as Nila and as part of a pack of children that varied in size, depending on any number of unforeseen misfortunes along the way, as they moved from the inland bush toward the coast."

He pauses and searches Lydia's gaze scaling the walls around them.

"Don't you dare look the other way," he almost barks. "I am preparing you possibly for the most important choice you will ever make. So, don't you dare look away. I will not have it," he adds; takes a breath and continues.

"The child seems to have no clear recollection of where exactly she came from either or what the purpose for her trek to the city had really been. But it shouldn't require too much imagination to speculate that food has ultimately and always been the ever-dominant theme that has run through her existence; that eating in itself is a preoccupation that colors everything in her world — a world that to her is made up solely of children it would seem.

You should know, Lydia, that it was only recently too that the child for the first time wrapped herself in the sheets of a proper bed. And what I would really like you to understand is that by now some of the older girls she once came to the city with get to feel bed sheets much more often than she, because they are now older and therefore able to accompany gentlemen sometimes to places where sheets indeed exist.

For the time being, however — and this may come as somewhat of a consolation to you — she does not accompany gentlemen yet, but finds her own comfort and refuge at the steps of the São Francisco Church at night. And most importantly, you should know that diving for coins is in fact one of the things the street children of Salvador are most famous for."

Lydia reaches across the table to touch the skin on the girl's forearm and to look into her eyes. The child seems tired and many times more fragile than she had before. And then for a moment she and Lydia connect; and Lydia no longer needs to plot her words.

"Is there any place you would like to go, Edmilce?"

It sickens Lydia to think that after all the conspiring she has been doing, it not once occurred to her to ask the child this one simple question.

The girl's eyes remain fixed on her for a moment and she says, again in clear and near flawless Italian:

"How will you know that the girl has kept her promise, if she doesn't go with you to wherever it is you are going, Lydia?"

"What promise?" Paxi asks surprised.

"That the girl will not dive for coins again — Signore," Edmilce answers.

58

A Third Heart

Even years later, when asked how Edmilce had entered her life, Lydia would always give the same answer.

"As contraband and on little more than a whim," she would say.

But it would take much longer before she understood that Edmilce was in fact part of a pattern – one she had not coincidently stumbled upon, but a pattern that had actually been devised for her by a place called America; her life scripted up to this one leap of faith.

It is well past midnight when they leave Paxi's quarters, a pair of blotchy stains pacing over the boards with scarves wrapped around their heads in disguise. The ship has become a sleeping frame again, the domain of the rodents that have multiplied exponentially since Madeira and reign freely at night down the corridors and the decks. The crew has been spraying arsenic in every nook of the ship and has been doing so with increasing frequency.

It surprises Lydia that the functionary has not waited up for them to welcome the new arrival. She can hear his breathing evenly on top of his bunk as they enter. He seems far away somewhere. She points the girl to the top bunk across from hers, all the time searching the whites of the girl's eyes as the only part of Edmilce that is actually visible to her in the dark.

Of course, sleep comes to neither one, as they both wait out the night by staring at the jarred window across the length of the cabin; for the dawn to shed light on the thing that has been done. The functionary's voice replays inside Lydia's head as she tries to make sense of the thing that is occurring, the actual weight and magnitude of the responsibility she has taken on. But, mixed with that, every time, what makes her own thoughts so deafening is the alarming fact that Paxi occupies a place in them now as well. She tries to imagine how the functionary might summarize the situation for her, as he surely will in the morning. But every time, it is the scent of tobacco on her clothes and hair that blurs everything.

So far, Lydia has only known the functionary to be a rather melancholy man, whose gentle nature is often smeared by a moody side that is at its strongest - and meanest — right before his medicinal morning brandy, as he calls it. In the end, the liquor is what thaws him out enough to where any kind of communication becomes even remotely possible beyond sneers and barks with anyone around him. But this changes with Edmilce.

Right after daybreak the functionary propels himself out of his bunk and proceeds to hop around the cabin on bare feet at the end of white, hairless legs. He seems delirious, unsure of what he should say or do with himself.

"My, you're absolutely gorgeous! And what skin, my child!"

He turns between the two of them with a wild look in his eyes and it strikes Lydia that his Portuguese is downright perfect.

He besieges the girl with his famous elaborateness; introductions to which Edmilce can do little more than sagely nod her head and smile at the unhinged drivel that is almost as strange to her as it is to Lydia. He seems beside himself with excitement; as if he at last has been allowed to divert his thoughts away from his daily worries and can finally curve around to reveal who he really is. Or, at least, whom he wants them to think he is, at that particular junction.

He cups his child-like little hands over the girl's puffy cheeks.

"Your face! My dear God, your face! It's a chocolate doll, Lydia! Where did your find her?"

"Her name is Edmilce..." Lydia attempts, but he isn't asking questions, or really listening to anything either of them might have to say.

He just wants to talk. And before long, in his frenzy, he also begins to paint pictures — even if measured in mere glimpses — of the Brazil he knows, mysterious and far in every sense.

"Do you realise, Lydia," he says, only briefly ungluing his eyes from the girl still sitting in her bunk, "we're in Brazil now. This is the face of this country, the Negro face.... I hadn't realised how much I love this place. And now — now..."

In particular, it is the open fields in the South to which, in his crazed song, he will return every time. Next to cities Lydia has indeed heard of before, like Sao Paulo and Rio de Janeiro, he seems particularly gleamy-eyed about places like Belo Horizonte and Mato Grosso do Sul, and other such places that might have been pure fabrications on his part, as far as she is concerned. But he says that Edmilce reminds him of them all the same.

With intervals he talks about indigenous tribes he wants to visit in the North, as well, who supposedly go around wearing nothing but tree bark to cover themselves and sustain a diet consisting of various roots, ape and snake meat and other such atrocities, as he calls them. But before long he is back in the South again; again constructing flowery prose around the swamplands in the interior and especially a town called Trés Corações, his final destination, and which Lydia finally understands to be the matter-of-the heart he has talked about before.

Lydia is thankful for the functionary's stories; they help her to push through her own doubts and as he leaves the cabin to arrange for food later that morning, when he isn't there to animate them with the tales of this marvelous world of his, a vacuum seems to manifest itself between Lydia and the girl. Without him they seem shunted into an uncomfortable silence, divided by the barrier of language and culture, and a shared reluctance. In the functionary's absence they just observe one another; stare blankly into each other's eyes, which on both ends are filled with too many unanswerable questions. At times, the girl will become something of a ghost – an apparition to Lydia, distant and removed; a presence that is undeniable yet eludes all reason and purpose. There are moments the girl becomes so unreal, an idea so reckless that it is hard to imagine she is in fact even made of flesh and blood at all – that it lives, breathes....

It is only deep under the cover of night that Lydia will dare smuggle the girl out of the cabin. These excursions are strictly for practical purposes: to wash and do her necessities and perhaps some quick vampiric breaths of fresh air out on the deck and a view of the coast that is only shadows in the distance breaking up the night sky. It is with an anxious sense of duty that she returns the girl to the cabin unseen, pulled by the kind of fear that is far beyond making one fearful, for it is caused by the existence of humanity itself around them. Even the most fleeting of contacts with the other passengers Lydia now dreads. They are to be avoided at all cost, for she feels that even to show her own face now will surely betray the fact that she is truly hiding something, something as visible as a Negro child on a ship full of on-edged Italians. It is not a new thing for Lydia to know nothing of the future. Instead, her restlessness now comes from feeling pre-destined and bound.

<>

On the second morning the functionary is off early and disappears on a lengthy expedition about the ship, returning hours later with food and gifts, no less, for Edmilce.

He leaves the cabin with a contented whistle on his lips and as he tosses a devilish smile back at them from the doorway, it is clear to see how the added element to his journey has absolutely invigorated him. He directs his gaze musingly over their heads, at the light coming in from the pot-lid window and confides in them again how much Edmilce reminds him of places and people he has known on previous crossings, of whom he has grown quite fond and cannot wait to see again; adding:

"I am actually quite impressed, Lydia, by the choices you've made, even though I also find them to be quite reckless."

Upon his return he expands on this, expressing how much he enjoys talking with the girl, even if his definition of talking with is to practice his own Portuguese in the form of endless monologues, and which leave Edmilce batting her eyelashes and grabbing hold of both her knees with dizziness. But Edmilce appears to take to him well enough in spite of this, visibly savouring the cultivated manner in which the functionary addresses her. It is pure enjoyment of the fact no one has ever really spoken to her in such a way that makes Edmilce beam every time he opens his mouth.

When he isn't telling the child – and Lydia, though in far lesser terms - about Brazil, he stresses how important it is for them to brush up on their languages as well; Edmilce Italian and Lydia her Portuguese, and of course that their ultimate goal should be to learn Spanish, thinking ahead less than three weeks, to when they will arrive in Argentina.

He says it would be just too scandalous to still be communicating in that idiotic pantomiming of theirs, once they get to such a fancy place.

"If you'd dedicate yourselves just a little," he will say, "you will both be talking up a storm in no time!"

And, totally disconnecting himself with whatever he has initially been rambling about, he then goes on to demonstrate the phonetic similarities between all Roman languages; words like bread and wine and God and dress and so on, hopping right up to more complex sentences – and not without some impressive results, which he will duly reward with proclamations like, "You girls are a teachers dream come true..." and, "What I wouldn't give to be able to put my teaching skills to work on students that are trapped inside a crammed space from morning till night, with nothing else to do but practice, practice and learn!"

"What interests me the most, though, Signore," Lydia says, right in the middle of his specific recital about the double L phenomenon in the Spanish language and the N with-a-squiggle-on-top.

"And what would that be, Lydia?" the functionary responds, short and slightly annoyed by the interruption.

"What interests me, Signore Toffolo," she repeats, "is the fact that all this time you let me think it was some woman that was waiting for you in Brazil, while in fact it is a place. The three hearts, Trés Corações; it is the name of a town," Lydia says, again trying as best she can to accept that this is clearly a subject he wants to keep to himself – for now at least.

So, she decides on a different approach all together.

"You are also going to unmask your Nemesis, Ulisse Paxi. Is it not?"

"You seem to have memorised his name quite well." he answers, trying to sound more surprised than is in fact the case.

She searches his gaze as it slips away from hers, adding, "And once you have assured yourself, Signore Toffolo, that Paxi is whatever it is you suspect him of, will you then return to Europe feeling satisfied? Is this really the reason you traveled half the earth?"

His eyes magnify behind his spectacles, looking bewildered and a little hurt, too.

"What if you discover you are wrong, Signore," Lydia continues, "about Ulisse Paxi and perhaps discover that America is a better place than where any of us have come from? What if the authorities here in Brazil are actually giving away free land, to Italians and Germans, who cares? What then? Will you still go back and tell everybody in Italy you were wrong, and that they should all come out this way after all, as Ulisse Paxi has claimed all along?"

"Are you defending that rat? You don't even know half of what he has done and what he has said he would do – unless somebody stops him."

"Stop him from doing what exactly? Maybe it is you who should free yourself Signore. Maybe you shouldn't let yourself get so embittered by such nonsense."

"Lydia, I know Ulisse Paxi and I know what he is. Maybe you should meet him one day, so you will understand why I cannot stop until I have unmasked him for what he is."

"Maybe I will meet Ulisse Paxi one day." Lydia replies. "And who knows, some day I will realise you were right about him."

She has promised herself to never talk about her involvement with Paxi to the functionary. And all the more she is now convinced Emilio Toffolo must never know that Paxi has anything to do with Edmilce being with them. Yet, the more she absorbs the functionary's ranting the less she understands how such a gentle being, who can speak so lovingly about the world and the possibilities it offers, can at the same time be so cynical. There has to be something more, something much larger that connects these two men. And it is just too tempting to not seduce him to talk about it.

But every time she tries, however she flanks him, Emilio Toffolo will just end the conversation with, "I don't have to justify myself to anyone; not you, not anyone."

Every time this particular discussion erupts between them Edmilce just cuts herself loose by retreating into a world of her own, where she can safely just wait for these little storms to pass and for the functionary to resume his tales about a land called Brazil, which Lydia is convinced he adores infinitely more than the hatred he feels for Paxi.

On the fourth morning out of Salvador, after a restless and wallowed night, Lydia awakes to find the functionary is still in his bunk. So far he has been the first one up every morning and it surprises her he isn't already bouncing about collecting his things. An uneasy silence hangs inside the cabin now. As he lay facing the wall, his breathing is strained like a soft, mechanical, exhaustion-induced purring and the few thinning hairs he still has on his head are stuck to his scalp with fever.

She whispers his name. And when that doesn't incite a reaction, she carefully presses down on his shoulder with the tops of her fingers. When he slowly turns to face her, she can see his lips have acquired an opaque and gleam-less texture, which, rather to her surprise, at that moment, she somehow associates with the kind of leather she imagines Paxi might commission a pair of boots of. The whites of the functionary's eyes dance ghastly between different tones of yellow and his mouth pulls down to one side to intercept jabs of pain that seem to shoot through him on occasion. When he tries to speak, his words spill out of him in a disorderly fashion, weak and cracked, as a clear sign that his temperature is running dangerously high.

The fever is her first concern and she hopes she can bring it down far enough to where he might be able to communicate anything pertaining to his own condition – which might then provide her with ideas about what to do next.

He pendulously slips in out of consciousness for the rest of that day, ever tormented by spells of extended pain, it seems. None of her experience as an apprentice to the midwives at the nunnery could have prepared her enough to diagnose him properly. And the more this becomes clear to her the more she realises the magnitude of the problem this now also presents her – that Edmilce will not for very much longer remain a secret she can contain within the four walls of the cabin. Catastrophe seems eminent.

All Lydia can really do is stand back and listen to Edmilce whisper thinly, half to herself and half to the room around them, like a lullaby:

"No good – no good at all."

It is already dark when Lydia knocks on Paxi's door. He doesn't seem even the least bit surprised to see her — something she should have noticed, but doesn't.

"I need your help," she says.

He steps back to let her in.

"I promised myself I would not come to you," she says. "But there is no one else I can turn to for this."

The scent of his cigars inside his quarters soothes her immediately upon entering. It is a feeling she might have described as warm in some way, but far removed from safe at the same time.

"One of my cabin mates has taken ill, Signore Paxi," she explains. "He has been running a fever since this morning and it seems only to be getting worse. I don't think it would be wise to wait until morning before a proper doctor has been consulted."

She reluctantly concludes, "Either way, Signore Paxi, the girl will be discovered."

Paxi keeps silent as she talks. He hardly even looks at her. He just paces back and forth, making like he is actually considering the situation and the options available. There is nothing in his manner that suggests he even knows who the functionary is.

"Hide her," Paxi says.

"No. I don't hide."

"Go back to the cabin," he motions her to the door. "Wait for me there."

And within minutes after knocking on his door she is outside again, in the clammy dark of the early evening, shuffling herself back to the bowels of the ship.

The functionary appears to be sleeping almost peacefully when she enters. But then she realises that what makes the stagnant air so serene is the fact that the place has been tidied up quite meticulously. It pleases her to discover that Edmilce can be in control of far more than what she initially gave her credit for, that she can indeed be an asset - because, considering how things stand for now, she herself isn't much in control of anything.

Close to a half hour passes when an avid but delicate knock sounds on the door. A man in shirtsleeves; though distinguished nonetheless, stands in the doorway holding a small valise in one hand and a set of keys in the other - which throws Lydia off a bit and causes her to speculate about it. He introduces himself with some static of annoyance in his voice, as the ship's doctor. Only then does she see Paxi standing behind him, who is holding a cautious distance at all times, his eyes shifting between some invisible object down the hall and the tips of his boots, as they both enter.

The doctor's glare travels more freely through the cabin, however, from the patient to the valise in his hand and then eventually back to Lydia again. For only a second his eyes rest on Edmilce, who has seated herself in the most obscure corner she could find and remains there without making a sound. It is quite impossible for Lydia to guess exactly what thoughts creep through the doctor's mind at that instant, but she understands that this is not the time to dwell.

The doctor lowers himself and directs his attention toward the patient and after what could not be more than a minute, he concludes his routine by pulling down and up on the functionary's eyelids, turning his head toward the light and then abruptly rising to his feet again.

"Has the gentleman indicated any discomforts in particular?" he asks her.

"Yes" she whispers. "He complained of severe pains in his side. Other than that he hasn't been coherent since last night."

The doctor's eyes glide toward the dark corner again and remain there vacant for a moment.

"Is it what you think it is Doctor?" Paxi says in a rather urgent and commanding tone, though still wading in a whisper out of respect for the fallen.

"I regret to say that it looks like it, yes," the doctor replies, as he returns his attention to the functionary's bunk.

At the sounding of Paxi's voice, the functionary reacts with a light shift of the legs, but he is still too nebulous to fully grasp what is taking place around him.

The doctor opens his valise again and folds his stethoscope inside it, looking solemn but very much relieved his call is about to come to an end, and says, the volume of his voice a notch louder: "This is the fourth case of Yellow Fever we have had so far. All we can do is try to keep the patient's temperature down and pray for the best."

As is to be expected from a man who has clearly enjoyed something of an upbringing, the doctor addresses the only other man present – or standing at least - assuming perhaps, that Paxi is not aware of Captain Scola's generosity with rat poison.

"The day after tomorrow we should be arriving in Rio de Janeiro," he adds. "I urge you to see to it that the gentleman gets taken ashore – for the sake of the rest of the passengers primarily, of course.

The captain does not want to have any avoidable calamities on his hands, as you understand. And besides, in the city the patient's chances for recovery will be much better. Where is he traveling to?"

"To Rio de Janeiro," Lydia answers quick on her feet.

The doctor glances rather with disdain around the cabin once more and rests his gaze for a third time on Edmilce still inanimate in the corner, "Also, you should think of ways to avoid unnecessary calamities, Signore Paxi," he adds, as he takes a step toward the door.

Lydia gathers her breath to speak, but Paxi intersects her words before she has properly formed them.

"I appreciate your advice, Doctor," he says. "But if I didn't have a nose for avoiding calamity, I would still be in Italy."

A fierce glance is exchanged between the two men; filled with volumes of the kinds of words men like these rarely ever voice when in the company of women, even if these women are technically just children and one of them a Negro.

The doctor scrapes his throat and politely tilts his head in Lydia's direction.

"Good evening Miss...."

Again, Paxi takes a step forward to hinder her from speaking.

He follows the doctor out into the hall, pulling the door behind him to a slit. Lydia can hear them talking, but cannot quite follow the exact thread of what is being said. In the intonation of Paxi's voice, and from the muffled and complacent sounds the doctor utters in reaction to it she can tell that he is formulating instructions however.

Paxi steps through the door again, his eyebrows cast with real severity.

"I need to know everything there is to know about this man," he says, gesturing toward the functionary, who weakly shifts again taking the pressure off his side. "I need to know who he is and where he is traveling to."

"Rio de Janeiro. I just told you," Lydia says.

He turns to her without explaining any further and she, seemingly none to his surprise, readily accepts the fact that he is a man used to making decisions and should therefore better not be questioned. He lowers himself on the edge of the functionary's bunk and just looks at him with as much detachment as the doctor had before him, as if he is looking at just one of many elements to a problem he has been called upon to unravel. But, it also serves to solve the riddle Lydia has puzzled on for weeks; that Paxi has no idea who the functionary is. At least, this is what she wants to believe and hopes she has not wagered wrong.

As Paxi rises to his feet again she straightens herself to face him at near eye-level. She looks at him with the confidence and familiarity of an equal, and says: "This man is my uncle. When we get to Rio de Janeiro I will personally see to it that he goes ashore and that he gets proper care. I want you to know that I am not doing this because the doctor said that he must, but because I happen to think it is the best thing to do."

She becomes aware, cannot ignore, Edmilce observing them. She can feel the girl's eyes from the corner of the cabin twirling the ribbon of fate around them.

"My uncle was coming to Brazil, partly on official business," Lydia then says, with difficulty trying not to read the thoughts inside Edmilce's head. "He was coming to a place called Porto Alegre do Sul – do you know it Signore Paxi?"

On the day they met, he asked her not use the Signore bit when addressing him. But calling him anything else, as she blatantly lies to him without even batting an eyelid, is too awkward if not downright offensive.

"I have heard of that place" he replies. "Do you know what his business is there?"

"He doesn't talk much about his work. But he did say something about going there to catch a rat."

"Interesting. Is your uncle in the fur business – or in the pesticide business, a rat poison merchant?"

"Not exactly" she says. "But why don't you ask him yourself when he recovers?"

"It will be my pleasure."

He pauses and looks at her ponderingly, as though his thoughts have just taken him to a place faraway somewhere.

"I don't think this is the appropriate place to talk about this," he says. "But, would you like me to tell you a thing or two about Yellow Fever?"

"I see what you mean," she replies.

"I have asked the doctor to check up on your uncle tomorrow. Maybe it is wise to think about what you will do once you get to Rio. Things may look a whole lot different then. I will come around tomorrow as well."

He seems to hesitate.

"Just remember Lydia, that I am never far away."

"It comforts me to think that," she replies softly, glancing at the girl and then quickly turning her back to her. "Thank you again," she says with all the tones of a whisper that was meant to be intimate.

"How is our young friend?" Paxi then asks in a playful tone, reaching over to clamp Edmilce's toe with his fingers.

"Moito bem," she answers, emerging from the shadows to greet him with a smile.

<><><><><><><><>

They wrap a clean sheet from one of the empty bunks around the functionary and tuck him in for the night. His temperature has gone down some during the course of the evening. This brings peace of mind and much needed sleep. Even the humming from the engines, which in all of her time on board Lydia has not quite been able to get used to, retreats to the background and makes way for jumbled dreams the moment her head touches the pillow.

And in those dreams, no matter how random the imagery, Paxi is inside all of them. She watches him on the deck looking back at her, as she stands on a raft crammed with ballast drifting out to sea, symbolising, perhaps, all the little lies and untruths that hold together who she is turning into. No matter how insignificant the references to everything around her, in these dreams, either disappearing into the horizon or looking down through the surface of the water at herself as she sinks tied to a coffin, he is there as part of the summary of the realities she now faces.

The blue hue of the moon spills in through the locked window. It seems to purify the stagnant air that suffocates her more with every passing day. And from a distance, it is the voice of the functionary that pulls her back from the realm of dreams to the reality of steel cutting through calm, temperate waters.

Lydia, Lydia.

Reluctantly, she opens her eyes, fearing at the same time that if she does, she might not find her way back down there again for hours to come. But the functionary will not be dismissed and soon, again, there it is: Lydia, Lydia.

Almost as soon as her eyes open, her feet hit the floorboards next to the functionary, as he gargles up words thin and sunken.

"Lydia, it hurts so much."

"I know it does," she whispers back. "You have been gone for more than a day."

"I don't think I am here yet," he replies.

His eyes unable to focus and dipped ever deeper in that jaundice saffron dancing in the monochrome of the moonlight, he whispers, "I have something for you."

There is a short pause, as he bites his lip to negotiate another wave of pains shooting through him. "Something that belongs to me," he adds.

"But - "

"Listen," he presses, sounding overpowering, strong in the very fact he has no strength left in him.

She kneels on the floorboards, leans in closer and thinks of Edmilce somewhere off in the dark, listening in silence.

"I am not getting better," he manages, his words more like breaths already enveloped rather snugly in the sweetness of death. "I heard the doctor when he was here. I second his opinion to get me off the ship. I have become a burden that is too large for you to bear alone. And I am sorry about that. I hope I can make up for the troubles I am about to cost you," he says.

"But there is no need for that," she replies, though not quite sure whether it is against her actually wanting to accept a token of gratitude, or against the thought that plays inside of her that says a dying man doesn't really have the right to want much of anything.

"The carpetbag; you have seen me carry it. I want you to take it, all of it, and do with it what you must - once you get to where you are going."

"Yes, but...."

"I haven't the strength to explain. All you need to know is in the carpetbag. You will understand, once you get to where you are going."

"But how...?"

His wandering grin, devious as ever, begins to take shape around his sunken eyes, but the jabs inside of him prevent it from properly becoming a smile. He pauses to let his breathing acquire rhythm and become something of a steady panting again. A shadow divides his face; his chapped lips illuminated by the moon and his eyes a fluorescent yellow in the dark.

"I always knew I wasn't made for the tropics," he says, overcoming the pain to give her the almost-smile she will always remember him by.

She senses his body sinking deeper into the mattress, deflating as it were, in a final stand against turmoil, but giving into it in the end: surrender as the ultimate form of victory.

His strength briefly returns.

"Lydia, who was the other man with the doctor?"

"That; that was just a man - with the doctor," she stutters.

"I thought I could sense how you were looking at him. Am I wrong to presume, dear?"

"Not entirely."

"Would I like him?"

She looks into his face, and studies it for a moment before she answers. She wants for every crease on his leathery skin to remain permanently imprinted on her memory.

"That I am sure of," - her answers barely audible; a whisper more to herself than to him.

She softly presses her finger to his lips, letting him know that he needn't speak, that he has her blessing to rest.

"Dorme, Signore, dorme."

When day brakes she is still by his side.

If there had been tears that had run down her cheeks they had dried hours ago. If there had been tears at all, she had shed them measurably, not because they had sprung to her eyes but because she had willed herself to cry.

She feels Edmilce's bare feet gathering on the floorboards beside her, collecting like a solidified shadow in the meek light of the window. She lets the girl lift her hair gently off her back and twist it into a single braid, as her thin, coarse fingers slide gently along the length of it.

"Now he sleeps," the girl says.

"Yes, now he sleeps. And we have things we need to start doing, you and me."

She raises herself to face the girl, feeling as though her bones have aged a decade overnight. But she also feels the abounding energy she

73

knows she will need to carry her through the day ahead.

"Everything starts today, Edmilce," she says in a voice she herself does not quite recognise, and which reminds her of something or someone from her past.

The girl looks back at her, faithful but tensing her brow in an expression not of doubt or disagreement, but simply of trying as best she can to comprehend.

"You have to go to see Signore Paxi now, to tell him my uncle has passed away," Lydia adds. "He will know what to do."

The girl hesitates, but Lydia is quick to explain.

"It no longer matters, Edmilce, that people see you. By this time tomorrow, it will just be the two of us. And remember that it is they who hide from things, not you. Now go. I'll be waiting here for you."

Lydia pushes the girl toward the door, urging her - in Italian — to hurry. The functionary's lessons in Portuguese are simply lost on her right now. Edmilce briefly looks back, expressing her readiness to partake and disappears out the door.

It feels strange for Lydia to be by herself now, with only the lifeless body of the functionary to keep her company; like an intruder stumbling upon an event that is just too private. But he no longer is company, is he. And it has taken her the better part of the night to accept that one biting little fact.

She realises how careless she has been, sending Edmilce out onto the deck like that. But she needs to be by herself for more reasons than she can explain right now. She kneels next to the functionary once more and reaches under the bunk, accidentally, pressing her cheek against his hand gone cold under the sheets. She notices how, now that it has lost its human essence, his skin has become almost indistinguishable from the cotton draped wantonly around it.

She lifts from the suitcase the carpetbag he told her about, and which she has indeed seen him carry around many times before. She sits admiring the cracked surface of the leather, running her fingers over it to get a better sense of the man whose identity, whose past, she will from now on connect to her own. She has never really wondered about the content of the carpetbag before. And now, as she replays his last words in

74

her mind, she is overwhelmed by the feeling that whatever is inside will change everything. Without the slightest bit of tension in her fingers, she undoes the binding and lets it open to reveal three separate compartments, all at first glance containing no more than sheets of paper. Inside the first sleeve, she recognises the functionary's small and precise handwriting, like a series of tight curls drawn evenly, but interrupted on occasion by capricious scratches and squiggles around it in pencil: his notes.

She notices that in the second sleeve the papers have been more neatly kept together and make a far less erratic bundle; documents of some kind, anonymous and in that same baroque pomp she was introduced to in the documents she herself had received from the Italian port authorities back in Genoa. Some of them have been bound together with silk ribbon and some even in copper coil. She is able to decipher the writing in Portuguese only to some extent, a language that is still far too alien for her to fully measure. A series of official deeds of some kind, she assumes; important things she cannot identify beyond the seal that says something having to do with the department of urban development of the city of Trés Corações on the bottom of one of the pages.

"Your matter of the heart" she whispers in the direction of the cadaver stiff before her.

What intrigues her the most, however, beyond the fact that there are five identical documents that point in the direction of this one town in the Brazilian interior, is that either somewhere inside the bundles of paper or somehow attached to them, she might also find Paxi and thus broaden her understanding of the relationship, if any, between him and the functionary. But, whatever is on the papers, whatever they mean, she now has reason to see Paxi again and they may unravel the least tangible mystery of them all: her own future.

And if scanning the last of the functionary's belongings is actually brightening her view on things, what she then discovers in the third and last sleeve falls short of physically knocking her back, more with exaltation than real surprise, however.

In a folder tied loosely with black ribbon at the bottom of the sleeve, she finds the liquidities that clearly allowed the functionary to travel the way he did, staring back at her. And in that instant, the tip of the veil that made her future so uncertain only moments earlier, lifts abruptly. And once it has she knows that from now on, at the age of twenty-two, with infatuation taking possession of her with every passing day, and the responsibility she has taken on to continue her travels with a street child at her side, she will for as long as it will last, be rich.

It isn't unlike the way a sledgehammer might feel as it is slams on top of her, for it feels so absurd to realise that she can now travel across the ocean ten times if she wants – twenty, a hundred, judging by how much money is there. She can see the Scazzo sisters and understands that if ever she runs into the likes of them again, she will now no longer have to reproach herself for casting down her eyes and for praying that they will not notice the cuts and tears on her cloak and blouse. Because now, on this sad day, with her friend's corpse going cold and rigid before her, no more than an adjective to the man she had grown so fond of in a matter of mere weeks, she will – again, for as long as it will last, be one of them.

She can hear voices approaching outside and prepares to play what she hopes will be her last act of deception, a role yet again of someone she is not. She has formalities to take care of.

In what seems to her like a rehearsed pandemonium, with her in the middle of it, Paxi enters the cabin accompanied by the ship's doctor and two of the boys she has seen clearing chores around the ship on occasion. She recognises them at once and remembers how neither ever failed to tip the rim of an invisible hat to her before, whenever she had walked past them. A smile colors her face as both greet her with that same, somewhat downplayed gesture.

Immediately, quite guided by routine, the two boys remove the sheet and she notices how the yellow hue from the jaundice, which had rendered the functionary rather ghoulish during the two grueling days his illness had lasted, has all but disappeared. Somehow, she feels he looks more human in death than he ever has before.

A stretcher is poled past her into the cabin and positioned on the floor next to the bunk. The body is then craned onto it, a load that appears neither stiff nor languid and from the looks of how it handles it is hard to imagine that only hours ago it had actually been alive.

Through it all, she observes how Edmilce keeps a watchful eye on everything; how now and then she will plant her tiny fists on her hips, as though making sure everything goes according to some plan she has devised beforehand, as if the handling of the dead were her domain somehow. It makes Lydia wonder how telling this might be.

"Where will you be taking my uncle's body?" she hears herself ask in a voice that is weak and appropriately stifled by grief.

"We have a mortuary on the ship, Miss," the doctor replies, while the two boys get ready to maneuverer themselves and the deceased back out into the hall. "It is where we will keep your uncle until we dock," - and after a meaningful and rather biting silence, he adds that she shouldn't worry, that he will go to great lengths to ensure that her uncle is handled with due respect. "Signore Paxi has seen to it that we do," he says.

She notices that while the doctor directs himself toward her, his peripheral vision is clearly on Paxi standing next to him. She can furthermore not quite make out whether the doctor meant to be cynical or if being unaffected is standard procedure somehow, but it is primarily that he has caused her to wonder about it that strikes a nerve.

"Am I to understand," she says, "that it is on account of Signore Paxi that you treat the dead with respect?"

"If you must know, Miss, in my day - before Signore Paxi that is - we still performed burials at high sea," the doctor says with a clear tinge of added annoyance in his voice, as his cheeks pull at the corners of his mouth. He turns to face her. His eyes darken and his hand arches in a down-sweeping motion in order to illustrate.

"Well, that was a long time ago," Paxi interrupts, not much amused by the direction in which the doctor has decided to venture.

"You are absolutely right, Signore Paxi, that was a long time ago. I didn't mean to be insensitive."

"See Lydia," Paxi adds, "that is precisely what I love so much in learned men like the doctor here: they have such an extraordinary ability to self-correct."

"Indeed," says the doctor, motioning sharply for the boys to carry on, so he can follow them out.

"Oh, just one more thing, Miss," he then adds, turning around to face her again. "I will check the passenger log later on today, but just out of curiosity — it might spare me some time with paperwork, you see — what exactly is the relation of the young girl to your uncle?" he says, arching forward some, knocking Edmilce back against the wall by fixing his glare directly on her this time.

"I do not see, sir, how that would be any of your business. But, of course, if it will spare you the trouble of going through the passenger records; she is my uncle's adopted daughter," Lydia responds.

"All the way from Italy?"

"No. As a matter of fact, my uncle adopted her five days ago, in Salvador."

"Please forgive my impertinence, but you would be shocked to know the kinds of diseases that are carried by the local monkeys around these parts. It just isn't advisable to go around adopting them, is all I am trying to say."

She is unable to stop herself from taking a step in his direction. But Paxi, again, interrupts.

"That would be quite enough, Doctor. It goes without saying that I expect the utmost discretion on your part and that there will be no record checking, or anything of the sort. Can I be any more clear?"

"Rest assured, Signore Paxi. I only felt it needed to be said. It isn't the first time I have seen an outbreak of Yellow Fever after leaving one of these ports. And you know very well what I am talking about."

"And you, sir, know as well as anyone that whatever is causing passengers to become ill has nothing to do with these ports, or perhaps much with Yellow Fever even."

"I beg to differ, Signore Paxi."

The two men stand facing each other for a moment or two, like they had the night before.

"I could make you eat your words, Doctor," Paxi says standing down, and in doing so overstating his superiority in such a manner that it leaves Lydia flaccid in the knees and gasping for breath. "I will let you be, however, but only because I need to count on you."

"You are too kind, Signore Paxi," the doctor sneers in reply.

<><><><><><><><>

Five coffins get carried off the ship first thing the following morning, before too many of the passengers are up and about and it might hence sour up the general mood to see that death has begun to spread among them.

Lydia and Edmilce stand on the dock amongst the grieving and watch as the boxes are neatly stacked on top of a horse-pulled cart, which is to then lead the procession to the Cemitério São João Batista, in the city district of Botafogo near the harbour of Rio de Janeiro.

Already on the dock, only moments before departing, Lydia is finally able to spot Paxi up on the second deck, fixed against the morning sky indistinguishable from the steel around him. She accepts that their farewell is to be no more than a glance, at a distance and that the sharp, biting sensation she feels inside she will have to endure to its fullest. She isn't sure she deserves this and it is her abstinence that overshadows the sense that someday they will meet again.

At the grave site, a young priest directs his solemn words at each of the five boxes basking in the mid-morning sun next to a ditch with barely enough gape to fit them. He speaks in a New World brand of Italian she finds hard to place and fails to console in the end. His accent is in fact so off, so out of tune with anything any of them have ever heard before that it passes right through comical and straight into the rather alarming realisation of how far from home they actually are. In the words of the young priest, though by all means in reverence, he clearly lacks the first-hand knowledge of what it is to cross an ocean himself and therefore, in the hopscotch of his words is also palpable the rarity which they have all become.

Lydia holds a tight grip on the carpetbag. She has not yet read the letter the functionary has left her tucked next to the money. She wants to wait for him to be well and buried before she learns in which direction her next steps should be. And while the young priest utters the last of his verses she steps forward and places her personal documents, her past identity, wrapped into a bundle inside a silk scarf, on top of the coffin.

It isn't that she has thought this through to any great lengths, or that she has consciously been aiming at the poetry of this one gesture, but it feels right that those documents be buried here; now that she has made her crossing and like a token to the weeks the functionary's life had intermingled with hers, that it also be a farewell to someone she will never be again.

As she stares into the open grave she remembers the words Paxi spoke to her on the morning the functionary's body was taken out of the cabin.

"I am curious what will become of you," he had said, the moment the three of them were alone again.

"So am I," she had answered.

"Do you have any idea where you will go?"

"Not at this very moment. But I will soon."

They stood facing each other and the blood rushing past the back of her throat had turned her breath oddly sweet.

"Every time I have seen you, I have ended up thanking you for something," she had said.

"Do you have the feeling you are about to do it again?"

"It feels like the only thing I can do."

"How will you get to Buenos Aires?"

"I am not entirely sure that I should be going there at all right now. I hear it's crawling with Italians."

"I suppose that is one stripe it has against it," Paxi had replied.

"For better or worse, for now, Brazil has turned out to be my destination. Who is to say how long it will decide to keep me," she had added.

After the funeral she arranges to be taken to the most luxurious hotel available, as close as possible to the beach, from where she will have a full view of the Sugarloaf and from where she will continue to wonder which faraway world that strange rock might possibly have fallen from. Other than that one specification it matters little where they will settle in until she has decided what to do next. And that evening, from the balcony of their suite, on the seventh floor of the Tamanaco hotel, she lets the envelope dance in between her fingers, while on the cone of rock towering across the bay the colors change in the weakening light of the sun setting behind the city.

Never in her life has she been surrounded by such luxury. And she can only speculate how disconcerting it all must seem to Edmilce, who up until a week ago had never even had shoes on her feet let alone slept between the sheets of a proper bed. But the girl seems resigned, accepting her bath without much reflection or any sharpened sense of contrast with the place she has just come from, neither when she beholds the enormity of the bed they will later share or after Lydia had laced the water of her bath with oils and essences neither one of them have ever heard of before.

It is strange for Lydia to find herself in a position now that will most certainly have been denied her back home. She has awakened from a slumber to the dawning of the new century, with all its sheen and pace, electricity and ships crossing oceans every day and the sputter of automobiles in the streets below. More than ever she feels like a savage, however, a relic, but she knows that before long this too will become familiar; that in the end she will become part of this, however unthinkable it may have seemed less than a week ago. The sound of Edmilce splashing in her bathwater back inside reassures her that it will and that the time has come to learn who she will be in the morning. She undoes the seal of the envelope and produces a handwritten letter on stationary from the Doria Shipping Company, dated December 19th; four days ago.

She can sense the fever in the handwriting; almost taste the effort that went into putting jumbled thoughts into proper focus and onto paper. It all the more stresses the urgency of the words:

> *Lydia,*
>
> *Trés Corações – Three Hearts.*
> *What was mine is yours now.*
> *Find Corné Cunho. He will honor my wishes.*
> *Emilio.*

She stares at the paper for a long time, gets lost inside of it until she is brought back by the course touch of Edmilce's hand on her shoulder.

81

With a gasp that is more like a sigh that travels past her lips, she looks up into the child's eyes.

"Can you read, Edmilce?" she asks her.

"No."

"I am going to teach you."

They stay at the Tamanaco Hotel for three days, long enough to refurbish and to reciprocate the city's smothering embrace. They explore it by day and spent Christmas together in their suite, reminiscing about all that they have seen.

Lydia is quick to discover that she actually has a feeling for money, that she can manage it soberly, spend only what is strictly necessary, while still permitting herself and her young companion more luxury than either of them has ever known. She is quick to find a sensible balance between prudence and excess, keeping the money stashed inside a purse she wears crossed over her shoulder under her clothing at all times. The more she is in physical contact with it the more her confidence grows that she can indeed keep it from intoxicating her. At the same time, she feels she needs to detach herself from her newly found freedom to make choices as well, which she is confronted with each time she buys dresses and shoes for herself and Edmilce, and sits on the soft velvet of a horse-pulled carriage that transports them from one end of the town to the other. She has begun to see what she will later in life describe as the irony of riches, the paradox of wealth; how while there is monetary value to freedom itself, freedom is a burden that in turn requires great attention. Nevertheless, during their short stay in Rio, they hardly deny themselves anything. They hop from whim to whim, spending money she instinctively knows will last them for a very long time. At night they will stay up trying on the dresses and the hats they have bought, dancing like the children they in fact still are, inside some mock fairytale in the flood from the electric light pouring down from the ceiling. She feels her rebellious nature become bolder, now that she can pay her way past the gilded columns of the hotel lobby straight to her own suite, without having to humble herself for anything or anyone. And when not enough attention is being paid to them as the odd couple they certainly are, and the ladies hung heavily with jewelery next to the gentlemen in frock automatically assume Edmilce is in her service, Lydia makes sure that it is she who crosses the lobby barefooted carrying the exploits of their shopping sprees several steps behind Edmilce, just to raise some eyebrows.

<><><><><><><><>

She reserves two seats on a train leaving for Ouro Preto, two days after Christmas. And when Edmilce inquires as to the reason for their sudden departure, Lydia answers her with a question herself:

"You trust me don't you?" unable to explain why, or how, a longing for the countryside away from the city has gotten such a hold of her, as well.

The steam cloud that trails past their window the following morning is sweet with the smell of coal and the cattle country that spreads beyond the coastal mountains looks calm with abundance.

"You really should try wearing shoes, Edmilce," she says to the girl, who sits looking out of her window with her forehead pressed to the glass.

"But they hurt my feet."

"Try wearing them for short periods every day, until you get used to them."

"Do I have to?"

"Edmilce, whatever is to become of us; it will involve a life requiring you to wear them. In case you haven't noticed, prowling and scavenging around the harbour is in the past now."

"I will do my best," the girl replies and adds with some reluctance, "I would like to ask you where we are going."

Lydia looks over at her and seems to inspect the state of the girl's pigtails, and says, "I would like to say that it doesn't concern you, but I suppose it does. We are going to find a man named Corné Cunho in a place called Trés Corações. It is where my uncle wanted us to go. I would tell you more but there isn't a whole lot more I know about what it is we will find there."

Lydia stares out of the window for a moment herself and then turns to Edmilce again. She finds the girl's eyes are still fixed on her, but she is unable to tell what she is thinking. Her expression is too open, too clear of judgment and presumption.

"Whatever awaits us," Lydia adds, "whatever you do, I want you to never talk about money. I want you to never talk about all the things we did these past couple of days. Do you understand?"

"Yes."

They arrive in a town called São Thomé das Letras in the middle of the night. Edmilce has been asleep for hours, with her head rested on Lydia's lap. She shakes the girl gently and Edmilce is on her feet at once, finding her orientation as she springs to attention.

At the station, a porter places their luggage on a flatbed cart, which he pulls ahead of them slouched like a reed under the weight of it, through the streets of the town semi-lighted by gas torches. Occasionally, the man will turn to speak to them in a language even Edmilce finds difficult to understand. Right through the graveyard he has for dentures, caused by what Lydia figures is a lifelong regimen of cane spirits, he asks what has brought them to Sao Tomé and shares with them in passing that Trés Corações is still a way further west. How long it will take them to get there, he says, depends largely of the mode of transport they choose. He says that the roads going there are no more than cattle paths that coil themselves through the landscape and that if it doesn't rain — which it looks like it shouldn't — by automobile, much to Lydia's surprise, they could reach it in less than a day.

A rather stout woman opens the door of the hostel where the porter has led them to for the night. They exchange some words and with a brusque nod of the head, the woman agrees to extend her hospitality. She directs them without wasting more words than is strictly necessary, to two separate rooms, one of which is the servant quarters behind the kitchen area, where Edmilce is asked to settle and which, for this one time, Lydia feels just too tired to contest. The prospect of spending the night by herself seems to far outweigh this particular bit of injustice and she finds comfort in acknowledging that there will be plenty of these little battles to fight in the future, in regard to Edmilce, when they are both rested enough to win them again.

Lydia is led up mud-plaster steps behind the slightly German looking backend of the proprietress' to the first floor and back toward the front of the house. She follows the woman down a darkened hallway into what she assumes was once the master bedroom. Behind wooden shutters a large glassless window opens to a narrow balustrade and the street below. The breeze coming in feels kind and familiar to her. The place has all the compacted efficiencies of a private residence. There is also a rural quality to everything, something only one who is acutely familiar with it will recognise. The smell of barley that hangs in every corner brings to her awareness, with something of a bittersweet sting, undefined impressions and memories of the life that is now far behind her and only vaguely connects her with people and places she once knew. It is a wordless sensation that sweeps over her and takes her back to the foggy reaches of her childhood, with only shadows dancing dimly inside of them.

The room itself is simple, but it has been fitted with electricity nonetheless. In the darkness, while walking from the station, it was impossible to get a sense as to the actual size of the town of São Thomé. And the fact a train stops at a town, of course, says nothing about how big it is. But neither does the availability of electricity say much about the level of advancement of a country as vast as this.

She removes her dusty clothes and washes herself over a bowl that has been left there for her by the caretaker. It stands on top of a commode, along with a large jug of clean water and a bar of soap. She hangs her head over the bowl and pours the water over the back of her neck to rinse the dirt out of her hair. Feeling refreshed though far from clean, she slides her nightgown over her shoulders and the pouch that still dangles under her breasts, bulging with the money that does not feel is fully hers yet; not until she has stood face to face with the man named Corné Cunho and has learned who he is.

The bed is clean and soft and permeated with the scent of lavender. She stares at the light coming in from the street and as she watches the stars moving in the warm breeze hitting her face, the distant clacking of a horseman moving away from her and into the night sinks her into a dreamless sleep.

85

<>◇<>◇<>◇<>◇<>

When she opens her eyes again and strangely enough, the tanned wash of the plaster on the walls reminds her of the smell of bread. Again she feels transported back to those faraway mornings when she used to wander groggily down the stairs to find her father seated at the kitchen table and her mother busying around him. For an instant she is back there, in a place and a time when the world had still been small, engulfed by the same smell that overwhelms her now.

She wonders how the color of a wall can cause such an illusion, an optic trick so strong that it can arouse an altogether different sensation. It is bread, as unmistakable as the smell of freshly baked bread can be, though with something acrid and alien to it as well, something that might have passed for sourdough perhaps, but bearing the likeness to what she only guesses is a sharp tropical tang. Not only is it strong, enchantingly so, but it also completely destroys her otherwise so icy will that might have sprung her out of bed the moment she had opened her eyes.

She turns on her side and loses herself in a long stare into the streak of sun flooding in through the crack in the shutters, which she doesn't exactly remember having closed the night before. Her hand rises toward her chest to reassure herself that the money pouch is still wrapped around her, which it is. In the bright, smooth wipe of light coming from the window there is a multitude of voices and the occasional crunch from a wagon in rhyme with the hoofs of beasts pulling it along. From the sound of it, the empty street from the night before has become a public ground, a marketplace for sure, judging from the hollers that are the same the world over whenever fresh produce is being sold in the open air.

From the heat rising from the sun patch on the floor she can tell she has slept well past the time she had intended. And although, having probably lost almost the entire morning to something as dishonorable as sleeping, she is still too paralysed by the bliss of the sheets to do much of anything about it. She cannot remember the last time she has actually woken up alone. And in trying to, she finds herself forced to revisit a place that is now as unfamiliar to her as this room would have been back then.

It seems like an eternity since she has thought about any of that, the past she has disconnected herself from - when she still thought that memories could not be discarded.

But it is her unwavering aversion for sentimentality that helps her to finally climb out of bed. With her hair tied back, dressed in one of the skirts she had often worn on the ship, which she figures looks rundown enough to where there will be little speculation as to the fact she now has more money than anyone she is likely to encounter, she climbs down the stairs and heads in the direction of the kitchen.

Opening the door she finds herself in a space that seems much smaller than it had the night before and the table running down the middle quite a bit larger. Seated around it are three matrons before a large pile of bean shells next to a wrought-iron pan filled halfway with the bean pods soaking in water. She recognises one of them as the caretaker from the night before, as the woman rises to her feet and comes around to greet her broadening a smile. Officiously, the woman inquires if the room has been to her satisfaction. Lydia nods and thanks the woman appropriately for her good care. When the expected silence finally falls between them, Lydia disengages her eyes to glance further around the kitchen and notices the presence of a fourth person seated at the far end of the table. She might not have noticed the figure of Edmilce at all.

The girl casts down her eyes, however, startled and hiding a blushing that deeply darkens her chocolate cheeks. She stares at her own hands peeling indicating that she is doing it blindly, expertly.

"What are you doing?" Lydia asks, her voice calm, but with enough spite inside it that it causes a cat that had been sleeping in one of the corners to jump to its feet and dart out the door hissing.

"Waiting for you," the girl replies small.

"Seeing how naturally you have fitted yourself in a servant's role, Edmilce, hurts me more than she could have prepared for," Ludia says, though the question then soon arises of whether Edmilce will ever be her equal, Lydia keeps to herself.

"Show me where you spent the night," Lydia commands, tossing a series of short glances in the direction of the narrow door next to the stove to the room behind, a space she expects will be no more than a pantry.

Although, her first reaction is to slap the child across the face, as soon as they are out of view of the others, she cups it in her hands instead and pushes her down gently to sit on the edge of the bed next to her.

"You don't have to do that, Edmilce. You don't have to do anything I wouldn't do myself," she says. "We are guests here. It is we who pay them to do things. Do you hear me? Do you understand what I am trying to say to you?"

But the girl only blinks her eyes, as a clear sign that she most certainly does not.

"Are you angry?"

"Yes I am. But I also know that I am going to do things differently from now on."

<><><><><><><>

The claxon of the Daimler bellows in front of the house like some beast being bound for slaughter. It surprises Lydia in the least that the vehicle the porter talked about the night before is now standing in front of the house, considering the size of the monetary incentive she gave the old man to arrange it for them.

"If you leave at once," the porter says, still radiating with triumph as he stands in the doorway, "you should reach Trés Corações somewhere around sundown."

She never thought she could be this excited about a machine and remembering Edmilce's reaction to the trams slashing through the streets back in Rio, Lydia now wonders what it is going to take for the girl to even climb into one.

The driver is still seated behind the wheel. She can see he has a thick moustache that is pulled into two wild curls at quite a distance away from his face. He is geared up in a leather jacket, with goggles pulled up on the top of his head and judging from the reddish hue in the hedging of facial hair and the paleness of his eyes, she can tell he is a northern European furthermore. She finds his demeanour of determined anonymity rather agreeable — and thus comforting to think that it is next to him she will spend the rest of the day.

It is only once the vehicle has been put in motion that the man behind the wheel finally introduces himself as a German retired army colonel named Jens Rank. He is well in his fifties she figures and in several ways she cannot quite put her finger on, he reminds her of the functionary; something in his gestures and manner as he prims himself to speak. He came to a Brazil years earlier to find what he vaguely describes as fortune and happiness, without really letting on too much as to the form he has in fact found these things – or if he might possibly still be looking for them. Whichever the case, she thinks it most uncanny how much this sounds like something Emilio Toffolo might have said – and in fact did say, though not in exactly those words, when he himself had referred to this particular part of the world. It helps her to realise how close they are now to the place the functionary has destined them to go.

"I am the niece of an Italian businessman," she finally says. "He had once come out this way and before he died, only a week ago, he asked me to come here too. He was too ill, my uncle, to tell me why he wanted me to do all this, or why he wanted me to find this man whose name he only mentioned in a letter he left me."

They twist through the dusty streets of the town, which turns out quite a bit larger and certainly more elegant than Lydia had expected.

And with the ends of his bushy tusks flapping in the wind, the voice of the driver ever a purring growl, he asks her, "What is the name of the man you want to find?" - turning to face her and in doing so, unable to dodge a rooster that bounces out of nowhere in front of the car.

In a flash the animal disappears under the Daimler in a rapid clatter of breaking eggshells. Without losing her momentum however, and doing all she can to ignore the shrieks of laughter coming from Edmilce in the back seat, she answers him: "Corné Cunho. The name of the man I came here to find; his name is Corné Cunho."

The colonel seems silenced, clearly weighing in his mind what he has just heard, occasionally running his teeth over his upper lip.

"Is that correct?" he says, as the shredded rooster vanishes in the dust cloud behind them.

However, she can see the shadow of what might have been like a thin smile passing across the glint of his eyes. "My condolences," he says after another short but gathered silence. "May I ask the name of your uncle?"

"Emilio Toffolo."

"Is that correct?"

"Yes, it is."

"And what did you say your name was again?"

"Lydia, just Lydia."

"Well, Lydia-just-Lydia, it is quite a coincidence we meet then. And for your information, it isn't Trés Corações where you need to go. Where you need to go is a place right on the outskirts of it. We would have passed right by it on our way into the town."

"I take it you know this person," she says in the form of a question, which technically isn't one at all.

This time around, the smile that materialises on his face is so deliberate and drawn that she can see his teeth behind it. But, just as quickly as it appears, his face darkens again and his cheeks lose the rose color that has been visible behind the tan of his skin only moments earlier.

"Yes, I do know the gentleman you are looking for," he says "and it should not surprise you that I also knew your uncle then – quite well in fact. I suppose you are not bringing Dom Cunho very good news then?"

"No, I don't suppose I am."

"May I ask how your uncle died, Lydia?"

"Yellow Fever. He contracted it on the ship coming here."

"From where?"

"Genoa."

"And how much he hated to travel," the colonel then adds, but she isn't too sure he has directed those words at her at all.

"You really did know him," she then says, as if it were only now that she is starting to believe any of it.

"Yes, I did," the colonel says and turns to scrutinise her again, but in the most focused and gentle way one can ever scrutinise.

It gives her the feeling he is trying to register the likenesses in her face to the man he knew; likenesses she is absolutely convinced he will find besides, due to nothing other than the determination she sees in his eyes. For the longest time he drives blindly, studying her in the way a mother eagle might lovingly study her hatchling. And it is only once Edmilce's fearful cries coming from the back seat become audible does he return his eyes to the road, barely able to maneuverer around a knuckled root arching out of the dirt in front of them.

Cutting through forests and open fields, under the immensity of the tropical sky, Lydia recaps the story of how she has arrived at that particular moment in time, embellishing with great ease on the parts that best fit her new identity, while omitting the history only she knows about.

If there is one thing she has learned so far, it is that history is a subjective thing, something quite makable

In the hours that follow, from the German colonel she learns that the functionary had been coming out to these parts going on more than a decade now. Emilio Toffolo had indeed owned property here, he tells her. But as to the extent of it she could never have guessed. As far as Corné Cunho, he and the functionary had indeed been something like business partners. But for some reason she suspects that there are other chapters to that story, and which the Colonel himself is omitting from the tale he is telling. He says that there are things he has no place discussing with her, that there are matters she should learn from Corné Cunho himself and no one else; that he is sure the functionary had meant for it to be that way.

He explains that next to cattle farming, the region has mostly the mining to thank for its current economic boom. And having learned this, it makes every bit of sense to her that the functionary would still be collecting profits from it.

The further they drive into the interior, the more talkative the colonel seems to become. Especially, about the things that make this land particularly gorgeous and special to him – and rightly so, she has to admit.

By late afternoon they begin to pass pockets of habitation again. However, these are more like shacks cluttered here and there along the road. They are the temporary dwellings that house the seasonal hands that work the farmlands and the mines in the region, the colonel explains. When she

strains her eyes she can make out shadows in the shade staring back at them, figures fixed to the spot in the dirt where her glances catch them. They stare at the Daimler passing them; neither acknowledging it nor manifesting themselves in any way in its presence, like semi-invisible parts of the landscape and the trees they hide behind. On occasion, she can see children darting in and out of view, temporarily halting in mid-motion to stare back at her, before they too become vacant at the sight of the machine cutting past them. Not at any moment does the colonel decrease his speed. In fact, he rather seems to accelerate every time and on one or two occasions she also notices him tossing fixed glances into his rear-view mirror, toward the spot where Edmilce herself has somewhat begun to disappear as well. It is as if he were meaning to communicate to the girl something only she might understand and it unsettles Lydia every time to be excluded and ignored in this way.

The car slows and rolls onto a smaller road, passing in between two stone columns that lead straight into the forest. The road seems to twist without end through swamp to where it becomes hard for Lydia to imagine how a place as forsaken and rugged as this could ever actually belong to anyone. Now and then she will glance over at the colonel, but he no longer pays her much attention. His eyes he keeps fixed on the road, and his thoughts - who is to say....

All he says after a while is, "Corné sleeps between four and six every day. You will have to wait for him for at least another hour, I expect."

She keeps silent and continues to stare at the wall of green smearing past her, as the light of day, at times is shut out completely by the trees. However, as thick and as dark as the forest is after they begin to move away from the main road, as sudden is the clearing in which they soon find themselves. It opens to a trinity of sky and field and specks of grazing zebu and herons that stretch in a rolling motion for as far as the eye can see. Crowning the hill across the valley stands the house that ranks more into the likes of a fortress than any place anyone might think to call home.

"Welcome to Casa Cunho" the colonel announces ceremoniously, shifting in his seat somewhat with excitement. He puts the vehicle back into gear and continues down the breast of the hill. The zebu look up rather stupidly, as the car circles around them, treading over ground that is obviously best traveled on hoof and which Lydia figures will simply be impossible to brave on wheels once the rains have started. Climbing out of the valley, the colonel honks his horn to announce their arrival and heavy gates promptly open in the distance. Once inside them, the walls of the fortress prove much higher than they seemed from across the valley and they quickly find themselves in what Lydia can only describe as a sculpted jungle, deliberately manicured to the very last sprit of grass, it seems. Colorful flowers twist themselves through the garden like serpentines. Stone columns have sporadically been positioned together in clusters, each sprouting rhododendrons that hang like torches oozing heavy flames, giving the illusion that the rock itself is somehow fit to nurture them.

At the end of the garden, at the foot of the house itself, the colonel maneuverer the car around a three-basined fountain. It has a sundial made of what she suspects is pure gold at the head. As she studies it in passing the symbolism around her finally begins to dawn on her that almost everything around her has been arranged – or could be fitted most naturally – into patterns of threes - like the three hearts the functionary had mused so fondly about, she realises.

The colonel seems to know his way around, moving confidently like one who is a regular, if not an intimate part of it all; family perhaps. He leads the way up some steps that arch around the side of the house to a tiled terrace with sets of wicker furniture arranged, again, in a triangular form.

"Make yourselves comfortable," he says. "I don't expect Corné will be down just yet."

He excuses himself and enters the house. Edmilce has moved to the stone railing to fill her eyes with the view. Lydia follows her example and feels she wants to say something. But when she thinks about it, there isn't really very much that can be added to a scenery like this.

After a moment or two, however, Edmilce turns to her.

"They will want to know about me," she says.

"What do you mean?" Lydia asks somewhat confused and adds after searching the girls large, rounded eyes, "I guess there isn't much to tell, Edmilce. And besides, what if they ask about you?"

"I just wonder what you will say, when they ask you why we came here."

The girl pauses for a moment and turns to look up at the house. Lydia can read apprehension on her face.

"Why did we come here?" Edmilce asks.

"Are you sorry we did?"

"My place is with you now," Edmilce answers. "So, I go where you go. I just don't know why we are here."

"We are here, Edmilce, because my uncle asked me to come and talk to someone he used to know."

Lydia looks up toward the house, hoping she might discover what could possibly have caused the girl to have such doubts. She observes each window and counts three stories in total, plus what she assumes must surely be a rather spacious attic. It chokes her to think that there are so many questions she herself wants to ask, but she hasn't a clue as to where to even begin.

"You know," she then says, "If you are going to continue asking me so many whys, know I will always end up disappointing you in some way. The truth is, Edmilce, that I don't know that many answers to the why questions and even less to questions involving a how. Whatever is making you so doubtful, know that you are with me — that you will always be with me...."

Lydia wonders if the girl is only pretending to understand.

They have a perfect view of the entire property from where they stand and right as they turn their attention to the spectacle of the first ambering of the sky behind the hills, as night at last begins to fall, she notices the gates across the garden parting again. Through the vine and palm, she can see a figure moving toward the house; his rising and falling out of view tells her he is on horseback. The house springs to life around them. She can see people everywhere now, moving in at least as many directions. She can hear the clattering of dishes and cutlery inside as well, as if a table is being set in somewhat of a panic.

At last, the horseman clears the trees and halts next to the fountain exactly below them. He circles the colonel's Daimler several times before he slides off his saddle. His leather boots croon like a pair of live animals as he hits the dirt. As soon as he is standing, the man raises his eyes and looks up at them. Lydia greets him with the most cordial nod, knowing that she should by no means miss this opportunity to read as much as she can in the first few seconds his eyes have found hers.

She calculates that he must be about the functionary's age, slightly older perhaps. But in the way he moves and climbs the same brick-in-mud stairs to the terrace, it is clear he is far more agile and athletic than the functionary had probably ever been. In the way he pulls off his gloves and then slaps them into the palm of his hand, she can tell he is a man of authority. And by the way his shoulders heave as he walks, she can tell his head is probably filled with whatever is required from a man capable of ruling a modest-sized kingdom single-handedly as well.

His footsteps, as he walks toward them over the hard-baked tiles creates a complex rhythm she finds pleasantly distracting. And in spite of his horrific face, which, as he moves closer, looks more like it has been submerged in hot oil than simply having been afflicted by acne or smallpox as a younger man, she thinks him rather handsome; the kind of handsomeness rooted in inner grace and undisputed power.

Out of the corner of her eye, she can see colonel Rank hurrying out of the house now as well, stammering, "I went in looking for you. But they said you had gone out."

"I had some business I had to take care of," the horseman says, looking somewhat amused by the sudden commotion. "It kept me the whole afternoon," he adds generously, yet in no way apologising for himself. "I hadn't expected you back until the end of the week..." he says to the colonel, who stands nervously in front of him, tossing restless and almost anxious glances at Lydia and Edmilce, as he looks for the right words to begin his introductions.

The horseman takes a step forward and reaches out to squeeze the colonel's shoulder. And when they touch, in no more than a quick glance that passes between them, a certain bond is revealed that seems to go far deeper than any acknowledgment that might exist between two brothers. There is something far more intimate there, a brand of acceptance that goes beyond anything Lydia has ever witnessed before.

"That is what I wanted to tell you," the colonel says in a whisper that comes out of his mouth wrapped more in breath than in actual voice.

If communication had somehow flowed freely between them in silence earlier, it more than surprises Lydia to see the colonel get hopelessly stuck when he tries to verbalise any part of it.

"I want you to tell me everything, Jens. But first, don't you think you should start by introducing me?"

"I am not really sure how, if you can believe," the colonel responds in surrender.

"If no one else has the sense to properly introduce me, it leaves me no choice but to do so myself.

My name is Corné Cunho," he says, turning toward Lydia, performing a bow so subtle that it requires no more than defusing the focus of his eyes.

"My name is Lydia," she attempts, but the colonel interrupts.

"She is Emilio's niece from Italy."

"Is that correct?" the man says, studying her face more closely now, deliberately feigning a certain measure of delight.

For a moment all expression seems to vanish from his face. His eyes grow more stern and a couple of times they dart toward the spot behind her where Edmilce is standing.

"It is an honor to meet you," he says.

"Likewise."

"I apologise for having kept you waiting. Had I known you were coming, I would have received you myself."

"Colonel Rank, who drove us here, told us you would be sleeping," she then says.

Corné Cunho smiles and presses his hand to his chest, over-dramatising a meant apology.

"Dom. Cunho," she adds looking at the colonel, who in turn is looking back at her rather pleadingly, "I am not exactly sure why I was asked to come here. All I know right now is that it is rather sad news I am bringing. My uncle, Emilio, whom I understand you knew, died on his way here, two days before we docked in Rio de Janeiro.

If you would like I will explain and I am hoping you will do the same. For I am not entirely sure why my uncle asked me to come see you, as I mentioned."

His eyes go from stern to vacant. And even though they do not pull away from her for one second, she is sure he is no longer actually looking at her or really listening anymore.

"We met in São Thomé," the colonel adds, again trying to contribute as best he can. "The young lady was looking to come here. She said it was you she wanted to find" - and mumbles, rather to himself, "It didn't seem like a coincidence."

But Corné Cunho assumes command of the situation once more.

"You have traveled a long way to find me then. And for that alone, no matter what your real business is with me, please consider this as your home. I will see to it that your Negro gets settled in as well."

"Just to clarify a thing or two for you, Dom. Cunho. This child is not, as you call, my Negro. I would much appreciate if you didn't refer to her in that way.

Edmilce," she calls, not once disengaging her eyes from his. "Please introduce yourself."

"My name is Edmilce," the girl whimpers behind her. "It is an honor to make your acquaintance, Dom. Cunho."

"We are traveling together," Lydia says. "If you extend me your hospitality, which I accept gratefully, then you also extend it to her."

After a brief silence, he bows his head toward the young girl and replies: "I wouldn't have it any other way. Miss Edmilce, the honor is all mine."

<><><><><><><>

It is agreed that they should talk over dinner and take the entire evening if need be, to discuss what Corné Cunho refers to, quite tauntingly, as the hand of destiny that has brought them together.

Edmilce is shown to a room directly next to Lydia's on the second floor of the house. Both rooms are decorated with an uncluttered simplicity, quite in contrast with the nostalgic baroque style of the day. The place has an unassuming country elegance Lydia feels she should match by wearing a modest and simple black dress she bought for herself back in the city. In the adjacent room Edmilce is putting on the skirt and blouse Lydia bought for her the day before Christmas.

"We must look our very best tonight, Edmilce," Lydia says, as the girl drags her boots into the room by the very blisters on her feet.

But Lydia is oblivious to the limping and just appraises the girl much in the way a sculptor might appraise a chunk of marble before carving out the gem inside it.

"Tonight we honor the man who put us here," she adds, though unsure if the girl is even listening - or which man she is actually referring to.

"You know, Edmilce" Lydia continues musing out into the space before her, "I was just thinking of how far I have traveled and how distance can be measured in so much more than nautical miles alone."

The girl turns and smiles at Lydia, as though she were the one who is ten years older.

As they descend the stairs, they can see Corné Cunho and the colonel seated on leather armchairs facing each other inside a large space that covers the entire ground floor of the house. At a small distance away from the sitting area a table is set elaborately under several high-legged candle holders to illuminate the meal that will soon be served.

As they approach the two men it surprises Lydia that neither one rises to greet them. But she dismisses this as some cultural discrepancy she has yet to get used to, given that these men are probably no longer bound by the same customs she has observed all her life.

"I see you have put on new disguises," says Corné Cunho as they approach, emptying his drink in a flamboyant backward toss of the head.

"I am afraid your compliments are far too subtle Dom. Cunho. But I will take them as such nonetheless," Lydia replies, her smile as radiant as it has ever been.

"People rarely find me subtle Miss Lydia. Just Lydia was it?"

She sees the men exchange something of a conspiring glance.

"Dom. Cunho, this is a beautiful house," Lydia then remarks, anxious to break the silence that has worked its way around the room.

But she stops herself before saying anything more, wondering if she even has the vocabulary to describe what it is she actually finds so beautiful about it in the first place.

His reaction is no more than a quickening of his breath, as he smoothens the fabric of his dinner jacket before he rises to his feet.

"I am starving," he announces. "Jens, how about you? Aren't you just famished?"

"I believe I am," the colonel replies, getting to his feet as well.

The table is set for four. But, for a second it seems somewhat far fetched that she and Edmilce are actually about to be asked to sit at it. Corné Cunho seems to read thoughts as well.

"Please ladies," he says. "I am the most stubborn of skeptics, but I will not let my guests go hungry, no matter what their real intentions for visiting me. You and I have some talking to do," he adds almost in an accusing tone that in no way promises that the conversation he is referring to will at all be a pleasant one. "But I promise you that whatever you are walking away with tonight will not be an empty stomach"

"Thank you Dom. Cunho. But I am afraid I will never be able to match your gracious hospitality with what it is I am bringing you," she replies, regaining some of her confidence, even though her convalescence is purely cosmetic - and adds, "In fact, I believe it is me who is bound to gain the most from our coming here. So far, you seem to feel the same."

"Now you must explain," he says.

"I have every intention to."

She looks over at the colonel, who is staring at his hands folded on his lap again, the way he had done that morning, back in São Thomé, again looking rather lulled and uninspired.

"I suppose it is fair that I tell you how Edmilce and I happened to detour from our original journey to come out this way, before I show you something my uncle wanted me to give you."

"So far, Lydia, you have learned that I am not the most subtle person. Then you learned from me that I am a notorious septic And now you must know that I am also viciously impatient. So, please stall no longer," he half chuckles.

"Fair enough. My uncle died on the 18th of December, while traveling here. He died from a severe and swift attack of Yellow Fever out at sea. At least, Yellow Fever seems to be the official cause of his death, because I also have my suspicions about the amount of rat poison we traveled with....

Anyway, I am not exactly sure what his exact plans were, but for whatever reason, Trés Corações was on his itinerary. For your information, I was not traveling with him. As a matter of fact, it was something of a coincidence we were on the same ship out of Genoa at all. My own plans were to travel to Buenos Aires. And to tell you the truth, I didn't have that many plans beyond making it there.

However, before I veer off too much, let me return to my uncle. He ran a fever for three days; no more. And on the night he died, he left me his personal belongings, with instructions to come find you. I am hoping you will help me find out why.

He was too ill to explain to me who you were, let alone why he wanted me to come to you. But I had every reason to believe he saw you as a friend."

She pauses for a moment and looks around the table. She and the pockmarked Brazilian are sitting at the head of it facing each other. And even through the flair of the candles and the relative distance between them, she sees his eyes have filled with a festering kind of sadness, but which she finds somewhat difficult to place as well.

So far, Corné Cunho has seemed not in the least bit charmed by anything her being there might signify. She has gauged him as a man likely to be rather rotten inside - probably by vanity - and with every minute she spends in his presence the more puzzled she becomes as to why a gentle soul like Emilio Toffolo might so desperately have wanted her to come to him, of all people.

But she is sure that the more they talk the more answers she will gain in the end.

"For whatever it is worth to you," she continues, "there is a lovely headstone at the Botafogo cemetery that I feel matches my uncle's dignity and character quite nicely. Perhaps, now that I have honored his dying wish by finding you, you might consider going to Rio yourself sometime to pay your respects. For reasons that are still quite unclear to me, he wanted for us to meet," she repeats, though this time in a voice that is graver and clearly more cautious.

She becomes distracted by one of the servants who appears out of nowhere to set a plate in front of her. The sight of the food jumbles her thoughts. The servants skirmish about the room in perfect silence, delaying even further the moment she can resume by maintaining the level of wine inside her glass at all times. She can feel her cheeks glow like they haven't glowed since the last time she had known a winter. Edmilce has not passed on one of the wine servings herself, and had Lydia cared either way, it has already penetrated her veins too deeply for her to really do much about it.

With effort and with a tongue that feels like it has swelled up to twice its normal size in a matter of minutes, she does manage, however, "How did you know my uncle, Dom. Cunho? Do you have any idea why he might have wanted me to come to you — except for the food and the wine that is?" — barely succeeding in stifling a near-inebriated little giggle.

"Emilio Toffolo," Corné Cunho replies, bringing his empty glass to shoulder level to be refilled once more, "was a friend — and much more than that. It is true that we were also business partners."

He takes his time letting half the content of his glass run into his mouth. As he stares out in front of him whilst savoring the texture working its way down his throat, he adds, "We met more than twenty years ago, during Emilio's first visit to Brazil — in the city of São Paulo. I remember he had a strange fascination for the fact that so many of your countrymen were coming out this way. And as far as I know, this fascination remained with him until the last time I saw him, about five years ago, when he returned to Italy to fulfill his duty, as he called it."

He exchanges another private glance with the colonel, who, along with Edmilce sitting in front of him has not opened his mouth the entire time except to gorge up the food in front of him. His role at the table, like Edmilce, seems to be of an observer, as though they have been invited to join this gathering not to participate but to watch and perhaps detect particular subtle drafts in the conversation that might be of tactic importance somehow to the ones doing all the talking.

Corné Cunho continues.

"I had been in São Paulo on business and in time I was able to convince Emilio to see this part of the country as well, hoping that it would broaden his understanding of why people from all over were rushing to these shores – and still are, obviously. It was a thing he did come to understand later on I think, but was never really quite able to fully accept.

We decided to enter into some business together."

"What kind of business exactly?" Lydia asks, while she folds her napkin into different odd shapes next to her plate.

Not once does she take her eyes off the scars on Corné Cunho's face, which give him a rather ageless but still quite shredded look.

"How dull that you would ask that," he says, and for the first time she can hear the wine in the texture and width of his tongue.

"Why do you say those things?"

He sighs and sharpens his focus on her.

"If I confuse you, dear, it is because I have difficulty believing you."

"And which part of what I have been telling do you not believe, Dom. Cunho?"

"I am not sure yet," he answers, priding himself it seems, in the fact he can afford to be frank. "Do you yourself have any idea at all, why your uncle, as you say, might have wanted to send you all the way out here to find me?"

"I honestly do not. And I am having difficulty believing you are as clueless as you say you are, to tell you the truth."

He smiles and glances at the colonel again.

"Ah, the truth!" he says.

102

She then reaches down the front of her dress and removes from under her brassier the note Emilio Toffolo had given her, which she has stashed behind the money pouch. The moisture on her skin has made the paper damp, to where it is far less of a theatrical prop than she had initially intended for it to be, when she holds it up.

She pulls back her arm, squinting her eyes at the letter - flaunting the kind of confidence no one else really believes she has, and says, "In the middle of the night, before he died – after I had given up hope of ever hearing him speak again, he called to me. His fever had already reached deadly heights and when he spoke his words were no more than whimpers. He said for me to take whatever was inside the carpetbag he used to carry around everywhere he went."

She lets a pause break up her words, to make sure she has his full attention before she continues.

"The exact content of what was in the carpetbag I believe is none of your concern," she says. "What is, however, is this note, which I suspect he must have written while Edmilce and I had been asleep and must surely have taken him great effort to complete.

I have never doubted that he must have been quite delirious when he wrote it," she adds, still flipping the paper in between her fingers. "And I even considered disregarding it all together, in light of how ill he was. But because in this note he repeats exactly what he said to me that night, I have decided to carry on and do as he asked me."

At last she reaches over the table to meet Corné Cunho's extended hand. As he takes the paper from her, he exchanges yet another glance with the colonel, which this time makes her feel apprehensive and anxious to learn what that undercurrent between them is about, regardless that this time it is far less conspiring than before. Corné Cunho sits back in his chair as he slowly unfolds the paper, tossing up a series of somewhat weakened but still fierce glances in her direction. And for the first time that evening the colonel looks at her as well, in a restless and sullen way of one who is about to witness some kind of a tragedy unfold.

Corné Cunho sits motionless for a long time, scrutinising the writing down to the very last stroke and when he looks up again she thinks she can detect the glistening of tears in his eyes. He lets both his hands rest on the table still holding the paper and declares:

"You are an impostor"

"How dare you," she replies immediately, without needing to let the insult travel entirely through her first before responding to it.

A thin, bitter grin forms on his lips.

"But don't think I will judge you for being one. For I also know, in his own way, so was Emilio. And many with him I might add."

"I will not be called a liar," she hisses, her head quite clear suddenly.

"But you are. You are an impostor."

She wants to respond a second time, to defend herself in some way, to fight back with whatever she has, but her words are hindered from leaving her lips by the scrape of the choking lump that has formed in her throat. It tastes tart with indignation.

He leans forward.

"Lydia, when two souls of the same ilk find their way toward one another, the result is always pure and sincere. Now, let me explain something to you about the truth, as you obviously feel you are no longer bound by it. In the short period we had together, Emilio and I - before he was drawn back to his beloved Italy - I believe he showed me most of what he was about. He showed me his passions but also his fears."

He stops to light a cigar, which he gracefully pulls out of the inside of his jacket; a gesture that looks so familiar to her, so intimately close to what has caused her heart to ache since the day she got off the ship that she finds it almost offensive that he should smoke it in her presence. And it takes all she has to keep her composure, as he gets ready to continue behind a cruel cloud of smoke.

"You should know how much it saddens me to learn that Emilio didn't have enough time to complete the full picture I know he wanted to paint for me, of who he was," he says leaning back and bringing his voice down, directing it to her alone.

"Let me ask you something," he says, "you being Emilio's niece and all," - as she tries to ignore the scars on his face; the light from the candles emphasizing them quite dramatically from this angle. "What was his mother's maiden name, Lydia?" Corné Cunho then asks her, his voice the color of burnt coffee.

Silence; even the servants have temporarily been caught in a freeze, somewhere in the shadows around them. Lydia only blinks her eyes once or twice.

"What was his father's first name then? No? Tell me Lydia, I am sure you know he had only one sister, whom he had not spoken to in years. Do you know what the reason was that they finally broke off all relations?"

He sits back again caressing his lips for a while with the butt of his cigar, studying her and looking amused.

"Stop fooling yourself; this is how obvious you are," he says.

He holds up his empty glass again and one of the servants hurries out of one of the corners to fill it. She observes his confidence; precisely what is dwindling inside of her with every moment that passes.

"Stop insulting me, Lydia. I will not have it."

He rigidly looks down at the paper still in his hand.

"I would recognise Emilio's handwriting anywhere," he says. "This is clearly his hand, even though it is most unsteady – I must admit. But which, I suppose, verifies what you have so far told me about his being ill."

He looks up and she is surprised by the lucid but hurt expression in his eyes.

"For whatever reason, you must have meant a great deal to him that he should give you this," he adds. "It shows he deemed you worthy of pretending to be his niece, I suppose."

Again he directs his gaze toward the colonel and at last she feels she is beginning to understand the nature of the static that plays between them.

"Lydia, I have seen quite many travelers come through these parts – from places you wouldn't even have heard of. I have been surrounded by them all my life," he says. "And if there is one thing they have all had in common, it was the fact they were all looking for something. And in the end, it had always been to learn about themselves.

Now, don't look at me that way, because I know you know exactly what it is I am talking about. You see, Emilio was no different. He too was torn in that way. The last time we were together, the last time I failed to convince him to stay with me he finally admitted this to me - that it had always been his wish to be complete that drove him to travel. Even though he absolutely hated it; he hated it," he adds with a soft chuckle, flicking the crown of ash on the floor.

"And for what it was worth — which was considerable, travel was how he found out who he really was."

Corné Cunho takes a long pull from his cigar and pauses to let the thread of his words wrap itself around her, allowing her every opportunity to ask all the obvious questions - and to which he can then answer at last, and in doing so, freeing himself more than it would free her to know the truth, that what bound him to the functionary was something ardent and real, something that is reserved only for a few.

He looks at the colonel again. But the colonel does not return his glance.

They remain at the Cunho mansion for almost two months. In all directions away from the estate the roads have become unmanageable. Even the railroads leading to the major cities along the coast have in some parts been buried completely by mud. The rains are upon them.

"Once a year, for a couple of months, nature reclaims the land around these parts," Corné Cunho says to her, "just to remind us that in the end we own nothing. With luck," he adds, "it will be March before you can go anywhere."

But none of the speculations about the weather or those about the availability of transport seem relevant to her, next to the one question that looms over everything of where she will go — even if she could. Beyond fulfilling the functionary's last wish to find Corné Cunho, his lover, Lydia has virtually made no plans. She can barely conceptualise the future past this one event. Though unnatural as it is, next to her overwhelming need to be in control of all the things around her — especially her own destiny - she has come to realise that she isn't the only one scripting life around her.

Buenos Aires is still as hazy as it has ever been; no more than a series of disconnected images that make up the vague concept of it in her mind; neither a place that is desirable nor one to be avoided. But whichever way and whatever the backdrop; whether she stays in Brazil another year or leaves tomorrow, whether she travels to China or back to Italy even, she knows that she will eventually get there.

The documents she had found inside the functionary's carpetbag have turned out to be public stock, indeed issued by a local mining company some seven years prior, as she suspected. And she soon learns that in paper at least, she is now part owner of a great deal of the mining operations in the region. When she shows Corné Cunho the documents, seeking his advice as to what she should do with them he recognises them at once. She knew all along that the paperwork must have been valuable, by the looks of it, but now she also understands that they represent part of the base of Emilio Toffolo and Corné Cunho's relationship - and are therefore, worth a great deal more than just money. Also, she increasingly wonders to what extent Corné Cunho, if not exactly in a legal sense as much as a moral one, might feel entitled to at least part of whatever the functionary left her. But instinct tells her this isn't what he is interested in. And furthermore, she also understands enough about the world to know that there aren't any laws that will ever ratify such a claim in the first place, nor any that will ever sustain the claims she herself is making in regards to something as basic as her own identity. In that sense she and Corné Cunho are accomplices, equals only under the laws of chance.

One day, Corné Cunho announces that he wants to teach her and Edmilce to ride, being that on horseback is just about the only sensible way to cross the mush of the pastures surrounding the estate. He says he will instruct them in what he calls, the Brazilian riding style, which Lydia finds to be quite a bit crueler than those she remembers from childhood - when it had not in fact required gashing the horse's skin open with spurs in order to hurry it along.

As they cross the fields away from the house, dispersing the zebu with sharp whistles and the splashes of the hoofs beneath them, Corné Cunho summarises the situation, as he figures it stands:

"Knowing Emilio as I do — or used to," he calls from underneath the halo of water that surrounds him, as he pulls at the reins while an unexpected memory suddenly seems to make its way through him. "He would have wanted you to pursue whatever it is you need to pursue, Lydia, you are young," he says, his voice reluctant and with slightly more rasp. "And, you are independently wealthy now as well. And

with those two blessings, my dear" he adds, "know that you are also free to make mistakes; that you can afford to make them now."

He says he wants her to have a visual reference of the thing she now owns, that it will somehow give her a better sense of the possibilities available to her. Not far outside the mansion walls that seem to guard against an enemy probably long since forgotten, Lydia and Edmilce watch him circle his horse around a couple of young bulls grazing at a small distance ahead.

"These two are going to be champion breeders, you know," he calls back to them, referring to the two beasts that look up at them with that dim-witted gawk so typical of all grazing creatures. "They are going to make me rich someday," he adds laughing, his eyes fixed in their sockets in celebration of — well, himself.

But his face grows more earnest as he directs his horse back toward them.

"Before you leave us, Lydia, you need to make sure you fully understand all of this," he says motioning to the horizon and the magnitude of the landscape around them.

He adjusts his position on the saddle and nibbles at the butt of a cigar that materialises in his hand. He takes his time to stare at the tree line in the distance. She feels that he looks like a king savouring his own blood-earned conquests; that he clearly derives intense pleasure besides, every time he finds some excuse to look at his own realm and give it meaning.

"See, Emilio had come from a wealthy family," he says, turning to face her again. "To him wealth was like the sun setting and rising every day. To Emilio, all his life wealth had been a given of sorts, something that had always been there but never had any real taste to it, if you know what I mean. I believe that this is what he came here for, you see, to regain the flavour of who — of what he was. He knew that not his post at the treasury back in Italy, which he had held for more than thirty years, if

I remember correctly, nor anything else back there could ever give that to him."

"And?" she interrupts, "did he find what he was looking for?"

"Like I told you, I do flatter myself. But I believe he did, when he found me; yes."

A devilish grin appears on his face, as he briefly glances at her and maneuvers his horse in between the two of them.

He reaches over to adjust Edmilce's saddle by tugging at the straps, and adds, "Let's go see what is yours," - as he gives his animal only a light nib of his spur, catapulting it forward, calling back to them, "Try and catch up!"

The horses know the fields and obviously see the open space foremost as a place for running. In less time than it takes to close their eyes and shriek, she and Edmilce too shoot over the inundated marsh after him, delivered to a ton of muscle combined, sending flocks of birds up into the air around them.

Breathless and joyously terrified from the exertion of hanging on, Lydia and Edmilce open their eyes only once the horses begin to slow down to break the tree line. Corné Cunho is waiting for them; the smoke from his cigar mixing idly with the mist that hangs beneath the treetops behind him. Immediately, he corrects their technique like a lunatic lector and commands them again to follow him before he disappears into the growth, calling back a vague warning to watch for snakes.

The horses follow single file, as the treetops block the watery sun. A discernible twilight falls around them and the air feels many times cooler than the suffocating damp from the open field. Occasionally, he will toss back an approving glance toward them, as his horse crackles over the spongy floor, twisting deeper into the unknown over an unseen path.

Before long the trees clear again and they unexpectedly find themselves at the edge of a gape in the ground as wide as the field they have just crossed. It is a man made hole, deeper and wider than any hole she ever imagined human force could dig. She sees workers crossing over the bottom of it on planks that spiral up along its muddy walls with baskets of clay hanging on their backs and strapped across their foreheads.

She notices that the clay is being carried by human force only halfway out; mules cover the rest of the way to ground level. At the top the baskets are then emptied into larger containers to be carried out of sight by oxen. It is a sum of force, with human endurance at the end of some utilitarian chain that is as sinister as it is brilliantly effective.

"Don't tell me," she says in a tone that causes him to look up somewhat startled, though amused, "all our beloved Emilio left us is a hole filled with mud?"

"Hardly," Corné Cunho responds, but with a look that tells her she has not laid full claim to the pun she intended.

"Gold," he says thinly. "What he left you, dear, are half a dozen pits just like this one, filled with it."

She stares at him for a moment, not quite able, or willing, to fully grasp the meaning of his words. So, she turns her attention back to the pit and pantomimes coherent thought as best she can. She has never beheld anything like it before, though the whole spectacle strikes her as faintly familiar all the same. It pulls her back to the day Edmilce had dived after a coin in Salvador, the day she supposedly would no longer stand for injustice, no matter on what grounds it is ever committed.

Now there are maybe a thousand men moving about the bottom of the pit, barely distinguishable from the glistening greenish-grey around them. They are part of it, cast into it; worth no more than the short distance their bones can transport the muck. They are men only because one can deduct that they are indeed men, for humanity has been removed from the equation completely.

That morning back in Salvador seems like an eternity behind her now and the rage that had fizzed up inside of her then far less ardent somehow. She thinks of the things she had made Paxi out to be, the insults and the curses she had wished upon him for the thing he had done, and thinks of how different she feels now, now that she herself stands to gain so much from the thing she once so opposed.

"I want to make you a proposition," Corné Cunho says most matter-of-factly after a while, as if he is talking about the lunch that's waiting for them back at the mansion.

He slides off his horse swiftly and as part of one single gesture he walks around, takes hold of her reins and offers his hand for her to dismount. She is careful not to respond too quickly. Instead, she raises her eyes toward Edmilce, whom, none to her surprise, she finds still clamped to the neck of her animal, looking flustered still from their run through the field. Instinctively, Lydia makes a move in her direction, but Corné Cunho has already lifted the girl from her saddle and puts her down in the grass beside her. He combines the reins from the horses in one hand and begins to pull the animals along the edge of the pit away from them.

Encouraged by the feel of solid ground under her feet again, Edmilce skips out in front of her, joyfully petting the horses and talking to them, the way children will sometimes engage in direct dialog with animals they feel a particular connection with, often going from fearful to enamored in only moments. They move to where the mules are emerging from the pit and where the ox carts stand waiting to step-foot the mud away. They halt near the edge and she can almost taste the tension in the men emerging from the pit the closer Corné Cunho's moves to it.

"There is four ounces of gold to every half ton of clay we pull out of here," he says. "And this, dear, is of interest to you for two reasons. First of all, at this particular pit we will soon mechanise the digging and increase production tenfold. And second, we will be able to explore about as many new pits because of it."

She doesn't need to puzzle much on the numbers he is giving her and for the mind-boggling size of the fortune they are now standing on to come into view for her.

"What is going to happen to the workers, once the pits are mechanised?" she asks.

"I beg your pardon?"

She repeats her question and only then understands how out of touch she has sounded. She turns to look at Edmilce, who stares out in front of her now with a rather blank expression of her face.

"You said you wanted to make me a business proposition," she finally says, as if emerging from a short-lived spell.

"I did," he answers.

He flicks the butt of his cigar into the wet grass in front of him and presses it out of sight with the tip of his boot.

"Are you getting any sense of what the deeds and the stock Emilio

111

left you might be worth?" he asks, fixing his sharp, black eyes on her in a sideward glance.

"I believe so," she says.

"I should say that between the two of us, you and me, we own ten of these. Or will do so somewhere in the next few years. And speculating on you leaving this place before long, I propose to buy them from you.

At the bank in Trés Corações, they will give you a more accurate price of the stock. What do you say?"

"You are right, Dom Cunho, I could never live in a place like this. But even so, this is where I am now. And therefore, where I feel I should be."

She stares into the hole in front of her. One of the mules below seems to have got its hoof stuck in the clay and is temporarily holding up the line climbing up. Within seconds, one of the foremen approaches the animal and begins to flog it. With detached curiosity she observes and marvels at the rage with which the man beats the animal and how, even as some of the workers approach to help the beast out of its unfortunate predicament by pulling at it, and the whip now strikes human skin as well, does the man not let up.

She steps forward to the edge; stares down into the pit, appraising it like an extension of herself, and adds, "Here is what I propose, Dom Cunho: I will have the deeds valued at the bank, as you suggested and I agree that you pay me double whatever they're worth at this time.

My guess is that you will turn quite a profit from your investment in the years to come and this will give me enough means to sustain me for a while.

However, I will hold on to the stock itself. I feel it would be wise to maintain an interest in the area, regardless whether I ever come back here."

Even if it has turned out that she has an exceptional sense for money, her provincial distrust of it essentially remains unaltered. Like pebbles that will help her to retrace her tracks if she ever needs to, from Trés Corações to the port city of Santos and then on to Montevideo, before crossing the River Plate, she will spread the stock evenly between the banks at every town, planning to eventually arrive in Buenos Aires very much in comfort, but also with enough reason to exert herself once there.

It takes her almost the two months she spends at the mansion to learn exactly what role the sultry colonel plays in the history that comes to light there. For most of the time she is convinced that in Emilio Toffolo's absence Jens Rank became Corné Cunho's new companion, the man who replaced the functionary in the concealed intimacy of that place. But during the four days it takes the colonel to drive her and Edmilce back to the coast, once Corné Cunho finally concedes to letting them tackle the muddy roads, does she learn the real story about him as well.

Jens Rank, like the functionary, is what one refers to as a melancholy man, either out of lack of proper vocabulary, or the unwillingness to name things that are still quite unmentionable. It delights her to learn, however, that the colonel has faked his own death and the fact he left a wife and five daughters back in Germany seems almost trivial to her.

Back behind the wheel of the Daimler, as this is the one place the Colonel seems comfortable enough to really talk about himself, he tells her he met Corné Cunho around the same time the functionary had and that it had been in - one of those places frequented by - men like them - back in Sao Paulo. Musing, as it is clearly some story he has not had many opportunities to tell, he says that the thought of spending the rest of his life without having to make excuses, especially to the uniformed ranks in the army, about his personal preferences and his inclinations toward other men, was what finally drove him in the early nineties to arrange something of a disappearing act of his own.

"After I didn't return to Europe that year," he explains, all the while sucking at the ends of his moustache in the wind, "I must have been declared dead soon after," he adds almost with a song in his voice. "I was dead and free."

"And this is why you didn't believe me at first, when I told you Emilio Toffolo had died?" she asks.

"Well, it sounded all too familiar. See, as strange as this may sound, there is great freedom that comes from being dead, you know - especially when your life so far has been a lie — especially then."

She looks at him for a long time and decides that in several illusive but unmistakable ways, Jens Rank reminds her of the functionary. It could be in the benevolence in which he addresses her, or maybe in the way his eyes attempt to create images of the words she speaks back to him. There is far more that connects these men, this much has become clear to her, ties that go much farther than the simple business of accumulating wealth and things for which the world has not yet found the words to name.

"My feeling is that he had understood this too," she finally says, referring to Emilio Toffolo, "the freedom that comes from having the world bury the memory it has of you."

She wonders how many men like Corné Cunho and Emilio Toffolo and the colonel she herself has known in the past. But she isn't about to ask him.

Although, the roads are in far worse shape than they were on the inland leg of her journey two months earlier, they are less treacherous than Corné Cunho warned her they would be. Except for a few minor hold ups and some flooded fields around Sao Jose dos Campos, they arrive in little over four days at the port of Santos.

She arranges passage for herself and Edmilce on a timbre rig called the Garota bound for Montevideo, which is to push off the day after and will arrive at the Uruguayan capital less than a week later. The idea is to then cross the estuary to Buenos Aires from there.

At the docks, on the day of her departure, a choked silence falls between her and the colonel, the kind that often descends when indefinite farewells tend to approach. It makes the air somewhat hard to breathe, especially when those involved know all too well how impermanent farewells can be. Their words seem timed and colored by a teary chime hidden away in their voices.

"I think you will feel right at home in Buenos Aires," the colonel says. "If there is one city in the whole of South America that can trick one into thinking you are somewhere in southern Europe, it is Buenos Aires, you know."

"I think that for me that would be the last reason for going there," she answers him, but not quite able to express how much it touches her as well that he wants to put her mind at ease somehow.

She looks for Edmilce amongst the dockworkers and finds her in the distance standing by the water.

"I hope she doesn't dive in," she sighs to herself, but loud enough for the colonel to hear - and to react by asking her to explain herself.

"Why would she?"

"If you only knew what she is capable of," she replies scoffing.

"Who is she, Lydia?"

"I don't think I know her much better than you do, Colonel. She is a child that became a part of my big adventure so far. One day she was simply there and I couldn't really imagine being without her now. I guess she is what you see: a child that will always be a part of me, but one I cannot really explain. Not yet at least."

She glances over at him, sees that he has stopped fiddling with his tusks and now visibly puzzles over what she is saying.

"Colonel, there are still some things that are quite unclear to me about Emilio Toffolo. And I suppose that there will always be things I will never fully know. But still, you might be able to tell me a thing or two."

"Try me."

"Colonel, have you ever heard of a man named Paxi; Ulisse Gavino Paxi?"

"No dear, I have never heard of him before. Is he someone Emilio used to know?"

"Yes. Do you think Dom. Cunho might have heard of him?"

"It's possible. Did you ask him?"

"The truth is that I didn't even think about it. It is only now, sitting here that I remembered him. I guess it might have something to do with the sea, the smell of it perhaps; the way it sounds. I don't know." - and adds with a mischievous grin, "Whenever I get close to the ocean, I end up thinking about that man."

"I see," the colonel says smiling back, pulling at his moustache again.

Paxi

Contrary to what is often said and written about Ulisse Gavino Paxi, he isn't much of a dreamer. But this is only because with him thoughts never get the chance to bloat to such proportions. Whenever there is something to be wished for, with Paxi, action immediately follows — and always long before he has allowed himself to feel that brazen thing that fascinates him most of anything in the world: need.

To Paxi, there is something heroic about the idea that after a day's work a man can let his body sink into the softness of his bed, feeling the kind of exhaustion a night's rest can never erase, the kind of frazzle that erodes even the mind, the soul. He enjoys watching the men in the fields and in the factories, molding and bending steel and rock to the will of nothing other than flesh and bone, for he knows that he will never feel the way they feel things; that he just isn't meant to.

Surely, Paxi knows how to exert himself; exhaust every cell in his body if he wants to. But the truth is that he will never - ever — experience its physical pull to the fullest. And in that vein, he also understands — has always understood - that he will never know the necessity to fight for survival like so many around him do, or that he will, like the rest of humanity, at times be so utterly consumed by fear. No matter how much he simulates, like one simulates the steps to some dance to which there is no music; strife has always been something alien and mystical to him.

He wants to crave - to need and yearn like the rest of them; he looks for it in everything. And subsequently, it is the one thing he has never mastered and the one thing he sees as the single force other than himself that makes the very planet turn as his wheel.

◇◇◇◇◇◇◇◇

"I want to thank everyone for coming today," orates the functionary, as though he were about to start a scolding sermon, the kind to deflate the spirit even before it fully gets underway.

The functionary is much older than Paxi, but not only in years; there is something timelessly ineffective about him as well: a clerk body and soul — a natural.

The functionary removes his glasses, holds them against his chest in somewhat of a grave and pleading gesture and looks into the crowd he knows he will never fully reach. Paxi is seated in the chair to the side, smoking. And as the functionary fumbles to achieve only a string of short-lived stutters, Paxi in turn exchanges calmly amused glances with every person in the audience. Now and then, a ripple of annoyance will pass through the crowd, as it grows ever more impatient for the moment Paxi will at last let himself be heard.

"What is it you stand to gain by depopulating the Castelfranco region, Signore Paxi?" the functionary manages. "Why, by the time you are through here all that will be left are cemeteries."

Paxi straightens himself in his chair, admiring the craftsmanship of the cigar in his hand; artfully rolled Costa Rican tobacco rested against the octagonal lapis lazuli rock that decorates his left hand.

"Signore Toffolo, it is precisely because these lands have been toiled in faith by every person here today," Paxi then says, "and indeed, for generations in many cases, that the combined authorities should consider themselves privileged to be offered the titles you hold in your hands so precariously — as if you had just been offered a pound of cheese!"

A roar of laughter sounds through the assembly hall, clearly delivered at last. And it gains momentum. A sadistic chime can be heard inside of it, in spite of the devastating news they have all just received, that pretty much everything they own has been rendered worthless by the sheer size of the pile of properties being offered for sale in one single day. And that in fact they can consider themselves quite far from home already.

But this doesn't seem to matter much, nor whatever will come next, as long as Paxi continues talking and continues to stand before them. Every individual there is at the very core prepared to wager everything on Paxi alone, invest everything they own in the things he represents. He embodies new beginnings, America. Or, at least the illusion of it, because, based on what any of them really know about it, America isn't much more than a mirage of sorts, an air castle painted by the magnificent Lissy Paxi's own hand.

"Signore Paxi," the functionary continues, taking more of a distance now, "what is it you can exactly guarantee our constituents, whom you feel you need to represent here today?"

"A new world, Signore Toffolo," Paxi replies simply, "where for a fraction of the meager price the combined authorities will end up paying for the deeds in your hands right now - land it has been taxing for generations besides — new and fruitful horizons will be explored.

Signore Toffolo, what I offer isn't a guarantee, or mountains of gold. The only thing I promise is to open a door, which you and your combined authorities seem to want to keep shut for some reason."

Paxi turns to his carpetbag on the table and produces a single envelope. His movements are played down, making his every gesture all the more aesthetically appealing.

"Signore Toffolo; ladies and gentlemen," he says, opening the envelope and spreading a single sheet of paper out in front of him — the lapis Lazuli ring on his left hand in full view of the crowd, which he promotes every chance he gets by spreading anecdotes about the silver the stone is set in and the strange Inca idolatry carved on the inside of it.

"Perhaps, this will give you an idea of what it is I have to offer."

He pauses and lowers the paper, and purposefully holds the gaze of several of the adoring faces staring back at him.

"This document is not unique, ladies and gentlemen," he says. "Many like it exist through out the continent. But to share with you one example, this particular decree, signed by the Homestead Secretary and the Mayor of Santa Cruz do Sul has put approximately ninety families from the German city of Reutlinger and all its farming talent, right into the Brazilian heartland; each on ten thousand hectares of lucrative crops like soy, cotton and corn - for the symbolic amount of one Mark.

Now, tell me, of any of the deeds and titles you hold in your hands right now, Signore Toffolo, how many total ten thousand hectares or more?"

The functionary keeps his gaze on a fixed spot somewhere between the ceiling and the wall across the assembly hall, in order to keep from crossing it with the glares from the crowd. And at the sounding of Paxi's last question, involuntarily, his arm twitches upward, betraying how much he himself has come under Paxi's spell.

Again, the chill of disdain is felt passing through the crowd.

"Would you care to inspect and verify that the signatures of both the Homestead Secretary and the Mayor of Santa Cruz do Sul are real? Why, you might catch me in a lie yet, Signore Toffolo," Paxi then taunts, triggering another roar of laughter.

Paxi moves around the table, very much taking his time – in control of time itself, it seems.

"To tell you the truth," he then adds, "If this is what the Germans are getting for themselves, I believe we can at least do better" - playing the willing crowd into an absolute climax.

He hangs his head ever so slightly before he continues his stroll and dramatises suffering from acute boredom by yawning lightly into his fist.

But the functionary is still very much on his feet and says, "Signore Paxi, we all know that from the mosques in Constantinople to California's Golden Gate, people talk about you and precisely because people talk, you like to give them every reason to. You, Signore Paxi, represent everything the world should be but hardly ever is. We know this. The cut of your dinner jacket not so much reflects the fashion of the day, I'm sure, as it tends to inspire the one that will soon undoubtedly follow. But if you will, Signore Paxi, let me ask you this: who would you sell this abandoned land to, after the entire region of Castelfranco has been depopulated? Who is going to build here again, once you - and your flock - have moved on to this promised land of yours? See, I believe it is you who is the biggest cause for the plummeting property value. It is you, Signore Paxi, who will in the end be to blame for driving our honest and hardworking citizens to the edge of destitute. And you, Signore Paxi, will some day be called to answer for this."

"Is that a fact?" Paxi answers unimpressed. "And how poetic that you should mention gold, Don Toffolo."

"People, this is madness," the functionary then turns toward the crowd. "What is it that could ever compel you to gamble away everything you have on a venture for which there are no guarantees? Some of you are about to sell for scraps good, fertile ground that's been in your families for God-knows how long."

However brief, it is now the functionary's turn to take his time.

"And for what?" he adds.

"For hope, Signore Toffolo," Paxi interrupts, "hope and new beginnings, like I said." - and in a tenor that is crystalline and might surely be audible right through the thick stone walls of the assembly hall, he adds, "Surely you, Emilio Toffolo, should know all about how strongly a place like Brazil can fill one's heart and one's purse. Isn't it so, Emilio Toffolo, that other than myself - the traveled bastard that I am - it is you in fact, who knows better than anyone how lucrative a place like Brazil can be?

Tell me, Emilio Toffolo, why would you deny your constituents the fortunes you yourself have found in the New World? Why will you not tell us what it is like to find the freedom to indulge, even in our deepest perversions and become rich in the process - how only in a place like America we can become who we truly were meant to be?"

The crowd turns inward and in the silence, Emilio Toffolo speaks words only Paxi can hear:

"You will be destroyed. And when that day comes, it will be me standing over you."

He awakes to a polite knock on his cabin door. His eyes open, but his head is still all wads. He watches the milky sky and the rain that streams down his window. He holds his breath and waits for the knocking to return.

"One moment," he calls; voice a dusty rasp.

He slaps on some of the clothes from the night before as quickly as his unresponsive limbs will allow. On his way to the door he passes in front of the mirror, but turns his eyes away from it. Pushing down on the rat's nest on the top of his head he reaches for the door.

"What is it?" he snaps and is greeted by Captain Ulderico Scola himself.

The Captain tips the front of his cap to him and makes a jump backwards as a stream of water falls down the front of it and onto his shoes.

"Bad weather, Captain?" Paxi reacts, stepping aside and pulling the Captain in out of the rain.

"I suppose there is a slight situation with the weather," Scola apologises.

"Well, you have already convinced me of that," Paxi says, more jestingly than seems appropriate. "Did you come to tell me that it is raining, Captain? What is it?"

"I appreciate your sense of humor, Lissy. But it is something else I have come to talk to you about."

Paxi sits down in the chair next to the bed to pull on his boots.

"The weather conditions are worsening by the hour," Scola sighs, as though still quite mesmerized by the subject of climatic anomalies.

"Get to the point, Captain. Please," Paxi says growing annoyed.

"Of course."

The Captain straightens himself facing him.

"I believe some of your Sicilians have arrived."

Had anyone else, besides the Captain, said that to him, he would have thought it grossly out of place and downright disrespectful.

But Paxi knows Ulderico Scola well enough to know that being factual is just one of the Captain's more interesting shortcomings, a handicap of sorts, which Paxi has always been quite fond of.

"Well, we are shipping off tomorrow, Captain; I am not surprised. What's the problem?"

"They are insisting to board, Lissy."

"Let me repeat my question."

"No passengers are allowed on the ship until tomorrow eight o'clock," the Captain says, as though reciting a passage from a log book he has set out to memorise at some point. "You know the regulations and you know why."

"Yes, I know the rules and the port regulations," Paxi says. "But, I also know that the weather has not gone unnoticed by you, either. And as I recall, you yourself just now remarked that it was raining harder by the hour."

"Yes?"

"Well?"

Before the fierceness of Paxi's glare has fully burned itself through the Captain's skin, Paxi's eyes close to hide a resigned sadness that would surely have been visible in his eyes, as well.

"Take me to them," Paxi finally sighs, getting to his feet and pushing Scola to the door.

Stepping over the slippery gangplank, against the glistening grey stone of the dock, Paxi can hardly distinguish about twenty individuals huddled together like a pack of frightened dogs or just a lump of clay; his Sicilians. He walks at a steady pace, only to keep Scola at a trot behind him at all times. And as he gets closer to the group, as always, it is the hollow of their eyes and cheeks and the weathered hands he shakes that give him that old and familiar sense of determination, which always so reaffirms the path he has chosen in life.

"Gentlemen," Paxi says, as he realises that the group is made complete by two or three women, as well as a handful of children. "We will see to it that your luggage is collected - and that you are shown below deck and out of this miserable rain, for which I personally and most sincerely apologise." And to which he adds, "You are just going to have to take my word for it that Naples truly is quite a sight to see under more favourable conditions."

He turns sharply to face the Captain, who has not left his side the entire time, hiccuping to speak all along, but unable to get even one word in.

"Captain, see to it that these people are taken care of."

"Signore Paxi," Scola protests finally, addressing him formally now in the presence of such classless rabble no doubt. "Regulation says that there will be no boarding until eight o'clock tomorrow morning – like I explained."

"We arrived here late last night," says one of the Sicilian, wrapped in drenched wool and a rag on the top of his head that had once, most probably, been some form of head wear and adds in a declarational tone, which leaves no mystery about the fact that he is speaking for the rest of them, "We have no other place to go."

"Captain, I want these people in dry clothes and fed within the hour," says Paxi.

"But Signore Paxi," laments the Captain again, "you tend to forget that proper procedure must be followed. If I let the passengers board whenever they decide to board, we will soon have complete chaos on our hands. Boarding is at my discretion, Signore Paxi."

"Noon, and no later, Captain. And, if you must know, it is because you are the Captain of this great vessel that I trust you will do exactly what I ask."

"Signore Paxi, the procedure is that the medical team examines the passengers before they are allowed onto the ship," Scola insists, ignoring the fact that Paxi – a civilian – has actually given him a direct order – in public no less.

"We were examined ten days ago in Catania," pitches in the Sicilian again, before he empties his nostrils with a forceful blow, barely missing one of the women standing off to the side.

"Precisely," says Scola. "And that is why you all will need to be examined again – before I will let you board."

"Captain," Paxi says in a tone that is unexpectedly soft again, quite in contrast to the growing panic in Scola's own voice. "By the time we get to Buenos Aires, we will all have lice. Noon, e Basta."

<><><><><><><>

By mid-day the rain has cleared and the sun has already begun to put that smug grin back on the city - the one most travelers say they will always remember Naples by after they have seen it from the bay. True as ever to their communal nature, which Paxi feels he can always recognise particularly in Sicilians, the early arrivals have wasted no time striking up camp in the ship's hull. He fully expects his instructions will be followed to the letter, and not giving the matter another thought, for the rest of the morning he locks himself inside his cabin to prepare to join them.

He knows that eventually he will end up staying with them, as if it were even remotely possible to learn every personal detail about every single one of them. He will end up giving in to that urge to share himself not as a man but a substance fit for consumption. He wants to hear, to learn their expectations of the journey ahead and to then pretend that he too is crossing the Atlantic for the very first time. But as much as he wants to dissolve in their midst, there is also an ardent desire to parade himself before them, to shine on them the luminance that is invoked whenever his vanity and his altruistic nature are perfectly aligned inside of him.

Later that morning he will descend into the hull wearing his most impeccable suit. He will move through the corridors on his way down from second to third class until he finally arrives at the spot that is the farthest from the light of day. He will let his eyes crawl up and down the steel walls around him, every emotion known to him suffocating him all at once, yet feeling numbed.

As he moves closer to the small fire nearest to the engines, he will pass women already sprawled on the floor peeling potatoes and men huddled together in dark corners smoking. It never takes very long for his presence to be noticed. How could it? Don Paxi, one of them will soon exclaim and in Paxi's mind, as he cleans his fingernails in front of the mirror, he can already see the group gathering around him. As though caught in a spell, the women will abandon their menial chores and slither in wanting to touch and kiss his hands. The men will throw their arms around him in an undeniable expression of affection toward the one man who represents the very thread of every dream they have ever had.

He will always have bottles of liquor brought down too, which will then be shoved back in his direction immediately after being uncorked. He will accept gracefully and drink from the bottle without reserve. He will hold urchins in his arms and smoke rancid tobacco rolled with noxious rice paper. He will be urged to drink more and soon music will play until he has forgotten that there are in fact times that he isn't with them; a part of them, like this. And often by the time he sees daylight again, they will already be nearing the tropics.

He is still with the Sicilians when the rest of the passengers start shuffling in the following day, reluctantly zigzagging their way to the bottom of the metal stairs. Their clothes are still stained white with lice-powder and their faces look like how he imagines the righteous might look after they have accidentally stumbled upon the gates of hell.

He rises out of a pile of dusty blankets, feeling humbled by the scene unfolding around him. His feet direct him to the centre of the hull; his palms turned outward to the throng moving past him. For a while he stands like this, as if washing himself in the stream of bodies, hoping, as he has done so many times before, that it will rinse away the numbing fat around his heart. A handshake ruffles him out of his stupor as he finds himself staring into the face of a man he may or may not have met before. He watches the man's lips move, shaping words but they barely register. His responses are engaging, however, his own lips appropriately shaping the right words to everything the man is saying.

"Don Paxi, what a pleasure! Allow me the honor of presenting you to my wife…" – who's name Paxi forgets almost the moment he hears it, as he does the children's names, who obviously belong to the man; runny-nosed, underfed ducklings, who look rather cross-eyed to him from exhaustion and bronchitis, but who clearly know who Paxi is and understand quite well what it means for this man to have taken the time to shake their father's hand.

At last, he manages to tear himself loose and squeeze his way toward the stairs, craving the solitude of his cabin again. As he ascends he can feel on the surface of the metal around him that the Ostia Antica is already moving and wonders if the crowd below is aware of it as well.

The honor is all mine, he mumbles to himself.

125

<><><><><><><><>

The following morning the view of Naples from his cabin window has been replaced by the sight of the Genovese hills, draped in an ectoplasmic mist that licks its way down into the bay. Today another ninety-eight souls are to join the Sicilians for the crossing to Argentina. And again it is more than a sense of duty alone that drives Paxi to be seen among them.

There remains, however, a tactical matter he needs to take care of before he can descend into the hull again or down to the dock. He needs to properly thank Captain Scola for the magnanimous gesture the day before, even if letting his first arrivals board early was something the Captain would never have refused him. He knows it's in the best interest of the ship entire that Scola be duly reaffirmed in his superiority of rank, despite of the fact that it is Paxi who personally commissioned him for the crossing. Paxi understands like no other the importance of not challenging the hierarchy that is essential out at sea; that nothing can worsen an already fragile and tense situation, brought forth by an ocean crossing, like the lack of authority. Even if his wishes will always prevail, it is of utmost importance that he not oversteps his position as merely another passenger.

He enters the bridge and finds Scola bent over his instruments and charts, engulfed in that nervous energy that can always be felt during those erratic hours before either entering or leaving port.

"Thank you, Captain," Paxi says announcing his presence, quite oblivious to the fact that he might not have chosen the most convenient time to interrupt.

"Lissy!" the Captain replies in a tone of mustering patience, as if he were addressing a child he feels obliged to pay notice to. "What can I do for you?"

"Get us safely across the Atlantic, for starters," Paxi answers, but quickly adds, "Of course, I am most confident that you will, as always. What I came up here for was to thank you for taking such good care of my Sicilians yesterday."

"Cargo hull or not, Lissy; Sicilians or whatever other creed you might decide to ship off someday, they are my passengers as much as they are yours."

"It is humility and a magnanimous heart that makes a great man, Captain. You have proved to me yet again how true that is."

After avoiding each other's glances for a while and a draughty silence spawns between them and the moment becomes rather palpable in which the polite insincerities will dry up, both men finally come around to face the reality in which Paxi is in every way the captain's superior.

Paxi moves around the bridge, his thoughts wandering and bracing himself for the moment Scola will ultimately begin to bore him with details about nuts and bolts.

"How is it looking?" Paxi finally asks.

"I have been looking at the charts from the last time I sailed to Buenos Aires," Scola says, while caressing the matted beard that cascades down from his chin and fighting back all the while, the feeling that he needs to legitimise himself.

"How long has it been?" Paxi asks, leaning over the Captain's shoulder for his own look at the charts.

"It'll have been two years in February," the Captain replies, a distant chime sounding in his voice. "I was forced to skirt south around a storm after leaving Madeira that time. The crossing took us almost a week longer because of it. We took the Atlantic in full breadth – almost flat on the equator."

"Right over Neptune's roof," Paxi muses, his palm brushing warmly over the captain's shoulder.

"I suppose so. It was an exceptionally smooth sail, as I remember."

For the first time Scola actually turns to look at Paxi leaning up against him.

"How is the boarding coming along?" Paxi asks, moving with a confident stride to the window that overlooks the stern.

"Another two hundred and thirty - with paid-for boarding cards," Scola sighs. "But I don't expect there will be too much contraband today," he adds. "We are taking strict precautionary measures this time."

The Captain lifts his eyes from the paper for a quick glance at the window as well. "How many are yours?" he asks, seemingly preoccupied with other, quite unrelated matters.

"Ninety-eight." Paxi replies like a pup that's just caught its first bone. Scola now straightens himself to face him.

"So this is only the first wave. Is it not?"

"That's correct," Paxi replies, letting his eyes linger on the crowds outside. "During the past four months I've been recruiting hands for several building projects in Buenos Aires" he adds. "Most of them are due to join me here in Genoa."

"How about you?"

"I am to deliver them by no later than January tenth. After that, I am shipping off again to New York."

Scola lets out a sniffle that is partly dismissive and partly rather awe-struck.

"If I didn't know any better, Lissy, now would be the time I would ask you where, after all these years, there will be a place you will ever call home."

"And, if I weren't suffering from a bit of melancholy about the future as I am right now," Paxi sighs again, "I would answer you that it is right here, on a hunk of steel about to make for the open ocean, where I feel I should be."

Scola's earlier sniffle now ups itself into what Paxi can only interpret as something like a contained scatter.

"Melancholy, Lissy? In all the years I have known you that is one thing I have never seen you suffering from."

Scola moves to the stove and fills two mugs of coffee.

"What's in New York?"

Paxi turns abruptly toward the Captain, startled by the fact his thoughts had temporarily wandered away from the conversation.

"I have some business to take care of there, involving tenements I am helping to finance to the south of Hell's Kitchen."

He pauses.

"And which they can't seem to be able to complete without my personal attendance," he adds. "I believe I am dealing with a serious case of either utter stupidity or plain corruption. I don't know."

Scola's eyes search Paxi's face from across the bridge and squeezes them tight, as he tries to comprehend the nature of the apparition standing before him.

But, as always, Paxi knows what this look means. He has stood in front of enough mirrors to understand what a puzzling creature he can be at times. He knows that in all fairness he needs to explain.

"It is November now," he says, "and three more vessels are due to depart before the end of the year for the Atlantic, right?"

He reaches for the coffee the Captain extends him.

"There is Naples; there is Genoa and there is Barcelona. Respectively, the first two will be bound for Buenos Aires and the last to Boston, which is due to leave the Strait of Gibraltar on Christmas Day."

He pauses again to enjoy the hot liquid burning his lips.

"This year alone," he continues, "I have already arranged for passage for more than seven thousand souls from across Europe. By the time spring rolls around this year two ships had already have left the ports of Rotterdam and Hamburg bound for Philadelphia and New Orleans, carrying everything from Poles and Lithuanians to Germans, Russians, Norwegians, Dutch; all of whom with one thing in common: a deep bond with me personally, the one man whose mere name is often enough to paint in colors most of them could never have even imagined before, a true vision in their minds.

Yet my presence is now required for the start of one lousy building in New York City. You ask me!"

"Corruption! Definitely corruption!" the Captain says out of a lack of a more proper way to respond, then realising how condescending he just sounded. "Be careful though," the Captain then adds, hoping he can somehow correct his misstep by displaying concern.

Now Paxi looks somewhat puzzled, though quite amused at the same time.

"Why do you say that, Captain?"

"Lissy, not everyone loves you the way they do," Scola answers, pointing his bearded chin in the direction of the window.

Paxi lets out a short laugh. He turns away from Ulderico Scola, afraid that in his eyes an all-together darker emotion will become visible, one that might reveal how little he figures his chances are of ever actually having to face real adversity.

"New York, Captain, is to be the closing leg of more than a year of constant travel for me," Paxi answers after a while. "But do you want to know what really inspires me right now - and has inspired me for quite some time? It is that I simply refuse to look past this one particular event now, this thing in New York. It is as if no matter how hard my entrepreneurial instincts urge me to come up with some kind of a plan, a continuation of sorts, of the way things have been for the past twenty years, I refuse to give in to it."

The Captain looks back at him, his face drained and disoriented. Paxi's smile is warm, enchanting - affectionate almost.

"I will leave you to your preparations, Captain. What time do you suppose we will be pushing off?"

"Without any major setbacks, we should be on our way by early afternoon."

The Captain hesitates as Paxi places his coffee on the drawing table between them.

"Will you join me at dinner this evening?"

"I will be dining below deck, Captain."

The air is cold and humid and electric with activity. Two officers cross the gangplank onto the ship and off it again, shouting hysterically and waving lists in their hands. The mass moves around them like a liquid and even those who had stood about rather lethargically and lost seem to exude motion now.

Paxi knows the routine perhaps better than many of the crew and while the chaos never ceases to surprise him, he also knows it is precisely the charge that now hangs over everything that plays the biggest part in hooking him to the very thrill of travel.

He makes his way through the crowd and tries to pick up on the chatter around him, remembering that this is the language of mayhem and that, even if it is as legitimate a form of communication as any other, it is in essence unintelligible. Part of the throng seems to break free and begins heading toward the gangplank, knocking down several children and an old woman in its path. In a single sweep, Paxi reaches and lifts all three of them before they hit the ground. Pressed against him and dangling helplessly in his arms, the old woman now just stares into his face poised in a smile.

"Don't you worry, dear," he appears to be saying, whilst immovably anchored inside the stream still running past them, "I will not let go of you."

By now the old duck has gone completely limp in his arms.

"Let it be a consolation to you, dear," Paxi then says to her, admiring the creases on her face, as though he is able to read her personal history from them, "being hysterical is just how Italians achieve their highest state of effectiveness."

The old woman's eyes are wide open, but she may well have lost consciousness all together at this point; not necessarily from the start of having been trampled, or the fact she now dangles in the air, but she seems anesthetized rather by the mere sound of his voice.

"See, dear," Paxi continues in an inspired tone, "no matter how much pushing and shoving and how much shouting is required for processing warm bodies onto Italian vessels these days, the scheduled departure is almost never delayed. No matter how deep the delirium of it all, in the end the anchors are always lifted," he adds. "Make no mistake," - his voice as clear as the November air around them - "the whole of Italy is boarding ships nowadays. And they are all steaming in precisely the direction I am pointing them in. If any of this has startled you, please accept my apologies," he says. "See, the ruckus around us is my design; it is my symphony you could say. If you look hard enough, you will see my hand in everything around you today. Everything today carries my signature. But you probably already knew that."

He puts the old woman down and vanishes inside the crowd as quickly as he appeared from it. He finds his way back to the gangplank and onto the deck again, intermittently making himself invisible every time he is recognised in the crowd and his name is called out. Finally, he finds a spot behind some crates that have temporarily been left unattended. From there he decides to search the deck for a sight of Lydia, the girl who knows nothing about him and upon whom he will therefore bestow everything America has to offer.

Paxi has been in Genoa a week earlier, arranging for the arrival of his workers. And it is on the day before his train is due to depart for Naples that in the middle of the piazza Dante one afternoon, the indifference in this one individual, stops him dead in his tracks. Out of the thousands whose lives he has touched, the fact that this one girl, who is neither plain nor particularly pretty, not as much as looks up at him when he passed her, is at last the proof he has been searching for: that indeed, he may be human after all.

Even from across the square, the tone his boots produce as his heels hit the stone is usually enough to give away his identity, but not this time. That day, the motion of his coat, as it dances from his shoulders, invokes not even the slightest reaction.

Is she even human?

Her indifference inspires him like few things have ever before. And from that day forth he will spare himself no effort in finding out everything about her. He activates every resource he has to make sure he will follow her to wherever she is going, to indulge further in the fact that his magnificence, at least to one individual on the face of the planet, means absolutely nothing.

<><><><><><><>

As on every other crossing before this one, Gibraltar is well behind them by the time he emerges out of the hull again. The British fleet valiantly at the foot of the Rock is already a memory. Winter hangs in the air, but in a matter of days the Atlantic will lower its sensuous blanket onto his shoulders again and render him free once more.

To Paxi, Gibraltar has always represented the threshold to new beginnings. And then, in a day or two, Funchal, the very gate to the tropics, the last gem impaled by a European flag, the place that cures him of the Old World every time. In Madeira he will disembark to walk the gentle slopes and the town colored the whole year around by flowers native only to this one place. In a day or two he will get lost again in the fragrances that wash over him from the hills. A lukewarm breeze will creep through his hair as his feet hit the dock. Boys with north-African milk-and-coffee skin but tightly set Portuguese brows will climb in the opposite direction, carrying crates filled with orchid pods and fruits onto the ship and bags of mail back onto land. He will watch the mules working the cranes that unload the bales of fabric and Abruzzo wool out of the hull, along with about everything else that is required to maintain this island as part of the continent somehow.

As always, only a handful of passengers disembark in Funchal, usually first and second-classers who, for some reason, always fail to actually take that plunge across the ocean, like the poor are doing nowadays in unheard-of numbers.

On the dock below a man draws his attention. He is greeted by the two young women he remembers having spotted about the deck back in Naples and who by now have played out their role in his grander plan. He muses how much these two represent the emerging bourgeoisie of the day, which has finally managed to wedge itself between the working classes and the titled rich but without the merit or the grace to fit in with either.

He wonders what they are saying, but he needn't actually hear them speak to observe the ostentation with which an excessive number of times expressions like fantastic and marvelous and you-do-not-say are tossed around as part of the banner to the idea that standing no longer requires pedigree.

The man has come to greet them and Paxi feels he can recognise a certain reluctance in his bearing, similar to whenever he himself is confronted by the likes of these two tarts; by wealth without elegance — without any real virtue.

He turns his back to the wind to relight his cigar and smiles at the thought that he has yet again managed to escape — that yet again his destination is west: away from Europe, from precisely this.

He crosses the deck with a determined push in his step and disappears into the stairwell. He knows exactly where he needs to go, though he is far from certain what he is to do once he gets there. He moves through the corridors without diminishing his pace and counts the numbers on the cabin doors as he passes them until he gets to number ninety-four. He rolls the butt of his cigar several times over his lips as he

133

contemplates thoughts that should be forming in his mind, but aren't. After several blank moments he raises his left hand with the lapis ring to knock, producing a sound that isn't the sound of knock at all, but something of a sharp pinch that sends the rodents scrambling for cover around him.

Within seconds the door opens and the rather ruffled figure of Emilio Toffolo stands before him. A long silence follows, its edges sharp with shock, but mainly hate – and fear.

"What can I do for you?" the functionary says, in a voice that sounds rather unsteady but polished with dismay nonetheless.

Paxi calmly replies with a hint of tedium, "I came to see how you are holding up," he says, still not quite sure yet of what he is doing there – let alone if it has indeed been a proper answer to the functionary's question.

"I beg your pardon?"

"May I come in?"

"I do not see why you should. But if you feel you must."

The functionary steps aside, closes the door and stands motionless against it, gawking up as his nemesis invades the small space with the kind of eloquence of movement that could easily have brought tears to his eyes.

"I am going to repeat my question," he says, his voice still rather shaky, "what can I do for you?"

Eventually Paxi snaps to and turns to face him like a sleepwalker who only now has come to realise he has been roaming about.

"Emilio Toffolo, the righteous functionary from Bologna," he sighs, "The man who has taken to travel the world, just so he can hinder me. What am I to do with you? I have already prevented you from traveling in the comforts you no doubt are accustomed to. Shall I restrict your access to food for the remainder of the trip as well? Or do you think I should see to it that you are denied entry into Brazil all together? Please tell me. I am at my wits end."

"Do you think you are the only one with influence, Ulisse Paxi?"

Silence follows again, as though there were no language rich enough for the things that need to be said; it is a silence only Paxi has the strength to break.

"Do you actually hate me, Emilio Toffolo? Do you believe that if I were ever destroyed the world would stop being what it is?"

"Hate isn't quite the term that describes how I really feel about you," the functionary replies.

"And that comforts me; it really does. Why are you then on this ship? Is it pride? Is it because you feel I made you look like a fool that one time?"

"Everywhere you go, Ulisse Paxi, you leave a trail of devastation. It is for a greater good that you be stopped."

"Oh, I don't mind being stopped, as you say, or even destroyed. I don't mind that at all. Only, to be destroyed by you is a thought I cannot conceive of. And therefore...."

"Are you threatening me?"

"Do I need to?"

"My loyalty is with the combined authorities, appointed by the court in..."

"Yes I know; Bologna....

"And you, Signore Paxi, are a menace to them. See it as my duty to stop you in whichever way I can."

"And how I wish you could, Emilio Toffolo, how I wish you could be a match. I admire your passion. And I hope you will take me on my word that I do."

Paxi peddles his head from one side to the other, as though to shake his confusion out of it.

"You puzzle me, Emilio Toffolo; you really do. What on earth do you care what I do, anyway? And the so-called economic devastation, as you say — why do you even give a damn?"

"It's called loyalty," Emilio Toffolo responds.

"But to what? I know who you are; I know what you are. And I also know that it is only when your feet touch Italian soil that you become a slave."

"You are a thug."

Paxi hesitates, relishing the attempted insult, only wishing he could actually be stricken by it. He takes a few deliberate breaths and calmly lifts his hand to run his manicured fingers over the cool, salty metal of the wall.

"Perhaps I am," he then says, as he steps out into the hall again and the metal door slams shut behind him.

He had hoped that somehow the weight will be lifted from his heart by coming here. However, it now feels even heavier. The visit has given him none of the lightness he so had hoped for. Instead his feet drag and his limbs swing next to his body like lumps of meat from a dirty hook. And as he pulls himself back through the corridors toward daylight again it is the knowledge that no matter what, he — and not the functionary — will ultimately always win that makes him feel shattered.

You're no thug, Lissy Paxi, he whispers to himself, as he steps out onto the deck and feels the wash of the year-round spring in the air caressing his face once more.

You are just cursed.

Another week has passed by the time he finally emerges from his cabin again. The Atlantic and its gargantuan monotony has gone by almost unnoticed. And when he does rejoin the living, it is again the farmers and the factory workers whose company he seeks.

Since Madeira he has been neither awake nor asleep, but rather has bobbed around in a place that is neither a part of reality, nor one particularly imagined. His meals are brought to him at all the appropriate times by one of the boys from the kitchen, only to be removed from his doorstep untouched a day later.

One evening, however, as the tray is lifted from the floor, the door suddenly opens and there stands the creature the boy has unsuccessfully sought to feed for almost an entire week. In a spiked snarl the creature asks the boy what time it is, what day and finally, if the midway point of the Atlantic has been reached already. Like a trained monkey, the boy answers each question in the order it is posed; "almost seven-thirty, sir, it is Wednesday, November 21st and no, the midway point of the Atlantic has not been reached. God willing, sir," the boy adds, standing rigid, chest heaved forward and the heels of his shoes clicking against each other every time he speaks, "we should be reaching it sometime tomorrow evening."

Had the boy's answer been that they had all sunk to the bottom of the ocean, Paxi would have been equally unmoved.

The boy falls silent for a couple of seconds, clears his throat and, only once he is convinced Paxi has no more question of his own, which will far outweigh anything he himself still has to say, continues:

"A special dinner will be served in the captain's quarters tomorrow evening, precisely for that occasion," he says. "The Captain said that if I managed to speak with you, I should ask you if you would like to dine with him and his guests, Signore."

"Who is going to be there?"

The boy answers that he doesn't exactly know, but that he could inquire for him.

"Don't bother, I won't be attending," Paxi says, "But don't forget to thank the Captain for inviting me," he adds.

"I will Signore."

The following day, Neptune's day, around dinnertime, Paxi emerges and appears not at the Captain's quarters but at the mess on the second deck instead, wearing his best frock, as always looking groomed and as sharp as the edge of the razor which he had not touched since Funchal. Once in the mess he sits on one of the long benches to smoke and waits patiently for the crowd to start converging around him, men and women alike to become somewhat blushy-cheeked as they pass and greet him, as though they are greeting sunshine itself.

The first to take a seat at his table is a couple in their thirties, Paxi guesses, along with their young son, a boy of about ten. Paxi has never seen them before, but as is often the order in which contact with mortals comes about for him, it is the wife who first gravitates in his direction. The woman politely asks if the places around him on the benches are taken. And when he beams up at her, answering that they indeed are not, she promptly introduces him to her husband, Massimo and son, Renzo as well, who stand hiding behind her holding bowls of food and waiting for a cue to finally sit down to eat. The woman says her name is Dine.

"I don't suppose we have seen you down in the mess before, Signore Paxi," she says, as she takes up positions in front of him and appears to be paying almost no attention to the plate in front of her. "Do you often take your meals down here?" she asks.

"I suppose I don't often enough," he replies unassumingly, yet slightly amused as well, at the blundering effect he tends to have on women he speaks to for the first time.

"I don't mean to be rude," the woman says, letting her gaze glide carefully past her husband sitting next to Paxi, "but it does surprise me a bit you are not in the company of a lady, Signore Paxi — and please if you find I should mind my own business, I am hoping you will say so!"

Paxi lets out a chuckle and replies without a moment's hesitation.

"In spite of what you may have heard about me," he says addressing the young woman- but also turning toward Massimo and even the small Renzo as he speaks to her, "I am rarely seen in the company of a lady."

"Why is that, Signore?"

"The answer to that question is that I simply despise the sentimentality that often comes with that sort of thing."

"I must say," Massimo's voice unexpectedly breaks an oddly charged silence, even if it was far too short for it to have acquired any real meaning, "it is an honor."

The husband has strategically positioned himself beside him, just in case there is any truth to Paxi's reputation around women, and now extends his hand to properly formalise the encounter.

Paxi shakes the man's hand without hesitating and after doing so he extends it across the table toward the young boy, who has so far hardly as much as looked up him.

"Where are your manners, Renzo?" the woman hisses toward her young son. "Introduce yourself to the gentleman!"

"That's quite alright, Madam" Paxi says, and then to the boy. "The stew looks a lot more appealing, so I can't really blame you, Renzo."

He leans back, reaches into the pocket of his vest and comes forward again holding a copper locket in his hand.

"Renzo, do you know what this is?" he says, after which the eyes of the boy lock briefly onto his before he shakes his head most efficiently, causing one or two strands of black hair to tremble on his pale forehead.

"This, is a compass, Renzo. I bought in New Orleans some years ago," he says flicking it open with a single snap of the fingers. "The needle will always point north, you see. And the great thing about a compass is that once you know which way is north, you will never lose your way. And did you know," he adds, "that the captain of the ship uses one exactly like it?"

He places the compass on the table in front of the boy, leans back and takes a few short pulls from his cigar.

"And I would like you to have it, so you will always know which way you are headed."

"We are going to Buenos Aires," the boy replies without much expression and still not quite enticed, as though their actual destination pertains only vaguely to the compass he is now admiring in his hand.

"But Renzo, is that all you can say to the gentleman?" exclaims his mother again, giving him a soft but not-to-be misunderstood little kick under the table, followed by one exactly like it from his father across from him.

"Thank you, Signore," young Renzo mutters, wide-eyed and rather puzzled by the stranger's unexpected and hard to place generosity.

A contented smile appears on Paxi's face, as he allows himself to indulge in all the things that are not a direct product of his own brilliant and tempestuous mind.

<><><><><><><>

As the small family spoons up the stew, Paxi learns that the husband is a concert violinist, who has worked as an instructor at the Philharmonic Academy of Bologna for the past six years.

"In March of this year," the husband adds, "I took the family to Berlin, to see about a job offer at the conservatory. At the hotel where we stayed, we heard about some crossings you yourself, Signore Paxi, had organised once, on which you had got a great number of musicians, but particularly teachers, I remember, out to Buenos Aires, under the simple and brilliant motto that there is nothing more stimulating for a creative mind than to discover a new continent."

"And soon enough," Paxi replies, "you will be able to see it for yourselves."

As the young family finishes eating they talk about the cities of Europe they have visited before and the specific spots in them that have branded themselves in their memories the most. They examine Renzo's new compass and talk about the long history of sea travel. Of course, they talk about music, about their favourite composers and the styles that have inspired them. And Paxi in turn expresses how much he regrets not having had either the talent or inclination to develop himself any further in music as a child himself.

"Mahler, Signore Paxi, is no more than spiced up funeral music," the husband says at some point, "It is totally... without character," the husband whispers and then, as the excitement inside him appears to build, adds, "And do you know, Signore Paxi, if cauliflower had ears, what it would listen to?"

"No, I do not." Paxi replies, holding on to the sides of the table, feeling he might soon easily slide off the bench laughing.

"It would listen to Verdi!"

With every roar of laughter the crowd seems to grow larger around them until the entire table and even some of the ones around it, have joined in, over-shouting each other with each joke that is told. At some point a doctor joins them, who speaks about wanting to become a farmer and soon thereafter an engineer who claims he is an exceptional cook, if one is to ask anyone in his hometown of Potenza. The conversations, in multitudes and running simultaneously back and forth, meander between politics and the arts and move around to music again. Soon there is a seamstress, a carpenter; young and old, a crowd as diverse as the dreams they share.

"Lissy, you are not eating?" remarks the engineer with a heart for gastronomy, sucking rather ecstatically on one of Paxi's Costa Rican cigars, which he has passed around in the crowd.

As is often the case, Paxi's answer is cryptic — or at least betrays that he is from a world most can do little but imagine and at best fantasize about during private moments.

"I couldn't wish anything other than to be as I am right now," Paxi answers him.

Eventually, of course, as he has just begun to blend and to disappear almost completely inside the voices and the faces around him, the crowd disperses, as it always does. One by one, they take their leave, until again it is just him, left to relish only the memory of what it is like to be amongst them, to be surrounded by those to whom, in his view, the world ultimately belongs.

He reaches over and picks at an untouched strip of meat inside one of the bowls still on the table. In the distance he can hear the clatter coming from the kitchen, of tin being washed off and stacked to dry. And as if he is shaken from a deep sleep, the reality of his own itinerary flashes up in his mind again; in little more than a week he will have made it across one more time.

He calculates that it has been over a year since the last time he was in Salvador. And now, completely unprovoked, he feels a peculiar longing for it and annoyance as well that he still has solitary days to wait out before he can touch the plaster along its crooked streets again and hear the sing-song Portuguese of the empowered Negro of Bahia. He turns the butt of his cigar around between his lips and when he closes his eyes he can already hear the Bantu drums beating inside of him, as he remembers the very first time he heard them, when he had aimlessly walked over the Pillory.

He gets to his feet and pushes his cigar out in the soggy polenta inside one of the bowls. In the distance he spots two members of the kitchen staff wiping the tables and mopping the floors. He moves toward them, while fishing in the pocket of his trousers for coins that feel strange in his hand and without value, considering his current geographic location.

"Thank you so very much," he says, as he divides all the spare change he has between the men.

"Grazie, Signore Paxi!" the men reply.

He starts to move in the direction of the stairwell, already thinking about the sun that will soon be rising again, beating him yet again to the horizon he knows he himself will probably never reach.

"Signore Paxi," one of the men then calls behind him after his back has already turned. "Did you eat?"

Paxi swings around smiling, not caring much either way which one of the men has actually spoken.

"I could see on the faces of everyone around me how good the food was," he replies and adds, "That was sufficient for me," - his gaze unfastened from a tug of craving for the solitude of his cabin.

"Do you ever eat, Signore Paxi?" one of the men then asks him, determined to seize this unique opportunity to learn the answer to a question he has probably asked himself many times before.

"I think I do," Paxi answers, taking a step in their direction, his brow tensing as he searches for a better way to answer such an odd question.

"I think I do," he repeats.

"Or do you only eat when you are with the Captain?" the second man then moves in.

Now a smile stretches across Paxi's face and he moves in even closer, determined to be as candid as humanly possible.

"To be perfectly honest with you," he says, "it is with the Captain that I never eat. In fact, I don't think that while in his company I have never put food in my mouth at all."

<><><><><><><>

He is on the pier almost the moment the truss is fastened and heads straight into town; he wants to be there when it awakes, when the stalls are erected and the first carts of fish are rolled into the square. He needs to be a part of it again.

It is still early morning, but the bright wash of the walls is already blinding as he strolls along the asymmetry of the architecture and amidst the smells that so characterise this place. There is roasted coffee in the air and sugarcane, sweet one minute and strangely rancid the next. On the one side of a street corner it might be flowers that ambush his senses, while on the other, fish left to rot might be mixing with the fatty stench of unprocessed cacao and which assaults his every pore as he passes. He fills his mouth and his pockets with mango and plantain. He savours everything and it is as if the defiant smiles of the locals of Salvador carry in them the very weight of the city's history. Just as Gibraltar is the gate

142

out of Europe and Madeira the one that leads into the tropics of the Atlantic, for Paxi, Salvador is the stepping stone to America, but also one that is indicative of things to come, like a gauge to test what lay in store for him.

The first time he walked through these streets, he felt that the colors and the smells spoke of the decay of the continent he had managed to escape once again. And in fact, it is here where his eyes actually opened to the notion that his place has never been in Europe to begin with, but on these very shores. Because, so he reasons, if any town could arise from the pits of slavery baring a smile such as this, then it can only be his humble duty to show it to as big a chunk of humanity as he can ship in a lifetime.

Not far behind the cathedral, tucked away inconspicuously at the end of an alley lined with doors without names or numbering, is where these revelations came into being, the last time he was here. It was an event he will never forget and a spot he knows he will always return to. He suspects he has been led to it, literally, in the lightness of strolling aimlessly through these streets; guided as it were, right up to Mãe Franca's door.

He remembers she stood before him in a plain dress; her head wrapped in a white tunic and dangling from one of its folds a wooden cross, no larger than the buttons on his shirt. He remembers her door opening as he is passing it. He remembers how he greets her and that he might have walked past her without a second glance, had he not been struck by such familiarity in her yellow eyes, specked with obvious European lineage, set fixedly on the ageless slope of her smooth, caramel face.

"You've traveled a long way," he remembers her saying, leaving him little choice but to engage her.

Of course, it was not the first time a woman had addressed him in passing from a door opening, but this was clearly no appeal for his time or his money. Rather, Mãe Franca seemed to have addressed a thing far deeper inside of him, reaching much farther than any whore he had ever been with.

"Most ships in the harbour have come from far, Madam," he had replied. "So I suppose it is safe to assume that so have I" - amused mainly by her over-all manner and disturbed by it somewhat as well.

"Yeah, well, you have a long way to go still," - laying full claim on him by shrugging indifferently.

"I guess that would depend."

"And, have you found what you were looking for?"

"I wasn't under the impression that I was looking for anything. So, I guess that means No."

"It is a woman you are looking for, isn't it?"

"Not particularly and with all due respect, I hope you are not soliciting."

"I know you're not a fool."

"And how do you know that?"

"But you sure can say stupid things."

"What did you call me?"

The woman seemed unimpressed, but still the wooden cross in her tunic trembled wildly with an otherwise undetectable shake of her head.

He honed in on it, studying it for a moment.

"Now that we're agreed on that part, I am curious to know who you are then," he had said.

"My name is Mãe Franca, the student-daughter of Eshu, Yorubá god of crossroads and new beginnings - if you want the full of it. But that's the least of your concerns. Perhaps, it is you we need to be talking about."

"What about me?"

"Stay there," Mãe Franca then said and disappeared inside.

"You tempt, seduce with smoke," she had said almost accusingly, returning to her doorstep a moment later.

"Are you trying to sell me something?"

"On the contrary, I am going to give you something."

She extended her hand holding a bundle wrapped in white cotton. With her free hand she unfolded it with delicacy, which seemed unbecoming and rather out of place and let the ends of it drape down. Inside the bundle emerged three, crude-looking wooden figurines: one of what looked to be a dancing savage hung with beads, one of a hunter poised with bow and spear and lastly a seated old man.

"Choose one," she had said, raising the bundle slightly toward him.

144

"I would like to think I have a choice in the matter," he had said, as he reached for coins in his pocket, adding, "I will take all three."

"No, only one. You like to throw with money too, don't you?"

"Whenever I can, yes," he had replied almost mechanically.

He lifted the hunter out of its snug bed of cotton, driven by nothing other than the fact that it had been situated in the middle and seemed the most neutral choice to make.

Her face lit up into a smile, cunning, almost cynical.

"Do you know whose image you hold in your hand, dear?" – But she didn't really wait for an answer. "It is Saint George – the hunter-god, protector of all those who search for lost things: Oxossi,"

She had dug her eyes into his, connecting with him in a rude kind of intimacy older women usually adopt when they feel they lack more effective kinds of lure.

"For whatever it is worth to you, he represents your present and your future for as long as you need him to remain at your side."

He had laughed: "But you must allow me to pay you for it."

"Don't you know how to accept a gift? Keep him near. Give him a spot where he will always be safe; but always near. Hold him in your hand whenever he calls to you. Look at him. Think about him. Let him speak to you and if you keep him safe, he will do the same for you."

"You can count on it," he had replied, as he tilted his head to the side somewhat, in a gesture of meant appreciation for the joke that had been played on him. "Tell me though," he then said, finding Mãe Franca's yellow eyes once more, "What are the other two images inside the scarf? Just so I'll know what I wasn't allowed to buy from you."

"Don't you worry about them, they are just images. But come back for them, whenever you've squared off your business with your hunter."

"But how will I know when that is?"

"He will tell you."

"Nothing like this has ever happened to me," he had said, bringing his laughter down to a grounded and well-mannered sniff.

"Are you pleased?"

"I am enchanted, I guess would be the right word," Paxi replied.

"Don't count your blessings that quickly, dear, because like you, he is also a seducer and he does have a tendency to make enemies."

"I like him already."

It has been twelve years now since that encounter. And in those twelve years, Paxi and the figurine of Saint George, his metaphorical twin, Oxossi, have indeed been inseparable. It has never been far out of his reach and he has often turned to it to break the silence that has descended upon him since that day, a solitude so cluttered and thronged that it too has become something of a companion to him.

He has returned to Salvador many times since that day. But each time, he has resolvedly avoided going near Mãe Franca's shaded alley. It has been a place he simply forbade himself to go, for if he ever did it would mean what soon became unthinkable: ever having to part with his Oxossi.

To feel the figurine snug against the lining of his coat, whether it is during some formal function in Venice, Vienna, Philadelphia, or while he tempts fate on nights he walks the back streets of Port au Prince or Boston, the sensation of the wooden image pressing against him strengthens him and his sense that perhaps he too can be ruled by something larger than himself.

It has been twelve years - more than twelve in fact - and it is impossible for him to hide the shock at seeing that Mãe Franca has not aged one day since. He stammers when she appears, at a loss for words and he cannot remember the last time, if ever, he actually blushed as he does now, in the shine once more of her all-seeing yellow gaze.

Hurriedly and in somewhat of a panic he searches her face for a sign of recognition but he is quickly reassured.

"Did you help those who were looking for things?" she asks him, as he stands wringing his hands before her, twisting his fingers into odd shapes like a schoolboy fighting back the urge to wet himself.

"And then some," he replies, glad he still sounds like a grown man.

"Did you seduce?"

"Like the devil himself" - the gleam returning to his eyes.

"Did you make enemies?"

"More than I care to count."

"Did you search for justice?"

"As I will continue to," he answers her like a victor.

"Then what are you doing here," Mãe Franca asks, not in the least bit interested in flowering-up the bluntness of her words.

"I did not come to return my Oxossi," he says. "I came to choose another image alongside it. I don't feel I need to tell you much about my life for you to understand what it is that I need."

"Then don't." - her voice soft again. "You don't have to choose. In fact, something tells me a lot of the choosing has been done for you already."

She folds her hands in front of her patiently, like she is waiting to see the light change in his eyes.

"For now, perhaps, all you need to know is that smoke seduces her too."

"Her?"

"That is a long story I don't think you have the time to hear," she says, making him feel reprimanded and lost again. "Go back and remember that he is still a seducer; Oxossi is — that he still makes enemies." she repeats, her last words barely audible over a fit of uncontrollable laughter that takes hold of him; again, like that first time, twelve years ago: gutted and vain, as he retreats toward the open street away from her.

All the way through the Pillory and down to the docks again he laughs, roars at the joke that has been played on him; all the while, Saint George dancing in his pocket. He reaches for the figurine, tosses it up in the air and catches it again, only because he, Ulisse Gavino Paxi, chooses to catch it. He thinks of hurling it into the greasy waters by the port, belching up against the dock; that it might free him in some way to do so. But then again, it will be too much of an admission of what a fool he has been.

So, he returns his Oxossi to the pocket of his trousers, as a memento to that odd but negligible encounter and decides that from now on the hunter god will be his captive instead of the other way around. And as far as Mãe Franca, she can choke on her riddles for all he cares.

He climbs the ramp back onto the ship, as he wipes the sweat that has started to run down his face from the all the laughing and the coughing, and the choking on the hilarity of what he has allowed to happen. He composes himself while he re-lights his cigar and leans over the railing to stare at the dunes in the distance, happy again, relieved that nothing else is required of him now, that he has yet again saved himself and that again the future no longer matters.

He decides that for the rest of that day he will sit right on that very spot and smoke – and perhaps, even toss the rest of his coins into the water, just because he can and there is no one to stop him if he chooses to do so. It is up to him what he does or doesn't do; it has always been up to him and it always will be. It is a thing that cannot be changed, by nothing; by nobody.

They stare like thirsty lambs at the prattling glow of fireworks that dome over Buenos Aires across the estuary. It is New Year's Eve and not a breath of wind can soothe the surge of scurvy and lice eating at their skins. Mid-summer is cumbersome, like dead weight hanging from every limb and every word that is spoken. The forward motion of the ship is no longer a sensation, but a far-off illusion that by now has become hard to even believe in.

Since Naples, fifteen of the five hundred and twenty-two souls perished after the outbreak of Yellow Fever they had picked up on the shores of northern Brazil. Nine of the bodies were left behind in Rio and the rest of them traveled under a sensible layer of salt, in a room next to the infirmary, awaiting proper interment in the Argentinean capital.

The price of each crossing Paxi can always measure in the sunken glares of his fellow passengers upon arrival; whether it is Philadelphia or the port of Santos, it always looks the same. It is a look drained vacant of expectancy, an emptiness that goes beyond regret or doubt, all the way to that place where the spirit, raw and exposed, tends to forget it is ever even connected to the physical world in the first place. Just to look into their eyes, always provides Paxi with a rather seductive glimpse into an all-together different realm; and how he envies it and wishes he himself will someday be that affected by anything.

As things stand, he will deliver his cargo of Sicilians almost two weeks ahead of schedule – and only three head short of a complete package. He hasn't arranged for shelter until the handover date with the building company and therefore sees no other option than to quarantine them at the port until then. Of course, this means extra costs, but considering the small fortune he is still due to receive for them, this is hardly of consequence.

At the offices of the port authority a letter is waiting for him from his aunt Rosalina, whom he brought over from Italy nine years prior. In the letter she implores him to call on her before departing for New York. And it is the simple fact that he would never – not even in the seediest reaches of his imagination – ever even remotely consider not doing so the minute he disembarks that alarms him. The letter says that there are matters she needs to discuss with him, with the words, at once, underlined at the bottom of the page.

Still reeking from the lice powder not even he can escape after six weeks navigating the tropics, the very day of his arrival, he lifts the metal ring hanging from the door and clunks it twice on its copper base, sounding off the immensity of the house in the echo it produces inside. He could let himself in; he has a key. But after an absence of almost two years, he feels it would be downright disrespectful to do so, even if after all, this is his house.

When the door opens, the look in the housekeeper's eyes makes for a gaping void collect itself deep in his gut.

"Don Lissy," Doña Marta, the housekeeper, says. It is a sigh that sounds like an icy wind passing through her as well, upon seeing him. "We were wondering when you would be coming" - looking as though the mere sight of him has appeased her in her sense of dread.

"Martita, what's the matter? There was a letter...."

"It's your aunt, Don Lissy. But she will want to tell you herself" - and adds in rapid succession, "Come in, come in."

He enters the house and tosses a quick, inspecting look at the interior. Along every wall, inside every niche, he recognises the relics he personally has shipped over while the house was still being built back in the nineties. It is mostly paintings depicting a long family line that goes

149

well beyond his own Venetian origins and which, supposedly, has its roots in some displaced eighteenth century Franco-German nobility.

He built the house on Juncal, in La Recoleta district, when he first came out to Buenos Aires with the intention for his aunt Rosalina to eventually live out her days here. She is his surrogate mother since the time he was twelve years old and with that, to Paxi, she is also the only woman whom he feels has any real right to such a title.

His own pedigree, which some claim crosses that of the Savoys in the mid nineteenth century somewhere as well, has never made much of an impression on him. Let alone the dusty oil paintings of his kin, which display deep cracks and tares now from the journey they were subjected to while getting to South America. But he still believes that for his aunt they are much more than just daily reminders of the past she too has severed all ties with.

"Martita, are you going to tell me what on earth is the matter? Is my aunt well?" he asks the housekeeper standing before him in her two-tone starched cotton dress and her apron tied around her hips, still slim but now somewhat rounded by age.

"I will let her tell you all about that," she answers smiling, searching his face for subtle details that might somehow have faded in her memory since the last time she saw him. "I am just glad you are here," she says.

"Of course," he mumbles.

On every other occasion, whenever he has called on his aunt in the past, she has received him in the salon at the end of the entrance hall in which he is now standing. It throws him off and more than amplifies his already heightened state of alarm now however, that the housekeeper leads him up the stairs instead. She knocks softly on the bedroom door, inaudible almost; a gesture that is more like some ingrained reflex Doña Marta has developed over the years, above all to always be discrete. She tips her toes as she presses down on the handle and sticks her head inside. But she retreats with a quick gasp, pulls the door shut and turns to face him again.

"She is still asleep," she says. "She will be angry I did not wake her, but she needs her rest."

"Martita, it is me who is going to be very mad if you don't tell me —

right now — what on earth is going on."

"Oh, Don Lissy, it's so sad," the housekeeper says, pushing him back toward the landing.

"If you make yourself comfortable, I will fix you a lunch."

"Marta, no. Tell me what is going on."

"Don Lissy, there is an abscess, a tumour — and it is growing. They say there is almost nothing they can really do for her."

"Why didn't anyone write to me about this? How long has she been like this? Which doctor? How do they know?"

"We did write to you, but you had already left Italy, we think. We did not know where you were exactly. All we knew is that you would be arriving around the New Year, like you said," she adds, her palms upturned by her face before she grabs the railing again, apparently to steady herself under the strain of her own words.

"But how did this come about?"

"The doctor says it must have been there for quite some time, the tumour I mean, until..."

"Until what?"

"Until the day she lost her balance coming down the stairs, Don Lissy."

He is silent, cold and empty, as he lines up the words he is hearing inside his head to make some sense out of them.

"She suffers from spells," Doña Marta continues. "She has to stay in bed most of the time. She sleeps almost half the day and when she is up she complains about headaches and suffers from terrible mood swings. She is losing her sight to her right eye, which the doctor confirmed just two weeks ago. He says she will soon be completely blind on that side. When she does get out of bed, the only thing she does is complain about the fact you are not here, Don Lissy. She will be so happy, so happy."

"Martita, how do they know it is a tumour?"

"They examined her for everything else, Don Lissy and figured that since she loses her balance, and is now losing her sight, it can only be a tumour."

"I have to see her," Paxi says, and attempts a step in the direction of the door once more. But he feels the housekeeper's hand pulling him back from the sleeve of his jacket.

"Please don't wake her. She needs her rest. It will make her very, very happy that you are here now, believe me. But it will also take a lot out of her. Give her a few hours; make her happy then. For now, let me fix you a lunch. Please," she adds, and after a moment disappears in the direction of the kitchen, leaving him behind to calm the trembling in his legs – a sensation all together alien to him up until this point.

He has his lunch in the dining room, returning the blank and self-righteous stares of his ancestors with contempt. The meat is tender and he finds the taste to be distinctly Argentinean, comparable to nothing in the world. The wine is thick, like blood already in the process of clotting, but with enough tang to help dissolve the fiber in his mouth.

"Martita, see to it that my things are picked up at the offices of the port authority. I won't be leaving anymore," he announces, as the housekeeper retouches his glass and moves unobtrusively to the other side of the table to receive her instructions.

"You will have everything by this evening," she says, and disappears again toward the kitchen.

"And Martita...?"

"Yes, Don Lissy?"

"Leave the bottle."

With his glass still in one hand and the bottle of wine in the other, he steps back out into the empty hall. The scent from the silk inside the bindings of the books in the salon have already reached him. No matter where on the planet he might be at any given time, the smell of silk will always take him back to that room. A mosaic of books covers three entire walls and at the end a large glass door leads to the garden, which is set against countless shades of green and specked with an unmistakable level of artistry that characterises his aunt like nothing else, by almost every possible variety of orchids. His aunt Rosalina has always referred to her garden, where she nurses every possible variety of orchids, as her temple, the place she spends time in, in order to feed her soul, as she puts it. He places the wine bottle on the desk he always pictures her sitting at whenever she writes her insightful letters to him and runs his fingers over the smooth surface thinking of her. The memories come to him in unrelated flashes and he lets them in like a torrent he could not stop even if he wanted to.

He remembers the year he was finally taken to live with her in the town of Torre Pellice, near Turin, only months after the death of his father, a man who in no way ever imprinted himself in his memory and who now represents only a vague concept of absence he has never grown to either hate or love let alone miss. It was the year his mother met an Austrian politician as well, whom she soon followed back to Innsbruck where she wouldn't be inconvenienced by the tedium of having to raise her young son.

His aunt Rosalina is his father's younger sister and from the time he was twelve years old she was the one who provided his education and has taught him the difference between acceptable and outstanding. By providing him with the sense that he was deeply loved regardless, she was the one who has showed him the tweaks between doing things differently and actually making a difference. It was she, his aunt Rosalina, who paid for his tutors and the best schools in Europe, the one who showed him Florence at the age of sixteen. In almost every way it was she who has cut the raw diamond into the force he has ultimately become. Yet, also the one who caged him in and estranged him from his peers in the process, to the point that today no mortal can realistically call himself his equal.

He can still see her at the steps of the Duomo, the summer in Milan before his first journey west; how she had looked back at him with a gleam of unwavering achievement in her eyes and the confidence it gave him to see it – the gratitude, the love. He can still feel her bosom pressed against his tear-soaked cheek, after some short-lived romantic endeavour had come to a cruel ending during his adolescence – and also the times he had sought the warmth of her bed, or she his and the soft flesh she had pressed against him behind the silk of her robe - which never unfastened, no matter what pleasures her elegant hands and mouth sought to bring him.

He is jolted back by Doña Matra's knock on the door, a downplayed tapping that causes little more than a slight ripple in the cigar smoke inside the room.

"Don Lissy, your aunt is awake. She's asked me to show you in."

He is on his feet before the housekeeper has even finished her sentence, rushing past her up the stairs. The shutters inside his aunt's bedroom are still closed as he maneuvers his way toward her bed in the dark mainly on instinct - and memory. He lowers himself on the edge of the bed frame and extends his hand to squeeze her bare shoulder.

"Martita asked me not to wake you."

"How long have you been home?" she asks, her voice like thin paper, more brittle than he remembers.

"I got home this afternoon."

"How long have you been back in the city?"

"We docked this morning. I still have a couple of hundred Sicilians quarantined at the port," he answers, his eyes still searching for her face in the dark.

"When are you leaving again?"

"Never mind about that. I am here now. It is you I am concerned about. Martita told me more or less what's been happening. I am hoping you will tell me more."

He can see her face brighten up into a pensive smile.

"I think, a collapse is what I would like to call it," she says, "the machine collapsing under the strain of its own weight."

"At least, you haven't lost your sense of drama, which is comforting," he says. "What happened, though?"

"Oh, about two months ago I fell down the stairs. I don't know; I just lost my balance. The next thing I know I was on the floor, with Marta standing over me, looking like she had just seen the sky turn red. And from then on it went from bad to worse. I have lost almost all sight to my right eye; I can barely walk without having to sit down and I am always asleep. Lissy, I suffer from headaches and most of the times I feel too depressed to even speak. And it is because of those headaches that they have decided it is a tumour that's doing me in."

"Doing you in? What do you mean, doing you in? Now that they know, they can surely do something about it," he implores, able neither to convince her let alone himself.

She smiles again and only now can he make out the shape of her lips and the sharpening of her eyes.

"There is no way to treat this, Lissy."

"Well, I am going to have a talk with the doctor and make sure they do – something!"

"There are things not even you can fix."

"I am staying and I am going to take care of you."

"You, dear boy, are going to New York, as you promised me. You have business to take care of and you are not going to let me be the reason for neglecting them. Do you hear me? When are you due to ship off again?"

"On the twentieth"

"Well, that gives us two whole weeks together, doesn't it?"

"Lina, I can't leave."

"Yes you can and you will. If there is one thing I hope to have taught you it is that you should never let sentimentalities hold you back from doing what needs to be done. And especially if it's on account of me. I won't have it. Not you."

"Don't say that."

"Don't say that? Don't you forget it. Do you want to make me happy? Then go to New York, as you said. Take care of your business – our business, because, if I recall correctly, you invested on my behalf as well. Now, kiss me and get Marta in here so she can help me dress for you. I want to hear about your travels."

They spend the evening in the salon talking, hidden together inside the silken cocoon of the books around them, making up for times apart; Paxi full of wonder and awe about his Sicilians and she about a world that now extends no farther than the garden beyond the glass doors.

It has been years and long before her illness since she last set one foot outside the door. She has enough means, of course, to remain completely unaffected by anything that goes on in a city that has for the most part always remained rather strange to her and one that has never sparked her interest much either. Outside Marta, her housekeeper, loyal to her since the time she first set foot in Argentina, she knows no-one and seems to care little for any other form of human contact beyond that one evasive and highly ritualised relationship with her maid. She has her books to keep her company she always says and of course, her Butter Buds and

Flute Players that grow eagerly alongside her orchids in the shade of her trees outside.

With Lina it has always been that in Paxi's absence humanity somehow ceases to matter much. He is everything to her and has been since the time he came to live with her as a child. Whenever he is not around she all but switches off, puts herself into a state of preservation until the day he thinks to return to her.

"How was Italy?" she asks him, priming herself on the leather sofa, getting lost inside a long, dreamy stare she directs up at him while he lights his cigar.

He knows, of course, that the answer to that question will interest her far less than the mere sound of his voice. When she reacts he suspects she only pretends that it breathes life into memories she has buried long ago and represent something other than the time when it was only the two of them.

"Italy is lost," he says, his glass dangling over the shin of his boot on the leather of the sofa next to her. "It is not only lost to you and me, but lost to itself in my opinion."

"You have always said that," she replies, her voice weakened not only by her illness but also the wine now, so that it sounds even more like music to him.

"That may be," he says, resting his head on the back of the sofa and turning sideways to face her. "But I have never been more convinced of it."

Her eyebrows lift, either pantomiming or stifling a deep sigh and moves her fingers tips to her lips before she reaches over and slides them into his hair and over the nape of his neck. Their stare is reciprocal, knowledgeable and unaffected by the constraint of time or morality: they are together again.

"I am going to take care of you," he says in a voice befitting the fact that the universe has shrunk to the size no larger than that very room.

"Yes you are," she replies, "by going to New York."

He feels her fingers tensing lightly on his skin as he softens his guiltless grin to let her caress his lips.

"I am not sure what's to become of me, Lissy. I feel weaker every day.

But if there is anything I have to show for it all, it is you — and you are not to be my nurse, ever. And if you don't understand this, then please respect it."

He feels her mouth on his, full and warm, her breath the scent of cool water, just as he remembers it.

He arrives in New York on February 12th, after a long and uneventful haul that was filled with a nagging pre-occupation about his aunt's condition back in Buenos Aires. That it might have been the last time they will ever be together prevents him from focusing on much of anything else. The doctor was frank about his estimation that at the rate she is deteriorating she is unlikely to last until the end of the year.

Yet, in spite of the prospect that he is about to lose the only family he has ever really known, he accepts her wish for him to leave again as if nothing has happened, as though his path in life cannot be altered, even by her nearing death. He has never second-guessed her before and is not about to start now.

New York is ablaze with movement and noise. To Paxi New York, like Buenos Aires, is undeniable proof that civilization is a recipe of both courage and imagination; he can feel it rising from the very foundations of these cities. Every time he has been here, every time he has walked through its streets the energy of New York has left him restless and light in the head. Never before has it felt so ominous to him.

It has been snowing for two days when he arrives at his hotel on West 44th, only two blocks from one of the building sites he has bought himself into the previous year. He has gone into business with some local bosses, whose integrity has never been of more interest to him than their seeming lack of it. It's a rather quilted bunch comprised of some colorful characters, like the two Italian brothers, Renato and Salvatore Motta, who represent a labyrinthine family network that has spread itself from Philadelphia to Boston and has acquired an impressive fortune in the past decades, mainly from meddling in some way in housing development. There is a Portuguese loan shark amongst the few so-called bankers and an Irish priest meandering for profits on behalf of several local churches, whom the consortium agreed to allow in almost unanimously during its formation, in order to give the whole thing at least the appearance of ethical behavior.

Paxi has entered into a business venture and has made himself part owner of a modest collection of apartment buildings being erected around the lower West side, for no other reason really than to turn an extra profit from the steady stream of immigrants washing up on these shores every day, a stream that ultimately he himself partly controls anyway.

It is a stream not unlike the one he has rolled into Buenos Aires, though here at a rate that is far less mind-boggling as in the antipodal city from which he just came.

Of course, there are several factors that make New York inherently different from Buenos Aires and thus particularly attractive for investment, one of which being that the imports arriving here are far less homogeneous than in South America. While in Buenos Aires most of the new arrivals are primarily of southern European descent, to New York they come from almost every corner of the earth. And it is precisely the diversity of New York that makes the profits to be made from moving his two-legged assets into it all the more steep.

Housing is by far the business to be in right now. As a general rule it has a tendency to turn any kind of capital into notable riches almost immediately. Paxi has come to realise in the past years that in many cases New York can also turn businessmen of character into rabid, greedy devils, who will stop at very little to secure for themselves a piece of the riches to be made here. If there is ever a paradox New York has a tendency to underline the very definition of it. While in many ways this town is a free-for-all and opportunities do crawl even in the gutters here for all those creative enough to recognise them, it has a rather dark knack for shattering dreams as well, as intensely as it tends to promote them.

Until now, Paxi has always failed to see that America and especially New York, is often no better than all the European cities and countryside he has depopulated over the years, in order to fill his ships. And it is for the first time now, as the notorious modern-day pied piper that he actually worries; that the monster he has helped to create might actually end up being uglier than the one he thinks he is luring a generation away from. To Paxi New York is almost in every way the one symbol of what America could be. Yet, it is becoming increasingly difficult to ignore that it is already stained by the inhumanity prosperity usually produces, and has been for quite some time now.

The first of several meetings scheduled with his business partners in the coming months is to take place on March the second, at a cottage in Shawangunk Mountains up state. Father Doyle, the Irish priest, had suggested the location and motivated his choice by the tactical reasoning that this wooded environment will provide the consortium with little distractions. By motorcar it is three and a half hours out of Manhattan, by horse carriage at least twice that. It is a rustic place, a five-story structure built back in the sixties by two Scots - twin brothers - who added an element of absolute luxury to its interior without ever losing sight of the simple fact that in the end, no matter how outstanding the food, a mountain shack should always remain, well – a mountain shack.

As the members of the consortium begin to arrive from the city, lurking out of the snowy forest like children at the gates of a playground, the chimneys of the retreat are already smoking and scenting the surrounding woods with genial burning chicory. One by one they are received in a large drawing room lushly decorated in a style reminiscent of the days of its Scottish founders, with chairs designed for beauty rather than comfort.

The men move about holding drinks and making small talk about their daily endeavours back in the city, now as distant as any place can be. All agree that Father Doyle has been quite right about the so-called inspirational effects the location would have on the group. It tends to strip men bare whose identity and importance have far outgrown their individual intelligence or education. It tends to promote the concept that out here they are all just men.

Paxi mingles among them with the ease of one who needs no credentials, his grace rising naturally from him, visible in the way he holds his glass but never actually drinks from it or parades himself over the waxed sheen of the floors. In English, Paxi has a strange accent, a mixture of a Victorian stiffness with an Italian swing, as he tends to put slippery vowels at the end of each word, while constructing impeccable sentences with refined vocabulary. When in conversation it provokes a sense of disorientation with most North Americans, but above all impatience. His English also has a tinge of German in the way he often places his question marks at the beginning of the sentence instead of at the end. To most New Yorkers though, he is just European. And because he is also alarmingly well-dressed the men find him suspicious and can thus appreciate him more for his money than the things he represents, or the cut of his suits.

As always it is the Motta brothers who monopolise him first.

"Ulisse, you look like you're expecting female company – of the better kind, I hate to admit," says Renato while pressing against him in a gesture that from a distance surely looks like they had been shaking hands, even though quite the opposite could be derived from the tone in which Renato Motta slobbers his words into his ear.

"I like to be prepared," Paxi replies simply, exaggerating the fact that he could be referring to any number of things.

"How is Buenos Aires this time of year?" says Salvatore, closing in like an oil spill from Paxi's other side.

"Hot, but I thought you knew that."

"It's been a while for me."

"Say," Renato pushes in again, switching to a broken and rather Anglicised Calabrian dialect, which Paxi always finds rather comical. "Still shipping out of Italy?"

"Not only Italy," Paxi replies. "But again, I thought you knew that too. I am still shipping, yes, out of Italy and out of ports I think neither one of you apes have ever heard of."

He promptly excuses himself and moves across the room, as he shrugs off an unholy urge to wash his hands.

Father Doyle stands huddled by the fireplace with a couple of investment bankers out of Texas Paxi has never seen before.

"Ulysses!" the priest cries out, as he sees him approach, but is able to contain himself just in time, as he realises how tender and effeminate Paxi usually makes him feel. "Let me introduce to you Bill Trollinger and Don Henry from Houston. They're here on my account. I am hoping to persuade them to invest in the good cause. Bill, Don, this is Ulysses Paxi from Italy, one of our investors from the first hour."

"How do you do," Paxi reacts, and adds, "Let me warn you: I know how persuasive Father Doyle can be, when it comes to attracting new investors, once he has put his teeth into something."

"Is that so," says one of the Texans – Don. "I'm not so sure how far a fellow who has the same name as the biggest drunk in the Unionist Army can really be trusted though" – referring, most likely, to former United States president, Ulysses S. Grant, Paxi deducts.

Paxi lets silence in and keeps it there.

"Ulysses S. Grant... do you mean the Ulysses S. Grant who commanded several rather bloody battles against the Confederacy during the American Civil War and has acquired something of a reputation for excessive drinking while on campaign?"

"Ah, you are still fighting the war then, Mister Henry?" Paxi remarks.

"It is part of the Southern soul, young man," the Texan replies, blinking his eyes rather profusely.

"Then, wouldn't it also be part of the Texas spirit to remember that Ulysses Grant fought the Mexicans before the Civil War and gave the Union the great state of Texas?"

A growing silence gathers now between the men, until Father Doyle salvages, how only Father Doyle can salvage silence, by over-emphasising his Irish-ness as some fool proof charm:

"Mother of Christ, when is dinner going to be served?" he asks, while squeezing with all he has the empty glass in his hand.

In response Paxi waves an arm, mobilising one of the waiters lurking in the corner.

"I hate to see you standing around dry, Father," he says, and lifts his gaze briefly in the direction of the two Texans, who subsequently and quite involuntarily it seems, toss back their drinks as if on command.

"Welcome in our midst, gentlemen," Paxi says, raising the remainder of his glass of wine and putting it down untouched on the nearest table. "We can always use men of vision," he adds and brushes lightly against

Father Doyle's shoulder as he straightens himself up again.

"You're one strange fellow, Ulysses," says Father Doyle in a burst of short, uneven breaths.

"And a somewhat un-American one at that, from what we hear," adds Bill, the one who has not yet spoken.

"In time, gentlemen," Paxi says, moving his eyes back and forth across the room, already scanning his possibilities for finding less tedious conversation. "In time, you will think of me as the most American of all of us. But before we get into any of that," he adds, "you must explain to me a thing or two: why come all the way to New York to invest your money?" he asks the Texans, who, due to Paxi's direct tone, have positioned their legs slightly apart, which either betrays a deformation of the knees caused by spending too much time on a horse as children or that they are consciously suggesting one.

Bill responds: "Well, mister Paxi, if one is going to invest money, why not do it where the most money in the world is being made. We don't need to tell you that!"

"Well, in a few years, my feeling is that Panama will be just such a place. And for you it will be closer – distance-wise I mean – out of Texas."

"You really believe they are actually going to dig that hole down there, Mister Paxi?"

"I most certainly do, Mister Trollinger. Better yet: I happen to know for a fact that the digging will start in two years' time, at the latest. And when it does, as you will agree, it will be a goldmine, as far as business opportunities. A treaty will be signed that will give the United States complete rights to the canal for years to come. Think what it will do for the reduction in shipping costs. And what about the tremendous amount of infrastructure that is going to be required to manage all of it – and all of that right in your backyard, gentlemen."

"And how would you happen to know all of this, sir?"

"I will be the one that is going to be supplying the workers, of course. And when it's finished my ships are going to be passing through it.

162

The men are directed into an adjacent room which has been improvised as dining area for the occasion. Father Doyle, hoping to optimise the gathering to its fullest has strategically made the seating arrangements in a series of most intricately thought-through matchmaking compositions. However, his tactical symphony falls apart the moment the men begin wading their way toward the tables and groups begin to form naturally. Trying to save what is left of his scheme the priest now flutters desperately about the room in a round of musical chairs that leaves him as the last one standing once it has finally come to a close. His arms fall heavily to his sides in defeat and with something of a glazed gawk he wedges himself in between the Motta brothers who, being the only other Italians in the room besides Paxi, have navigated quite unaided toward the seats nearest to the kitchen.

From across the room Paxi can see Father Doyle's translucent hands clamped around a jug of wine, looking more lulled with every minute that passes. Directly in front of Paxi are seated two New York under-secretaries to the mayor's office. These two are also part of the consortium, but only in the capacity that it is from them that all the building permits will be obtained and could thus as easily be revoked, if they so please. It is necessary that all relevant functionaries be indulged, if any kind of building project is to come to some successful completion at all. The two sullen figures in front of him are drawn into conversation with absolutely no-one and seem furthermore not in the least bit interested in initiating any themselves.

To his right, the notorious loan shark, Beto Rodriguez, who operates mainly on the west side, sits motionless, either unable or unwilling to say much. His gaze remains fixed on the empty plate in front of him and on occasion he will scratch the teeth of his fork with the tip of his dirty fingernail, as if it were a miniature harp-like instrument that produces tones only he is capable of hearing.

To Paxi's left sits a youngster who can't be older that twenty, crunching his table manners behind an abysmal stare which he has fixed on his father, a contractor out of Jersey City, who has been building up and down Manhattan for the past thirty years and is by now considered something of a fixture at these gatherings. On occasion, the boy's gaze will dart nervously from one side of the dining area to the other, before resting on his senior, Dwight Paul every time.

"I believe it is snowing again," Paxi remarks to the youngster, trying to breathe some life into him by referring to things he will surely be able to relate to.

"It is," the boy answers in a voice neither dead nor particularly alive.

"I don't remember seeing you the last time we all got together like this," Paxi attempts again. "My name is Ulysse Paxi," he says, extending a hand in the boy's direction.

The youngster accepts it politely and says, "I am Michael Paul. My father - "

"I know who your father is," Paxis interrupts.

"I am sorry. I suppose you would," the youngster reacts with a short smile directed at his plate.

"Oh, it's not that. I saw you come in with him and felt there was quite a resemblance – if you don't mind me saying so."

The youngster forces a bitter gust of air out through his nostrils.

"Are you entering into business with him?" Paxi asks.

"It would appear so."

"You don't seem too pleased."

"Let's say that I have other plans and that my father and I differ somewhat on that."

"Study; university?"

"No, nothing that elevated. I want to travel."

"Well, I am certainly in no position to contradict your father, Michael Paul, but travel, in my opinion, is about the most elevated thing any young man could choose to do. And you can tell him I said so," Paxi adds.

"Oh, I will."

"And where is it you would like to travel to?"

"Europe."

"Have you seen the west?"

"Indian country, not for me."

"No, I mean San Francisco; the Nevada dessert can be quite beautiful. Mexico? But Europe can be memorable as well, I suppose."

"Do you like Europe, Mister Paxi?"

"Not particularly."

"Why?"

"Europe is dead. I believe that the future is here – in America."

"What is wrong with Europe?" the boy insists, coming to life and in a manner that is surprisingly articulate and reveals an excellent education.

"I am thirty-eight years old," Paxi then says, glancing at his table companions. "I have been back and forth across the Atlantic numerous times and every time I return to my native land, the place that should pull me in some way, I am instead filled with a feeling that I am stepping back into a world that is – well, caving in on itself. Whenever I am in Europe, any part of it, that feeling hits me like a downright stench – as if a shadow has begun to fall over it and all its ceremoniousness with its hollow traditions, are things I no longer want to be a part of.

See, Michael Paul, I am convinced that a dark chapter has begun to unfold around us and it won't surprise me in the least if Europe just simply implodes someday soon."

"What, you think there is going to be a war?" the boy asks, revealing his youth in more ways than he could suspect.

"War should be the least of our worries."

"You like it here?"

"As much as I like being in a place where civilization is forming, sure."

The youngster leans back in his seat and eyes the room around them again, comes forward and steadies his gaze on his table companions – a belligerent look Paxi thinks he can recognise from a time he might have had it in his eyes, as well.

"You call this civilization?" the boy asks rather measured, to which Paxi's eyes soften in complete understanding and becomes aware of the glares from the others.

"It is civilization in the making, Michael," Paxi continues, seemingly unhindered. "That is what inspires me."

"America is the future," Beto Rodriguez then volunteers, coming to life. "Mister Paxi is right about that," leaning his head down to glare up at the boy, his greasy locks almost grazing the empty plate in front of him.

"See, Mister Rodriguez agrees," Paxi remarks.

"That is right," then sing the two clerks from the Mayor's office almost in unison.

"And do you want to know how you can tell when civilization is in the making, Michael Paul?"

"I guess," the boy replies, tossing up his shoulders.

"Civilisation is in the making, Michael Paul, when pencil lickers like our two friends here, can make a fortune for themselves without contributing anything," - pointing the foot of his wine cup at the two bureaucrats, who have gone rigid in their chairs.

"Civilisation is in the making, Michael Paul, when thieves and thugs; rats like our own mister Beto Rodriguez here are allowed to enjoy the light of day with the rest of us. And that, my young friend, is what I call civilization"

The two bureaucrats slide back their chairs and march out of the room in dignified outrage. Beto Rodriguez remains motionless. He has gone back to staring at his plate. The only difference being that the lock of hair hanging down against his forehead now trembles wildly, signaling a far more tempestuous condition behind his silence.

"Sorry about that," says Paxi, tidying his cutlery alongside his empty plate. "I didn't mean to offend."

"Yes, you did," the boy replies. "You are a very arrogant man, Mister Paxi. And I have a mind to demand you apologise to our table companions before someone smacks you one right in the mouth."

"Don't make any promises you can't keep, young man," Paxi replies. "My guess is even you have more sense than that. And so do the two pencil lickers. They'll recover; I am sure of it, just like Mister Rodriguez - won't you Beto?"

The loan shark doesn't move.

"The thing is, Michael Paul, that my share in this project is far too large for any one of you to take offense to my abuse. You will not punch me, as I am sure the two gentlemen from the Mayor's office will be back in their chairs long before our first course is served. You will see. And to answer your question, the great thing about Americans is that they will endure anything if it means ensuring a profit."

Paxi straightens the front of his jacket and stares blankly above the heads of the consortium around him, before he turns to the youngster once more, and says. "And that too is a sign of civilization."

It never ceases to amaze Paxi the extent to which the human animal is prepared to deceive itself. One by one, he counts the faces around him — as he always does; studies them like a cat studies a prawn on a hook, faces shadowed over by spite and folly, yet faces he knows he will do anything to illuminate once more.

Throughout the entire meal, Paxi's table seeks refuge in the cutting of meat and the shoveling of green beans and potatoes onto forks. A curtain of complete disengagement falls around him, placing him in a sphere all his own. Paxi is no longer there, the crowd around him has been pushed to oblivion by the thing that is at the root of his detachment: his aversion for the thought that he might ever be claimed.

Coffee and brandy are served; he reaches into his inside pocket and lights a cigar. He takes in clouds of smoke deeply into the base of his lungs and then exhales them with parted lips and flared nostrils. He turns the coffee around in his mouth several times before swallowing it, his eyelids partly veiling as he surrenders to the pleasure. He dabs the corners of his mouth with the napkin from his lap and rises to his feet, vaguely even aware of the whispers and the glares that get stabbed into his back as he walks to the hall and up the stairs to his room.

Enemies; he has become so proficient at making them that the conspiracies devised against him throughout the years are simply without consequence; he just lacks the ability to even pick up on them. If he had ever detected evil converging around him, somewhere along the line he has lost the ability to really feel it. Had he not been so detached, he might at some point have picked up on the fantasies that play inside men like Father Doyle or anyone of the others, have sensed perhaps, in the way they look at him and verbalize behind tensed lips and quivering chins the ills they wish upon him.

Had he done that, then he might have been able to ask himself to which lengths men might be willing to go to reprimand him for his arrogance - for Beto Rodriguez' notorious switchblade to cut into his skin one day, in the wake of all the insults Paxi has directed at him throughout the years. What might Michael Paul's fist have actually felt like, had it landed on his face that evening — as it probably deserved to? He knows what the Motta brothers are capable of, but it never occurred to him — not for a second - that a thing like that might ever apply to him.

He taps the tip of his tongue on the butt of his cigar to extract the nectar that clings there, as he climbs the stairs and takes the inconsequential steps that will lead him to some destiny in which he will always win and always be out of harm's way. He searches his pockets for the key to his room and thinks about his share in the projects being discussed downstairs without him. He wonders in what context he himself plays a part in their conversations. Does it really matter?

He sloppily calculates the extent of his interests here in New York and those elsewhere around the world, but he finds it difficult to grasp the concept of what he actually owns. He takes off his jacket, hangs it over the chair by the window and stands before the mirror unbuttoning his shirt. There is a jug of water on the nightstand. He pours himself a glass. He might have wondered how easy it would be for anyone to poison him, for instance, and might have thought — perhaps - of all those who can and might; all those men — and women - who would. He barely understands that of those particular individuals there are in fact many.

He douses the lamp and admires the snowy forest outside the window, how the light of the moon plays on the tops of the trees, casting shadows in the froth around them.

"You are cursed, Ulysse Paxi," he mumbles to himself, half laughing and half whimpering, "Cursed."

He lay on his bed staring into the blackness around him and thinks of his aunt Rosalina. He tries to analyse a certain feeling that has come over him, but it is too new, too alien. It rather chokes him; it causes his fingers to cramp up and his nails to dig themselves like deathly claws deep into the sheets of the bed, once he realises that this thing he is feeling is an all-enveloping longing for home — that there actually is such a place. In the darkness he ponders on this feeling, in the way one might ponder on the movement of water, or something so elemental that it is beyond human comprehension – an idea so rooted in a mystic realm somewhere that so many find it impossible to give it words. It is something he has never felt before.

Eventually, though, sleep settles over him, decisively and with little warning. It is always something of a dreamless mire that lays claim on him and which often has little to do with rest or some sort of act of replenishment. Eventually, thoughts drain away from him until there is nothing but the faint echo of the forest outside his window.

When something opens his eyes again that night, he can sense that morning is still an unfounded promise of sorts. His body is still immovable, yet his eyes fixed with hawkish intent on a single spot between the back of the chair and the dark velvet of the curtains. With his mind he scans the room, his ears as sharp as a bat's, his breath suspended. At last, he forces his body to turn on its back. He remembers the jug of water on the nightstand; he sits up and puts his feet on the floor to fill the glass. Blindly, he drinks what is left inside it. He refills and drinks again, and groggily takes some steps toward the window to reassure himself that it is indeed still night.

He pulls back the curtain and feels the cold draught gliding down through the window frame and over his bare feet. He can see that the light from the moon is more direct now than it had been before and figures he must have slept for a couple of hours, at least. And had he ever felt fear before, he would surely recognise in himself the feeling of absolute terror when he senses the shadows rouse in the darkness behind him. But the truth is that fear happens to be one of those things that have always eluded him. Had he felt himself in any real danger before he might, just might, have turned quicker – who knows - when he hears footsteps spring toward him over the floorboards.

The sound of the window breaking is as unreal to him as the birds releasing icy shrieks in the night around him or the frozen air sanding his skin as he falls. The light from the moon has a porcelain quality: beautiful and menacing. He opens his eyes to it, squinting into its sheen. For a split second, the Lazarus around his neck makes itself felt, right before the world goes still and black around him.

Saint I

If there is ever an impression the town of Montevideo leaves on Lydia it is probably that it leaves none on her at all. It feels like a forgotten corner to her, literally in the shadow of all the grandness and the promise that is Buenos Aires across the estuary.

They arrive in Argentina on March 10th, 1903, to at last see the place half of Europe is talking about and to which not only Italians have been drawn to for generations, but migrants from all over Europe just the same. Clearly, this place doesn't need much of an introduction as the capital of the Americas.

Back in Italy, in the damp Genovese streets, whenever Lydia had thought of the future, Buenos Aires was always the place her mind had drifted to. It became almost synonymous with the concept of future and whenever she had thought of herself as anything more than just another empty belly pointing her wild dreams west, she had always thought of herself here.

As the child she was before embarking, she was prepared to arrive with little more than some coins in her hand and once here to then slug her way right through every fight that crossed her path, because if there was a future for her at all, then fights could be fought and won. But the memory of that child now seems distant, an entity in the third person, a stranger to who she has become in only months. Money has changed her and distance has fitted her with any identity she might want to adopt. What has not changed is what Buenos Aires stands for, the ultimate destination.

She has often heard talk about La Boca, the ghetto by the waterfront where the European vessels unload their cargo, along with all the by-products associated with the mass flux of souls pouring in from the Old World. From the carriage that takes her and Edmilce out of the port and into Palermo, she realises how for many of her countrymen La Boca is where the Atlantic crossing usually strands, but which she has now bypassed due to nothing other than the simple grace that she did not arrive from Europe at all but from neighbouring Uruguay.

It is strange to hear Italian spoken on every street corner again, even if it has that baritone of an elastic kind of Spanish running through it. It tends to give it hips and swoon, she feels. Or is it the other way around; is it the Italian that runs through the Spanish here that makes the most banal conversations sound dirty and sexual? Even Edmilce, who by now has acquired a considerable vocabulary in Italian herself, has not failed to pick up on the unmistakable croon of the Porteño talk.

Palermo is an affluent residential sector with numerous guest houses and hotels lining large avenues and parks. The carriage driver recommends a pension, which he deems most appropriate, after sizing them up, probably by the craftsmanship of the riding boots Corné Cunho had commissioned for them before leaving Brazil. The driver emphasises that the Pensión Olga is run by Palestinians like himself as the biggest advantage – but who later turn out to be Russian Jews, who had only spent a couple of years in Palestine before ricocheting to South America. The place is in a brownstone building near the Plaza Güemes, which dates back to the seventies and had served as a rope factory until coming into the hands of the Koifmans. It is named after the wife of the proprietor, a woman in her late forties who advertises right off her almost pathological obsession with tidiness and hygiene, and which in all seems to fit quite perfectly with her personal fascination with cabalistic numerology, as well. And indeed the rooms have not a speck of dust. Yet, no matter how much Doña Olga has scrubbed the floors and the walls over the years, as part of some epic battle to rid the place of that brazen smell of dried hemp, which is still detectable every time even the slightest breeze travels through the rooms, there is still a strange, rather phantasmal cosiness to the place that unnerves Lydia, but seems to inspire Edmilce somehow.

Whenever Lydia passes the matron in the hall, she will always be carrying either starched linen or buckets of water laced with vinegar for one of her ritualised scrubbing sessions. Her greetings always come with a wild and distracted look in her eyes and they will always precede some reference to either the smell or the exorcism of ghosts only she, Olga Koifman, seems passionately unwilling to live with.

"This is the cleanest place in Buenos Aires," she will say almost every time and to which Lydia will always respond:

"Yes, it is very clean, Doña Olga, thank you," which will subsequently trigger some elaborate apology for the spirit of the hemp that still haunts the place.

But it is right after their arrival in Palermo, during a time that Lydia's focus could have wandered in any other direction that a particular side to Edmilce becomes apparent to her, as well. Right away, Doña Olga and Edmilce seem to find common ground on some vibratory level where no words in a shared language are much needed to strike a melodious chord. While Doña Olga's esoteric view on the world around her is generally met with disinterest and downright scoff by most, with Edmilce she appears to have found a rare ally, an accomplice in all matters intangible. They take to one another. Whenever Doña Olga speaks of all that which haunts the pension or the mystical role prime numbers play in the reality of everyday life, Lydia notices that her eyes will connect with Edmilce in wordless understanding. Yet, of what exactly is something quite beyond Lydia's comprehension.

With increasing frequency Edmilce begins to disengage herself from Lydia's side during this period. She will offer to help Doña Olga with her chores around the building while Lydia explores the city. It angers Lydia at first, to see with how much ease Edmilce is willing to let herself in with the servant caste, to which, if nothing else, she herself no longer belongs and seems to show almost no interest in what Lydia considers to be more elevated matters like learning how to read and write. Soon though, even Lydia has to admit how the gleam in Edmilce's eyes reveal the enjoyment she actually derives from keeping busy with the sweeping of floors and the stirring of pots and pans in the kitchen.

For the time being, Lydia just surrenders to what she hopes will only be a temporary defeat, and thus leaves the girl behind with the matron as she sets out on her own to explore the city she has fantasised so much about. In many ways it reminds her of how she set out to discover Genoa, but with none of the aversion she felt then toward a place she only explored as some sullen way to kill the days before embarking. This time she has an insatiable appetite to discover, to take in the city to the very last brick. She wants to feel the electricity the Scazzo sisters had talked about and to experience first-hand how sweetly one can be dwarfed by the pompous architecture of the Plaza Lavalle and the chaos Paxi had described, as he told her about the market halls in the Abasto district and how he too had once dissolved inside of them. As she wanders through the streets it is as if every step she takes inspires the one that follows, as now all the stories she has heard about this place are allowed to acquire shape around her. It is as though she were developing a new sense of herself to be here at last, a new reflection of who she is becoming.

Usually, it is only after her feet have become sore from her walks that Lydia will return to the pension every evening. There, Edmilce will bring her up a sumptuous meal after she is done soaking in the hot baths the girl draws for her. With a vacant but attentive look on her face that begs neither a question nor a remark about anything that either of them have done that day, the girl will just watch Lydia eat. Whenever Lydia does ask her about her day, the girl will answer diligently, but never return the question. After the meals Edmilce will take the dishes back down to the kitchen and return shortly with a hot cup of tea laced with brandy to warm and soften the sheets Lydia then crawls into for the night. She will find her nightgown spread out on the bed and her clothes washed and folded in the dresser. At first glance she assumes it is Doña Olga's meticulousness behind the way the room is tidied every day. Upon closer inspection, however, she notices the imperfections that are there as well, like a corner of the bed sheet sticking out from under the mattress the one time, or her woolen slippers symmetrically arranged next to the nightstand, but with left to right facing in the wrong direction. A ghostly draft goes right through her when she finally realise that it has been Edmilce's hand all along in the way the room is kept.

One evening Edmilce, arranges the pillows on the bed and lays over

Lydia's feet an alpaca blanket Doña Olga has given her in payment for her invaluable and still unassuming help around the house. It is on this particular occasion that Lydia's increased interest in those subtle but unmistakable changes in Edmilce begin to take hold; changes that would not have drawn Lydia's attention at all, had the girl that night not exchanged the usual tea and brandy with a steaming calabash of mate.

"Everybody drinks it here," the girl explains. "It's very bitter, so you need to drink it with lots of sugar."

Lydia takes in the steaming holly rising from the opening.

"I missed you today," she then says, interrupting herself in the middle of singeing her lips on the hot metal of the mouthpiece to search Edmilce's face.

The girl responds with a reluctant smile: "Doña Olga says that the mate leaves grow nowhere else in the world but here...." – ineffectively avoiding the subject.

"It's lovely, Edmilce.... Doña Olga is very kind to send this up for me.... And you are very kind...."

Again the girl smiles, politely perhaps, but falls silent and evasively turns her attention elsewhere.

"I wish you would see the city with me," Lydia adds, but stops herself in time before she says any more and thus might flounder into something that will underline the differences between them even more.

"You enjoy staying behind to help Doña Olga, don't you?" she stammers instead.

"I enjoy waiting for you; to wash your clothes while you are away – and cooking for you for when you get back," the girl replies, as though some unexpected turn in their conversation has urged her to explain herself.

"You know you don't have to do that," Lydia says.

"But it is what I should do."

"What do you mean? Wouldn't you like to see the city with me?"

"If you want me to I will."

"I want you to do whatever," Lydia starts to say, but stops herself again to rethink her words. "What I want, Edmilce, is for you to go to school like other children - eventually."

"If you want me to I will," Edmilce repeats, casting down her eyes.

It surprises Lydia to hear her say this, for at the same time it couldn't be more obvious that Edmilce is definitely not like other children - and never will be; and that therefore no matter how many books Lydia manages to ram into her tropical skull, Edmilce will never be bound by the same realities as everyone else.

"Edmilce, you will be more than a girl that washes and folds my clothes. Do you understand that?"

"But I want to take care of you."

"And it is because we need to look after each other that you need to learn how to read and write. Don't you understand?"

"I do."

"I have decided that we should move out of here and into a place of our own. There is a building not far from here. We will be moving there at the end of the month. You can still come over a couple of days a week if you want, to help Doña Olga. But you will no longer be helping her for free. If you are going to work, for anyone, you should receive proper pay. And this new rule will go into effect immediately."

Lydia reaches inside her brazier for the money pouch and produces some coins.

"Here, take this," she says, extending her hand. "This is payment for watching over our things while I have been away."

Edmilce takes the money with that benign stare that often falls over her face, whenever Lydia places demands on her.

"I have decided to start looking for work myself, you know."

"What will you do?" Edmilce asks, her face temporarily lightening up in the hope the conversation will veer off permanently away from the thing that will always remain vague and quite ungraspable to her; money.

"First thing though," Lydia then says, sitting up straight on the bed, pushing back her damp hair behind her shoulders, "we are going to talk to Doña Olga about paying you for the work you have been doing around here so far."

Edmilce's eyes move to the alpaca blanket and then up to Lydia again.

"Edmilce, what will you do if something happens to me?"

"I don't understand."

"If something were to happen to me, how will you take care of yourself?"

"In the same way I took care of myself before you were brought to me," the girl responds simply, not in the least aware of how absurd her answer has been.

But Lydia is too determined to not let herself be distracted by the girl's occasional riddles.

"I wonder: would you go back to pick-pocketing again? Back to diving for coins?"

The girl's gaze for the first time becomes fixed, as she now too struggles to choose the right words to respond.

"Even you dive for coins, Lydia."

The apartment at the Plaza Italia is on the fourth floor of a residential building overlooking the botanical gardens. When they stretch on tiptoe on the balcony they can see the zoo over the chestnut trees across the street and beyond it the hazy, temperate waters of the river. With its two bedrooms, the flat is relatively modest in size but it is semi-furnished and equipped with modern conveniences like a gas-burning stove and electrical outlets in every room. But what impresses them the most and gives the new place a certain decadent status, is the uniformed doorman, whose only apparent claim to existence is to open the heavy brass doors to the street for them.

The foremost reason Lydia decides to take it, however, is that it feels fresh and clear of ghosts especially. It is to be the place where she and Edmilce will at last make a start of things.

Back at the guest house it is not without the expected amount of resistance from Doña Olga that Lydia manages to secure proper employment for Edmilce for three mornings a week after they have moved out. The girl is to continue her chores as before, but at a wage Lydia feels is reasonable enough to compensate for what she is beginning to regard as Edmilce's rather 'subservient' ways.

Claudio Tapia

Lydia begins to buy every book and every newspaper she can get her hands on, as if at any moment the spell could be broken and they might soon wake up to find themselves unworthy after all of the blessings that have come their way. She teaches herself Spanish and in the process embarks on a stoic mission to teach Edmilce how to read and write. The brandies the girl has grown accustomed to bringing her in the evenings are abolished, as everything they do now is fitted inside a strict regimen of excelling beyond even their own expectations. They need and will become proficient in the art of self-sufficiency.

In the afternoons Lydia now takes the girl out to see the city. The same grim method that has now fallen over every aspect of their lives together is applied here too. Every district is studied over a map before it is explored at length. Edmilce responds as neutrally to the changes as she does with every new demand Lydia places upon her. She accepts it without question, ready to become anything Lydia wants her to be.

As they watch the fish being unloaded off the carts from the harbour at the Abasto markets one day, Edmilce asks her, "Do you know how to clean fish, Lydia?" - in a disconcertingly mature tone and ahead of a rationality that is eerily clear.

"As a matter of fact, I do" Lydia replies, wondering whether the girl intentionally tried to expose in her some hidden traces of vanity – or something else altogether perhaps. "Why do you ask?"

"Well, it just looks like they could use a hand cleaning them and you said you wanted to find work for yourself, that's all," the girl responds, as though no condescension could ever be meant by the simple thing she is suggesting and to which Lydia can respond with nothing but the truth: that deep down she does think that cleaning fish is now beneath her.

The same episode repeats itself not long after, when they are leaving the building and have to wade their way through the sloshing of mops past the cleaning woman near the entrance.

"Have you asked?" Edmilce whispers, leaning into her as they pass the doorman.

"Asked what?"

"Well, if they might be looking for someone to help them with the floors. You said you wanted to work."

"Do you think I should mop the floors in our own building, Edmilce?"

"Well, there are lots of other floors in other buildings you could clean."

"Do you really see me doing that?" Lydia gasps, unable to hide a mounting sense of torment in her voice.

"Well, you said you wanted to work; this is work. I clean floors."

"I am afraid I wouldn't be very good at it, Edmilce. Besides, I don't believe I would like cleaning floors very much."

It is an answer that comes close enough to being factual, but which in no way accommodates the truth. It merely buys her some time before she has to admit to herself that the impossible has indeed occurred, that the sheen of the functionary's fortune has begun to corrupt her - that it has begun to chip her stoic nature and limit her in her choices. It humbles her – after it infuriates and saddens her too that Edmilce will hold a mirror before her in this way. But after the anger and the hurt ebbs, there remains an increased sense of astonishment as well, that the crude child she picked up from the streets not even a year before can be so insightful, so well equipped to ignite inside of her such a bright flame of self-judgment And with this she now knows that if nothing else, Edmilce can also protect her in a moral sense.

"To be quite frank with you" Lydia says, after Edmilce has confronted her again, as they watch the whores beginning to parade themselves at dusk near the docks in La Boca, "if you really want to know, I do feel I can do better than to clean floors, or fold linen at some hotel, as you suggested yesterday – or even sell my myself for wine or spare change," she adds, pointing her chin toward the women huddled together sharing a cigarette. "And the reason I feel that way, Edmilce is because I'd probably not be very good at it, like I told you before. But I don't want you to worry; because there are things I am good at."

Lydia pauses and pretends not to get lost in the sharpness of the girl's eyes.

"If you didn't enjoy helping Doña Olga, Edmilce, I would be the first to suggest you reconsider going back to the pension every week." she says, gathering up some of her own pride now after the girl has spilt it on the street stones around them again. "It is no different for me," she adds.

They listen to the chatter of the whores across the street.

"Remember I used to tell you about the time I helped deliver babies?" she says. "I was pretty good at that. But the thing is I sort of promised myself that I would never do that again."

"Why? If it used to make you happy..."

The girl seems to take a deep breath, and says: "I change, Lydia. I think I change every day," she says. "But you cannot and never will." — again, surprising Lydia to the point of sheer horror with how astute and sharp the girl can be.

Edmilce takes a languid look at the whores moving about under the streetlight like a flock of ducks, as they wait for the first ship of the evening to enter the harbour, and adds, "If you want you could teach me to deliver babies. I could help you."

Lydia looks at the girl for a long while and then back at the whores, but this time with added interest.

<>

They continue to read together in the mornings and plot their walks through the city in the afternoons, and in their tireless schedule of processing as much information as Lydia can ingest for them both, which only intensifies in the weeks that follow, they at least have found common ground again, re-found strength in their elemental differences.

With increased frequency, come nightfall, their daily excursions through the city end down by the docks, where they settle at the Vuelta de Rocha to watch the street merchants pack up their stalls and make way for the whores to turn nightfall into something of a feline dance around them. They will sit and draw the flags of every ship that comes in, so that they can check the origins of each at the library the following day. They quiz each other as to each new thing they see and practice the bits of Spanish they learn until darkness has completely fallen around them before returning to Palermo.

"If I had even the smallest grain of musicality inside of me," Lydia says one evening, as she muses on the heartfelt sounds of a Neapolitan fiddle and guitars spilling out from some dimly lit tavern across the street. "If I could make any music at all, beyond being able to whistle for a second or two I think I would try composing songs like that," she adds, giving in to the long embrace of a yawn.

"I have never heard you whistle before," Edmilce responds tuning in to the music now herself; to the heavy hearts of the men shuffling past them and the whores taking up positions under the scattered street lamps along the embankment.

The clattering of bottles mixing with the music, in violent strokes and complex timing, roll over the stones of the street and seem to gather at their feet.

"You know," Lydia continues, "that La Boca is a direct reference to the mouth of the Riachuelo River?" as she points toward the muddy waters below them. "And the funny thing is that this so-called mouth isn't really spilling the river into the sea at all. It works the other way around I think; I think this is a mouth that drinks whatever floats this way from the sea — like us."

Lydia looks at the contours of Edmilce's pigtails in the dark, before she jumps to her feet and heads straight for the open doorway and the throbbing wall of men's laughter.

Edmilce hurries behind her, she too ignoring the sneers coming from the whores they pass. But once inside, they are grabbed by a thing far more engaging than the tough whore-talk that in the end isn't really tough at all but rather breakable and distant. It is the music at first, that weird chopped up time they had heard around the city on occasion and which seems to always give men something of a collective aura; sad melodies put forth by the fingers of musicians making love to their instruments. Tango.

The mood inside the tavern is thick and acridly masculine, the kind of energy that for Lydia sooner has a tendency to paralyse than inspire movement of any kind. The men hang listless over jugs of beer and wine, too worn down from the day's work, it seems, to extend even a finger in the direction of the women standing around them. The whores looking like vultures on a stick appear to be waiting for action that, from the looks of it, will probably never come. The music, this new sound, is too unhinged for it to; too sad, Lydia feels.

But it is right after she has arranged for her own jug of wine to share with Edmilce and to partake in some of the meat sizzling on a grill out back that the ground seems to get pulled from under her.

Years later, Lydia will look back on this moment and still she will be able to dissect every second that leads up to it; the faces of the men around her, the tartness of the wine softening the muscles in her face and even the wobble of the bench they sit on, when the scent of Costa Rican tobacco reaches her.

Her body goes rigid and her nostrils flare. But at the same time she feels faint and overwhelmed. With a sharp and hawkish glare she finally is able to hone in on two of her countrymen seated near the entrance; at least, judging from their excessive use of hands, even as they whisper to one another, she assumes they are Italian. And who, had she not been sent twirling the way she had by the mere smell of the smoke that is coming from their direction, she would surely have mocked, the way she usually mocks whenever she observes her countrymen.

She rises as though commanded by a will other than her own and crosses the room toward them. She waits patiently for the men to raise their heads before she addresses them in Spanish, though she isn't sure what she will exactly say until the second her lips begin to move.

"Your cigar, Sir — I am almost too embarrassed to ask," she stammers, somewhat regaining a sense of where she is. "You probably will think I am a complete idiot for asking, but you don't suppose you could tell me where it is you... "

"Would you like one, darling?" one of the smokers interrupts her, glancing briefly at his companion with a look of granted victory in his eyes.

He leans back in his chair. It is the gesture of a man who, especially in a place like this, expects no other type of exchange with a woman that isn't some form of solicitation on her part. He then extends his arms forward and rests his wrists on the table in front of him.

"Oh, if you would be so kind, sir, I would be much...."

"Is that correct, darling?"

"That is correct, sir, yes. I would be most appreciative."

The men turn to each other again and exchange words in a dialect

Lydia cannot quite place. But the tone of the man's jest reveals the extent of it. While they laugh, revealing uneven teeth and tongues stained with wine, she in turn speculates freely about the oil stains on their hands and the dismal dockworker existence these reveal. Her expression becomes more passive as their laughter grows, both in size and level of taunting. And with every roar and every belch the more determined she becomes that she will never speak Italian again.

One of the men reaches for a rusty metal box on the table and pulls a cigar out of it, which somewhat to her surprise, he then extends in her direction. For a moment their laughter subsides as they both look up at her with discerning expectation on their faces.

"Sir, you are too kind," she says, as she twirls the cigar between her fingers and keeps her gaze focused on anything but the man's eyes. "You do not know what it means to me to get my hands on one of these. Would you tell me where you got them?"

"Well, darling, if you sit with us we might tell you," says the younger man, the one who has not yet spoken.

Lydia turns to study the boy's fuzzy moustache, which grows tentatively between patches of late-bloomer's acne and says, most matter-of-factly and feigning a sheepish smile:

"I am already sitting somewhere else, thank you."

"That so?" says the first man.

"Yes," she replies, her tone darker and her eyes slightly sharper.

Another round of dialect flies back and forth and again their laughter rolls through the room, from the sound and feel of it clearly at her expense.

"In light of that, as you are probably not going to tell me where it is you got a hold of these cigars, kind sir, there is only one other question I would like to ask you and your friend."

"And what would that be, darling?"

"What are you two buffoons laughing about?"

For several seconds the two men do little more than stare at her, as if something lumpy had just shot down their throats without warning. But after their wits have returned to them, the older one says, "Somebody ought to teach you some manners."

She has chosen the right moment to slide the cigar into the side pocket of her coat to keep it safe from whatever is coming. She senses that Edmilce has come to stand behind her and that she has positioned herself out of sight of the two Italians.

"If I am in need of a lesson in good manners, I will be happy to indulge," she says. "However, I hope you are not suggesting that a cunty piss stain like yourself is going to teach me, are you?"

At this the men rise to their feet, though the younger one more reluctantly than his companion. Still there is a certain degree of routine and clearly not the first time they both have menacingly towered over a woman. And without taking her eyes off them she realises that it isn't so much a question if a punch will be thrown at her, as much as when and with how much force.

She can still feel Edmilce's body pressing against her from behind, preventing her from stepping back - and so ruling out every hope of dodging the violence that will soon come her way. She thinks how ironic it is that right when she is about to gag on her own teeth certain specific, though unrelated nuances in her surroundings will stand out so sharply in her mind, like the fact the musicians have not dropped one note throughout the whole exchange and that so few people around them have taken even the faintest interest in what is about to happen. Through the open door she becomes aware that raindrops have begun to hit the street as well and of all things she might have become conscious of in those poignant seconds before she gets socked, she counts that only one of the whores in the street has moved in closer for a better view.

And at last, there it is: the tensing of the man's eyelids and the slight shudder of his shoulder as he pulls his arm around the side of his body. With the calm that comes from merely replaying an occurrence that has already taken place in one's mind, Lydia closes her eyes and waits. But other than a faint shifting in the air around her, there is nothing; she feels nothing. The only physical sensation is that of her weight being pushed to one side but softly enough to keep her from falling. When she opens her eyes again, before she hears the man in front of her bleat like a drowning lamb, she sees the buck of one of Doña Olga's dinner knives, the ones with the crafted horn handles, sticking out of the man's cheek. She watches him stumble backwards, hands covered in blood holding the side of his face. And as he opens his mouth to actually scream the scream his eyes have already been expressing, she can also see that while the serrated edge of Doña Olga's dinner knife has perforated his pale face right through, it has severed his tongue almost entirely in the process.

She cannot help but think back how shiny and well-polished Doña Olga's cutlery always was at dinner back at the pension. She notices how elegantly the metal of the knife reflects the light in the room inside his mouth now. And as she thinks of Doña Olga, only then does she think of Edmilce. The little thief!

At some point, Lydia instinctively reaches back in a protective gesture, for she still thinks Edmilce is standing behind her. Now the girl's upright pigtails dance in front of her, however, and it is in fact Edmilce who reaches back and has a hold on her now, as they both face the crowd gathering around the injured man.

Through the commotion Lydia spots the younger man hovering over his friend as though frozen and seeming to have all but forgotten about her. The musicians have finally stopped playing and they too now hurry over to tend to the man squirming and stumbling wildly through the room, falling over chairs and tables and staining the floors and the walls with blood.

Vaguely she feels Edmilce pulling her along in the direction of the door. Still no one seems to be paying any attention — a blessing she is sure will not be a lasting one. Within seconds she can feel the cold rain and her feet been pulled into a sprint by muscles that now seem ten times heavier than she remembers them. She feels Edmilce's hand clenched tightly around her wrist as they run down the embankment choosing the most darkened paths.

A hushed woman's voice in the dark makes them stop. Aqui, por aqui... And it is on account of nothing other than animal instinct that they let it lead them further into the shadows. They can hear the commotion from the bar behind them beginning to spill out into the street, which only means that someone will soon be looking for them.

They follow the voice blindly through a door and into what Lydia can do little more than assume is a dwelling of some kind, because she can no

185

longer feel the rain. The bolt of a lock falls into place with a clunk behind her, muffling the sound of the men outside. The woman's voice looms up again and Lydia is startled to discover how closely she now stands.

Callense la boca, las dos. Tu tambien mantonsita.... the woman says, directing her words at Edmilce specifically, though Lydia can't see it, calling her little brawler.

They do as they are told and turn their full attention to the noises in the street again, drawing near at times, too near, and then dissolving again into the distance. And only when it seems that the danger has slackened do they allow themselves to breathe again. They take turns precariously clearing their throats and nostrils, in an attempt to appease the darkness they are standing in, this tomb-like enclosure that for the time being has become their shared sanctuary.

Eventually, the intervals of calm out in the street become longer until in the end all is quiet again.

"Stay here, the both of you. And don't make a sound. If you as much as open your mouth, little brawler, you're going to need a lot more than just a knife to save your skin — do you hear me?" says the woman, as she ruffles what sounds like a rough linen skirt while she talks.

The woman undoes a lock opposite to where they have entered, which from the smell of soap that hangs inside the enclosure, Lydia now presumes is used for laundry or the storing of brooms and mops. The woman swings open the second door and as the light spills in Lydia recognises her as the whore who had stood watching their exchange back at the bar. A sense of dread descends upon her, as she wonders how safe they in fact are.

The woman in the doorway stops and turns toward them again, outlined against the light. She stands motionless; her face now shadowed over, a silhouette whispering to herself this time: Matonsita, very much in judgment but with morbid admiration ringing through it as well.

A half-hour passes after the woman disappears through the door and it takes almost that long for Lydia's thinking to regain its normal throttle, to where the events of that evening can pass before her at a somewhat graspable speed.

"I am not done with you yet," Lydia finally whispers, inclining her head and feeling Edmilce's pigtails brushing softly against her cheek in the dark.

"I understand," the girl whispers back, solemnly, small.

"If we get out of here in one piece, Edmilce..." she whispers.

"Yes...?"

"We are paying Doña Olga a visit in the morning...."

"Yes...."

"... And when we go there...."

"Yes...?"

"You - are going to offer working - without pay - until you have compensated her for the silverware you stole...."

"Yes...."

"As for that other thing tonight...."

"Yes...?"

"Thank you."

"For what?"

"For saving me from a broken nose...."

"Yes...."

<><><><><><><><>

The bolt on the door rattles and lifts again, the light blinding them this time. The woman motions her head for them to step forward.

"Nobody is going to think to look for you here," she says. "Not yet anyway."

They step into a kitchen, which looks like it could serve any number of other purposes, as well. The almost ethereal quality Lydia attributed to the woman earlier has vanished completely now and seems rather far-fetched; absurd even. The whore is handsome and somewhere in her late twenties; not much older than Lydia is herself. From the iciness in her eyes there is little speculating as to the woman's profession. She seems defensively dignified, alternating her conversations with long, spiritless stares into the distance.

"My name is Rosario" the woman says, then coughs, "and in the eight years that I have been prowling the docks," she adds, addressing

187

Edmilce directly now, "I have never seen anyone do what you did tonight."

"Is that why you called her that earlier?" Lydia interrupts.

"Pero coño, I hope it wasn't a thing you do very often" the woman replies smiling, creasing her rather sunken forehead, based on which Lydia has already concluded that Rosario probably has Spanish or Portuguese blood. "But don't worry," Rosario says to Lydia, as though to comfort her, "I was impressed with you too."

"I am not sure how glad I want to be about that," Lydia replies, striking a softer tone now but with some effort all the same and she quickly adds, "But before we say another word Rosario, I must thank you first. I don't know what we would have gotten ourselves into if you hadn't helped...."

"In the river, probably: at the bottom of it," the woman says, laughing and openly revealing teeth that are both stained by smoke and sporadically capped in gold.

She points her guests toward a couple of chairs around a small table in the middle of the kitchen.

"Let me guess," she belches, "you two have no idea whose face you mutilated tonight."

"I am afraid I don't," Lydia answers; her courage sinking into her shoes once more, as she braces herself to hear the rest of it. "Who was he?"

"A two-bit pimp named Loli Tomasso. He bosses some of the girls around here and has been trying to recruit more for himself for as long as I have known him. Most of the girls, here at least, are independent, you see. So, let's just say that he is not very well liked.... And what you did tonight - well, it did not go unnoticed, believe me."

The whore looks at Lydia for an instant and then at Edmilce again.

"There isn't much else that can really be said about Loli Tomasso," Rosario continues, "other than that he is mean and best of all: stupid. I don't know which is worse to tell you the truth. But he won't be doing much talking after tonight."

She wrinkles her nose and pulls the content of her nasal cavities with a single and very loud snort, and adds, "Do you know you sliced his tongue almost right through?"

"I somewhat suspected that," Lydia smiles sullenly and turns briefly to look at Edmilce, who continues to stare back at her, as always, asking her for answers to questions that are always larger than them both.

"I didn't even ask you your names!" Rosario then jeers, impatiently panning her gaze back and forth between them.

Edmilce shifts her weight and Lydia can feel the girl's glare burning on her skin without really having to see it.

"My name is Lydia," she then says. "And this is Edmilce."

"Don't worry" says Rosario. "You can trust me" - pointing both thumbs at herself in a playfully boyish gesture. "I'm no stranger to brawls either," she adds.

"You are taking quite a risk by having us here then," Lydia says.

"Yes, and did you see the amount of blood?"

Lydia nods, biting her lip and looking terrified.

Rosario lowers herself onto one of the chairs and leans forward, almost scratching the table top with her chin.

"What were you and Loli Tomasso talking about that ended so unfortunately for him?" she asks. "I have to know."

Lydia stares back and the more she fixes her eyes on Rosario the more she feels she needs to suppress laughter. She reaches into her pocket.

"What's this?"

"This is what he gave me before he swung at me," Lydia replies, carefully placing the pimp's cigar in front of her on the table.

"He gave you a cigar?"

"Smell it."

Rosario lowers her face further, wrinkling her nose as though it were a dead bird.

"It smells like a cigar. I don't get it. Is this why you would cut that imbecile's face in two?"

"I don't suppose you know where he might have got it from."

"Are you serious?"

"Well, Rosario, there are only a few places this particular cigar could have come from. Let me ask you this then: have you ever heard of a man by the name of Ulisse Paxi?"

Lydia's question is met with an arrested silence, as Rosario appears to be scrutinizing her now.

"Who are you?" Rosario asks, as though her question should instead have been what on earth she is doing in that part of town in the first place, if she isn't a whore and seemingly has no interest in entering the trade either.

"I will let you know when I figure that out myself," Lydia answers. "But you haven't answered my question."

"Oh yes, about Lissy Paxi."

"You said Lissy."

"Yes, Lissy. Signore Ulisse Paxi. Ulisse Gavino Paxi, right? Your question is if I had ever heard of him."

Silence.

"Lydia, I don't know what it is you want. But doesn't everyone know Lissy Paxi — Ulisse Gavino Paxi?" she taunts.

Lydia becomes aware of the blood pumping through her veins as she realises that with her answer Rosario has implied far more than she has bargained for. She does not want to know anything more and cringes at the thought of what might possibly connect Paxi to the woman sitting in front of them now.

<><><><><><><>

Although she seems most certain that the authorities will not be involved in connection with the incident at the bar, Rosario still insists they wait until closer to dawn before venturing back outside. She also argues that Loli Tomasso probably has good reason to steer clear of the law as much as he can, even if it is in the role of a victim — especially in the role of a victim.

"He probably won't show his face around here - for a while," Rosario says.

A silent understanding seems to have been reached between the women, though it could just as well be nothing more than a feeling that has taken hold around the kitchen table, to not touch the Paxi subject again; it has cost a pimp part of his face after all and Lydia reasons that enough damage has been done for one night on account of that topic.

During the course of that night, the contours of what is Rosario's life come to pass instead and even if they are primarily flashes of an existence spent prancing the streets, it is still much more than what Lydia feels is prudent to reveal about hers. But the trade-off seems well balanced upon discovering that Rosario likes to talk and especially to talk about herself.

"Do you live here?" Lydia asks.

"Of all the girls I am the one who spends most of her time here."

"What do you mean, 'of all the girls'?"

"Well, officially, it is my house, but what it really is, is something of a general-purpose refuge for some half a dozen girls that work the docks. So, if you're wondering, this isn't the first time women have come here to hide from some thug or other. The house fronts as a linen hall; we wash and iron during the day and at night women can come here to rest or eat a proper meal if they want to – basically, to get off the street for a couple of hours, if they want."

According to Rosario, aside from some of the girls, few know of the place and even fewer have ever actually been inside.

"We see ourselves as something of a collective," she then says. "We look after each other here. And that is why we don't need filth like Loli Tomasso to pimp us around. And that is also why – as far as I am concerned," she adds, "the two of you are welcome here."

She rolls one cigarette after another. She offers them one and looks surprised every time Lydia and Edmilce kindly decline. She draws the smoke deeply into her lungs, arching her back with every pull and then comes forward again exhaling whilst studying them with an investigative gravity in her eyes.

"My advice," she offers, "is that you two not show your faces around here either, for a while, because you will be recognised," and adds licking her lips and intensifying the severity on her brow. "Believe me, you don't want the likes of Loli Tomasso coming after you. You might be better off in the hands of the police – if you know what I mean...."

Rosario peppers her warnings with anecdotes to give Lydia and Edmilce a better sense of what they are dealing with. But every time she does, admiration and something of a personal sense of victory can also be seen in her eyes and which seems to grow larger as the night wears on.

"Almost all the girls I know carry blades, you know; for protection. But as far as I can remember not one of them has ever done what you did this evening," she says, directing herself toward Edmilce again in near triumph.

She pours cups of tea and roasts old bread over her stove, while she explains the logic at the base of her personal business strategy like a veteran tradesman.

"In a town of immigrants like this one," she explains. "- take a wild guess on the number of women as opposed to men," she challenges with growing fire in her eyes.

"I wouldn't know," Lydia responds; not quite sure whether to broaden her smile or to allow herself a deep frown.

"It is about one to a hundred," Rosario punts. "So, it's just plain stupid for any woman not to get out there and shake out some of those sailor pockets."

She halts in mid-sentence again, as she has done several times, to look at the two of them and assess the trading potential that has so unexpectedly made its way to her table.

"The trade isn't entirely without peril, of course. But tonight you've proven that you can stand up to any of those thugs out there. It's just hugely lucrative, is all I am saying."

<>< ><>< ><>< ><>

Close to sunrise, after the curtains vaguely begin to pale with the dawn, footsteps unexpectedly sound on the second floor.

All Rosario offers in reaction to the sudden commotion is a look up at the ceiling before she gets to her feet and rushes off with a creased and diligent look on her face.

They can hear her ascending the stairs whilst mumbling words both to herself, as well as to whoever just made the floorboards creak.

"No Sofia, you hard-headed goat," they hear her say in a reprimanding tone that is shortly followed by the voice of a second female pleading weakly in resistance.

They follow the tumbling of feet with their eyes on the ceiling and then back toward the stairwell as Rosario descends again.

"She shouldn't be walking around," she says, crossing the kitchen toward the kettle on the stove.

She pours a cup of tea and after she knocks the tealeaves out of the strainer into the sink, she directs herself toward Lydia and Edmilce, who just stare back like cows watching rain come down.

"Sofia is one of the girls I was telling you about. A week ago she discovered she was 'blessed with child', as they say, and two nights ago she did a javelin on herself..."

"A javelin?" Lydia asks politely, though she has less trouble unraveling the metaphor than she leads on.

"A self-inflicted abortion, with a knitting needle," Rosario says, adding with disgust, "A nice bit of knitting too."

Again she rolls her eyes as she illustrates with both index fingers the length of the needle Sofia had done her so-called knitting with.

"How is she?" Lydia asks, with added authority in her voice.

"She showed up here bleeding like an animal, barely able to stand. I took her in and got her off her feet and eventually the bleeding stopped - I think."

"You think?"

"It's stopped. But she shouldn't be walking."

"No, she shouldn't be."

"That is what I have been saying."

"May I see her?"

"Why?"

"I used to be a midwife — well, I was almost one in another life."

"Have you ever performed an abortion?"

"No, but I have seen — what a javelin, as you say, can do."

Lydia is already on her feet and only now does it become evident how much taller than Rosario she is — and to what extent Lydia is able to impress with just a look of determination on her face.

Rosario places her free hand under the cup.

"Follow me," she says.

A narrow hall divides five small rooms on the second floor. And at the very end, directly above the kitchen, Rosario opens one of them. She motions for Lydia to follow. The bed the woman is in takes up most of the space of the room, so that they have to slide in edgewise to fit themselves in.

"What's this?" the woman in the bed asks, peeping a sideward glance at them through the slits of her eyes. "It hurts like a bitch again," she murmurs.

"This is Lydia," Rosario says in a clear whisper. "She used to be a midwife - in a past life, she says. She asked to see you."

"And what does Lydia exactly do in this life?"

"Staying out of trouble as best I can," Lydia answers, pleased by the woman's good disposition considering. "I want to have a look at you, to see how you are coming along."

"I brought you some tea," says Rosario, not quite ready to let the conversation between Sofia and Lydia take off without her.

"I prefer rum," says the patient crooning with irony, but more so with physical pain.

"No liquor," Lydia says with sternness in her voice she doesn't quite recognise. "It is precisely what could cause you to start bleeding again," she adds. "Have you been drinking?"

"Just Rosario's tea, I regret to say."

"Don't try to sit up - let me have a look at you."

"I haven't bled to death, so I think I will be alright."

"You are still in danger of things that are far worse than bleeding," Lydia says right back, but this time much more conscious of the tone in which she speaks.

She feels she sounded oddly calmer than she thinks she would have - and if not necessarily calmer she feels that above all, she has sounded able, which are two things Lydia has never compared before. She feels her hands become warm and steady, a feeling she now remembers from when she used to assist the nuns back home, now that again she reaches down to heal.

She examines the damage the knitting needle has done to the woman's insides, but beyond some raw lesions she is soon satisfied that for the time being the girl isn't in any real danger. She straightens herself

up again and smiles down emphatically

"A couple of things," she says, as she smoothens the front of her dress, confident her hands are stained with nothing that might dirty it. "Do not get out of bed. There will be no drinking. And most importantly: do not do this to yourself again.

She is conscious of the silence her own voice seems to be able to command inside the small room and decides she is not entirely displeased by the effect.

"If by some miracle," Lydia adds, "you ever do get like this again" - hardening her tone to give her words the greatest possible weight, "come to me for help. I have seen women die from doing what you did," Lydia says, turning to Rosario now but thinking back to the conversation she and Edmilce had the night before, before Loli Tomasso.

"Next time, you may consider me part of your collective. Capice?"

It isn't until somewhere near the market halls on their way home that Lydia finally speaks.

"We will never be able to go back there, you know," she says, though feeling herself cringe at how redundant she has actually sounded by overstating something that obvious.

But this bothers her far less than knowing that the woman they met that night — not the man Edmilce almost killed with Dona Olga's dinner knife, but the whore who runs a collective down by the docks - will eventually pull her back there. It makes her stomach almost turn to think that no matter how foolish, the truss of fate will prove many times stronger than any amount of common sense.

"Edmilce, do you remember what we talked about before?"

"What, about becoming whores?"

"No Edmilce, about delivering babies. And remember how I told you that I never wanted to do that again?"

"Sure," the girl says, with her eyes still fixed on the empty street in front of them. "What about it?"

"It seems odd to me now, that's all."

"What should I tell Doña Olga when she asks me to return the knife I stole," Edmilce asks.

"Tell her you lost it," Lydia says, short and vexed by her own flawed moral logic, which makes her wonder if she will ever be able to educate Edmilce to always do the right thing.

"But that would be like lying, wouldn't it?"

"Then tell her you left it sticking out of someone's face down in a bar somewhere, Edmilce," Lydia responds, her voice surprisingly clear of all irony.

<><><><><><><><>

There is a knock on the front door of the apartment, late one evening. It is the knock they have been waiting for.

The doorman comes up with the message that a young lady has asked to speak to Señorita Lydia. She is waiting downstairs in the hall he says.

Lydia follows the doorman and with every step the clearer her head becomes.

"Did the young lady in question also give a reason why she wanted to see me?" she asks the doorman.

But, of course, given that the young lady could only be Rosario, the reasons that might have brought her all the way to Palermo in the first place are probably not the kind Rosario would exactly have wanted to share with the doorman anyway.

He confirms indeed that the visitor did not specify her business.

It startles Lydia how different Rosario looks standing on the marble floor of the hall. Instead of the sensuous blue dress she had worn the night they met, she now wears a man's woolen coat, buttoned all the way up to her chin. Instead of the high-heeled shoes Lydia remembers she now wears heavy work boots and that the moisture from the drizzle outside has darkened the toes, which suggests furthermore that she has probably walked all the way. Lydia does not recall having specifically noticed rouge on Rosario's lips and cheeks the night they met either, or that she had worn any form of eye shadow. Now her face is atonic without it. She looks older. Yet, everything about her now has the abandoned look of a beaten child, with nothing of the self-determination that had so characterised her less than two weeks earlier.

"Are you in trouble?" is the only thing Lydia can think of to ask.

"Like I promised you, nobody knows I am here," Rosario says in a nasal tone that suggests furthermore, that she has a cold. "But I felt it was worth taking you up on your offer," she adds reluctantly, almost smiling.

"Come up," Lydia says, glancing at the doorman, who is staring blankly at an upside-down newspaper in his hands.

"No, I need to head back. Can't we talk outside?"

The cold wind bites through Lydia's poncho and the light rain hardens her face once she steps out of the copper and glass from the lobby.

"Are you in trouble?" she repeats, though this time not so much as a gutted reaction to Rosario's appearance, but with real concern.

"I am trying to prevent another needle job," Rosario says. "It's about a girl I know. I am afraid she will hurt herself unless somebody helps her do it. I want to ask you to come down to the house again."

"You yourself said that I should not go back there. And I think you were right; I think it would be very unwise if I did," Lydia says, though already weighing the consequences of the words she is to speak next.

"Bring her here."

They intently search each other's eyes for all that which Lydia has not actually said with those three words.

"When can you get her here?"

"Tomorrow; I have money," Rosario adds, pulling a wad of bills out of the pocket of her coat."

"I don't want it," Lydia replies, pushing back Rosario's hand. "And don't offer it to me again."

"You are quite a number, Lydia."

"So I have been told."

<><><><><><><>

To Lydia prostitution has always been a hazy concept, something either fleetingly touched upon inside the abstracts of conversation, or when moral judgment is passed in the third person. She has never even visualised the mechanics of it before; and it is with cool sobriety that she now accepts this intimate invitation into its sweltering core.

Rosario returns to the apartment the following day with a nineteen-year-old girl who calls herself Pilar - a homely thing who wears that liquid glare of a rape victim like a crown to years of abuse, with her anger duly turned inward. But there is something in the way the girl prims at the world around her, which suggests that the term rape somehow no longer really applies to anything having to do with Pilar, but simply to the way the world just happens to be. From the moment Lydia looks into her eyes, shakes her hand and hears her weathered voice say angry words she knows that to Pilar, somewhere along the line, pain has long ceased to hurt.

Although performing abortions is certainly not what the nuns back in Castiglione would ever have described as part of their mission as midwives, during her time with them there was plenty of opportunity for Lydia to observe and practise the very art of performing them. In fact, delivering babies was only a small part of what women in the region turned to the nuns for. It was a thing that was never talked about, but nonetheless performed with little scruple, by powdery, sacred, steady hands. And it was probably because of the very clandestine nature of these types of interventions that the hooded saints in Castiglione performed abortions to such meticulous perfection. During her time at the nunnery Lydia had pretty much seen all there is to know about such procedures and she feels confident that little is likely to surprise her here.

Immediately after their fateful night by the docks Lydia prepares one of the spare bedrooms of the apartment in anticipation of Rosario's inevitable visit, expecting that if it isn't days it would likely be a matter of only weeks before she is asked to return to her old vocation. The following day, with the sight of the bleeding Loli Tomasso still fresh in her memory, she begins to stock up on everything she will need for when that time comes. She buys surgical instruments, towels, gauze and linen and in less than a fortnight she graduates herself out of the apprentice role she had played back at the nunnery to one of the seasoned abortionist she will soon become. And now, as the angry Pilar stands before her she feels confident, a welded certainty, that the girl is in the best hands she could hope to be in in the whole of Buenos Aires.

Whenever she thinks about the first abortion Rosario will inevitably ask her to perform, Lydia often tells herself to remember to pay special regard to the human element of the whole procedure and the consequences of the thing she is about to do. Now, however, as Pilar opens herself, it just sickens her to look into a soul this damaged. Her touch soothes the pain not as something Lydia specifically learned from the nuns but like a reflex, a thing that happens not out of compassion or even empathy, but out of a pure necessity to cleanse. There is hardly any bleeding at all and Pilar is still fully conscious by the time Lydia straightens herself and moves away to dispose of the bed pan containing the fruit of her efforts.

Throughout the procedure Edmilce stands beside her, assisting her through the most painless abortion Pilar has ever had. And, of course, Pilar will not be the last. Over the next three years Rosario marches an entire army of women through the apartment and as Lydia's record of service grows so does her reputation. Soon the apartment at the Plaza Italia even replaces Rosario's original place in La Boca as the safe house for the ever-growing collective. There is always some girl there during that period, either recovering or waiting to abort – or just hiding from the discords of the street. Soon there isn't a whore in Buenos Aires who hasn't heard of the apartment at the Plaza Italia, as in those three years Lydia herself becomes downright legendary.

It is her demeanour, they say; her serenity and ambivalence to the thing she does for them that puts something of a saintly aura around her. And in particular it is her hands that among the whores acquire the biggest fame. It is Lydia's ability to heal and alleviate by way of nothing more than the heat she is able to channel through them – a thing she discovered about herself back with the nuns, and which she had hoped the ship and the Atlantic would have erased, for it belongs to a world she had hoped to change and herself along with it.

<><><><><><><>

It is three years Lydia and Edmilce spend submerged inside the thing occurring around them, which, for as long as it lasts, has also freed them from too much inner reflection.

It was never Lydia's intention to run a profit from what they were doing. The money they have arrived with still suffices in providing for their basic necessities and whatever is earned additionally is invested directly back into the practice — not to make it profitable in any way but because there is nothing else they can really think of doing with it. During those three years the apartment becomes like a machine that turns and sputters tirelessly to the beat of their dedication to it; an entity unto itself that grows whether they mean for it to or not.

It is Rosario who insists they accept payment for their services, arguing that they might otherwise deny the girls their only way to express their gratitude for the help they receive. Lydia yields and the small, symbolic amounts she charges the girls are primarily to satisfy Rosario's entrepreneurial nature; a concession on Lydia's part, which results in the practice becoming profitable beyond anyone's comprehension. A true obstetrical goldmine, Rosario called it once.

Inevitably, however, it becomes increasingly difficult to properly balance between the practical reality of what they are doing and the need of some of the women to raise Lydia onto some saintly pedestal, which is ultimately what baffles her the most. And while it greatly amuses her as well that anyone might see her in such an absurd light, and occasionally jokes about how she is slowly becoming Buenos Aires' patron saint of fallen women, it does disturb her greatly nonetheless when she considers the darker side of this type of adoration and the flaw in the human soul that tends to bring it about.

By the time the third autumn rolls around and day or night whores can be found outside the door of the building and in the park across the street, waiting to catch even the smallest glimpse of her, the fair one, Lydia the merciful, the one who performs abortions without pain or bleeding; immaculately, her restlessness begins to return and her focus shifts to the horizon once more. What makes it even worse is that no matter how much her aversion grows, she begins to realise as well that to Edmilce the mystification of her person makes sense somehow.

As the water of the river begins to acquire its wintry brown once more and the vibrant colors of the city ebb away along with all the fragrances of summer, in June of 1906, that far-off gaze has already fixed itself in Lydia's eyes again. And when early one morning Rosario comes around to the apartment to fetch a girl who had been helped the day before, it becomes hard to deny that once more change is at hand.

It is on a morning like any other. The procedures the night before went without event and after a good night's rest Rosario is to walk out of the apartment with a young woman — or maybe two — with their bellies fit to commence work within no more than a few days. On this particular morning, however, Rosario seems troubled, off-balance somehow. Lydia takes her aside the moment she sets foot in the apartment.

Lydia has learned that on occasion, like Emilio Toffolo back on the ship, Rosario too likes to line her insides with a morning glass of brandy whenever things are troubling her. Lydia fetches the bottle of Peruvian Pisco from the kitchen, which she got as a present from one of the girls the summer before and touches up a glass for her.

"Tell me about it," she says, as she searches Rosario's eyes, reaffirming as much as she can the level of depth their friendship has acquired by now.

Rosario responds matching the intimacy with which Lydia has spoken by resting her gaze on Lydia's lips, and says, "On the night we met you told me the whole ordeal with Loli Tomasso was about a cigar he gave you."

"Yes, I did."

"You showed it to me, remember?"

"I do remember."

"I am going to wager that you held on to it — that you still have it after all this time."

"Why are we talking about this, Rosario? Has Loli Tomasso done something?"

"Hardly."

Rosario sighs fidgeting and stares down at the glass on the kitchen counter. She moves her hand and turns it around its axis with the tips of her fingers.

"I have no idea what it will mean to you, but for whatever it's worth: Lissy Paxi is in town," she says.

Lydia's gaze cools and the amber-green of her eyes lock on the other woman's face as though they were teeth.

"You wouldn't have the faintest idea what it does to me that someone like you tells me she has seen him."

"What do you mean by that?"

"What I mean, Rosario, is that it turns my stomach to think what could possibly connect you - or anyone else you might know – to him."

"Had anyone else said this to me," Rosario whispers sweetly, but still with poison casting shadows on her face, "I would have smacked her across the room you know."

"Please don't forget what happened to the last person who felt the impulse to do that."

"And this is what I like so much about you, Lydia, Saint Lydia, the immaculate Lydia, with her healing hands: that deep down at the core you are the vilest cunt I have ever laid eyes on."

"It takes one to know one," Lydia says calmly, walking back into the study to fetch a glass for herself this time.

She moves back into the kitchen and pours herself a glass, which she places right next to the other one and stands looking at it, pressing her weight against Rosario, challenging her to either press back or step away.

"Now I am going to need one of these myself," she says still in a whisper, turning her glass in the same way Rosario just turned hers.

After a long stretch of silence Lydia looks Rosario in the eye again.

"Where is he?" she asks.

"No, no, no." Rosario says loudly. "You first. What is he – to you?"

"I met him at sea."

<><><><><><><>

Lydia sits motionless on the wooden bench; her back rigid and her hands folded in her lap. She listens to the drone of voices in the other room and the chiming of keys hitting the metal bars of the nearby cells. She has never seen the inside of Caseros Prison before. It stands next to the orphanage she has visited several times before with Rosario whilst holding some unwanted urchin she delivered back at the apartment. The prison stands in a tree-less and a rather forlorn part of town, in an ash-barren nothingness which seems like the perfect location for an institution such as this.

Across from her the only other visitor in the waiting room is an Indian woman with two young children who could easily pass for moving bundles of rags hanging over each leg. In a series of snot-ridden croons she can detect the vague frameworks of the infant's world that can seem neither pointless nor show any immediate purpose. She assumes the woman must have been no older than thirty, but in the far-fetched event that a creature like that might actually talk to someone like her and told her she is fifty Lydia would surely have believed it. There is defeat in everything about them; that conquered, self-preserved look of the Indian that reflects a history in the process of erasing itself, a future as luminous as the inside of a Mapuche crypt. At no point during the entire time they sit across from each other has the woman or have even the children once looked at her; their eyes like a wet mop on the tiles between them.

A uniformed guard appears in the doorway and announces, as though over the heads of some invisible crowd he has been instructed to contain, "La Señorita Lydia."

She rises and takes a step forward.

"The prisoner is ready to receive you. Follow me."

She is led through a corridor lined with iron bars before a dozen empty cells and is asked to take a chair before the one at the far end. Without another word the guard turns and walks back down the corridor, leaving her by herself for another ten minutes or more.

She wonders if Loli Tomasso will even recognise her, and if he does what his reaction will be when he sees her. A few months before word reached her that he beat and stabbed to death one of the girls who used to work for him down by the docks. An argument supposedly erupted into a fight between them and escalated into its fatal climax right in front of more than a dozen bystanders, who — so the accounts of the incident went — did little or nothing to prevent the girl from bleeding to death on the sidewalk.

Loli Tomasso was arrested and convicted, but no matter how disturbing or to what extent the incident somehow characterises the kind of man he is, she still puts in the effort to see him and would have done so even without the metal bars that will now separate them. There is a greater necessity to do this, to see him; she is there to free herself.

A lock rattles across the cage and a man who looks much smaller, thinner and certainly much younger than the one she remembers from the night of their encounter, appears before her. His eyes are heavy but watchful - alert in the way a beaten animal might look as it senses danger. The side of his face where Edmilce rammed Doña Olga's dinner knife looks like a badly stitched cloth. It seems to fold inward, which gives him a rather tart look; his lips set in a permanent pout, as though he were sucking on a slice of lemon or about to begin a soft, unmelodious whistle.

For a while he looks nervously around the cell and when he can find no one else except for the guard standing behind him, he focuses his eyes on her. She feels it almost rude to make even the slightest movement except with her eyes to study him further. He approaches with the hint of a drag, not of his feet but visible in an almost ape-like sway of the shoulders. As he nears her, bending slightly forward, she can see him searching his vile memories in the hope of connecting them to the sight of her somehow. He stands for a while, seemingly unaware of himself. He bends down further and slowly lowers himself into the chair facing the bars of the cell. Then, at last, there it is: the recognition they both have been waiting for. She can see the muscles of his face relax somewhat, as his brow tenses and his eyes become slightly more shiny and dark.

"I was about to get quite offended that you didn't recognise me, Señor Tomasso," she says in a voice that is even - and terrifyingly sweet.

She can tell he is still too dizzy and off-balance to produce words, so she continues.

"I can't say that there is any better place to find you than in a cage."

"What are you doing here?" he presses through clenched teeth.

"I am not here for you if that is what you were thinking. I am here for me. I am here to let you know, Señor Tomasso, that I forgive you for being what you are."

"Forgive me? For what?"

"For being what you are," she repeats. "But I don't want to dirty too many words on spelling it out for you."

There is a long pause, a frozen wedge of time in which he might have laughed in her face or crawled into the farthest corner of the cell to digest the horror of what she has just said to him.

"Could you be the craziest bitch I have ever come across?"

"Today I put you behind me, Señor Tomasso. And remember that whatever is to become of you after today you have been forgiven," she repeats. "See it as a curse I am bringing down upon you. Surely we both know how susceptible we Italians can be to such a thing."

Her fingers rise warily to the side of her face and makes a cutting motion in the air.

"A curse, Señor Tomasso."

She makes a move to rise but he beats her to it, snapping at her between the bars of the cell like a dog.

"When I get out of here I am going to come looking for you. See if you will forgive me then."

"You will do no such thing," she says in her softest voice again, blinking her eyes each time he thrusts up his wrists that are shackled to his belt.

"You will think about what I have said to you and I trust that you will honor my wishes."

"What, that you have come here to put a curse on me?"

"No, señor Tomasso; that I also came here to free you — of me."

<><><><><><><>

It has been exactly four years since she crossed the Atlantic on a ship that taught her, if anything, that to take control of one's own destiny is to put oneself at its mercy and that her paths will never again be familiar ones; that they will forever wind themselves before her according to some erratic and mystic plan. So far, destiny has brought unheard-of fortunes into her life and individuals like preludes to things to come. Yet Loli Tomasso was one that required closure from the very beginning.

She knew from the moment she stood in front of him that night by the docks that there would be no place on the face of the earth for both her and the menace he represents. Buenos Aires is big but it would never be big enough to keep him out of her life forever. So, she was left with no choice but to find him first and pro-actively command him out of her life, in the vague knowledge perhaps that if she did destiny would take care of the practical details for her that will make it so.

She wagered right; because not a week later news reaches her that the pimp from La Boca has been found dangling form the end of a rope in the latrines of the prison. Rosario bursts into the apartment that afternoon to bring her the news, but Lydia's sole reaction is to say that Loli Tomasso indeed had many reasons to hang himself. She does not ask for details nor does she care much to listen to Roasrio's unsolicited account of what supposedly happened. Lydia merely says that it is a chapter they can all at last put behind them, while she folds towels in the kitchen and lowers needles and syringes into a pan of boiling water, preparing for the first abortion of the evening.

"Does anything ever affect you, Lydia?" Rosario asks her, rather at her wits end by how passive Lydia can seem at times.

Lydia continues to stare translucently at the towels in her hand, her lips repeating her cold logic like a mantra, that Loli Tomasso indeed had many reasons to hang himself whilst in her mind different words altogether keep repeating themselves; words pertaining to the real reason Lydia has sought closure in the first place; the fact she now again shares the streets of a city with Paxi.

Immediately after she receives the news about Loli Tomasso she goes off in search for the address Rosario has given her: 44 Juncal. In the lush shade of the chestnut trees that line his street, as she looks at the mansions hidden behind them, she keeps having to remind herself that these are indeed residences, for they look more like palaces erected not for real people but to accommodate some far off concept of the completely unattainable. Yet the paper in her hand insists that this is the place where she needs to be.

She crosses the street away from the house so as to not draw attention to herself, as she stares up at it and tries to put her head around the thing she is about to do. She reaches down to straighten the wrinkles on her dress, out of habit and going back to a time when her dress would have been little more than rags, which she would have tried to pass for one and herself for the kind of lady not even remotely worthy of presenting herself at the doorstep of a dwelling like this. She keeps having to tell herself that she is dressed in the latest fashion now; that this time around she indeed is a lady and in every way worthy of – what exactly?

She lets the heavy iron ring fall on its copper base and closes her eyes, the way she always does whenever she needs to pretend she is in control of things. She can sense no movement inside the house. All she can hear is her own blood beating in even thrusts from her throat into her cheeks and like an even drum on her tongue. She lifts her hand impatiently to knock once more, but this time she clearly distinguishes the steady clank of officious footsteps approaching from the inside. The door opens heavily with a single high-pitched creak as the housemaid appears before her.

"How may I help you?" Doña Marta asks with an inquiring but unpretending expression on her face.

"I am here to see Señor Paxi," Lydia answers almost mechanically, as unaffected as she can.

She does her best to appear confident, but after the word Please comes out of her mouth in a voice that is too small and far too watered-down with hesitation, it frightens her to hear how unprepared she is. For a quick second she feels the impulse to turn and walk away, but it is a shadow that passes across the housekeeper's face that keeps her standing where she is. She then remembers how Rosario had mentioned something about an accident in New York. At the time, she had stored this bit of information away and reduced it to little more than a passing murmur she had not been able or willing to acknowledge. But it seems more than significant now.

"Who may I say is calling?" the housekeeper asks.

"My name is Lydia."

"Lydia..."

Doña Marta savours her name like a tasty morsel that is familiar yet illusive and strange.

"Is Señor Paxi expecting you?"

"It would surprise me greatly if he were," Lydia replies.

The woman studies her for a moment longer but without falling out of her role of one who is required to always comply with a smile, the woman casts down her eyes.

"Please come in, Miss," she says, and steps aside.

Lydia's eyes scale the walls over the series of portraits that represent the long pedigree of the man she has longed to see since Brazil. It isn't exactly the formality with which she has been received or the crystal chandelier that hovers over her, but more the scent of his cigars inside the house that weaken her legs and she has to remind herself to continue breathing.

She waits as the housekeeper moves away toward a door at the end of the hall and through which she promptly disappears, leaving her in the watchful care of Paxi's gawking ancestors, all bearing a resemblance that is difficult to pinpoint but unmistakable nonetheless. As she scans the paintings, the housekeeper's silhouette outlined against the glare of the slit in the curtains startles her, a ghostly apparition that makes her wonder about the bolts and locks with which the woman has secured the door behind her a moment earlier. She can see Doña Marta nodding her head ever so slightly and only then does Lydia understand that the idea is to follow her into that room.

The first thing she notices is that the curtains inside are drawn shut as well and that the crepuscular scent of silk from the bindings of the books that line the walls mixed with the scent of his cigars make the room even duskier. Only from the stinging in her eyes and the scrape of her throat as she enters does she realize the library is filled with smoke.

The matron whispers his name in the dark and hearing her say it makes the years since she has seen him acquire something of a thorny texture. She senses movement in a far-off corner. Making a vague scratching sound a squatted shadow then begins to move, but halts halfway before it becomes fully visible.

"What can I do for you?" the shadow asks in a dry, grinding voice she can neither place nor dismiss as that of a complete stranger.

The figure sounds bloated besides; as if the tongue with which it speaks has been numbed somehow, damaged, much in the way Loli Tomasso had sounded.

"I came to see if you had kept your promise," Lydia says, diverting her eyes for a moment, "...with regards to diving for coins," she then adds, sure she will validate herself with a reference to something only Paxi would know about, or whatever is left of him inside the creature now lurking in the dark.

"I did keep it, rest assured," the shadow replies. "Lucky for me too, because if I recall correctly, fulfilling my punishment, had I not kept it, would be quite impossible now given my condition. Martita, you can go. I don't think the lady is here to assassinate me. Not yet anyway."

"Would you like me to make tea?" Doña Marta asks.

"Lydia, would you like some tea?"

"Only if you are having some. Thank you."

He remains invisible and stationary, revealing himself only through his floundering articulation.

Lydia sits down on the edge of the sofa and waits until the housekeeper has closed the door on her way out.

"Do you mind if I sit down?"

"Please, make yourself comfortable."

"You seem to have remembered my name," she says, but in no way attempting to conceal how much it annoys her that she is still speaking to a dark wall.

"And you have remembered quite a bit more than just mine," he replies, audibly smiling now.

"I also remember you had a face and a certain eloquence of speech to go with it."

"I had a lot more than that," the shadow replies. "Look, if you are looking to rekindle some memory from the time we met, I am afraid I will have to disappoint you."

"That is quite presumptuous, even for you," she says.

He finally pushes himself forward and only then does she realise he is in a wheelchair. It embarrasses before it shocks her, but it could also have been the other way around, to realise this. He picks up on it and appears to search for words.

"You obviously heard I was back in Buenos Aires, so you must also know why I came back, and what happened while I was away," he says, pushing up his shoulders and upturning his palms on the wicker of his armrests.

"I have no idea."

"Well, you certainly seem different from how I remember you," he then says with a smile.

"It has been almost four years."

"Yes, and a lot can happen in four years, as you can see. What can I do for you?" he repeats, this time slightly more pressing.

"You could tell me what happened to you. We could take it from there," she replies.

It is hard to convince herself that she isn't indeed talking to a complete stranger. He is thinner than she remembers; his skin much looser around the bones. His complexion seems to have no color furthermore and is lacking in all the vibrancy that used to define him so well. His hair is cut short, no longer the sheen of curls touching the back of his neck and dancing around his face as he moves and talks. She notices that his face is somewhat slanted as well and that one corner of his mouth has a tendency to drop into something of a sullen, near-anguished expression.

"What makes you think I will want to tell you about that?" he asks, just short of a bark.

"It has been almost four years and I am only curious to hear what has happened during that time."

The words, you said you would always be near, form in her mind but never come out of her mouth.

"Are you here to collect on some promise I may or may not have made to you?" he says reading her thoughts.

"You helped me back then and I felt that you would probably want to hear how things have worked out for me, and Edmilce; remember her?" she says, without any of the scorn that has begun to close around her throat.

"I appreciate you being so direct," he says. "The more I listen to you the more I remember the impression you made on me – and why I felt so compelled to help you in the first place. But in case you haven't noticed..."

He lowers his damaged gaze.

"Whatever is in this chair is not the man you met back then. What you see is a parody."

"I never expected to find self-pity in that man either," she half-mumbles in a voice suddenly quite drained of strength, and hope, perhaps, too.

"Whatever landed me in this chair, Lydia," he retorts, but also with a playful chime in his voice, "was fortune failing me, at last. I just want to gauge your expectations."

"People feeling sorry for themselves has always made me rather sick, señor Paxi."

"It used to make me livid," he replies.

While they talk she soon realises that behind her aversion for self-pity, none of his physical impediments remain noticeable to her for very long. She senses that beyond her annoyance she could become rather oblivious to them and that his feeling sorry for himself is nothing more than a symptom of whatever it is that has happened to him – the accident Rosario had tried to tell her about; that it must not only have broken almost every bone in his body but apparently much of his composure and pride as well – which isn't necessarily a bad thing. She also understands how, because of this, much of his vanity runs rampant now, like some exorcised demon with nowhere to go except to hide behind the books and the paintings that cover every wall. His depth seems hollow and it reminds her of the emptiness in the whores Rosario brings to her doorstep. They too have a tendency to ignite a healing fire inside of her.

"This is something I will probably never understand," he adds, "but this chair, this vehicle for self-pity is also my life's triumph; it freed me, you see, and it has convinced me that I will actually die someday."

"What happened to you?" she repeats; a felt whisper that completely dissolves her earlier harshness.

He throws a series of nervous glances at the door, perhaps hoping the housekeeper has timed her return with the tea in such a way that it will provide him with an excuse to stall or maybe, with a bit of luck, ignore her question altogether. He turns his head sideways and looks at her.

"I fell three floors out of a window. I have severely damaged my spine; cracked my skull, shattered my hip and collapsed my lung on a snowy rock. It was very cold, though I don't exactly remember feeling the cold; I just know that it was, like I know that it was the middle of the night, around three. I was not found until the next morning," he continues, "I should be dead. I was in a coma for five weeks after that and I wasn't quite amongst the living when they repaired most of the immediate damage. There was enough damage to last me a lifetime, as you can see; the fact I now talk like a half wit and am unable to get out of this chair for much of anything defines me now."

"How does one get to fall out of a window in the middle of the night?" Lydia then asks, picking her words carefully.

"That is actually quite simple; I was pushed."

"Who?"

"You know that I have never actually asked myself that question. I've always figured that if ever there were those who felt affection for me, then there surely must at least be that many who would wish me dead or hurt. It doesn't matter who actually pushed me or on whose behalf they acted. All that matters is what I have become as a result. Having said that, I will repeat my earlier question: what can I do for you?"

She rises to her feet.

"I came here to thank you for what you did for us. For what it is worth know that I am grateful and that I will never forget you. I can find my way out."

Seeing Paxi has brought the functionary back into her memories more vividly than ever before. She has often thought about Emilio Toffolo and of all the things they would have talked about; seen and done together had he lived. She can often almost smell the sweet-rancid cologne he used to douse himself in after his morning walks along the decks of the ship and at times can even hear the soft mumbles that used to roll over his lips as he sat slumped down in his bunk sifting through his notes. At times, she thinks she can even hear his voice reaching out to her through the jumble of other voices in the street. It fills her with a strange, almost daughterly longing for him every time.

She drags her feet past the cemetery and then skirts the shores of the river north, back to Palermo. She sits on one of the benches along the iron fences around the park and thinks dully about loss and longing and the sweetness that connects the two; to explore the chaos that can seem so unavoidable at times, along her own path to order. She thinks of herself with a sneer and of the trickeries of destiny. She listens to the leathery tapping of the ferns against the metal railing behind her and wonders if indeed she herself will ever take root. She thinks about Italy, or at least she tries to, for her memories no longer reach that far back it seems. They tend to disintegrate in her mind on the decks of a ship and the weeks she had watched the ocean go by like an immovable crust of rock.

She knows that eventually she will succeed in picking up the routine of her life again, the way it has been for the past three years, as if nothing has happened; as though the sun has not actually warmed her that day with hope, while at the same time the pathetic sight of Paxi in his wheelchair has not frosted her soul right up again. It leaves her nauseated with sorrow.

She decides she will never speak about her visit to the Paxi house, not to Edmilce or Rosario. Instead, she will simply submerge herself again in the realities she has so far created for herself, that relentless stream of victims of fate and folly but for whom she will now be strong again, even if she herself has her own lost illusions to mourn.

No matter that in so many ways Buenos Aires has become home to her, today that has changed. And in spite of all its invigorating complexity she knows it will now also begin to annoy her, to put a moody and impatient energy around everything she does and sees. After today life will be just motion again, like it was before the Atlantic: movement without purpose.

<><><><><><><><>

As expected, Edmilce has left the light in the dining room turned on for her. Lydia has never noticed before how much the place reeks of antiseptic, how rolls of gauze and piles of towels are almost permanently strewn in almost every corner of the apartment. And it would not have surprised her if a strange woman suddenly crosses her in the parlor either, slouching her way to the kitchen for a cup of tea perhaps or some fruit from the basket on top of the table; some woman whose face she hasn't as much as glanced at before, with a name she never even bothered to remember.

She finds Edmilce sleeping on the bed in the guest room. She immediately recognises the girl's spongy pigtails like giant spider claws against the pillow. She pulls back quietly, carefully shutting the door and removing her shoes so as not to wake her and retreats down the hall. But a groggy growl calls her name behind the door before she can move away.

"Where have you been?" Edmilce whispers, as she half-sits up and then collapses softly back on top of the sheets again.

"Out, about; no place in particular"

"Tutto bem?"

"I am not sure. But it will be," Lydia replies. "Go back to sleep now. What are you doing sleeping here anyway?"

"Can never sleep...." The girl begins, but knows she needn't finish that sentence.

"Yes, I do know," Lydia says smiling.

Whenever Lydia isn't with her Edmilce is usually too restless to sleep and during the few times they have actually been apart that long she has paced up and down the apartment the entire time, like some panic-stricken animal looking for shelter. And each of those times, whenever she returned, Lydia found her either waiting up or sleeping in some strange place where in the end exhaustion had got the best of her. She knows Edmilce doesn't like being alone and that she will always be afraid of the dark.

She enters the room and sits down on the side of the bed. She gently pulls the covers up over the girl's shoulders and says, "Can I ask you something?" - as she studies the shimmer of the girl's skin in the dark. "How do you like this place, this town?"

As soon as she asks this she realises how predictable Edmilce's answer will be, as she also realises that in the past three years Edmilce has barely been outside.

"You thought it was a harsh place once," Lydia laughs. "And you were right about that; for the kind of women we see here it would be dangerous anywhere."

She cups the girl's round cheeks with her hands.

"It will always be you and me, won't it?" she adds, not quite revealing all she actually means to say.

"There is always a you and me," the girl whispers back.

"I have been thinking that it might be time we saw some of the country you and I."

"What country?"

"Well, this country, of course."

"Of course."

"Now, I just hope Rosario will let us leave. What do you think?"

It is now Edmilce's turn to laugh: "I think she will."

Saint II

Rosario turns up at around ten, as usual, to collect the two girls Lydia has treated the day before. It has been less than a week since Lydia saw Paxi and everything around her has felt off since. She can't help but notice that Rosario is slightly more agitated and ruffled than she usually is. Lydia watches her as she works herself out of her coat and flings it over the back of one of the chairs in the kitchen with a theatrical sweep and plants herself in front of her with an expression of one bagging to be interrogated.

"Somebody has been asking about you," she says, unable to wait for an invitation to divulge. But in Lydia's case that can take a while.

"What do you mean?" Lydia asks in return, unable to hide the fact she is bracing for just about anything by placing her spoon too delicately on the saucer, and wrapping her fingers too tightly around her cup of tea.

She adjusts her focus on Rosario's face from across the table, as she gets ready to speak again. But she decides against it. Instead, she watches Rosario play up the red on her cheeks from the cold morning she has just come in from.

"Let me see, what could I have meant when I said somebody has been asking about you.... It-was-a-MAN..." Rosario mocks with adolescent suspense.

Lydia only blinks her eyes once or twice, and carefully wets her lips on the rim of her cup.

"What man, you ask?" Rosario continues in light of Lydia's persistent silence. "Well, I don't know; I wasn't there. But one of the girls told me. She said some man she had never seen before — an Englishman - at one of the bars in Retiro, asked her if she knew a woman of about your age, named Lydia."

"What makes you think he was asking about me?"

"For one, when my friend asked what his Lydia's last name was, he said he didn't know; but that the woman he was talking about probably went by just Lydia – that his Lydia probably didn't use a last name at all."

"So?"

"So, nothing; my friend asked him if he was in the mood for a stroll around the park. He said no, gave her some money, and left. A true gentleman, she said, too."

"There could be a thousand women in Buenos Aires named Lydia, Rosario. What makes you think it was me he was asking about?"

"He described you pretty accurately, that's why."

"He described me? Who was this girl anyway? How does she know me; let me guess."

"Are you kidding? The immaculate one, all the hookers know you. Saint Lydia, remember?"

"Do you think it was the authorities – the man I mean?"

"I don't think so."

"You don't think so! In case you haven't noticed, I am performing abortions out of a residential building in the middle of the city, Rosario."

"Well, you are really famous in certain circles. I thought you might like to know that some man was asking about you. It might do you good, you know; a man," Rosario adds.

"Very thoughtful of you, but I don't like the idea of men asking about me in bars. Especially in bars frequented by you and your girlfriends."

"Oh, that's right, I forgot: you will have none of that. Again, it might do you good, a man."

Lydia rises slowly out of her chair.

"I believe it is time we concentrated on more pressing matters, don't you think?" she says, turning towards the door to the parlor. "Number one was still bleeding late last night. Unless you have a way of transporting her to a clean bed, I suggest you leave her here until tomorrow. Number two...."

"They have names, Lydia. Number one is called Carla, and number two, Julia."

Lydia turns to Rosario, but looks right past her.

"I don't care to know their names, Rosario. After what I do to them, I prefer not to. But if it's so important to you: Julia will be fine to leave today."

"You are a saint, you know that," Rosario then says rising out of her chair as well; her tone is filled with genuine affection and with a rather unique yet jaded form of gratitude.

"Please be careful," Lydia says at last, unable to resist.

She unsteadily takes a step forward and adds, "And you will let me know if this man, whoever he is, appears again?"

"You know I will."

They enter the spare bedroom where the girls, Carla and Julia, lay side by side on a large, matrimonial bed.

"Good morning, honey farts," Rosario sings, downplaying the moral crunch most of the girls usually struggle with after a night in the apartment.

"Julia, honey, I am going to help you with your clothes, so I can walk you home," Rosario says, and then turns her attention to the other girl, Carla, "How are you feeling? I hear you had a bitch of a night."

The girl whimpers lightly, and pulls the covers over her chin.

"Lydia says you should stay here another day, to get some strength back into you. I'll be back for you tomorrow."

"You will have the bed all to yourself," Lydia adds, still standing in the doorway and looking out into the hall. "And you will have enough time to think about how you are going to do things differently after you leave here."

"Why do you say that?" Rosario asks, reaching down to remove some strands of hair stuck to the girl's forehead.

"This is the last time she will be able to come here," Lydia replies, still directing her eyes away from the bedroom. "She has been here twice in the last year. And like I told her last night, her body won't take this a third time. She is simply not built for it. Not even considering that she is probably infertile by now, the next time she could kill herself. So, it is time she thought about things, that's all."

"I know," the girl responds, even though Lydia has not addressed her and turns away pulling the covers all the way over her ears.

"Some people's flesh is thin and softer than others'," Lydia continues, examining her own fingernails now. "Carla's flesh doesn't take stitches well, see; she rips and bleeds right through them. Maybe you can help her understand this."

"I understand," Rosario says, leaning in closer to the girl, who is still completely submerged. "But it isn't always a choice that is completely theirs to make, you know. Do you understand that?" Rosario adds, turning to face the door.

"No, I don't," Lydia says simply. "And that's exactly the point. I am not part of that, you are," - pushing herself forward to disappear down the hall.

Rosario follows after a moment and finds Lydia seated in the kitchen again, her arms stretched out in front of her and turning her tea around on the tabletop, her gaze spilt over the rim; her eyes not seeing. Rosario moves behind her to the stove and pours herself a cup as well. Julia appears in the doorway and remains standing, chin to her chest and fidgeting with the ends of her over-sized sweater with the air of a repenting child.

"Julia has something she wants to tell you before she leaves," Rosario says.

There is a pause before Julia utters thinly: "It's about what you said to Carla. I want you to know that I have thought about things; about what happened here last night, and all that."

As the girl begins to speak, a faint galloping in her words draws Lydia's attention to a stutter she has not noticed on the girl until now. She wonders if it had been there the night before, or if it is that they have not spoken enough for it to have become evident.

"Thank you for helping me," the girl stammers, "but I don't know how I can promise you that I will not be back to see you some day."

"Of course not," Lydia sneers, "and don't look for vocabulary you don't have."

Rosario starts to roll a cigarette, which Lydia has grown steadily into the habit of accepting going on two years now and meaning she could easily call herself a smoker by now, but doesn't.

"I've seen you with your hair down, so to speak, remember. The only way you are going to be able to promise yourself that you will not be back here and end up like your friend in there, is if you change your vocation.

And if you can't do that, the only advice I have for you is cotton balls."

Julia's gaze becomes unsteady and rather bumpy, while Rosario does all she can to keep the tea in her mouth from traveling up out of her nose behind a burst of laughter.

"Not sure I understand," Julia says after a while.

"You don't do you." Lydia replies calmly, in the least bit moved. "Stuff yourself with cotton balls before the next time you turn a trick. It will reduce your chances of you having to go through this again."

"How do you know this?" Rosario bursts out, quite unable to resist the temptation of kicking in an already open door.

Lydia ignores her.

"After you finish, remove the cotton and rinse yourself out. That is about all I can offer you."

Lydia tosses a frosty glare at the girl, and holds it there until Julia winces back.

Edmilce, who has been peeling bean pods in the corner of the kitchen and has remained perfectly invisible throughout the exchange, now stirs.

"I am going to make soup today. Is anyone staying for lunch?"

"No, thank you, honey bird," Rosario replies, chipper again. "I need to get this young lady home; she is actually looking a little pale to me suddenly."

"We got some meat yesterday," Edmilce quickly adds, as a way of upping her offer.

"If we could, you know we...."

But before Rosario can finish her sentence, Edmilce rises from the floor and leaves the room wiping her hands on her apron. She returns seconds later with a large wad of cotton, which she then pushes into Julia's hands before going back to her chores.

"Cotton balls – I will spread the word...." Rosario declares giggling while stuffing her scarf down the front of her coat.

<><><><><><><><>

That afternoon Carla's stitches rip for the third time, her insides too raw and damaged by now to sustain any kind of repair. Soon the hemorrhaging proves unstoppable, and she slips into shock within the hour.

Nothing like this has ever happened before, and no plan has ever been devised for an event like this. And now that it is upon them, they have no choice but to improvise to save the girl's life. Different options are discussed as to what should be done, but after closer consideration not one seems feasible. Arranging for outside help or transporting her anywhere will be far too costly in terms of time, which the girl clearly doesn't have. The risk of having to explain more than they can, once they make it to a hospital is also far too great.

Of course, Lydia has taken all sorts of measures to safeguard the clandestine nature of their activities. And inexplicable as it seems, none of her precautions even remotely cover the possibility that anything like this might ever actually happen. Has she started to believe all the nonsense that is being said about her, about her abortions being famously painless and always rather miraculously clear of complication?

Early on, Lydia doubled the salaries of each of the two doormen working in the building to ensure their absolute discretion. But asking either one of them to carry a bleeding prostitute out into the street?

Together with Edmilce, she works on Carla that entire night but they can do little more than collect the blood gushing through her stitches with fresh towels and prevent the mattress from getting soaked all the way through. In mounting desperation, they even attempt plastering the cervix with a mixture of candle wax and potato starch, in the hope it might help to slow the flow of blood. Carla, number One, expires in the matrimonial bed early the following morning.

As usual, Rosario returns to the apartment at about ten, and it takes little explaining once she sees the looks on Lydia and Edmilce's faces and the blotches of dried blood stuck to their faces and hair.

Hija de la gran puta – is how she sums it up - accurately.

221

The hardened edge of Rosario's streetwise demeanour proves a welcome breath of sobriety as she naturally takes charge – or seems to at least. But it is to be mid-afternoon before any real ideas begin to make their way around the kitchen table as to what should be done.

As far as anybody knows, Carla, number One, as Lydia morbidly insists on calling her, even well after they have wrapped her in a sheet of canvass Rosario manages to get her hands on, probably crossed the estuary from Uruguay some years prior, possibly around the same time Lydia did. Even if they want to, it will be close to impossible to inform any family, if there is any, without actually involving the authorities. The good news being, of course that the girl will thus unlikely be missed.

"Maybe we should come forward and face the consequences of what has occurred," Lydia argues at some point.

But to which Rosario barks back, "Do you need me to explain to you what those consequences are?"

"But it's absurd to think there are any other options, Rosario."

"I believe you have been to Caseros, haven't you?"

"Yes, I have been to Caseros."

"And have you thought what a detriment a jail term will be, to a lot more people than just the three of us here? Where is the sense in that?" Rosario argues time and again, as the three of them conspire around the kitchen table.

"And what kind of a sentence do you think we are going to get for burying a woman in the park, Rosario?" Lydia pushes back. "Make no mistake about it: whatever we have been doing here is over. Our choices are very simple, we either turn the situation over to the outside world, or...."

"Or what?" Rosario says, as she gargles and spits the remainder of cold tea in her cup to wash away the taste of dust that keeps collecting in the back of her throat.

Lydia sighs into the palms of her hands covering her eyes, and then in a tone that is severe, like clouds parting after a storm, she adds, "Will you let me take care of things my own way? Do you promise me you will not ask questions?"

"What are you thinking about?" Rosario asks

"I am thinking; let that be enough for now."

Lydia slowly rises glancing at her two companions with a determined sparkle that almost fools them into thinking that somehow, some yet undisclosed plan has already been set in motion. She reaches down the front of her dress and pulls out the money pouch that has become an integral part of her dress; an undergarment that has become as natural to her as the brassier it is always attached to. The size of the wad of bills causes Rosario to drivel unintelligibly as her eye balls dance in prefect time with Lydia's fingers counting the money.

"There is always a way to buy yourself out of a situation," Lydia says. "And what I need now is for the two of you to stay put until I come back."

"Where are you going?" Rosario manages, regaining her voice.

"For starters, I think it is time to pay out Don Aurelio's yearly salary," she says, referring to the doorman on duty downstairs. "But please, no more questions."

"Do you need me to come with you?" Edmilce offers, but wanting to say something quite different.

"Stay here, Edmilce."

"But you will need my help" the girl insists; though again her words a complete mismatch with wanting to express how terrified she is.

<><><><><><><><>

Edmilce, the pet, with her keen instincts and her gift for prophecy, has gone around chanting disassociated mantras for the past few days; punchy little verses pertaining to saints and other characters Lydia has never heard of before.

That night Lydia leaves the apartment feeling disemboweled and carries inside her mouth the familiar, bitter aftertaste of death. It is a foul dryness that can only be quenched by enduring the fact that here she is again toting around dead bodies. It is as if in the scheme of things, death is a way to announce that drastic changes are at hand. And what terrifies her the most is how well she can recognise herself in the midst of it all.

The doorman is sitting at his lacquered desk, situated between the stairwell and the heavy doors that are set with colored glass and iron in that curvy spaghetti-style that has blown over from Europe in recent years, and has steadily been marking the face of Buenos Aires. It seems almost comical that she should think about such a thing, and it only serves to underline the absurdity of what she is about to do.

She can see that the doorman is reading that morning's newspaper, probably for the tenth time by now, and the headlines on the front of it remind her she has been up for almost two days. Her hands still glow and feel strangely dry with the heat they still radiate.

"Good evening, Don Aurelio," she says descending the last of the steps to the main lobby; her voice in check, avoiding harsh and sudden bursts so as to not startle the old man too much. But in spite of her caution he crushes the paper with a single clap of his hands and springs out of his chair.

"Señorita Lydia, good evening," he stammers.

The doorman hops in place before her; as if she has just caught him hanging on the wrong side of the bottle of brandy she knows he keeps locked inside the second drawer of the desk.

"Well, that is a coincidence if I ever stumbled upon one," he adds, ineffectually adjusting the collar of his uniform. "Is there anything you need?"

"What do you mean, Don Aurelio, what is a coincidence?"

"Oh, that you happen to come down just now," he flounders. "I was just talking about you."

"You were talking about me?"

"Oh, nothing like that," he says, still fretting. "There was a gentleman here a little while ago asking for you. I said that if you weren't expecting him, I was not going to disturb you at this hour. I know you are quite keen on your privacy, see. But the gentleman didn't insist."

The doorman straightens his arms along the sides of his body and stands in attention.

"He did, however, ask me to give you something," he slowly adds.

From the way his eyes drop away from her she can tell he immediately regrets what he has just said.

"Well, I was going to come up," he pleads.

Lydia remains silent, letting him twist himself into the web he is spinning for himself and letting it be clear above all that coercion is to be the tactic she will use.

"I figured it was late, so I was going to walk up tomorrow morning."

"Don Aurelio, am I understanding this correctly?"

"No, Señorita Lydia, no. Please."

"Why didn't you come up sooner? I feel almost like you are leaving me no choice but to express my concerns to the superintendent."

"No, please."

"What were you asked to give to me?"

He reaches into the drawer of the desk, pulls out an envelope and extends it toward her.

"What time was the gentleman here?" she asks, as she runs her fingertips over the paper, as if trying to divine its content by mere touch.

"It must have been a half hour ago," the old man answers, a sense of looming catastrophe becoming painfully visible in the expression on his face.

She knows he is lying to her, but she also knows that beyond this point he will do anything she asks of him. She turns away to open the envelope and he discretely retreats against the wall.

Dear Miss Lydia, the paper reads.

I have been asked by a friend to find you, and to let you know that even in his current condition, he would much rather face the consequences of throwing coins into the river, than to have to live with the thought of never seeing you again. (his words)

I will return to speak to you in person.

Sincerely,

Roger Persival

She steps forward toward the doorman, who has turned himself into a salt pillar behind the desk.

"Did the gentleman say when he would be back?"

"No. What would you like me to do if he does?"

"Do not show him up. Do not tell him you have seen me. Tell him I am not receiving calls. Can I trust you will do this?" she says, sliding the sheet of paper into the envelope and then handing it back to him.

"Of course, of course. Would you like me to give it back?" he asks, holding the envelope in between his thumb and index finger away from his body — as though it might explode in his face at any second.

"Tell him you lost it. One look at you and he will have no problem believing that," she says and walks out into the street, her head spinning but still quite lucid about the fact that, as one of the very few certainties she still possesses, come morning no matter what, the body of a young whore will be good and buried somewhere.

Had anyone asked her which specific events would ultimately lead up to that particular point in time — and in which order - Lydia would probably have hidden behind her evasive silence to keep from having to lie.

But there is at least part of an answer in the fact that somebody is obviously looking for her. And therefore, that there is only one place she can go.

"I need to speak to mister Paxi," Lydia announces to Doña Marta.

The skin around the housekeeper's eyes looks swollen and taught; who is to say, from having dozed-off while reading on her bed perhaps. The housekeeper looks more confused than surprised now to see Lydia standing there.

The housekeeper doesn't seem to recognise her at first, but after a couple of weary squints her memory of a week earlier finally falls like cold syrup over her face. Although there isn't much hesitation to let Lydia enter the house, a discerning ripple of suspicion darkens the woman's face.

In the far end of the scarcely lit hallway Paxi's wicker chair emerges out of the study, easing forward on bicycle wheels. Lydia can tell he has had his hair cut since the last time she saw him. His face is also shaven and she feels that he makes a much cleaner impression overall, which also make his skin quite luminescent in a pumiced sort of way, too angled by the shadows that fall over it, reminiscent in every way of his ill health. He pushes himself forward and as he gets closer it is hard for her to read the expression on his face. There is a trace of victory there somewhere, but not the kind that expresses winning. It is a face cast rather on the receiving end of mercy.

He remains silent, waiting for her to speak.

"It isn't you throwing coins into the river that brings us together, you know," she finally says.

"What is it then, you suppose?"

"Death, Lissy. It's death."

He pushes his head slightly forward, studying her more closely in the shadows.

"I sent someone out to find you. Did he find you?"

"Of course he did."

"I will have Marta fix you a cup of tea. Let's go in," he says.

He skilfully flings the chair around and propels himself back down the hall. Lydia follows calmly; taking her time, as though all the urgency she felt getting there has faded by the fact she is now in his presence.

Once in the study he goes straight to the desk.

"Please forgive the state of the place," he apologises. "I have forbidden Martita to touch anything in this room."

The desk and the floor around her are littered with paperwork, as is the sofa to her right, which faces the glass doors to the garden.

"It looks like you are keeping busy," she comments.

"I am sorting through my life and it surprises me how much of an administrative endeavour it has been. I am planning to write my memoirs, I don't mind telling you."

"Isn't that something one does at the end of one's life?"

"I suppose," he replies, somewhat hiding a mischievous smirk that takes shape on his sunken cheeks, which only remotely reminds her of the man she met on the ship "But I take it you didn't come here to talk about me," he adds.

"That is not entirely true."

"Well, whatever the occasion it means the world to me that you are here," he says facing away from her, which leaves her wondering somewhat as to the extent of the sincerity of his words.

"You seem well," she then says, somewhat surprising herself.

"Flattering words," he replies; either a reaction or indeed quite a question. "And to think that it was ultimately my vanity that landed me in this contraption," he says lifting his palms to the air to refer to the wheelchair underneath him, very similar to how he had done the last time she saw him. Though only now does she notice how the rings on his fingers look far too large and heavy dangling from his papery hands. "It is my narcissistic streak that in the end is teaching me to be humble, Lydia — and isn't that just amazing?"

"I meant it," she presses. "You look quite capable, even in a wheelchair."

He keeps his hands suspended in the air and stares back at her; again with that expression on his face that so marks the self-absorbed moral high ground of the weak and the injured.

"The man you sent out to find me wrote me a note this evening. In it he seemed to have quoted you," she says. "He wrote to me that you couldn't bear the thought of not seeing me again."

Paxi smiles.

"I am sure he expressed it more eloquently than that."

"Yes, he did,"

She takes a step in his direction and at last does he lower his hands, grabbing the armrests as though it had not been she that moved but the chair itself.

"I can help you too," she says, not quite in command of herself anymore, but letting her words take shape inside the room all by themselves.

"There was a time when I would have laughed, had anyone said that to me. Now I don't mind telling you that I think you are probably right."

"But for now it is me who needs your help" she adds. "I think you are the only person who can help me."

"Death, you say?"

He moves his gaze away from her as she lays out the situation for him in backward chronology. She speaks evenly, her voice in perfect time with the metronome of her objectivity; as if the girl Carla and all the implications connected to her being dead at the apartment, are all part of a history that again is spawning out of her.

"You do understand for how long they will put you in jail for performing an abortion?" is all he says, directing his words toward the shadows around them, as though it were taking him great effort to actually look at her.

He lightly taps the skin on his forehead with the tips of his fingers, like one thinking through some complicated equation for which he no longer needs to address her directly, but has become abstract and disassociated from a realm in which it is just the two of them.

She notices his thumb turning the lapis lazuli ring from the inside of his hand. And quite unexpectedly, she imagines what it would be like to be touched by him, the way he is now, if indeed his touch would feel the way she has always imagined it would.

"Of course I know that I will rot in prison for performing an abortion," she replies. "But what worries me, Señor Paxi, is that I have been performing them for past three years - a hundred of them. What worries me, Señor Paxi, is that my house has become something of a butcher shop we happen to live in. Now, that is the thing that worries me."

He stares at her in mocking disbelieve, doing all he can to pretend he is being thrown off by what she is telling him.

"I would say you are joking if I didn't know better...." he then whispers, right before he scatters out laughing.

"And to think that I had started to lose my faith in humanity...." he says.

"Well, I am glad I was able to humor you."

"Strange, because if there is one thing that is absolutely essential for doing what you have been doing, it should be a sense of humor. Obviously, I am still learning something new every day."

He falls silent for a moment as he tries to think back to the last time he had actually heard himself laugh. Meanwhile she realises that she never has. He lifts his hand and she instinctively raises hers to meet it; his touch making her light-headed and she closes her other hand over it to keep herself from toppling over.

For a split-second, their eyes morph into a single view of a future that for the first time is not being written by some destiny running rampant, but one of their own making. His hand is neither cold nor clammy but soft and clean, and clearly belonging to a body that has been broken yet in complete control of itself.

He pulls her closer and presses his lips against the roof of her hand, as though he has been reading her thoughts. And as she fights back the urge to run her fingers through his hair, she remembers all the metaphors that describe a thing like this; how the feel of a man's breath can ignite flames when held against a woman's skin; that merely the touch of a man's lips can evoke inside a woman a peculiar craving she so far has only likened to being devoured entirely.

She might as well have been spinning around the room by the time his lips finally come loose from her hand and her feet touch ground again.

He lets go and stares up at her, his face filled with the tracks of self-reflection that have passed over it in recent times. He pulls back his chair as well, but never disconnects his eyes from hers and motions toward the sofa.

"Please wait for me," he says. "I won't be long"

He pushes himself toward the door.

"What are you going to do?"

"Help," he answers rather dark, but amusing himself at the same time, it seems, with private thoughts, and adds, "I sense travel in the air."

"What do you mean?"

"It isn't rhetorical; that is exactly what I mean. I won't be long," he repeats and disappears through the door.

She lowers herself on the edge of the sofa and wrings her hands, reflecting on the fact that they have just been inside his. She looks around the room at the strewn papers everywhere, as they remind her of when the functionary used to work through his notes; he too had been a man who could afford to bother with such detail, she thought to herself.

She reaches down for a sheet out of the pile next to her and lets her eyes feather over it, barely picking out the content. She notices that the writing is neither in Spanish nor Italian. From the occasional squiggle over the vowels, she precariously assumes it is Portuguese. A portion of the text then seems to jump at her from the bottom of the page. She feels she recognises the order of the words, as though she has seen them before. But her focus is too loose to really connect it to a particular place or time. She lets her eyes dance over the bottom of the page a bit more, and then a date: 1899, which initially seems to hold no meaning, dances before her as if nudging her to pay close attention. She marvels at how the wavy curls dance around it to form an illegible signature she is almost certain is not Paxi's underneath it. And it is then that the writing falls into place: Trés Corações.

In a way that could easily suggest that the paper can unexpectedly catch flame, she returns it to the exact same spot she has picked it from and fixes her eyes on the black window across the room. Looking away from the paper pile requires more strength than she expected. She rises to pull herself free from it and walks toward the window. She cups both hands on the glass to obscure the reflection of the lamp on the desk, taking a dishonest interest in the view outside - anything to keep from being pulled back to the papers now palpitating on the leather.

Only minutes later, although it feels like hours, the door finally opens again and Paxi re-enters.

"I promise I will explain," he says, halting before her, seeing her eyes aflame with vex and surrender at the same time.

"In case you are having trouble dealing with the inevitable right now," he says, "know that it isn't out of disrespect. But there is little you – or I, now that I am implicated, can do about any of this. I think it is pretty obvious what should be done," he continues, not in the least bit hindered by the fact that he still isn't making much sense to her.

But he repeats, "There is nothing anyone can do."

"Can you help me, Lissy?" she then says in a voice weary and frail. "Because," she adds, "I need to get back – and I need to get back with answers either way."

At that moment the door behind him opens rather soundlessly. She has to bat her eyes twice to stall the rest of what she has intended to say, things that were meant for no-one else but Paxi to hear. It isn't the housekeeper that enters the room, as she had expected. It is an elegantly dressed man instead, whom she has never seen before – but who needs little introduction at this stage.

"Lydia, I would like you to meet an old friend of mine, Mr Roger Persival," Paxi says, tilting his head to the man standing behind him smiling handsomely at her.

Roger Persival has the kind of posture one might associate with the sway of sunflowers or heads of corn perhaps. There is a lightness about him, but also a stillness in his gaze, which seems to point to a history that is unnerving as much as dark, and which draws her attention due only to the fact that he keeps it hidden so well. He is also clearly a man who enjoys the type of grooming that reaches much farther than mere upbringing and has more to do with lineage than anything else. She can tell he is at least ten years older than Paxi and that in spite of his red curls, his tailored suit and the handmade boots on his feet, one might also wager that he and Paxi are related somehow – or at least that they can easily reach common ground in just about everything. The words inside her have stalled permanently it seems, deep inside her.

He greets her cordial; carefully dozing not his words but his gestures.

"Roger has been my presence in Buenos Aires, for years," Paxi says. "He is the person I have trusted to watch over my affairs in my absence, since I first came to this town."

He turns his chair to face both of them now.

"But, as always, I am being far too elaborate. I almost forgot that the two of you have already corresponded," he adds dividing his gaze between them.

"Does he know?" Lydia asks, unable to get a full grip on her tone of voice, and therefore revealing.

"Everything," Paxi replies, shrugging carelessly. "You asked me for help and this is help. Roger is the best you could hope for in light of the predicament you're in – the predicament we are all in."

He rolls his chair to face her again, and adds, "I mean, you don't expect me to do any heavy lifting, now do you?"

"What are you talking about?"

"Lydia..." Roger Persival then speaks for the very first time.

She finds his voice rather flat – too ordinary, perhaps, and it matches in no way the impression he has made on her so far. He speaks the kind of Spanish one often hears by the docks and the market halls; pitch of voice a bit too high and his delivery too nasal for a man dressed the way he is.

"I am going to drive you back to the apartment," he says. "Lissy is going to be coming with us."

"I wouldn't miss this for the world," Paxi cuts in and it is the childish gleam she sees in his eyes that greatly adds to her concerns.

However, in the next half hour, the more she learns about what they have in mind the more she understands that there is nothing else that can be done.

<><><><><><><>

It hasn't been very often that Lydia has surrendered so completely to a situation in which she herself has had so little a hand. And the fact Paxi has played an indispensable part in two of those instances, she can not have found any more significant.

Within the hour she is seated next to Paxi in Roger Persival's Studebaker, heading back to Palermo. Hardly a word is spoken the entire way; there is just the streets rushing past her in the window, as the stranger maneuvers his vehicle through them with ease and routine. Paxi is slouched on the leather next to her and does not for a moment take his eyes off her, boldly studying her; either remembering or perhaps relishing a future that has not been there for him before tonight.

The car stops in front of the apartment building and through the flowery patterns on the glass door to the entrance she can see the doorman breathing heavily with his chin on his chest behind the desk, as she expected. The stranger shuts off the engine and the three of them sit motionless for a moment, silently running their thoughts over their plan; a plan that seems perfectly sensible, if not for the fact that it seeks to gamble them straight into the arms of destiny.

Finally, Roger Persival pulls the gloves from his hands and slaps them together into his bare palm, signaling it is time to proceed. He climbs out of the vehicle and walks around to open the door for her. As she reaches to take his extended hand, she feels Paxi gently gripping her arm from the

233

back seat. She turns to him and tries to measure the mischievousness of the grin that has stretched across his face, one that is lopsided and hollow now, but which, for her, will still distinguish him from any other man on earth. And it is at that moment that she understands that it is more than the broken bones of a cripple she will eventually set out to heal but the mind of absolute lunatic as well.

"There are places, not very far from here," he says to her, "where no human being has ever been before, you know," in a voice strangely filled with reflection — as he savors with his mad glare the texture of her lips.

She does not respond, afraid somewhat that if she makes even one sound, moves even one finger, the thing she now feels will be cut loose forever. So, she tries to envision the kind of place he is attempting to describe.

She walks into the building and holds the door for Roger Persival, who follows closely behind her pushing Paxi's empty wheelchair. The only reaction from Don Aurelio, still sunk deeply in his boredom-induced slumber behind the desk is a faint shift in his breathing, which escalates into a series of broken-off snores, before it rolls back, with a smacking of the lips to start the whole process all over again. And it isn't until Lydia is standing directly in front of him that he finally opens his eyes, springs to his feet, licking his mustache like a cat being tickled.

"Señorita," he stutters, still disconnected from his body, still mindless from the lather of sleep.

"Good evening, Don Aurelio," Lydia says formally.

"Is it? — evening?" he says, groping a glance at the clock on the wall and then to Roger Persival next to her.

"Don, Aurelio, there is something I need you to do," she says, placing her palms flat on the desk and leaning in toward him.

"Of course," the doorman fumbles on.

"Actually, Don Aurelio, there are several things...."

"Of course."

She turns her head toward the end of the hall and then back towards the doorman again, who stands biting his facial hair to shreds now.

"First, I will need you to listen very carefully," she says. "You must first forget that you ever saw me tonight — we never spoke. Is that clear?"

The doorman nods his head reluctantly, but still aware that he is condemned to do whatever she asks of him.

"Then," she continues, "I would like to lock you up in the broom closet for about half an hour. I will need you to give me your keys and remain inside it very quietly, until I let you out again."

"But Señorita, you cannot ask me to do that. It's impossible — it could cost me my job — or who knows, worse...."

"I considered that, and that is why I also want to give you this...."

She produces an envelope from the side pocket of her coat and places it on the desk between them. She takes her hands from it and looks intently into his eyes once more.

"If it ever comes to that, Don Aurelio, I think you will find comfort in what I am giving you now," she says, glancing at the envelope. Think of it as an incentive to make up for the fact you neglected to give me a most important message earlier this evening, and for your snoring being the only greeting I received from you upon my return just now."

He drills his eyes into hers, buttons up the jacket of his uniform and fixes the cap on his head.

"I was in the Brazilian war, you know."

"I did not know that. Were you a brave soldier, Don Aurelio?"

"One of the bravest; never captured and never injured."

"There is valor in getting out of a war in one piece, I always felt," she says. "There is no doubt in my mind that you have an instinct for it, survival I mean."

"I survive, Señorita. I always do," he responds, oozing slightly too much pride as he steps out from behind the desk pulling at the hem of his jacket one last time and then slowly leading the way to a small door underneath the stairs.

"You should know that it is thanks to the bravery of our soldiers that we are the great nation we are today," he says.

"I could not agree with you more."

She places the envelope in his hands as he continues to march away from her. "I hope this will help to remind you how much we all have to thank the men who sacrificed so much."

He opens the door to the closet and remains standing for a moment, sunk in thought, musing almost.

"It was an honor to serve," he says gaping into the narrow dark space before him, as he shakes his head at the disarray the brooms and mops were in.

He reaches in, wraps his heavy arms around the poles and stacks them neatly up against the wall.

"War is a nasty business, you know...."

"I can only imagine how gruesome," she replies soothingly.

He inspects the closet one more time.

"But you are a brave woman, Señorita."

"I sure try to be."

He bends forward and upturns one of the empty buckets in the corner of the closet, wipes off some cobwebs and dirt from the metal surface, and then, with the sultry, self-fulfilled melodrama so often found in military men, sits down on top of it; his back as straight as he can possibly line it, as though he is unwilling somehow to allow himself even the smallest amount of comfort.

"Your keys, Don Aurelio."

He reaches into his pocket and sorts through the bunch, before he presents her the right key.

"We are a great nation, Señorita," he repeats.

"That we sure are, Don Aurelio," she says shutting the door between them and turning the lock.

<><><><><><><><>

She hurries past Roger Persival, who has not moved away from the desk the entire time. He follows her silently, and it isn't until they stand inside the elevator that he finally speaks.

"I feel there is a difference between a country that has great things and one that could actually be considered great" — a remark that seems thought-through. Yet, it surprises her all the same to hear him reflect on such a thing.

She calmly directs her eyes away from him and gets lost in a stare directed at the bent metal that decorates the railings of the stairwell sinking past them as they ascend toward the fourth floor. Lydia rarely uses the elevator, which runs in a shaft through the middle of the apartment building. Other than when she needs to help Rosario escort one of the girls back to the street after a stay at the apartment she generally prefers using the stairs, a self-inflicted discomfort that has always had a purifying effect on her – something that helps to remind her she is still bound by earthly things.

She motions for Roger Persival to wait while she enters the apartment first, so she can prepare Rosario and Edmilce for what is about to happen. Once inside she is greeted by the rolling sound of the chairs in the kitchen, as the women spring out of them upon hearing the front door. Through the familiar smells that characterise the place she has called home for the past three years, she feels rather overcome by the sweet, discerning aroma of death in the air as well; the perfume that rises right before decomposition begins to take hold on flesh.

Edmilce and Rosario run out to meet her, both jabbering at once demanding explanations as to what took her so long to return. But she pushes them back into the kitchen and lays out as evenly as she can the extent of the situation. She says that there isn't much time to explain and does her best to not reveal how numb and disengaged she feels.

She waits for a torrent of questions and the protests against the decisions that have been being made on their behalf to pass. But neither come. If anything, Rosario and Edmilce look tired, worn, though also angry all the same from having waited for her almost the entire night. The apartment makes her feel feverish and cold now.

She eases out of the kitchen and into the hall again to signal for Roger Persival to enter. So far, she has only seen him in dim-lit corners and in the darkened interior of the car. And as he stands in the cold, electric light spilling down from the ceiling, it is the skin of his hands that now sends a disconcerting wave of emotions through her. His fingernails are perfect squares based solidly on the tips of his fingers. The skin around them is not only translucently white, with the veins and joints erratically marking them with shades of blue and pink, but they are quite handsomely wrinkled as well, which makes them rather immaculate-looking, precisely the way she remembers her father's hands had been.

"Ladies," he says, "I trust it has been explained to you what it is I am doing here," - with an accent that is still hard for Lydia to localise and which she rashly fantasises is neither Spanish not Portuguese but something of a combination thereof; Basque perhaps. "I am going to need you do exactly as I ask," he adds with a look on his face that is almost priest-like.

Rosario glares back, innately resisting probably everything that will come out of his mouth. Edmilce next to her just balls her fists; it is anybody's guess what she is thinking. Then, simultaneously, their eyes move to Lydia, who now rests her entire weight on both arms like poles on the table. All she can do is to nod, feeling too wrecked to actually lift her head to look back at them.

"Sweetheart, you need to sit down," Rosario says once she notices how Lydia is about to topple over with exhaustion.

She moves around the table and wraps an arm around her. A mere glance from Rosario is all Edmilce needs for her to spring into action as well. She reaches over to relight the fire under the kettle, a reflex she has developed at Lydia's side and which adheres to the rule that in times of crisis one must always have hot water at one's disposal. As Lydia slides sideways into the chair in front of her, Roger Persival too steps in her direction and places his hand on her shoulder.

"Do you need me to explain to them what we discussed?" he asks her in a fatherly tone and with the kind of expression on his face she prefers not to see.

"I will be alright," she says.

"You must rest," he argues softly.

"Just give me a moment."

He turns to Rosario and Edmilce and says, "Could either one of you please show me to the young lady?" — referring, so they assume, to the dead body in the other room, attributing a human quality to a thing that has become quite abstract to them already, subsequently putting an eerie but sobering chime on the situation. All heads turn toward him as he speaks and it leaves them wondering at which point they each had stopped remembering the dead girl they hardly knew, but whose death they caused, each in her own way.

"And what do you think you are going to do there?" Rosario hisses under her breath, putting up her usual street-fighter-front, the one she tends to reveal whenever she is feeling particularly lost.

Roger Persival arches his eyebrows and elegantly abstains from the expected reaction. Instead, he intensifies his attention on Lydia, who seems to have shrunk even farther onto her own frame.

"I am going to put the young lady in this chair," he finally says in a tone that is even more sugar-coated than before, and takes a small, controlled step in the direction of Rosario. "And after I do that," he adds, "I am going to walk out of this apartment with her. For now, this is all you need to know. Will you show me where she is?"

Rosario's face twists itself into an over-expression of hostility, the way a small child might do whilst arguing on the playground as to whose turn it is on the swing. But she moves slowly in the direction of the door nevertheless, somewhat over-dramatizing her reluctance.

"This way," she says moving past him. "She is starting to stink."

"It hasn't been long enough," he responds sagely.

"Then it is me that smells," Rosario says, leading the way through the hall.

Lydia wipes her hair from her face and looks at Edmilce, who stands staring back at her no longer expecting answers. But Lydia doesn't seem to want to offer them either. Edmilce turns to pour boiling water into a cup and then places it in front of her.

"I think it is best if we left," Lydia says, as she motions toward the chair next to her for the girl to sit.

Edmilce cocks her head and seems to hesitate; seemingly struggling with what Lydia is trying to say.

"By this time tomorrow, Edmilce, we will have left Buenos Aires. We have outstayed our welcome here."

She pauses to allow the girl to ask her all the obvious questions. But Edmilce remains mute and unassuming.

"Is your husband coming with us?" she asks instead.

"Who do you mean?"

The girl cocks her head again, genuinely confused by the absurdity of Lydia's question.

Lydia smiles.

"He is downstairs, waiting in a car. He will be back for us tomorrow evening."

"What about Rosario?"

What about me? - sounds from the door opening.

"I don't know what your friend is planning to do in the bedroom. But he asked to be left alone," she says entering the kitchen and pulling out a chair for herself.

Edmilce sits up and Lydia follows her example, with effort.

"What about me?" Rosario repeats, revealing tension; not in her voice but in the way her eyes fix themselves on the two of them.

"You need to go home Rosario," Lydia says. "Nobody knows you have been here. This doesn't need to be your concern."

"You seem to forget," Rosario says, snapping at once, "that it is me who brought - the young lady — here," - mocking Roger Persival by pursing her lips and lifting her nose into the air. "Who do you think they are going to want to talk to when the young lady turns up missing? Not my concern, you say?"

"That's fair," Lydia says almost whispering. "But do you understand what needs to happen now?"

"What do you think?"

"And are you willing — or able to face those consequences?"

"Do I have a choice?"

"You always have a choice, Rosario."

From the sound of the footsteps in the hallway they can approximate the added weight of Carla's corpse now in the wheelchair. They listen to Roger Persival halt by the front door and then as his footsteps move back toward the kitchen. He stands in the doorway looking at no one in particular, but lingering his gaze unseeingly on Lydia several times.

"You don't need to go back down with me," he says. "I trust you will take care of the rest."

"Yes" Lydia replies. "As agreed."

"I think you would be wise to rest up."

"I think we all would be," she adds. "I feel like thanking you."

"Then thank me," he says.

Lydia's smile, being even more weary and tired than before, is somewhat brighter now and actually shows relief.

◇◇◇◇◇◇◇◇

In the distance, from the inside pocket of her coat hanging in the hall, the dreamed jingle of Don Aurelio's keys jolts her out of her sleep. It is almost half past one in the afternoon. Edmilce is still breathing evenly next to her on the bed. In the window hangs the nothingness of a Sunday morning. But she has lost track of her week all together. Like a smudge, the image of the daytime doorman, who was due to start his shift at eight that morning pollutes her thoughts. And subsequently, so does the image of Don Aurelio locked inside the broom closet.

She shakes Edmilce.

"Get Rosario up and start packing," she says, before she slides into her boots and hurries out of the apartment and down the stairs, either unable or unwilling to fully imagine the extent of the situation she is running toward.

Before the last curve of the stairs she pauses. She hears the daytime doorman, Carlitos, talking to one of the cleaning women. Mixed inside their conversation she distinguishes the clunking of buckets and the sloshing of mops on the stone floor. She fixes her hair blindly as best she can and tentatively descends into view.

"Señorita."

"Carlitos, is everything alright."

"Well, yes. Why?"

She pulls the keys out of her coat.

"I found these on my floor. Had you not missed them?"

"Well, no, Miss Lydia. I wouldn't know how they got there. Aurelio said nothing to me about them being missing."

"He was...."

"He left this morning, a little before eight, after I got here."

The daytime doorman then pulls an almost identical set of keys out of the drawer of the desk, and holds it up to her.

"This is the bunch he gave me, as he always does."

She figures it must be the look of confusion on her face that encourages him. He tosses a quick and rather gloating glance at the cleaning woman, who has her ears pricked up to catch every word that is said.

The doorman turns to Lydia again and relaxes his shoulders somewhat.

"We keep a second set of keys, you see. Just in case — obviously."

"Obviously," Lydia repeats.

"I will ask Aurelio but he didn't mention anything."

"Now, no more than out of curiosity," she says, "where do you keep them? The spare set I mean."

"Well, Miss Lydia, you do understand that we are not in the habit of sharing that particular bit of information with just anyone," he says with smugness well camouflaged inside his dutiful tone. "But, of course, you are not just anyone," he adds quickly. "We keep an extra set in the broom closet — behind the bleach and the vinegar," he concludes, pantomiming a whisper that is loud enough for the cleaning woman to hear loud and clear.

Lydia just stares at him, not even bothering to react.

"I am so embarrassed," the doorman then says, the grin on his face underlining his insincerity as ever before.

"And Don Aurelio, he did not mention anything at all?"

"No, Señorita, he did not."

He unassumingly takes the keys from her and begins to move in the direction of the closet. He jovially tosses the bunch around his finger several times and then stops halfway there.

"But now that you mention it, Aurelio did say something rather strange to me before he went home this morning."

"Really? What was that?"

"He is a funny old man you know," he adds, ineffectively stifling a mean little giggle.

"He asked me if I knew the lyrics to the national anthem. Crazy!"

"And?"

"And what?"

"Do you know them?"

"Of course not."

"Well, perhaps, you should learn it," she says, burning her glare right

242

through him.

She turns away from him and starts up the stairs feeling the fever in her legs and more than a bit suspicious about her own need to be invisible, that longing which will at time rise inside of her, of wanting to be smoke or nothing at all; a memory if that.

Back in the apartment she finds Edmilce and Rosario standing in the parlor, surrounded by a pile of trunks and baskets. In her hands Edmilce also holds a glass jar. Inside it flutter a half dozen moths she has been collecting around the house for the past two days.

"What's this?" Lydia asks.

But it is mainly the look of complete helplessness on their faces that infuriates her.

"We packed, as you said," Edmilce responds in a tone that sooner belongs to a child ten years younger than to a young woman probably of about sixteen or seventeen, or whatever her exact age might be at this point.

"I don't have anything to pack," Rosario adds, defending herself but quite unsure from what exactly.

"You won't need much, Rosario," Lydia says, perhaps more crassly than she intended, before she turns to Edmilce again and the jar of moths in her hands. "You are allowed one valise, Edmilce. No bugs. Please, no bugs."

"But they're everywhere," the girl says. "Haven't you seen them?" she adds pointing to the curtains as she holds Lydia's glare pleadingly. "They are in the beds, inside the pans in the kitchen – everywhere!"

"What are you saying, Edmilce, that you would like to take them with you?"

It has not been very often that Lydia has seen fear in the girl's eyes, and it sickens her to think what it means to see it now.

"No bugs, Edmilce" she repeats. "And as for you" – she turns to Rosario, "I have clothes that will fit you. Don't worry." she pushes out, banishing with all her strength from her voice the contempt she feels toward them both.

Just a few minutes past eight o'clock that evening, as has been agreed, they descend the stairs single file and out through the front door of the building, led by Roger Persival, to the Studebaker parked on the curb. Each of the women carry no more than one suitcase and an erased expression on her face to go with it.

Don Aurelio has just started his night shift and stands in attention behind the desk as they pass him. He stares blindly into the distance as Lydia pauses at the front door. She puts down her suitcase and turns to him. He shifts his weight, clearly hiding his discomfort as she approaches.

"I want to say Goodbye, Don Aurelio."

He tenses his lips.

"All the best to you," she adds and moves away again, respecting his silence.

Then he says, in a sultry whimper, dry and grinding and producing almost no sound, "You forgot about me last night."

She turns to face him.

"You let yourself out. The envelope I gave you, did you open it?"

"No, I did not."

"Will you?"

"Eventually."

"You're a good man, Don Aurelio."

"Yes Miss."

<>◇◇◇◇◇◇◇◇

In the back of the car, Edmilce wedges herself between Lydia and Rosario. She hasn't said a word the entire day. But then again, Edmilce isn't one to ask too many questions in the first place. As always, she follows in whichever direction Lydia's path might happen to pull her, simply drifting on the consequential stream of Lydia's life.

They drive away from the Plaza Italia, out of Palermo and on toward the outskirts of town. They leave Buenos Aires in the choke hold of a reverberating kind of silence, which remains with them until they have well entered into the countryside, where night predominates and is broken only by an occasional speck of light from a bonfire along the road.

Had anything been said at all before then, it would undoubtedly have been in the form of questions none of them have the right answers to anyway; beyond perhaps, how much they now are part of some traveling pack of misfits, strange to the world at large but drawn together by the histories each carry inside.

On occasion, Paxi will brave the pain it causes him to turn around in the front seat to glance at the three of them. His eyes will be watchful, but his gaze will never last long enough for it to be considered too observant. Still, a peculiar alertness has pulled itself taut across his face, as a mischievous flicker clearly shows how much he has missed the adventure of travel.

It is Rosario who finally speaks.

"I don't believe I have properly introduced myself to either one of the gentlemen," she says, glancing meaningfully over at Lydia, who has not stopped jabbing at the night outside with an uninterrupted stare. "I feel that I should," Rosario says, "before I carefully ask where it is they are taking us."

Roger Persival, never taking his eyes off the road, briefly tightens his eyelids in the mirror in what Rosario only guesses is a smile. She watches his eyelids widen as Paxi clears his throat to speak.

"My name is Ulisse Gavino Paxi — or at least, what is left of him. Before I became a cripple my friends used to call me Lissy."

"I still call him that," Roger Persival interrupts, adding. "Even now that he is a cripple."

"And that is what I would like you to call me as well, Rosario," Paxi continues, ignoring the comedy at his expense. "If you care to, of course."

He pauses for a moment and glances at the road ahead.

"You may even have heard of me."

"Please tell me more" Rosario says, "I may start to remember," - she now too is unable to resist the invitation to be cruel.

"There will be plenty of time for that," Paxi replies. "But I believe it were introductions you wanted. So, if you will allow me, the gentleman conducting this sublime piece of machinery is my good friend, Mister Roger Persival."

"I am delighted to make your acquaintance, Rosario," Roger Persival says. "And you are right, we didn't get of a chance to talk much yesterday."

"Are you an Englishman, Mr. Persival?" Lydia then asks, coming in from the night outside.

"Welsh, actually. I helped Paxi arrange a crossing back in '92. We've been friends ever since."

"What kind of crossing was it?" Rosario asks, coyly confused.

"Lissy and I helped some of my countrymen settle in the mid-western United States – wheat fields mainly."

"What is it you do, Mr Persival?" Lydia then asks, her tone slightly more amber.

"I am a businessman."

"That doesn't really cover any specifics," Lydia replies.

"After Nebraska, Lissy convinced me to visit Buenos Aires. And there are quite a number of specifics, as you say, that have kept me here ever since. I own an interest in several construction companies back in town and also in a place at the foot of the Andes, which I hope you will enjoy as much as I have over the years."

"Is that where we are going?" Rosario asks.

"For a while, yes." Paxi replies. "Mendoza is where we will wait for spring."

"Why?"

"Because I want to show you the Pacific."

"Does you being a businessman include burying young women in the night, Mr. Persival?" Lydia asks, as though remembering something she had meant to touch upon.

"No, it doesn't, generally," he replies, unflinching. "But if you are referring to the young woman, whose death you caused, Lydia, I lowered her body into the river. The bottom of the estuary is quite muddy, you know. Whatever sinks into it is most unlikely to ever come up again. But, I am also curious," he adds quickly, "now that we are getting to know each other. Where did you acquire your skills as a midwife?"

"You are the last two I would have suspected of such bad taste," Paxi snaps, his voice going off on a badly controlled slip.

It makes silence descend upon them again, either merely to reflect on Paxi's dominance or privately to reject it.

"I may be a cripple," he adds, "but I can still demand sensitivity from those who have bound themselves to me."

"You sound as insane as you ever did, Signore Paxi," Lydia remarks from the backseat.

"And that is probably the best bit of news I have heard since you showed up at the house yesterday, dear."

"But he is right," Edmilce says. "We should never again speak of the dead girl," - in a voice that is a bit sinister, only for the mundane reason that she has not yet opened her mouth today. "Instead, we should all be grateful" she slowly adds.

"Oh, you are just superstitious, like all Brazilians," Rosario then says, and to which Edmilce replies in a way that is as cryptic as it is simple and unpretending.

"There is always a plan, Rosario. Even you being here is part of one; just don't forget to be grateful."

Edmilce's words echo inside the car as the night expands around them, a black, dusty blanket brushing up against the flare of the headlights. It hangs over a flat and invisible landscape that only magnifies the reasons each one of them has for being stuck inside of it.

<><><><><><><><>

It's just a few minutes before three in the morning when they pull off to the side of the road and halt in front of a two-story building, which, had they been able to actually see it, might have turned out to be as wide as a small city block. The outline of the structure is a loosely contrived shadow against the night sky, except for the flicker of a single oil lamp suspended right in the middle of it.

"Are we there?" Paxi asks, lifting his head out of his chest.

"We are there," Roger Persival answers him.

"What's happening?" Rosario croons, coming out of a suspended sleep as well.

Both men simultaneously turn toward the backseat to watch the reluctant wave of movement that passes over it, as the three women take a moment to regain their sense of orientation.

"We will stop here for the night," Paxi says. "In the morning we will arrange for petrol and continue."

"To the foot of the Andes?" Rosario asks, her voice warm and still somewhat sugary from a surprisingly replenishing sleep.

"Yes."

Roger Persival climbs out of the vehicle and comes around to Paxi's side.

"It'll do you good to stand for a while," he grunts softly into the other man's ear, under the strain of lifting him out of the front seat and onto his feet. "Get the circulation going," he adds.

He then locks his arm around him and begins moving toward the watery flame up ahead. Rosario too stumbles out into the open, but she remains with her back pressed against the side of the car; the darkness around them perhaps a bit too vast and abysmal; without a horizon, seamlessly blending sky and earth around her. She lights a cigarette and bends forward stomping her feet to shake the sawdust out of her head.

Edmilce climbs out as well and follows the two men toward the house, cautiously testing the ground under her feet as she moves. She sees them halt at a door that materialises in front of them. She is now able to distinguish them better against the solid surface, on which Roger Persival pounds his fist after releasing one hand out of the hold he has around Paxi. But her habitual sense of devotion toward Lydia somewhere behind her, out of sight in the dark, beckons her attention back to the cloud of dust that still envelops the car.

As she step-foots her way back, she can see Rosario's face lighting up orange, as she intermittently puts the cigarette to her lips to take in smoke.

"It is some kind of pension, I think" Edmilce says once she reached her, though quite in passing; a statement in no way meant as conversation.

She leans in to look inside the car, but finds the backseat empty and quickly turns toward the night again. She could ask Rosario as to the direction in which Lydia might have walked off, but she doesn't. Instead, she walks right past her and steps into the blackness once more, hardly aware of it now, thinking only of Lydia and of Lydia's obsession she has come to recognise so well over the years of needing to prove to herself - and to everyone else - how easily she can still walk away from everything to tread her own path.

"Lydia! Lydia!" Edmilce calls, breaking up the night around them with the rising pitch of anguish resonating in her voice.

Less than a minute goes by like an eternity, until she can finally hear footsteps grinding their way toward her, but approaching her from different directions all at once.

"Lydia?"

When Lydia's voice is finally upon her, reassuring her with soothing words, as always, I am here, Edmilce. I am here, the fact that it emerges from behind her gives the girl a start that makes both her feet temporarily come up from the ground.

"I am here," Lydia repeats, only too familiar with the effects her disappearing can at times have on Edmilce and gently rests her palm on the spongy surface of the girl's scalp. "It isn't often we get to experience total darkness," Lydia says, matching perfectly with her tone the cruelty of her words to the affection she also feel for the girl.

And, as always, Lydia wonders to what extent Edmilce has understood that her stroll through the dark had been just another way of testing her.

Edmilce wonders if she will ever possess enough vocabulary to express how she feels the following morning, how on the Pampa, morning itself is a process; that it comprises no more than two primary elements: color and heat.

She could express that the landscape is flat alright, uneventful perhaps, too. But will Edmilce ever be educated enough to describe that it is the bellowing emptiness that actually makes it rich with diversion, with surprises behind every dusty stone? Or that it awakens her senses only because if there is nothing but sky every anomaly has the tendency to provide a spectacle? Every bush and every rock at sunrise goes from a shadow to a blotch of indistinct browns and creamy greens, to something that in the end is always just a variable to the color of sand.

It will not be long before she can take off her shoes again, until she will feel the cool sand under her feet pushing up between her toes. It is that old urge again, which she always feels whenever Lydia isn't around; it is for Lydia that she wears them at all, shoes. She feels shackled by them, always has, a choke hold she has never quite got used to. Whenever she frees her feet, still, even now, she feels transported back through a blind man's knot of memories to a time before Lydia - before time itself, in a way.

She steps outside and begins to walk away from the house, feeling dwarfed by the all-consuming silence around her. The leather of her boots meanly cuts her skin, strangling her from the bottom up. She walks past the car, cutting a line with the tip of her finger in the dust that has settled over it. She crosses the road and follows the fading tracks of Lydia's footsteps from the night before, and it surprises her how far they go. Eventually, much farther than she had imagined the previous night the steady line they make abruptly implodes and then runs back toward the car again. But she continues bravely beyond that point, letting the thrill it causes her to do so tickle her belly and the oxygen in her lungs to leave her body in short little gusts — not unlike the times whenever she secretly touches herself in a certain way and makes herself feel cool winds blowing inside of her. She feels silly about it now, that whenever she touches herself like that it always reminds her of the first time she ever tried a sip of soda water, the way the bubbles had tickled the inside of her mouth, evoking a sensation not unlike the one she feels whenever she explores her own body.

She feels her heart trotting faster inside her chest now and understands that this has everything to do with the fact she is now on uncharted territory: touching ground Lydia has not touched before her, and to not be connected with Lydia, even on this level, has always made her feel alone in a strangely exhilarating way.

Once she is far enough away from the house, out of sight, she stops to undo her shoelaces and indulges herself by clawing the dirt with her feet, letting the dust massage the tender skin underneath her toenails. She can almost feel the winds inside of her already; though, of course, not nearly as strong as those other times. But still, it is enough to be considered a pleasure, one of the few private pleasures she knows she will ever have.

There is no calculation or any reason in particular to halt where she does. And neither does she feel the need anymore to glance back in the direction of the house, a mere spec now amongst the patches of bush behind her. She ties her boots together by the laces, flings them over her shoulder and continues a little further until again, quite randomly, she kneels in the dirt and pulls from her pocket some empty flasks of peroxide, which she collected before leaving the apartment. She has brought about a dozen of them, some with screw tops turned tight and others simply closed off with gauze and string.

The fetuses inside, some of them no larger than a kidney bean – and some even smaller still – look sad and meaningless now, having long since passed from the bloodied state they had been in on the day she retrieved them out of the wads of cotton, as she had pretended to clean off the mess after one of Lydia's so-called procedures. But even if they are now little more than vague, brownish stains on the inside of the glass, it feels right that they be brought back to the dirt, where, so she knows – still knows – all things ultimately belong.

She reaches into her pocket, and pulls out one of the candles she had got in the habit of taking from several churches around the neighbourhood as well, whenever Lydia had sent her out on errands and she had secretly attended mass instead. She digs several holes in the dirt with her fingers just large enough to fit the flasks in and carefully places each inside - not so much with a sense of ceremony but more with a delicate and precise kind of attention.

After a while she straightens herself and looks down at the arrangement before her, a semicircle of tiny graves, which curiously move and thrill her with a dutiful sense of accomplishment. The discoloration of the tissue inside some of the flasks caused by the peroxide draws her attention, as it had before, but which has so far not ceased to fascinate her. She lowers herself to inspect it more closely, observing the odd phenomenon with disconnected awe, not unlike the way she still observes cars and trams rolling over the streets, which to her the fact they don't need some beast to pull them along still very much represents some strange form of magic.

She covers the flasks with the dirt and digs down the candle in the semi-circle before them. As she flicks her fancy lighter, which she has kept hidden from everyone, even Lydia, since the day the Gods and the saints came into her life, she lines in her thoughts the faces of the women each blotch had once belonged to, quite unaware besides of the staggering level of detail with which her mind is able to draw those faces, even months later, in some instances.

She lets her thoughts wade back to the car and the night before, as she says prayers for all of them too: Lydia, her everything, the one to whom she knows she will always be bound — even if it is by a truss larger than she will ever fully understand. She even prays for Rosario; that mean Portuguese whore, with her harsh laugh, her foul mouth and coffee breath. She prays for Paxi and also for his friend, Mister Persival, with his handsome, freckled hands and eyes the color of the sky in wintertime.

Edmilce never prays in words, but rather in a series of disjointed moans, sung to random images she creates in her mind as she goes along. Most of the times, prayer - and when she can afford to be elaborate, is accompanied by the incorporation of incidental objects that are usually as random as her thoughts, but which very much symbolise whatever it is that fills her heart on any given day. It is always a strange symphony of rituals, with her, which have collected themselves in her memory over the years, but which she is now scarcely able to really trace, like the liquor she sometimes forces into her mouth and spits on the ground around her; all copied acts that are somehow connected to prayer and magic alike.

Rituals are a way for Edmilce to create order, to package and make digestible a world that is always as large as it is simply unfathomable; to make somewhat bearable the very concept of future and to make sense of her own existence.

After letting her mind wander for a while, she digs into her pockets again and pulls out the cigarette butt Rosario wastefully flicked into the dark the night before. She had picked it up out of the dust the moment Rosario's back had turned, and stashed it quickly inside her purse.

She bends forward and lights it on the flame of the candle. With the butt dangling from her lips she draws a cross over her chest and face, and rises to her feet again.

She hurries back toward the house; already lamenting the fact she will soon have to commit her pretty feet to the hard leather of her boots again. From a distance she can see the Welshman, Mr Persival, out by the car. The front end of the vehicle has been folded open, and he seems to be pouring something into it from a large tin can. She then remembers Paxi mentioning something to that effect the night before and she figures that whatever the Welshman is doing has something to do with that.

She remembers that last night Mr. Persival had been dressed quite elegantly too, quite the kind of gentleman that always makes her — and also most of the white women she knows - feel rather disheveled But this seems less to be the case now, being that he is not wearing his jacket and his shirtsleeves are rolled up past his elbows. He looks rougher, dexterous and quite a bit younger too.

He has his back to her when she approaches, improvising a whistle in the cool desert breeze to announce her presence. He turns and a generous smile materialises on his face.

"Good morning to you," he says, radiating and genuinely happy, it seems, to see her.

She returns his greeting and with her eyes and insolently follows a single droplet of sweat that crawls down the side of his face. She thinks it's funny that he doesn't seem to notice it, because it looks like it tickles.

"Been out walking have you?"

"It is very quiet here."

"Not a soul," he replies, pulling his back straight and then directing his pale eyes toward the horizon.

For a moment his face seems to be searching as it turns slightly more earnest and then quickly shrugs off whatever has crossed his mind.

"So, what brings you out this early in the morning," he asks her, as though he were having some trouble redirecting his attention back to the here and now.

"I just like walking by myself some times," she replies.

"I know what you mean. I am an early riser myself. Say, have you seen the horses?" he says, pointing his chin toward the back of the house.

But her eyes remain on him, as she tilts her head ever so slightly surprised that he should pull her back so violently back to the reality in which to most people she will always be child.

253

"I don't like horses," she answers quite unable to curve a pubescent sulk from escaping her lips, making her all the more conscious of all those things about herself that will always make her inherently different.

"What are you doing?" she asks him, raising herself on the tips of her boots to look over the raised hood of the car.

"Refueling, so we can be on our way," he replies eager and officiously; adding, "I suggest you have yourself a good breakfast. We have a long day ahead of us."

"I don't eat in the morning."

"Well, I suggest you get some food to take with you then, because we will be traveling the rest of the day."

"I'll be alright."

"As you wish."

"I like your car."

"She sure is beautiful, isn't she."

"You say she?"

He laughs, at last swatting the droplet of sweat that by now has almost reached his upper lip. In the same single sweep he wipes his forehead and the tip of his nose, as well.

"Oh, very much so," he says. "She is a she in every conceivable way" – as it takes Edmilce a moment to realise he is still referring to the car. "She is strong and fickle, just like a woman. Or, at least, the way I prefer them."

He studies the girl with mock-suspicion for a moment or two.

"Where are you from, Edmilce? What's your story?"

"I don't have a story."

"Everybody has a story. And you surely must have one."

"I am with Lydia; that is all the story I have" - closing herself off, but not in any way the Welshman will ever really notice.

She observes the way the light plays on the color of his eyes, realising also that besides Lydia no one has ever asked her that before. And back then, when Lydia had asked her that same annoying question, she had given her no more than a thinned-out summery of what her life had been – or whatever she can really remember of it. Now she finds it almost impossible to answer; it's such a handsome man asking!

Will it satisfy him if she tells him the truth - that as far as she knows and cares she really has no story; that the story she does have only begins on the day Lydia appeared on the horizon? She has a name, but that is merely practical – everything is called something and for no other reason than that so does she. Who might have given it to her is part of another story all together, one that is in no way connected to who she is now.

The Welshman was right about the day ahead; the monotony of the Pampa is relentless and by noon every one of them has come under its spell. Even Rosario with her big mouth, by the end of the day, can muster little more than dead ringer-stares at the gaping plains around them.

However, it is Paxi, by far, who seems to experience the most discomfort. Edmilce watches him from the backseat, as he twists himself into different positions trying as best he can to alleviate pains he furthermore seems to want to keep to himself at all cost. He never complains, except perhaps, by letting out breathy whimpers on occasion, as he courageously tenses his lips and continues to stare through the windshield at the flatness still ahead of them. And each time he does, Roger Persival will veer his attention away from the road to look at him, his face dimorphic with worry one minute and eager to cover distance the next. At some point, Lydia reaches forward and rests her hand on the back of Paxi's neck, much in the same way Edmilce remembers she used to sooth the girls recovering back at the apartment – a gesture that seems infinitely more significant now, however.

She has never seen Lydia touch a man before and wonders indeed if Lydia ever has. Perhaps, the babies she buried back in the desert that morning have something to do with that; that her little rituals have liberated Lydia in some way to do what she probably has been dreaming about doing for years, that without all the death she has caused binding her to the past, she is at last free to touch Paxi - to change yet again.

255

Mendoza is no more than a chance gathering of lights in the night, something temporary and quite out of place. From the road, the Andes have been visible for hours. Or at least, the light ricocheting on its snowy tops from the setting sun to the West gives the illusion they are there, before the valley is slobbered over again by the tongue of dusk.

Unlike what any of them expected, Roger Persival's house is a simple structure. Holes have been punched into the mud-washed walls to represent windows that look like they provide neither a view nor much ventilation, and have thus obviously been put there only to maximise the coolness of the shade inside. There are no servants rushing out to greet them either when they drive up to it and neither are they received by anyone once they stumble over the threshold and stand huddled together while the Welshman searches for lamps and candles to light their way.

Edmilce watches him fumble around the dusty wicker chairs and tables, endlessly apologising about the state of the place, which has clearly fallen into a state of total decay in his absence. The more he attempts to explain himself, while the spiders and the rodents scurry along the walls from the light of the oil lamp in his hand, the more Edmilce actually takes to him, as he seems to shrink to human proportions before her very eyes.

He swings his arms wildly through the stale air at the cobwebs that over the months have effectively connected the ceiling to the floorboards, and says, "No one ever comes here. It is my neighbours that keep the orchard and they have no reason to ever come into the house at all,"- adding, "But don't worry; I have clean sheets, and beds for every one of you"- as a boyish smile tightens across his face.

There is a short pause in his ranting and Edmilce takes the opportunity to ask what kind of trees he grows in his orchard.

"Olives, dear," he replies. "But I also have lemon, peach - some avocado too,"- as the sparkle temporarily returns in his eyes. "If you would like, I could show you around in the morning," he says.

"Please," she answers. "I would like that very much."

But she is not the only one who notices a peculiar ring that clings to her words as she speaks them, and which leaves everyone wondering to what extent horticulture is actually the thing she is really interested in.

The Welshman just smiles and lets the freckles on his cheeks play with the blue shimmer of his eyes in the candlelight.

"Please let us help you, Don Persi," Rosario then says, just short of clapping her hands when she speaks. "Just you tell us what it is you need us to do," she adds.

"I hate to have to trouble my guests," he replies, still trying to grasp the exact tone of the chord Rosario has just snapped. "Indeed, it would be helpful if you could... help me make this place somewhat live-able again. But first, let me show you to your rooms," he corrects himself in mid-sentence. "And in the meantime I will start a fire and fix us all a cup of tea."

He hurries out to the car to untie the wheelchair from the roof and rolls it in for Paxi to sit.

"You are looking quite exhausted, my friend," he says smiling, as Paxi lowers himself into it.

Paxi waves his hand in the air dismissively, to which the Welshman reaches into Paxi's inside pocket to remove one of his cigars; puts it to his lips and lights it for him.

"Don't go anywhere," he whispers softly to his friend before he disappears into the hall followed by his own shadow dancing on the wall from the glow of the candle in his hand.

Edmilce starts to follow him toward the back of the house, but something like a draught, almost a phantasmal sigh or breath on the back of her neck makes her stop before she turns the corner. From the darkened hallway she glanced back at Paxi still parked in his chair in the middle of the living room, looking quite immovable and exposed, and she then sees Lydia, whom she had not heard or seen since getting out of the car, come in through the front door and move slowly toward him. She watches as she then lowers herself before him, takes hold of his hands and stares up into his eyes with the kind of intensity she has never seen in Lydia's eyes before; never known her to exude such intent and such hunger of soul.

A rather unsettling feeling sinks into Edmilce, and along with it the realisation that what she is witnessing is in fact the end of things as she knows them; that soon the thing she just saw in Lydia's eyes will ultimately be the thing that is to squeeze her into the periphery of Lydia's affection somehow. Not in a million years would she have guessed that she could ever feel anything like this and that — whatever 'this' is - would feel so much like a jab of betrayal — but she hasn't the vocabulary to name the thing others might call jealousy.

<><><><><><><><>

That night she lay quietly under the sheets of the bed, meandering her thoughts on the even rhythm of Lydia's breathing next to her. She listens to the chirping of the crickets outside and the mice racing over the baked shingles on the roof, and tries to see herself as anything other than what she has been all those years — a mere extension of the woman that is everything to her. But her thoughts scramble and she becomes distracted every time by image of the Welshman appearing before her - and the question he had asked her that morning:

What's your story, Edmilce? Surely everybody has one.

In the dark Edmilce tries as best she can to answer it, piecing together vague memories about herself; about who she was before clean, scented sheets and eating at tables set with glass and silver — and shoes on her feet. Through the veil of all those changes she can see herself as a young child seated on the cracked clay in a clearing in the forest, and then as she is pulled into the arms of an older child whose name had been Nila. She can see herself being carried through one field and into another, through one patch of forest and into the next, until there is a long, narrow road, which, as her failed memory serves her, leads straight into the city.

In fragments she can see herself surrounded by hordes of other children as well, though none as young as she had been then, all moving in the same direction, on this one even road. She remembers the days turning to night, heat being followed by shadow and that with every one of these changes more children joining the trekking herd. She remembers the hollering around her, that aimless quacking of children that seems constant, but which, when one listens closely, isn't constant at all, for it tends to rise and ebb into itself again deliberately in measured waves. Other than that, her memory continues to fail her in terms of any real detail. From those days all she really remembers is thirst, hunger and above all heat, for she had probably been too young to ever have really felt frightened or lost.

What is quite a bit clearer, however, is the day she and Nila entered the town. And what a sight it was, the first time she saw the ocean; memories not only images but also the smell of it, that odd mixture of rot and freshness rolled into one, which greeted her in the breeze and became stronger every day she got closer to it. Even now she can still hear the sound of the waves heaving lazily against the side of the dock and the friendly smell of burning coal rising from the ships anchored in the bay.

From Nila she learned all she needed to know for a life down there; she learned to beg and also to steal; to fight, especially to fight, either for respect or more immediate necessities like food and a dry place to sleep every night. By the time Nila herself had simply vanished, like the ships that enter the harbour only to disappear a day later into the vastness beyond the lighthouse, she was proficient in just about every skill required for survival down there, even after Nila was finally found dead in a pile of fish heads on the beach some days later, beaten and ravaged in the way only European sailors can ravage children from time to time.

There simply wasn't much time to dwell on things. The hunger reflex just doesn't allow it; that neurological twitch that can focus the mind like nothing else on earth can, and which is found even in the simplest of creatures. And for that matter Edmilce could just as well have been a jellyfish, her young brain at some point reduced to the size of a pigeon stomach.

She awakes to the soft caress from the breeze coming in from the crack in the window. Inside it she can smell the lavender buds on the windowsill, and thinks to herself how sprinkling rum will achieve the same effect of keeping the scorpions at bay. The sky outside is grey; clouds tempering the early-morning light in such a way that it encases the countryside entirely. Next to her Lydia still sleeps, the way Lydia always sleeps: without doubts; peacefully.

She collects her shoes from the floor and slips out of the house, drawn by the impulse to see the olive trees Roger Persival had talked about the night before — for his words to become real, something she might be able to touch somehow. She wants to see the peach and the lemon with her own two eyes. Yet, what excites her the most, of course, is the prospect of running into him.

The morning air feels cold; a cold much sharper than the cold back in the city. For a long while she stands to the side of the house, absorbing the silence around her, waiting for the Welshman — as if by some miracle - to materialise in front of her. The occasional barking of a dog in the distance, and the deflated cackle of chickens foraging in the thorns lining the ditch tell her he isn't around, however, that the orchard is yet another extension of the solitude that has always surrounded her. It isn't the kind of silence she sensed out in the desert either, the kind that is clear of life all together. Ironically, here, at the foot of the Andes, it is filled to excess with the proximity of humans.

The house stands on a small elevation away from the town and from where she stands no dwellings are actually visible. In the breeze around her still hovers the smell of grass burning and it makes her think of the times Lydia had sent her out to the incinerator of the apartment building to dispose of whatever was left from the abortions of the previous day and how the smell of it, whenever she opened the shoot, as it rose into her nostrils, had been enough to make her sob every time. She thinks how whenever Lydia had entrusted her with these macabre little chores, she used to console herself by walking around the neighbourhood instead, collecting candles from the churches and then burying the aborted fetuses in the park across the street. Because — and this she was pretty certain of — the ground is where all things ultimately belong.

She must have done it a hundred times, and now she is doomed to always wonder if she could have prevented poor Carla from following her baby right into death herself, had she got to the park on time to bury the bloodied sheets - or at least, had she found a moment or two to properly light even one candle on her behalf. It feels strange to not actually be burying things at this hour, the way she had for the past three years.

She notices that the trees in the orchard are still fruitless, lined up perfectly in symmetrical tracks that slope gracefully down the side of the hill, as they seem to be waiting for spring to get a proper foothold in the Mendoza valley. And then, just as she contemplates descending down past them, from a small distance behind her, the voice of the Welshman reaches her, at last, though softly mocking.

"Did you know that olives produce a kind of fungus that makes grapevines flourish quite beautifully?"

Edmilce takes a moment before she turns, to let the dim-witted grin ease up from her face before she does. But the astonished gawk that falls over it once she sees the mountain range behind him must surely look as stupid.

"Puta madre" — an expression she has picked up from the crowd they had been frequenting - escaped her lips now in a single breath.

She splits her gaze erratically between the Welshman and the wall of rock that disperses the clouds above his head, not quite sure which of the two sights have temporarily impeded her speech the most. He must have picked up on this, for he briefly turns to look at them as well, and then back to her, amused and gloating somewhat.

"That is exactly what I said, the first time I saw them," he says.

He pulls up his chest in a sigh filled with finality and then crunches his boots in the dirt moving in closer.

"And just think that we will be crossing over them soon...."

"Everything had been so flat," Edmilce says, still distracted. "I didn't expect that they would be so huge — and that we had got so close."

He laughs.

"What did you think the Andes would look like?"

"I guess I hadn't thought about it."

"Up early, are you?"

"You too."

"Always."

"I wanted to see the orchard," she says, "and I wanted to see you" - in a declaration that is as unambiguous as it is dry and completely lacking in self-reflection.

"And here you have," he responds neither acknowledging the huge confession she has just spilt before him, nor quite ignoring it.

Mostly, it is the intensity of the smile on his face, which has remained unchanged that makes her unsure of herself.

"I remember I said I would show you around," he says. "Would you still like me to?"

"Yes."

He steps through the trees and motions for her to follow. He talks incessantly as he walks ahead of her, pushing low-hanging branches out of their path, but not once actually looking back in her direction. But, to whatever he is saying, she isn't listening. Her mind is cleared — washed clean. All she can focus on is the cracking of his leather boots and the smell of his skin filtering through the clean cotton of his shirt. At some point he stops and waits for her to catch up, turning sideways to let her move past him, and as she does the scent that rises from under the pits of his arms makes the sides of her tongue cramp up a bit.

Had she been a few years older she might have been able to recognise the signs that announced what would come next. Had anything like this ever happened to her before, it would not have surprised her when he cupped his hands over her breasts from behind and his mouth sucked itself onto the back of her neck.

She feels herself falling to her knees, her hips pushing yieldingly skyward and into the sharp sting as he enters her. She clenches her fists and rests her head on top of them to catch the intensity of his pillaging, lifting her gaze only on occasion toward the mountains turning liquid behind the tears in her eyes. She has never known pain could be this pleasurable, or that the sex of a man could a singeing blade for which she might ever hunger in this way — and the more he harries her the more she hungers.

As suddenly as it erupts, however, the tumbling behind her stops. She feels the Welshman go limp and slither out of her, panting with the high pitch of a cowering dog. She remains as she is, head still on top of her fists and her breath dispersing the dirt that has found its way into her mouth and has crunched itself between her teeth. She has no notion of indecency, of how exposed and beast-like she might look in the position she is still in, for in her mind she has never been much of either; has always been something rather undefined and in between: meat without much purpose, without a story indeed.

She watches as the sun randomly illuminates the peaks of the mountains in the distance. They seem almost within reach. All the while she is hoping the Welshman will regain his strength at some point and climb his way back in to her. But there is no movement behind her, only the sound of him heaving for each breath, as he leans against the peach tree; licking his wounds like a man some twenty years older.

"Cover yourself," he says, his voice still too weak to be anywhere near commanding.

She sits up and pulls her dress past her knees as far as it will go. She finds it hard to look at him. Let alone fully interpret the expression on his face – if the expression of a man drowning could be called an expression at all that is.

"You must never mention this to anyone," he says.

"Why would I?"

"Precisely."

"There aren't many things that are mine, Mr. Persival. This is, and there is nothing about it that I want to share with anyone."

"I am glad to hear you say that," he responds, squeezing a short pause into his asthmatic wheeze.

"No man has ever done this to me before," she says.

"Is that a fact?" - for the first time actually focusing almost all of his attention on her since relieving himself; the contempt in his voice she barely picks up on, however.

"And, was it all you thought it would be?"

"When I look at you, Mr. Persival, you look strong, and so smart..."

He pretends to contain a burst of laughter, but all that comes out of him now is a dry scrape of the throat.

"You look like the kind of man that could give a woman much pleasure. But instead, it looks like trying to almost killed you."

"You little whore."

As she smiles he can see the dusty line of saliva across her cheek change its angle, and for a reason he cannot explain, it sends a wave of passion right through his very heart, which, once it ferments for a second or two inside of him, sends a mean, hot surge of pure anger back into his extremities. She can see viciousness in his eyes, as he looks her over, and also in the fact his sex no longer hangs in the dirt. And then she hears it in his voice as well, as it turns ever weaker and more delicate from it.

"Turn around," he says, "so I can give you what you came here for."

263

She closes her eyes and turns away from him again, face to the dirt and hips open to the clouds above.

He stretches on the grass, his shirt floating loosely around him. Edmilce sits beside him and studies him like a kitten following rolling marbles. He wiggles his toes behind the wave of a warm and draughty yawn. Words don't seem necessary for communication between them to be any more complete, or for the air around her to feel any more perfect as his cool white hand leisurely searches under the hem of her dress.

Then, as though in some minor detail, in the way perhaps the breeze might rouse the hairs on his chest, or in the way each sprit of grass somehow manages to produce a distinctly different taste inside her mouth each time she bites through one, she remembers his question from the day before, the one that keeps resurfacing in her mind, bouncing inside her like a bird determined not to be caught.

"I don't remember having had a mother or a father," she says. "Or brothers or sister either. But at night I would always have a place to sleep. But this was all before Lydia - at this house that wasn't a regular house at all really," she adds.

"It belonged to a lady everybody knew as a Mãe-de-santo, who used to take in children from the street."

Roger Persival briefly lifts the straw hat covering his face, but other than that he does not react.

"It means mother-of-saints," she says, assuming that by lazily changing the angle of his head he has somehow asked for an explanation. "It's a person who helps people," Edmilce adds. "A Mãe-de-santo is somebody who understands everything about people, you see. I always take care of people too," - as if this too is some detail that needs proper clarification and just cannot be left out.

"So, you were something of a street child then?" he mumbles, just to encourage her to continue talking.

"I was at first," Edmilce replies, deftly spitting out a ball of mashed up grass and replacing it with a fresh blade she plucks from the ground between them, as she continues in the tone of a child not quite used to forming complete sentences.

"After a while, when I was a little bigger, though, I almost always slept at that house; I almost never slept outside anymore. So, I wasn't really a street child, by the time Lydia came for me. I was still a thief though — but there is a difference.

Hey, are you asleep, Mister Persi?"

A smile appears on his face. He nods his head No, but his eyes remain closed.

"I knew that things would be different for me some day. I just knew that the stealing and the running around in the street would not always be how I lived my life."

Edmilce turns and glances at the house, brings up her knees and wraps her arms around them smiling.

"But Lydia was already with me."

"What do you mean by that?" he mumbles, as he pushes his straw hat further down the length of his face to shield his eyes from the sun rising across the valley.

"Just like I say," Edmilce replies. "Lydia was already with me then. I have known Lydia since the time I was very small, you know, from Mãe Franca's terreiro, standing behind the Xangó and the candles — behind the ashtray and the cigars. People used to dance in front of her all the time."

The Welshman's eyes open briefly and he squints in her direction, clearly measuring her.

"I wasn't supposed to see all that," she continues. "But I did. It was one of the rules Mãe Franca had; children were never allowed in the terreiro. She used to say that some things were not meant for children to see."

She pauses again and removes a small twig that has tangled itself on the hairs of his chest. She holds it in between her fingers for a few seconds, and then breaks it in half.

"Mãe Franca probably didn't know about all the things we saw when we weren't there; when we were out," she adds pensively. "Of course, I did use to sneak into the terreiro anyway, on the nights when people came to dance — especially on those nights. Mãe Franca only used to pretend she didn't see me and let me get right up to the front, to watch the dancing and the drumming anyway. And this is where I saw Lydia for the first time – and I think she saw me too."

A crystalline giggle tweaks her smoky voice. Slowly, Roger Persival rises on his elbows and pushes the hat away from his face to look at her. And again he does that thing with his eyes, which amuses her so much, of jamming ten different expressions into them, while still looking like nothing will ever confuse him. He grabs her face with both hands and kisses her on the mouth. She smiles back, as her attention then shifts back to picking at the scab on her knee, looking quite lost between fact and fiction, as though there would always be a big blurry gape between the two.

"It was at Mãe Franca's house that I learned that one day I would leave that place," she then says. "And that I would someday be a lot happier too - than most of the children I used to run around with.

I didn't know her real name back then – Lydia I mean. All I knew was that someday she would come for me – I already knew what she would look like; the color of her hair and eyes; I even knew what she would be wearing.

It took me a long time before I had the courage to ask Mãe Franca about the figurine on the altar; who she was and why I felt so attracted to her – why I felt like she was telling me things. And maybe if it was because it was attracted to me."

"What did you think it was telling you?" the Welshman asks, his head resting in the grass once more.

"That she would someday come for me, like I said, and that she would make me happy! What else?"

"I don't know. What did Mãe Franca say?"

"That if I was respectful of it, the orixá – that's how she called her – would come to me with blessings. And this is what happened years later, on the day Lydia and Mr. Paxi came to Salvador. They brought blessings."

"That's a great tale," the Welshmen says, laughing at his own remark and like most northern Europeans, charmed by his own sobriety.

"Sometimes I wonder if you really are as clever as I think you are, Mr. Persi."

He sits up again, leans in towards her and says, as he searches her evasive gaze:

"I am not that clever, Edmilce. You're right about that."

She stares back at him in mock-reproach and then lowers her eyes to examine the scab on her knee again, which, all the while, she has not stopped picking with her nail. A trickle of blood finally rolls out of it and down the front of her leg; purple looking against her dark skin. He watches her run her finger through it in an upward motion to stop it before it reaches her ankle, and then licking it clean.

"Mãe Franca said that I had always been connected to the figurine and that I therefore would always have to honor her – that I could always turn to her if I needed help, and also that all the changes in my life would always come from the sea."

"You mean, like fish?"

"You are not always funny either, you know."

"I am not trying to be. I just don't understand," he chuckles. "How did Mãe Franca know all this, Edmilce?"

'She was a Mãe-de-santo," the girl replies, growing ever more exasperated by his jesting, but she continues. "She knew that I would always be connected to that spirit – and the sea of course."

"I didn't know the sea had a spirit."

"And there is still a lot you don't know, Mr. Persival."

As Edmilce speaks she turns her gaze in the direction of the mountains again and lingers there, as though she instinctively knows that the shortest distance to the ocean is right over them, however irrational, given how tall and massive they look.

Then startling him a bit, she reaches down, and gently squeezes his arm.

"Meet me tomorrow again?"

"You're insatiable."

"What does that mean?"

"That you never get tired."

She searches his face and then examines the rest of him, making him feel actually naked for the first time.

"But I do get tired, Mister Persi," she says, as she jumps to her feet and runs through the trees in the direction of the house.

Every morning, during the month they spent at the foot of the mountains, Edmilce and the Welshman meet behind the orchard. But Edmilce isn't the only one who adopts new routines during this period — or ones that involve such awakenings either.

As she returns to the house with the taste of the Welshman still bitter on her tongue, she will often run into Lydia and Paxi out on their morning walks. It is part of Lydia's efforts to kick out what she calls the laziness that has got into Paxi's legs after the accident. The wheelchair Lydia will leave by the front door and then, locked tightly in an embrace for support, she will head him out toward the road. Edmilce will sit on the porch and watch them disappear in the distance. Often her eyes will fill with tears, until her initial jealousy dilutes out of existence to make way for gratitude, for the fact that she now too has a lover, even though she does wonder if Lydia will actually prove strong enough to heal her handsome Paxi to where he will ever be much of one.

It is still winter, officially, though everything around her tells her spring will soon be upon them. It is as though the ground under her feet were announcing it by vibrating right through her with anticipation; ever sharpening the hot imprint the Welshman has cast by now between her legs. Even the scent traveling in the breeze from the eucalyptus trees that line the road seems heightened and poised for the pending changing of the seasons — like a promise that life will always find a way to renew itself, no matter what one ever decides to bury out in the desert. She is beginning to understand that with every start, there is always a farewell to bite through — and so, that before long she too will leave this place, and perhaps, everything else that since the streets of Salvador has become so familiar to her.

And what a foolish thing, Edmilce also thinks; to be running from fate, as she and Lydia have been doing for the past four years, as though they might ever be able to outrun it somehow. Isn't it precisely the other way around? Isn't fate the very thing one runs toward when one runs?

Could Lydia still not see this? Had Paxi, with all his worldliness, not discovered by now that this is so? Or is it that he too is compelled to run, like Lydia? What will it take, Edmilce thinks, for all of them to finally see that there is just no escaping what they are?

She watches Lydia and Paxi small in the distance, as they start to head back. She thinks of Mãe Franca and the terreiro, and of the time she had watched the figurines reveal her future for her — the Goddess and the Lazarus.

She jumps to her feet and runs out to meet them, stomping and yodeling blissfully as she flings her arms around them.

"What is the matter with you?" Lydia protests, as the girl almost knocks her over.

"I am just so happy Lydia," Edmilce replies.

"You are so happy that you would push a cripple to the ground?" Paxi joins her scattering, steadying himself on his cane with one hand and pulling at Lydia's hand with the other.

"You are not a cripple," Lydia corrects him, right as the tip of his cane slides off the side of a rock on the dusty road, causing him to begin to topple over. Instinctively, both women reach to steady him, with a level of coordination that is a direct product of the years they have hardly been apart.

As they pull him up, the silver chain that hangs around his neck dangles into view, revealing Paxi's wooden amulet around his neck. Edmilce just stares at it, not in the least surprised that it has revealed itself to her at that particular moment, but still quite in awe in the face of providence. And without meaning for it to, the word Lazarus escapes her lips.

For a moment, Paxi stares back at the girl and then down at the amulet still dancing in the open.

"It's so easy to forget where you are from," he says, "but then when you think of it..."

But he seems to reconsider whatever he has started to say. He steadies his cane in the dirt instead, and with his right hand he reaches inside his collar, a laugh no larger than a sniffle escaping him as he does. He closes his hand around the figurine and his eyes fill with remembrance and the truss that connects him to it.

Edmilce glances at Lydia, as the scene on the pier flashes before her and the words that were said, as if it had only been yesterday:

I like your lighter.

What lighter?

The one you just used for your cigar, Papi.

Thank you.

Can I borrow it?

Why?

To light a cigar.

You are too young to be smoking.

And you are too good-looking to be traveling all by yourself.

What am I going to light my next cigar with, after you've run off with it?

Why do you think I am going to run off with it?

What should make me think you won't?

Toss me a coin, Papi.

How about you earn it?

"Let me come up there - and earn it."

How about you tell me from down there what you can do to earn it.

You can toss coins into the water, and I can fish 'em up for you.

Can you swim?

It will only cost you a coin to find out. And when I come up with it, Papi, you give me your lighter too.

She remembers how Paxi had stepped away from the railing for a moment, and then re-appeared holding up a copper piece between his fingers.

The lighter is yours, is all he says as the tiny dot breaks the surface of the water with a sucking sound.

She feels herself breaking the surface as well, reaching down toward a speck of light that is becoming ever fainter as it travels surprisingly fast down into the murk. She knows she has to reach it before it gets to the bottom. She knows that once it buries itself there it will be lost forever, and that the real danger to this stunt is in being stupid enough to dig your hands into the slick, where you are sure to cut yourself on the debris buried there, or perhaps even get stuck too. But the coin reaches the bottom before she gets anywhere near, and feeling particularly brave that day she does the one thing she has seen go bad so many times before. She rams her arm deep into the oily slime.

The events that follow are rather sketchy to her now; all she really knows is that once she breaks free she has the coin in her hand and the distinct feeling of absolute victory in the knowledge that in addition to the coin she's earned the pretty man's fancy lighter, as well.

She climbs back onto the pier, and as she blows oil and salt out of her nose she searches the spot where the man stood. But he is no longer there. All she can make out now is a commotion down the end of the pier and distinctly a woman's voice entangled somewhere inside it, the way only a woman's voice can sound when it is enveloped in all out fury. It is at that very moment that she sees that the statue of the Goddess that had so enamored her back at Mãe Franca's house has come to life and is now heading straight for her consumed in anger.

She clamps the coin tightly between her teeth and prepares for the beating that will soon surely follow, judging from the size of the storm approaching, hollering in a language that sounds like fiddles being played at an extremely fast pace; Italian, she knows now.

Again, her memory of the precise events that come next are still a blur to her; of how she hides her face in between her knees and covers her head with her hands to guard off the blows from the Goddess-become flesh, unleashing her wrath upon her.

What she does remember though - quite well - is how at some point the gentleman lowers himself before her; how fresh his breath is as he gets in closer - and despite the smell of cigars that permeates everything that is connected to him and the words he then whispers:

Did you get it?

She nods yes, her lips and her jaw still tight, biting down on the coin for dear life.

Show me.

Reluctantly, she parts her lips just wide enough to let him see the copper resting on her tongue, and then quickly locks her mouth again.

You are a good swimmer.

271

She remembers nodding and blinking her eyes once too often, to where a torrent of tears can no longer be stopped. She feels his hand come down gently on the top of her head, as his other hand moves up holding the silver lighter she inquired about earlier, but which she hasn't actually seen until this moment. It is even more beautiful than she imagined it.

"I believe this is yours," the gentleman then whispers, placing it in her hand out of view of the Goddess still standing over them. He then points with the nail of his thumb to a word that is engraved on the side of it.

Can you read?

She nods No and wipes the salt from her eyes to better focus on it anyway.

It says Paxi. That's me.

Edmilce could have imagined herself being anything, as long as it was spawned by Lydia. She was her echo, her shadow and the pillar Lydia could always lean against to steady herself. What is unthinkable, however, just because it would go against every law of nature and divinity — for they are one and the same, and always have been — is that she will ever be Lydia's equal. And, if that, the unthinkable ever occurred, this will then be the day that nature and heaven — and everything that exists parallel to the world they live in — will extinguish like the wick of a used up candle.

Spring is upon them in every conceivable way. The colder winds from the Pacific, not the temperate ones from the Atlantic, which in so many ways has made them what they are, and the fate they share, will soon be reaching them. From the realm of the Atlantic they are about to sever themselves, as their journey is about to take them into the Andes and beyond, into the realm of the Pacific, the iodine that belongs to Gods unknown to her, and therefore fickle in the laws they prescribe.

Of course, Edmilce has known transition. She understands it perhaps better than any of them, but to cross the mountains means far more than just change: it means the end of a history she herself has helped to write. The signs of it are everywhere and that she now carries the Welshman's child is merely one part of that story. Rosario has the town of Valparaiso waiting for her to be laced with her whoring ways, and the Welshman his reasons to vanish from sight the moment she has announced her pregnancy. Lydia now has her Paxi and that in itself is history finding closure.

Change is upon them all; she can feel it rising through her feet, the way only the animals can sense the unrest gathering beneath the crust of the earth, before it causes havoc in the human world. From the deep rumbling that causes the dogs to bark at night and the horses to push their moody snorts out into the dust, she knows that soon the Atlantic will no longer shape her world.

It might still be weeks before they actually reach the West Coast, but the Pacific with all the change it will bring, can already be felt. It can be felt in the tightness deep inside her belly now and in the scent of the eucalyptus. It tells her the snows will soon melt and that the last leg of their journey will finally begin.

Of course, it is impossible to say with any certainty at all if they will ever actually reach the port of Valparaiso. Though, that it is a place ruled by different forces Edmilce hasn't a doubt. The earthquake will come, and when it does, as on August 6 of the year 1906, exactly twenty-seven days later, as she stands at the shores of this new and unknown horizon, what once was granted, on that day might be reclaimed.

Acknowledgments

Exploring the traditional paths of writing, I queried literary agents as much as any first-time writer out there, I suppose. But this was while I was still quite blind to the fact I already had the best agent in the world, even though she will never let herself be cast into such a traditional role.

A pivotal moment was the day my dear friend Angela Capo listened to my story of how my father's grandmother had traveled from Italy to South America as a child, right around the turn of the twentieth century. The little I know is that this rather intangible lady from the distant past had become a midwife at some point, played some on the stock market, and ended up leaving a modest fortune at the time of her death in the early seventies.

My memories of this individual being sketchy at best, for they are fogged over by the distant view of the small child I was at the time of her death, provided me with the basis and the opportunity to let fiction take over. And the fact that there is no one in my family, furthermore, who can really explain to me how she exactly managed to accumulate all the assets she left behind, was ultimately the void that got filled by this book.

Angela helped me to understand that the book I was to write should therefore, not be about my great grandmother but inspired by my sketchy images of her instead whilst telling the tale of the millions who left the European shores during that period in search of new beginnings. That summer day, as we collected empty bottles of wine in the back yard of my Amsterdam home at the time, and prepared dinner and talked about books and music, Angela said that if I wrote this story down, it would someday become a book that is read by all.

I rarely contradict her.

Thank you, Angela, for staying on top of the project; for encouraging me and being critical when you needed to be and for being devoted throughout.

As I shaped the book into its current form, chucked flawed versions left and right and started from scratch on numerous occasions, I am much indebted to individuals who provided their sharp and selfless critique along the way. In this capacity my gratitude goes out to Judith Tijman,

Barbara Mazzotta, Francesca de Châtel and Jolanda van der Toorn in particular. A HUGE mention goes out for Marlies van der Meer, who quickly went from fan to friend to my committed editor and with whom I e-mailed every single page, as I applied the last coat of paint to the manuscript before submitting the final version to Reagan Rothe, my publisher at Black Rose.

It is true what they say, you know, that writing is a lonely business. Of course it is! But it is also a big part of the lure, is my guess, as well. As writers, we are masters of realms as big as our own imaginations. But, as clichés are always the truest of truths, it can also get quite lonely out there.

And what a delight it is when you have sat in silence for days, massaging your keyboard with loving taps of your fingertips in the creation of that realm on the page, and you gather with ten other writers to exchange ideas or just simply to talk about the thing often no-one else knows about or really understands! A writing group can help to remind you that you are not alone. And when it is your turn to submit work-in progress, when ten authors critique it professionally and with utmost respect, your work gets lifted to an all-together higher level.

My humblest gratitude goes out to my talented friends in the Amsterdam Writing Group; to our fearless leader and Steinbeck champion, David Lee, science-fiction writer and sharp critic, Carolyn Chang, mystery/thriller writer and Texas rose with a pen as sharp as a killer's blade, Barbara Austin; our genius and soon-to-be mega hit (I just know it), Peter Crowe, short story writer and mistress of ghosts on the page, Milla van der Have, the ever-elegant Francis Cox and not to forget our latest two additions, Paco Cantu and Mike George.

And how could I not be eternally thankful to the talented photographer, Anja Robertus in whose intimate company I first-drafted the book, alongside our beautiful children, Mo and Camil, to whom I have dedicated this debut. Thank you, Anja, for your design and photography for the book's cover – and your advice and your support in the beginning stages of the project. You were there!

Thank you, Rene Ahoud at JohnnyRaw, for helping me to expand my writing with the spoken word and for helping me to discover the possibilities of 'Lit-Cinema'.

An honorable mention here for the winners of the facebook competition, who shared online in their own creative ways, how they were personally touched by the story I was about to tell. Thank you for letting my work inspire you, Elly Trampenau, Petra Vlaskom, Maureen Barkey and, mentioned once again, Marlies van der Meer. I hope I will live up to the promise.

Completing this book has been a process to which many contributed. Many will know who they are, but the important thing is that I do.

There are many who were a part of this, many names that need mentioning with gratitude. All of these are names of inspiring souls who believed in me and the project, some even before I ever started it. I should close these acknowledgments by thanking my parents, my family and my personal friends, for their love and their support every step of the way.

Thank you Ingrid, my lover, companion, accomplice and friend.

Amsterdam, December 2012.

CPSIA information can be obtained at www.ICGtesting.com
Printed in the USA
LVOW121027310513

336230LV00003B/3/P